DARKNESS I BECOME

E.S. LUCK

Contents

For the girls who aren't "nice," who won't smile, who aren't sweet or demure; and the women who are a little rough around the edges, who are "bitchy," who show us that the spectrum of femininity is vast and varied and intriguing in ways that allow us to examine the strange multitudes and contradictions that exist in all of us.

Content Note

Darkness I Become is a post-apocalyptic dark romance. It takes place in a world without laws and without mercy, where survival is a daily struggle. While the book of course features a HEA, its themes and events are often difficult and disturbing, and I encourage you to take the time to review the full list of content notes to safeguard your mental health.

- graphic violence & death
- murder
- rape (not by the MMC, fade to black)
- torture
- sexual assault
- human trafficking
- cannibalism
- child sexual abuse (past, mentioned, not graphic)
- domestic violence (past, mentioned)
- family abuse
- mild drug and alcohol use
- explicit sexual intimacy between consenting adults
- domination and submission
- praise and degradation
- spanking, genital spanking
- impact play (belt)
- sensory play (blindfold)
- bondage (hands only)
- threesome (FFM)

Chapter 1

Spring 2097

D rowning was a choice.

That's what Asha's father would've said in her situation. When you can no longer keep your head above water, just paddle harder, and if you can't—because of exhaustion, or pain, or because you just don't have the will to keep on fighting—that's your fault. You should've tried harder. When you opened your lungs to water, it's because you were weak.

Spoken like someone who's never had their head held underwater, Asha thought bitterly. *Sanctimonious prick.*

Now, lying beneath the smooth surface of the water in a filthy old bathtub, she opened her eyes and wished she could drown. That might be preferable to what awaited her above. The last few days replayed in her head like a distant, horrible dream that she couldn't wake up from.

Four days ago, she'd been living in the safest place that still existed, thirty years after the world ended: The Cave. A secure, walled compound where laws, schools, and technology still existed. A bastion of hope amidst a post-apocalyptic Wasteland.

Until they came, in black masks painted with gold eye symbols. She'd just gotten home from work when it happened: a colossal, ear-splitting bang that set her teeth on edge. Peering out the window of her small townhome, she saw black smoke rising from the centre of the compound—an explosion of some kind. It was a strange juxtaposition with the trimmed curtains and floral pillows of her small living room.

Quiet, contained domestic tranquility crossed with sudden, inexplicable chaos.

Her husband wasn't home yet, and if she was being honest, she hadn't even thought of him at that moment. Instead, she stared in shock as screams started to fill the air, and demons dressed in black descended on her neighbourhood, gold eye emblems emblazoned over their black masks. Her neighbour down the street—a kindly older man called Dylan—was the first to die.

At the explosion, Asha watched him step out of his house in confusion. Two of the gold eye masks advanced rapidly up the street, guns in hand. A second later, she heard another loud bang, and then Dylan was lying face down in the middle of the street. A river of red began to flow out from underneath him.

It was hard to process what she was seeing. For a second or two, she simply stood there at the window, stunned. No one told her what it would be like to see the life she'd always known suddenly shatter apart, all in a fraction of a second.

Her shock cost her, however. The two men in masks turned their heads in her direction and spotted her in the window. For a split second, neither party moved. Then the one on the left raised his rifle.

Asha screamed as she threw herself to the floor, narrowly avoiding the bullet that blasted through her window, showering her with glass. She scrambled across the floor towards the kitchen at the back of the house. Meanwhile, the men pounded on the front door. She breathed a momentary sigh of relief that she'd always been that person who reflexively locked doors as soon as she got home.

But it wouldn't hold them off for long. Asha heard the splintering of wood as she clambered to her feet in the kitchen, and she flew to the back door, where she made her escape into the tiny yard. It wasn't much more than a patio and a comically small patch of grass lined with shrubbery, but the fence was only knee-high—easily climbable. She raced for it and vaulted over, right into her neighbour's thick, untrimmed rose bushes.

Thorns pricked her all over, and Asha winced, but knew she couldn't afford to stop. Her thoughts were racing as she crawled along the line of rose bushes, using them for concealment. All around her were sounds of chaos and slaughter: screams, gunshots, heavy footfalls of people fleeing for their lives.

Where can I go? She thought, her heart pounding in her ears. She didn't know if the masks were all over the compound, or where they'd come from. More than that, she wondered, *why is no one stopping this?*

The Cave was heavily militarized. It was necessary to protect them from the Wastelanders outside its walls, and it made no sense that so far, she'd seen little to no signs of resistance.

Asha decided to try to reach her mother's house. She lived just down the street, and she worked for the government. She'd know what was happening.

Asha managed to move forward through people's backyards, using shrubbery and patio furniture to conceal herself as best she could. She thanked her lucky stars that her pursuers had obviously been diverted and weren't actively chasing her anymore.

Another stroke of luck: nobody was searching the yards yet, probably because they were too busy killing people in their homes. The thought chilled her blood, and she had to push it down to keep going. She had to shut out the screams and the growing stench of death or she'd never make it.

She finally climbed over the fence into her mother's backyard. The yard itself appeared undisturbed. Asha dared to approach the back door of the house and peer through its window. The house looked empty. She tried the knob, but it was locked.

Cursing under her breath, Asha trembled, trying to decide what to do. There were no sounds from inside the house, and her gut told her that her mother, for whatever reason, wasn't home. She could try to break in and hide there, hoping no one would notice her...or she could keep moving, try to find someone else she knew.

Hiding and waiting for help to come was tempting. But it would also make her a sitting duck. Some primal voice inside her whispered, *No one is coming. We're on our own.*

Because based on everything she'd ever been taught, an attack like this should not have been possible. The compound had complex alarm systems for intruders, and the military ran rapid-response drills for Wastelander attacks. There was no response at all, as far as she could tell. No emergency sirens. No firefights. Just slaughter.

So, something had gone terribly wrong. Worse than she could possibly imagine. And she didn't know what it would mean—she couldn't have, not then. But she knew, deep in her gut, that staying meant certain death.

Claire. The name of her best friend came to her mind as easily as breathing. She lived a couple blocks over, and her husband was an emergency room doctor. He might know more about evacuation efforts, or where to find help.

Heart in her mouth, Asha charted a course to Claire's house through people's yards, praying to every God she didn't believe in that her friend was alive.

Asha resurfaced, coughing, as a short, ugly man with a handlebar moustache banged open the dilapidated wood door.

"Get the fuck out!" he yelled. "You've been at it long enough."

She flailed uselessly in the rusted old tub, trying to cover her naked body, but the short, toothless man who'd entered the room just laughed.

"No secrets between us, sweetheart," he said, grabbing her cheek. She recoiled, but he held fast. "We'll be getting to know each other much better soon."

She didn't think about doing it; she simply reacted. She turned her head and sunk her teeth into his hand. He tasted like dirt and something salty she didn't want to think about.

He roared with pain and released her, then cupped his bleeding hand and examined the distinct tooth marks in his flesh.

"Bitch," he bit out. "Don't know where you came from, girlie, but you're about to learn your place."

Asha gasped in surprise and pain as he grabbed a handful of her black hair and pulled, forcing her out of the washtub. He threw her to the floor, still naked and soaking wet, and pain lanced her side as he kicked her in the ribs. She doubled over, trying to protect herself with her arms, but the second kick didn't hurt any less than the first.

"Don't get carried away there, Pike, or no one'll want her," a gruff male voice said from the door. "No good if she's all roughed up before auction."

Auction? Asha snapped to attention. She hadn't been told anything about these men's true intentions since they'd kidnapped her a day ago. She'd been wandering through the dense forest with nothing but the clothes on her back, desperately searching for food.

When she at last spotted a rabbit roasting over an open flame, all good sense abandoned her. The smoky scent of sizzling meat was dizzying. She'd gotten sick from drinking the water from a stream a couple of days prior, causing her body to empty itself of every shred of nourishment via painful vomiting and diarrhea. She'd eaten nothing in a week and was dangerously dehydrated.

But of course, when she'd approached the campfire, she'd walked right into Pike, and into this waking nightmare that refused to end. Four smelly, grimy Wastelander men had tied her up and forced her to walk for what felt like forever, until her legs gave out and they were forced to feed and water her, lest she not make it to wherever the hell they were going. Any questions about where they were taking her earned her a sharp slap across the cheek.

They led her to a much larger campsite, where more brutish, dirty men greeted them. Asha hated the way they openly leered at her.

"Such a pretty one," a man with greasy hair and missing front teeth crooned. "Such lovely skin...like polished copper."

She recoiled as his clammy, meaty hand touched her cheek, leaving behind a mysterious oily substance that she hastily wiped on the sleeve of her worn winter jacket.

"She's a prize," Pike had replied, showing off several blackened, rotting teeth. "Never seen one like her before. So untouched. So pretty."

Asha wanted to vomit, but wisely decided against it. She needed all the calories she could get, because who knew where her next meal might come from. As the sky darkened, they brought her to a copse of trees several metres from the main campfire. She was surprised to find two other women there, tied to tree trunks. Both women were fair-skinned and blonde, and thin as a rail, their faces smudged with dirt. There was a bone-deep weariness to them that showed on their faces. It was only their lack of wrinkles or expression lines that gave away their youth: neither could be more than eighteen or nineteen years old.

At twenty-six, Asha knew she looked younger and healthier than either of them. It didn't bode well that, in the company of these men, a couple of vital young women looked *this* haggard and unwell. She wondered how long they'd been there as they watched her, wide-eyed, while Pike made her sit and be tied to an adjacent tree trunk.

"Go to sleep," he ordered, smacking his lips unpleasantly. "No talking."

They weren't wrong about Wastelanders back home, Asha thought, wrinkling her nose. *They're repulsive.*

Pike wandered back to the main campfire, leaving Asha and the two women alone. Asha glanced in their direction. Both of them studied her with an intensity that made her uncomfortable.

"So, where'd they get you?" the blonde on the left asked in a low voice. She had a smudge of mud on the tip of her nose, and her blue eyes were wide and curious.

Asha stayed silent. She wasn't sure what to make of them, and she didn't want to provoke Pike or the others by talking.

When it became clear she wasn't going to reply, the other woman said, "I'll bet she's one of the volunteers Daddy told us about, Becks. Too pretty to not be."

"Ah, you're probably right," Becks replied knowingly. "Is that it, pretty girl? You offered yourself up to the men?"

"What?" Asha said indignantly, startled into speech. "No. As if I'd ever volunteer to be tied up in the woods by a bunch of Wastelanders."

The girls blinked at her. She realized too late that they'd probably never heard the term before...which meant they also didn't know that it was mostly used as a pejorative, thank God.

Get your shit together, Asha, she scolded herself. *These people are dangerous.*

"What's a Wastelander?" Becks asked, raising her eyebrows. "That another gang?"

In a manner of speaking.

"It's a word for outside people," Asha answered cautiously, and when they gave her another look of confusion, she sighed.

"Outside?"

"Never mind," she hurried out, not eager to explain. She had no idea if she could trust these women, but she could gather information from them. "Who are you?"

"I'm Brigid, this is Becks," the girl on the left said. "We're twin sisters from Milton. Settlement owned by the Skulls."

"The Skulls?"

"The gang these guys belong to," Becks answered, nodding back towards the main campsite, where a dozen men were laughing and drinking around the campfire.

The Skulls? Asha wrinkled her nose again. *Did they get a bunch of edgy teens to name their gang?*

"How did you end up here?" she asked, nodding at Brigid.

Brigid shrugged. "Our Daddy owed them a debt, and he couldn't pay."

Asha's eyes widened. "He sold you off to them?"

Becks scoffed. "Not like they gave him a choice. You from one of those free settlements? You got your nose in the air like you are."

Free settlements? Asha wondered. At the Cave, they'd always said that the entire Wasteland was dominated by vicious gangs. So far, her experience bore that out...but Becks was implying that not all settlements were under gang rule. She filed that away in the back of her mind.

"I'm from a compound," she finally answered.

"That's why she looks so different!" Becks exclaimed to Brigid. "Old Alex said they have microchips in 'em to make 'em prettier. That true, miss?"

Asha couldn't help but roll her eyes. "It's an implant, not a microchip. And they're not for looks; they're for health. But yes, I have one."

"Old Alex said he knew someone from one of them places," Brigid said wisely. "Guess he was right."

Asha frowned. She'd never heard of anyone escaping or leaving the Cave. The general policy had always been *no one comes in, no one goes out.* But then, she'd also never known about the violent rebellion brewing inside the compound...so clearly, the place was good at keeping secrets from its residents.

"What does it do?" Becks asked, sounding more excited than Asha felt the situation warranted. "Make you invincible?"

She scoffed. "No. Feeds us vitamins, hormones, and other stuff to slow the effects of aging and maintain health. Blocks sun damage. Speeds healing a bit. That's about all."

She didn't bother to add that it prevented pregnancy. Control over fertility was part and parcel with compound living.

"That's all, she says," Brigid repeated incredulously to Becks. "Sounds like a superpower to me."

Asha opened her mouth to retort, but then Pike was back. His furious face glowed red in the firelight.

"Go the *fuck* to sleep!" he screamed, obviously tipsy. "One more word from you *whores* and I'll whip you raw."

Definitely not feeling super right now, Asha thought as she cringed.

"They'd probably enjoy it," a man jeered from the campfire, and Pike laughed. "Don't worry, ladies, soon you'll have a new owner to do it for you."

Owner. The word struck fear into Asha's heart. It was the first time she understood that these men didn't see her as a person. Not only did they not care if she was frightened, they reveled in it. She, and the Wastelander girls sold off to the highest bidder, were chattel.

Nothing more.

Chapter 2

"**U**p," Pike barked at her. "Get up, bitch."

Still wet and naked on the floor beside the filthy bathtub, Asha coughed hard. Her ribs ached fiercely in the wake of Pike's kicks. Thankfully, she didn't think they were broken. She cautiously got to her feet. Purplish bruising had already begun to rise on her smooth brown skin.

An auction, she mused. *They intend to sell us off to…who, exactly?*

"Barney!" he called out the open door. "Bring the whore something to wear. Don't want to give away the goods before they're paid for."

Asha's heart stuttered at his words, and as much as she tried to think clearly, to keep her eyes open to the possibility of escape, fear filled her entire body. Her muscles felt rigid, and her judgment was clouded.

That morning, she'd been woken with the Wastelander girls after a night of uneven sleep and futile plots to escape that never panned out. The Skulls had tied them together with rope, forcing them to walk together in a line with their hands bound. They walked all morning, and by noon, they'd reached what looked like the ruins of a small village…except people were living there, in the skeletal remains of whatever buildings were left.

The village was fenced in. The fence was well-maintained, while the rest of the place was a mess. Holes in buildings were boarded up or simply filled with mud. Everything looked to be in a state of disrepair. A river flowed through the centre of town, but the water reeked so badly that Asha's eyes watered.

The residents themselves were a sight to behold. Most were sickly-looking, missing hair or teeth or both. Some had open sores on their bodies. All were painfully thin as they worked, tilling tiny, withered-looking gardens and hanging up pathetic-looking fabric scraps that barely qualified as laundry.

What the fuck is wrong with these people? Asha wondered, wide-eyed. *Why do they live like this?*

She quickly realized that the gang members in the settlement could be easily identified, since—although most of them also lacked the hygiene standards one would hope for—they looked more or less healthy. At least they didn't look like they were starving to death the way the residents did.

"Welcome to Little River," Pike said to Asha, Brigid, and Becks with a toothless grin. "Home sweet home."

They'd stopped in one of the dilapidated houses, where they forced her and the other girls to bathe. They also made her un-braid her long black hair, letting it fan out down her back. Now, Barney came into the little room and threw Asha what looked like the equivalent of a burlap sack with arm holes.

"I'm not wearing that," she said immediately, without think-ing. "Give me back my clothes."

"Shut your hole," Pike snapped. "You'll wear what we tell you. Your new owner decides if he wants your clothes or not."

Somehow, she'd found her line in the sand. She wasn't going to let these beasts march her out practically naked in front of the world. Her dignity was the last thing she had left, and death would probably be preferable to whatever they had in store, anyway.

"Fuck you," she spat. "Give me my clothes, or you can shoot me right here. I don't give a shit."

Pike looked ready to murder her, but Barney rolled his eyes.

"Whatever, Pike," he said. "Auction opens in five minutes. Let her wear whatever. She's the best one anyway; it won't matter what she's got on. She'll go *fast*."

"Fine." Pike left the room in disgust, then returned a moment later with Asha's dirty shirt, pants, and underwear. He tossed them at her.

"Be ready in thirty seconds, or I'll drag you out in whatever you're wearing."

Asha dressed quickly, hating that they watched and leered at her the entire time. But at least she got to keep her clothes, filthy and stinking though they were after a week outside. They were likely better quality than anything else she'd find out here.

Once dressed, they marched her outside again, where Brigid and Becks waited with a couple other gangsters. Both wore the burlap sacks, and Asha's heart tugged at their expressions. Both girls, in contrast to the night before, looked absolutely petrified.

"We thought they were bringing us to live here with a man," Brigid whispered frantically. "But they're going to sell us to—"

"Shut up," one of the men said, slapping her upside the head.

Brigid quieted, her bottom lip trembling. She suddenly looked so terribly young, and Asha couldn't help feeling sorry for her. She desperately needed to escape, but for a moment, she wished she could save the twins, too. They may have been Wastelanders, but they didn't deserve this, at least.

We don't get what we deserve, Asha thought bitterly as the men led them down a dirt road, deeper into the village. *But if I live through this...these idiots will. One day.*

They bound all three women's hands in front of them. Pike and Barney, along with their cohort of gangsters, then led the three women to a village square—an open marketplace where people worked stalls and sold things like sad-looking dried food and knitted sweaters. The only thing that didn't look scarce was the gun stall, where ammunition and various other supplies crowded the table.

The market was full to bursting, and Asha got the impression that wasn't its usual state. The residents seemed agitated, and it wasn't hard to tell why: the vast majority of visitors were large, relatively healthy-looking men, sporting what she could only assume were various gang paraphernalia. Most of them had an identical feather tattoo, crudely drawn into their skin, while others wore a skull crest on their jackets. Still others wore a strange, inverted crucifix around their necks.

They were the only ones who looked like a light breeze wouldn't knock them over, and as the crowd parted to allow them to pass, many of the men stopped to leer at them. Asha trained her eyes on the ground, refusing to look any of them in the eye.

You won't break me. You won't.

She may have had nothing left—not even Claire—but she wouldn't let them see how scared she was. They'd only ever see her teeth. Her rage. Her hatred of every last one of them.

They approached a raised platform at the back of the square. It was already filled with a dozen young women in similar burlap sacks. Asha scanned their faces. Some were as nakedly terrified as Becks and Brigid; others were resigned. A select few were smiling, confident, and had pushed their way to the front, where everyone could see them. She wondered how on Earth those girls had ended up here, where fear generally clung to everything like an unpleasant stench.

The Skulls men hoisted Asha, Brigid, and Becks up onto the platform.

A moment later, Pike ordered, "Line up, ladies! Best ones at the front, slow sellers in the back!"

Asha swallowed another surge of terror as they organized the women into three lines, one in front of the other, facing the market square. She tried to tuck herself in the back, between two women with horrible burn scars, but Pike scowled at her.

"You're our top seller today, cupcake!" he sneered at her. "To the front. If you're lucky, maybe there'll be a bidding war."

A bidding war...over my body, Asha tried to process. *Fuck this man to death with a rusty chainsaw.*

A throng of men gathered in front of the platform, yelling out insults and catcalls in equal measure. Asha tried to look anywhere but at their jeering, *hungry* faces; they would make her show fear. She lifted her eyes above the crowd and unexpectedly locked eyes with a man she hadn't seen before.

He was tall, muscular, and dressed in all black, with a black helmet, body armour, and neck gaiter that covered his nose and mouth. Only his eyes were visible, with heavy, dark eyebrows that gave him an intense appearance. He was outfitted similarly to the soldiers that guarded the Cave, with the barrel of a rifle visible over his shoulder. Unlike everyone else, he stood out of the fray, away from the crowd, leaning against a market stall with his arms folded over his chest.

He bore no mark of his gang affiliation that she could see, and he stared at her with a fierceness that was disconcerting, a crease forming between his brows. Did he look...*concerned* for her? But this Wastelander didn't know her. No one did anymore.

Asha couldn't have explained it, but a lingering intensity passed between them in that second-long exchange of looks. She also couldn't have explained what made her do what she did next, other than sheer, stupid desperation. Without breaking eye contact, her lips formed two words: *help me.*

He abruptly looked away and gestured to another man nearby, and had a brief, terse exchange with him. The other man—dressed identically, with skin like burnished bronze—didn't look happy about whatever was said, but he nodded and hurried away.

"Auction's open!" Pike boomed out over the crowd. "First up, we have this prime piece of ass."

He grabbed Asha's shoulder and pulled her forward, out of line. She resisted, glaring at him despite the pounding of her heart in her ears.

"Move," he ordered in a low voice, his breath stale and sour-smelling over her face.

His awful breath, combined with the malice in his features, awakened the beast of wrath inside of Asha. How dare this Wastelander scum do this to her. How dare he sell her, and all these girls, like they were at a cheap garage sale. She recalled a line Claire had once quoted to her: *hell is empty, and all the devils are here.*

She reared back and spit in his face. The hot saliva hit him on his cheek and rolled down slowly, painting him with her scorn. Whatever happened next, he would know she thought him no better than the dirt beneath her feet.

For a split second, no one moved or said anything. Then all hell broke loose.

She felt the acute pain of the punch to her face, knocking her over, and the angry screams from the crowd. Her ears were ringing, her head was pounding, and she didn't understand what was happening when Pike was hauled off the stage.

"Discount!" she heard some man yell. "Damaged goods!"

Visceral disgust was all she could feel. They didn't care that he'd hit her; they cared that he'd damaged the object of their desire. No one moved to help her to her feet—not even the other women on the platform. She struggled to her knees, feeling dizzy, as chaos still reigned around them. Some men in the crowd had, for no reason she could tell, started a fistfight, and others were trying to break it up. That was where she saw the man in black again: in the crowd, putting himself between two warring factions, along with a bunch of others dressed like him.

"Guys! Guys! No need for bad blood over a bunch of bitches. Stand down."

The command came from a new man who approached the crowd, his voice low and silken. The tone of someone who was used to being obeyed. He was a thin, lean man with short black hair and almost sickly-pale skin, though it was hard to see much of it with the sheer number of black tattoos that covered his face and body. His clothes must've been all white once, but they were greyer now, marred by dirt, dust, and grime. Most strange of all, he wore a crudely-formed gold circlet on his head, like a prince.

To Asha's surprise, heads snapped up to look at him, and the fighting slowed in response to his command. She finally managed to stand, her jaw aching fiercely.

"Angel!" one of the men called out. "It's not fair that they'd ask full price for her, you saw—"

Angel. What kind of name is that? Asha wondered. She shivered as he came to the edge of the platform and met her eye. His eyes were dark, almost black, and his face split into a smile of gold and rotted teeth. A shiver went down her spine. It wasn't a friendly smile; it reflected a darkness that she wanted to pretend she'd never seen.

"I did," Angel confirmed, turning to face the crowd. "But you asked me here to keep the peace. So, to keep the peace...I'll take her. You Skulls and Devils will have nothing to squabble over. The auction can go on as usual."

"Fuck that!" the same man yelled back. "You're just out for yourself as—"

"Shut up!" Angel roared, startling Asha. She took an involuntary step backward as Angel stared down the dissenter. He'd gone from perfectly calm to explosive rage in a single second, and it was that, more than anything else, that stopped her from speaking up for herself.

This man was volatile. Unstable. Unpredictable.

"If you want a war over this, by all fucking means," Angel continued furiously. "Give my guys a reason. You asked for peace, though, so think really fucking hard before you try me again. The girl belongs to me now, and you'll thank me for taking her off your hands. The end."

There was a tense moment of silence that Angel finally broke by gesturing from the man in black to Asha. "Cade. Get her in hand."

Cade nodded from his spot in the middle of the crowd. He and his men had managed to subdue most of the fighting, and though the crowd looked unhappy with Angel's orders, Asha was surprised that they seemed ready to comply.

Cade made his way to the edge of the platform and held up a gloved hand for her. She hesitated, but took it, and he helped her climb down. He began to lead her through the crowd. She jumped as another man in black brought up the rear behind her, until she realized—her fear edged with disbelief—that the two of them had formed a protective cage around her, protecting her from the crowd and preventing anyone from grabbing (or more likely, groping) her.

When they made it to the edge of market square, Cade led her down a dirt path into the village, past a line of ruined houses. He stopped at what once was a shop of some sort, where a few more of the men in black waited. A couple other guys in plain clothes hung around nearby, casually chatting, and Asha noticed that they bore the feather tattoo on their wrists. There were regular villagers here too, thin and threadbare as everywhere else, looking at the gangsters with thinly veiled distaste.

"Where are we going?" Asha asked.

"Angel's place," Cade replied, his tone clipped. "Tomorrow, we go home."

"Home?"

"The old capital," he said. "But let me give you some advice that'll serve you well, both here and there: don't ask so many questions. Just keep your head down."

Great, so it's like the compound, but without the security or the conveniences of modern living to make having no control over our lives bearable.

The former shop—Angel's place, apparently—was cracked concrete walls and blown-out windows and not much else. The interior walls were badly decayed to the point that it was now mostly one room, with not much inside except a pile of furs on the floor, a lantern, and a couple of well-worn chairs. Fear pulsed unpleasantly under her skin again when Cade entered the building behind her.

"You'll stay here tonight," Cade continued. "You should try to sleep before the long walk tomorrow."

"Yeah, good luck to me," Asha scoffed. "Surrounded by dozens of horny gangsters who all just watched me onstage."

Tiny creases formed at the corners of Cade's eyes, and though his mouth was still covered, she could've sworn he smiled.

"Not sure they'd mess with you after that display," he replied, then turned serious again. He met her eye for the first time since she'd spotted him over the crowd. They were steel grey and serious, and they stopped her in her tracks.

"But I'll guard the door," he said, his voice low and gravelly. "My men won't touch you without my permission."

Somehow, the way he said *permission* sent a different kind of shiver through her—one she wasn't prepared to entertain.

"Now I've got a question for you," Cade continued, and she braced herself. "Anyone looking for you? Is someone gonna storm those gates tonight and take you back?"

Asha studied him, trying to gauge what he wanted to hear, but he didn't reveal much. Rationally, she knew he was asking if he needed to be prepared to fight. But the way he said it almost made it seem like he hoped the answer was yes.

Unfortunately for both of them, however, nobody was looking for Asha Agarwal, in part because there was no one left to look. It didn't feel like there was much point in lying, either, because he wouldn't let her go regardless.

"No," she said, straightening her spine, trying to adopt a bored, haughty tone. "I don't need saving."

She thought he'd laugh in her face at that, and if she was being honest, she would've, too.

To her surprise, however, he said dryly, "I believe it. What's your name, darling?"

"Asha."

"Pretty. Well, Asha...goodnight."

He turned to leave, but Asha's thoughts suddenly went to Angel and his explosive rage. Whatever she said, fear bubbled in her gut. She tried to keep her bored façade going, however. *Give them nothing,* she reminded herself.

"Wait...what about Angel?"

It didn't work. Her voice sounded as scared as she felt.

"Wouldn't worry about him tonight," Cade said over his shoulder. "He'll be drunk as a skunk, and some of my guys will probably have to babysit him. Happens every time we come here."

"And after that?"

He didn't answer. "Get some sleep."

Cade turned to cover the doorway with the makeshift door, sealing her in. Asha let out a long breath, and though the sounds outside—of men talking, laughing, fighting—still made her uneasy, she felt safer than she had since her ordeal began.

She didn't know what to make of the man who'd come to her aid, but she somehow knew he had. She got the sense from the crowd that Angel's appearance had been a surprise, and there was no reason for him to have intervened without Cade.

Still, she worried and wondered, as she lay on the bed of furs on the dirt floor: what on Earth could he have said to make a gang leader willing to speak on her behalf?

Chapter 3

The next day was long. Asha slept fitfully and was awoken at dawn by Cade gently shaking her shoulder.

"We're heading out," he said. "Be ready to leave in five."

He led her outside to a cluster of trees and turned his back while she squatted to pee. For a brief moment, Asha thought of taking advantage of his turned back to hit him and run, but quickly dismissed the idea. Where would she go? Her home was destroyed, and everyone she knew was dead—even Claire, who she'd escaped with.

An uncomfortable twist of guilt stirred in her gut at the thought of Claire, but she shoved it aside. There was nothing she could do for her friend now. She had to do what she could to survive. There was no room for the kind of sentiment she would've felt before. This was a cold, brutal Wasteland where having a conscience made no difference in one's chances of survival. Based on what she'd witnessed so far, it seemed to be a liability more than anything.

But even if she'd had somewhere to go, she couldn't have convinced herself to hit Cade. She may not have trusted him, but it seemed that he'd helped her when no one else would've. He was in a gang, and was probably far from a good guy, but...he also didn't leer at her while she relieved herself—a shred of dignity denied her by her previous captors.

The bar is on the floor, Asha thought bitterly, *but beggars can't be choosers.*

Once she'd finished, Cade approached her with a rope in his hands.

"I'll have to bind your hands," he explained, and she swore she heard a note of apology in his tone. "But we'll keep them in front, so you can walk normally."

"Not afraid I'll use that to my advantage?" she asked wryly, eyeing his black tactical uniform. She was surprised when he snorted at her cheekiness.

"If you can take me down, by all means," Cade replied. "You'll have earned your freedom at that point."

"Freedom is not something to be earned," Asha replied with a sigh.

"Beg to differ, darling," he said as he secured her hands. "The price of freedom is always death. Now, let's get going."

She frowned as she followed him. His words had triggered the odd sensation of *déjà vu,* though she couldn't have explained why. She probably should've been put off by his response, but his light tone made it clear that it wasn't intended as a threat. And his casual use of the word *darling* made her feel tingly, even as she berated herself for feeling one iota of attraction to a man who was holding her captive...even if he seemed like a much less appalling option than anyone else in this wretched place.

Cade escorted her to the entrance to Little River, where they met a crowd of men gathered around a crudely-built carriage pulled by a single horse. Built from logs, it had a tent-like structure stretched across its frame with curtains at its entrance, concealing its occupants. She could only assume that that was where Angel would be spending the trip.

The crowd seemed split into two distinct groups: roughly a dozen men dressed as soldiers like Cade, and a couple dozen regular men wearing a variety of different outfits, but all seemed to display the feather symbol she'd noted earlier, either on their skin or their outfits. The soldiers all carried rifles and handguns, along with tactical backpacks. Only a few of the other men did; the others carried clubs, bats, and even swords. She wondered at their lack of firearms, but then realized that most of the men in the Skulls hadn't carried them either.

Two soldiers approached Cade immediately, looking for orders. The man on the left was light-skinned with blue eyes, and his fellow was the same soldier that Cade had spoken to the day before, when Asha had begged him to help her.

"This is Leo," Cade said to her, gesturing at the light-skinned man, then turned to his brown-eyed, bronze-complexioned companion. "And this is Dom."

"Good to meet you," Leo said, in a far more pleasant tone than Asha would've anticipated. "I'm the resident medic. If you have issues during the trip or once we're back, come to me."

Medic? She wondered. She hadn't even known anyone practiced medicine in the Wasteland. They were all supposed to be clueless, ferocious brutes.

"Oh," Asha replied awkwardly. "Alright. What do we mean here by 'medic'? You're not going to tell me to piss on my wounds, are you?"

To her surprise, Leo laughed. "No. Promise."

Dom didn't react, just averted his eyes from hers. He seemed far less friendly than the other two.

"Orders, Captain?" he prompted, nodding at Cade.

"Move out," Cade replied. "Each of you will take turns guarding the asset as we go. I'll be up front as usual. Angel's already boarded?"

"Yeah." Dom didn't blink often enough for Asha's comfort. "We're good to go."

"Good."

Cade turned to Asha. "This is where we part ways for now. I'll be hanging back and guarding Angel's carriage with a few of my guys. You'll go ahead of us with the others."

Asha nodded, then couldn't help herself. "What's the asset?"

His eyes shone with humour.

"That's you, darling. Leo or Dom will be with you for the trip. Be a good girl for them."

With that, he left, and Asha cursed him for the way her stomach flipped on the way he said *good girl.*

It should be illegal for a hot, muscular man with a gruff voice to ever utter those words.

The trip was long, much longer than the one to Little River, and after five hours of walking through mostly wooded areas, Asha's feet were screaming for relief. The men didn't seem as bothered; they must have been used to a lot of foot travel.

Leo stuck to Asha's side, and she soon realized that this was as much for her protection as it was to prevent escape. The soldiers in black only stole curious glances at her every so often, but the plainclothes gangsters openly ogled her at every opportunity. She supposed she should be used to it, but she still didn't enjoy being looked at like a piece of meat. It was too much like she'd always been treated by past partners, and, eventually, her assigned husband in the compound.

Eric always been the 'fuck her and fall asleep' kind of guy, and he barely paid attention to her when he used her. She doubted he would've noticed if she'd decided to read a book midway through. After the first couple times of him essentially jacking off with her body, she'd refused him...and that had exposed what a sham the marriage was. He had zero interest in her when she wasn't acting as a warm hole for him to fuck, and she had no interest in being his human sex doll.

It probably makes me a bad person since he's dead, but I sure don't miss that asshole.

"The Blackguard wouldn't do anything to you," Leo said conversationally at her side, rifle pointed at the ground as they walked. "But we can't be sure that a few of the regulars aren't stupid enough to try something. We've been traveling around for a couple weeks, so they haven't been around women that much lately."

"Charming," Asha replied sardonically.

"Hey, there's only so much ball sack you can see before you get desperate for an alternative," Leo said, amused.

She was surprised at his humour and openness with her, since so far, most of the Wastelander men had treated her like she was subhuman. Leo spoke to her like a person, perhaps even an equal. It was jarring after the last few days...but it was also nicer than she'd expected.

"What's the Blackguard?" Asha asked. "That the name of this gang?"

He hesitated, then replied, "It's complicated."

She frowned. "The name of your gang is complicated?"

"Yeah. Short version: guys in black, like me, are Blackguard. The rest are Guardians, but technically, we're also all Guardians."

"That cleared up nothing."

Leo grinned. "Told you it was complicated."

"Who's Cade, then, in this group? He acts like your leader, but isn't Angel the leader?"

"Yes," Leo replied, looking discomfited. "Cade is more like our commander. But I wouldn't worry about it now. Just focus on putting one step in front of the other."

She took his advice for a while, walking alongside him for a long time in silence.

"So, what's the plan here?" she felt comfortable asking after a couple hours on the road. "Cade said we're going to the old capital."

"Yeah," Leo answered. "We live in what used to be a gated community, I guess. For the elderly, in the Old World. Had a golf course. Must've been a nice spot, back in the day."

She swallowed. "And it's not now?"

He chuckled. "Well...it's better than a lot of places."

Not exactly reassuring, given the state of Little River, but whatever.

She tried not to allow her anxiety to win over her, which was no small task, given that she had no home, no family or friends, and no real idea of her future. She focused again on putting one foot in front of the other.

At noon, the men broke for a meagre lunch of dried meats, which they seemed to have no intention of sharing. The carriage was stopped, and Angel was consulting with his men as one of the others led the single horse they'd brought to water.

Asha's stomach growled as she rested her back against a tree trunk, but she pretended that she had no interest in their food, even as her mother's succulent butter chicken turned in her mind's eye. She hadn't eaten in more than a day.

Cade left his place by the carriage to join them. He'd lowered the covering over his nose and mouth, and she more clearly saw his face. He was unfairly handsome, just as his stormy grey eyes had suggested, with a sharp jawline, full lips, and shockingly nice-looking teeth. Everyone else she'd encountered so far, except for Leo, had had teeth practically rotting out of their heads. He was mostly clean-shaven, but there was a hint of five o'clock shadow along his jaw. He'd removed his helmet to reveal that his hair was cropped close to the scalp, in the closest approximation of a buzzcut one could get without electric clippers.

"Cap," Leo said in acknowledgement, with a tip of his head. "How's things?"

"All's calm," Cade replied, but he was looking at Asha. "Why don't you go check on His Highness over there? He's complaining about his back again."

Leo sighed and rolled his eyes as he got to his feet. "There's only so much I can do if the man won't do the exercises I prescribe. He's just gonna yell at me for not wasting drugs on it."

"I know," Cade said with a shrug. "Nobody said he was a great listener."

Leo left with another huff. Cade dropped his bag on the ground and took a seat in the grass across from Asha, who had started to feel paradoxically nauseous with hunger.

"When's the last time you had water?"

Asha shrugged. "Don't know, but I learned my lesson on drinking water direct from rivers. I was the sickest I've ever been in my life last time I did."

He reached for a flask at his hip, unfastened it from his belt, and held it out to her.

"Here," he said. "The trick is to boil it first. This stuff is fine."

She hesitated briefly, but she was so thirsty that she couldn't stand it. She took the flask from him with shaking hands, and the first drop of water on her tongue was pure heaven. She couldn't help it—she started to chug.

"Hang on," Cade warned, catching her wrist. She flinched, and he let go abruptly. "You'll make yourself sick if you drink too fast after being dehydrated. Go slow."

She surprised herself with a small giggle. "I thought you were stopping me because I was drinking all your water. Sorry."

A small smile curved those attractive lips of his. "No. Drink up. Just...slowly. You hungry?"

Starving, she wanted to reply. It was the honest answer...but she was still wary of showing weakness, even though he'd helped her. She didn't want to need him in any way, if only because he might be gone tomorrow. Just like everyone else she'd ever known. Besides, his kindness was such a rarity that it made her strangely nervous.

Unfortunately, her stomach answered for her, choosing that moment to growl louder than ever. She flushed, embarrassed, but Cade chuckled.

"That's what I thought," he said, rummaging in his bag. He unwrapped a bundle of cloth to reveal a sparse meal of dried jerky and a small stack of dense, hard drop biscuits. He held it out to her. "It's not much...but you can have it."

Asha hesitated, but her hunger had grown too powerful to ignore. She devoured the jerky first, which was dry but flavourful. The biscuits, however, were hard as a rock, powdery, and tasteless. A flash of amusement crossed Cade's features when she coughed after biting into one of them.

"Tastes like shit," he agreed, "but it's better than nothing. Ask Dom nicely, and he might find you some plants to eat."

Asha raised an eyebrow. She got the odd impression that he was distracting her on purpose, but it wasn't working. For hours, she'd wondered what she'd gotten herself into with this group—Guardians, or Blackguard, or whatever the hell they called themselves—and Leo had given her a bunch of non-answers.

"What's going to happen to me?"

Cade pinned her with a look from those steely eyes. She didn't like how his gaze made her feel exposed, naked, like he already knew all her secrets.

"I guess that depends."

"On?" she prompted. "Look, I need to be prepared. I'm not an idiot; I know you helped me for a reason. So, if that reason is to sell me on at the next stop...well, a warning couldn't hurt."

He studied her for a moment in silence, making her even more uncomfortable. She crossed her arms and stared pointedly at the ground.

Finally, he replied, "It depends on whether you'd rather be my woman or not."

Her eyes snapped wide. "*Your* woman? Like...how? Like ownership?"

"Yes," he said, point-blank, and she scoffed. "Look, that's how it is with the Guardians. Men are in charge; women are extensions of their men."

"And I'm sure you delight in that," Asha shot back.

"My opinion is irrelevant," he answered coolly. "Just like yours. It's how it is, and we have to make the best of it."

She chewed her lip. "What's my other option?"

Cade mimed covering his heart with his hand. "I thought you liked me, darling."

"My liking you or not is irrelevant."

"Now, that's where you're wrong," he said, a sly look in his eye. "Choosing me means that you get to live with me, instead of in a crowded dorm with all the other unattached women. It means that you'll get more rations. And it means that you won't have to open your legs for every man here and back at the Nest—including Angel."

Asha's eyebrows had risen so high they might've disappeared into her hairline.

"And for you?" she asked. "I'm assuming this generosity isn't free."

He shrugged. "You're not wrong. You'll work for me. Fight for me. And yes, I'd like to fuck you. You're a good-looking girl, and it's been a long time. I won't force you...but I won't lie to you, either."

Asha laughed bitterly. "I guess I have to appreciate your candor, at least."

He grinned, showing those surprisingly perfect teeth.

"It's what I'm best known for."

"Why can't you just let me go?" she asked. She hated how fear creeped into her voice, but reality was starting to sink in: she was never going to be free again.

Cade blew out a breath. "Because they'd know it was me. And I don't want a bullet in my head."

She considered that. "We could make it look like an accident—"

"It's not an option," he cut in forcefully. "If I could, darling, I would. You don't have to believe me, but it's true."

Even if he could, she thought, *where the hell would I go?* She'd be lost and alone and starving to death, the way she'd been before Pike and his goons had found her. That was a one-way ticket to a slow, painful death.

"Anyway, we need to move on," Cade continued. "But think it over on the rest of the trip to the Nest. You won't have much else to do anyway, since Dom is practically mute most of the time."

Cade stood and returned to Angel's wagon. Asha watched him go, chewing her lip some more. Anxiety was alive in her veins. She hadn't known what she was getting into when she asked Cade for help. Now, it was a choice between servicing him—a strange man who had, at best, questionable ethics—or being passed around to a bunch of gangbangers, who might hurt or kill her before or after they were done raping her.

Their lack of basic hygiene doesn't help, Asha thought ruefully. *At least Cade looks like he's bathed in his life.*

If he hadn't helped her, would it have meaningfully changed her options? She doubted it. At the slave market, those men wanted one thing. The best she could've hoped for, as much as she hated it, were the choices she now had in front of her.

Cade had been right about Dom; he barely spoke to Asha as he escorted her through the woods. Compass in hand, he helped steer their direction, but other than that, he left her to her thoughts. Which was good, because she was a little preoccupied at the moment.

I don't think he'd hurt me, Asha mused, glancing over her shoulder towards Angel's convoy. She couldn't see Cade clearly from this distance, but she felt his eyes on her. She scolded herself briefly: *You've known him all of a day. How can you possibly know what he's like?*

But he *had* helped her, hadn't he? Yes, maybe he was getting something out of it, but he also hadn't had to offer for her. He could've left her to Angel's men. Maybe he was helping her in the only way he could. Who knew how long he'd been living amongst the worst kind of people, after all? Maybe this was all he knew.

Asha's gut told her that Cade was the lesser of two evils, and it wasn't particularly close. He was the only one who'd treated her with an ounce of dignity during her captivity, and he'd never shown signs of aggression toward her, which was more than she could say for the men who still occasionally catcalled at her as she walked. It said enough that Cade had ordered Leo and Dom to guard her against his own gang; even he didn't trust them.

She would've died before she admitted it out loud, but she also had to concede that fucking Cade—who was unnaturally good-looking, especially compared to the other men—was far more appealing than the alternative. It was hard to see his body under the tactical uniform, but he was clearly in good shape. Maybe seeing him naked wouldn't be the worst thing in the world.

It made Asha feel cheap and crass, to sell herself off to some guy she barely knew. Her parents would've been ashamed of her. But she wasn't an idiot. She knew that he was the only realistic chance she had for survival. She would do what she had to.

Chapter 4

They walked the rest of the afternoon. Finally, the shape of shadowy buildings appeared on the horizon, and they entered the city outskirts.

"How much farther?" Asha asked Dom, who grunted. That was all he seemed capable of doing half the time.

"Another ten."

"Minutes? Hours? Days?" She wouldn't have been shocked if her feet were bloody stumps at this point, they hurt so bad.

He grunted again, not amused. "Minutes."

They weaved through the derelict ruins of city buildings, down broken streets and alleyways, stopping every so often to wait for Angel's convoy. As they went, they came across various people, who waved at them as they passed.

"Who are they?" Asha asked, a little nervously.

"They're our people," Dom replied in an imperious tone, as though she were stupid.

"Your people?"

"The Guardians," he said impatiently. "You didn't think we brought the whole gang with us, did you?"

"I didn't know what to expect," she answered, irritated. "I've never been here before. You don't have to be so rude."

Predictably, Dom grunted and didn't say anything else as they continued on, deeper into the city. Ten agonizing minutes of walking later, they traveled up a decaying road to an iron gate, with a tall fence that wrapped around a whole community. An extremely faded, barely legible metal sign said *Sunnyside Acres: Luxury Retirement Community.* Rusted, with ivy climbing its edges, it looked ready to crumble into dust. Someone had painted over it far more recently, with graffiti that read *Angel's Nest.*

"Welcome to the Nest," Dom said with zero enthusiasm.

"And what is that, exactly?"

He answered without bothering to look at her. "The home base of our territory. Everyone who lives here is in Angel's inner circle."

As they drew closer to the gate, Asha recoiled. Someone had sharpened the iron spires to a point, and the three tallest spikes impaled three worn, desiccated heads. Hollow eye sockets and yawning mouths faced skyward—a clear warning to all who passed by this wretched place.

These are barbarians, Asha couldn't help thinking. *What the hell are you doing, Asha? Making deals with these guys?*

"They've been there a while," Dom said, startling her out of her thoughts.

"Is that supposed to be comforting or something?" she asked incredulously.

He shrugged. "Take it or leave it."

There were several more of the Blackguard at the gate. Just like the Blackguard in the convoy, they stood out from the rest, dressed like soldiers. They acknowledged Dom with a nod, though they stared at Asha curiously as he brought her through the gate. They waited for the convoy to pass through and catch up with them at a fork in the old road.

The tent flap on top of the wagon opened, and Angel appeared for the first time since they'd left Little River, looking disheveled. Asha had no idea what he'd been up to that whole time, but she guessed it had to be better than walking. He hopped down from the wagon, and a couple of the men led the horse away.

The Blackguard surrounded him on all sides, with Cade at the front and Leo bringing up the rear, and they followed Dom, Asha, and the other Guardians deeper into the gated community. They acted like a private security force, which, for all Asha knew, they might be. It made her wonder what Angel had done that would necessitate that much security.

"I want everyone at the clubhouse," Angel was saying behind her, and when someone objected, he interrupted, "That wasn't a question, Khalid. I want a report before it gets dark. Then we'll have a little party, if it'll stop you being such a pussy."

He then called out to Dom, who turned slowly to face him, as though wishing he were anywhere else.

"Yes, sir?" He sounded like calling Angel that was literal torture, and Asha had to hide her amusement with a loud cough.

"A ray of fucking sunshine, as usual," Angel said with a dark chuckle. "Bring the girl to the clubhouse, too. I have plans."

That sounded ominous, but Asha looked at Cade, who gave her the tiniest nod.

"I'll do it," he said to Angel. "Dom can help round everyone up. He looks like he needs a break from her, anyway."

It was hard to deny that it was true; Dom looked like he wanted to crawl under a rock and stay there. Permanently. *I wonder how a man who obviously hates people ended up living in this place.*

Looking relieved, Dom ran ahead, and Asha saw Cade suppress a smile.

"Fine," Angel said irritably. "But I want her there, at the meeting. And get the girls to clean her up."

He wrinkled his nose as he looked Asha up and down, and she crossed her arms over her chest. She knew she was dirty, sweaty, and disheveled, but she was still offended. Angel looked like he hadn't seen a bath in a long time either, so it was a bit rich for him to judge her.

Angel walked down the lefthand path Dom had followed, his entourage falling in line behind him. When they were out of earshot, Cade said, "Wouldn't take it personally. They care more about how the women look than the men."

"Oh, sure, not personal, just sexist," Asha scoffed. "It's not about you personally, just everyone like you."

Cade shrugged. "I'm not saying they're correct. Just stating a fact. Now, have you thought about our bargain?"

"Is it really a bargain if one party has no other choice?"

"You do have another choice," Cade countered. "It just pales in comparison to the incredible opportunity to be with me instead."

She rolled her eyes. "You really are irritating, you know that?"

"Dom would agree with you," he replied with a grin. "Then again, he'd agree about most people. Anyway...quit stalling."

Asha let out a long breath. Her hands were trembling, so she laced her fingers together. Despite her fire, she was still afraid—afraid of what this new life would be, and afraid of these people who most certainly didn't have her best interests at heart. She swallowed hard before answering.

"I accept the bargain," she said. "I'll be your...your woman, I guess. But I have one condition."

He waited for her to elaborate, but she nervously chewed her lip instead.

"What is it, Asha?" he finally asked, and she was surprised at how his voice had gentled. He saw her fear. She screwed up her courage one more time.

"You...you can't hit me," she said. "Not if you're mad, or if I do something wrong. Because if you hit me, I might as well take my chances with the others, since they'll almost certainly do that to me anyway. If you hit me, our bargain is broken."

Cade flinched, almost like *she'd* hit *him*. He took a moment to answer, his throat working. He looked like he went somewhere far away.

"You have my word," he answered solemnly. "I'll never raise a hand to you. Ever."

The bar is in hell at this point...but it could be worse.

"Alright," Asha said awkwardly. "Then it's a deal. What now?"

Cade seemed to snap back to reality, shaking his head. "We have to go to the clubhouse, and at the meeting, I'll claim you as my woman. Then, everyone drinks themselves into oblivion, and I'll show you where I live."

"What exactly does claiming involve?" Asha asked nervously.

He chuckled. "I just announce to Angel, in front of everyone, that I want to take a woman. I already told him I was interested in claiming you, so we've already haggled over it a bit."

He started walking down the right path, and she hurried after him. "Haggled?"

"Yeah. You don't honestly think anything's free in the W—with the Guardians, do you? We trade for everything: food, supplies, women."

"Love that for me," Asha said bitterly. "So, what was I worth, then? A couple strips of jerky?"

"Give us some credit," Cade replied, amused. "Even we value people more than that."

He didn't answer her question, but Asha was distracted by the scenery unfolding in front of them. The place was heavily overgrown with trees and shrubs, but in the distance, she could still see small, single-storey homes dotted the gently sloping landscape. All were connected by crumbling roads. Some even had hollowed-out, rusty cars still parked next to them. A narrow stream wound through the place, providing a source of fresh water, and a crumbling stone bridge offered passage across. It had probably been beautiful once.

"This was an old folks' community in the Old World," Cade said conversationally. "Luxurious at the time. Every tenant had their own house. The clubhouse, on the old golf course, is where Angel and the girls live, and where we have meetings. Everyone else lives in and around the old houses."

"You have one too, then?"

He nodded. "I live on the opposite end of the settlement, though. More secluded, which is how I like it."

They passed one of the old houses, and Asha was surprised by how relatively intact it was. Ivy snaked up the walls, partially concealing several small holes, and there were deep cracks in the foundation, but it was otherwise in much better shape than any of the houses she'd seen in Little River.

It gave her some small hope that living here might not be as terrible as she feared.

Cade led her to the clubhouse, a sprawling brick building with a sloped roof and a large entryway that must've once been a reception area. Now, it seemed to serve as a common room of sorts, with hard metal chairs and sagging sofas lining the walls, and to Asha's surprise, potted plants that seemed to be well cared for. In the centre of the seating was an old metal barrel, sawed in half to create a makeshift firepit, in which flames were already dancing, warming the space. Three young women lounged on the sofas, chatting and laughing.

Upon seeing Cade and Asha, the young woman on the left—a pretty Black girl with long braids—called out, "Lana!"

Asha frowned, but a second later, a tall woman with long, flowing strawberry blonde hair appeared, wearing a mid-length eyelet dress that seemed inappropriate for March weather. She was probably in her early twenties, and Asha couldn't help noticing her voluptuous figure, with full, perky breasts, wide-set hips, and ample thighs. She swallowed hard and looked at the floor.

"Hey, Lana," Cade said in a friendly, familiar way. "We have a new addition. This is Asha."

Lana's bright blue eyes sparkled in the firelight, and she gave Asha a warm smile that made her flush.

"Hi there, sugar," she said brightly. "Welcome to the Nest."

Asha nodded mutely, earning her an odd look from Cade.

"Angel sent her to get cleaned up before the meeting tonight," he continued, a crease still between his brows.

Asha felt Lana's eyes on her, studying her. "She need a bed, then?"

"No," Cade answered easily. "After the meeting, she's mine."

"Wow, settling down already, Cade?" Lana teased him, in a way that made Asha's stomach flutter. "We'll miss you around here."

His grey eyes lighted, and his broad grin at Lana's obvious flirting was undeniably charming.

Why are they both so hot? Asha thought, half-protesting her own reaction to them. *People who hold you captive are supposed to be ogres or some shit.*

To be fair, most of them might as well have been, which made Cade and Lana's beauty that much more obnoxious.

"I'll see you again at the meeting," Cade said to Asha by way of goodbye. "It shouldn't be too long."

Despite her general distrust, Asha's heart beat hideously at the thought of him leaving. He was the only thing standing between her and the unknown abyss of her future. Their newly negotiated bargain was an anchor in the sudden storm that'd overtaken her life.

"It'll be okay," Cade murmured, evidently sensing her unease. "Once the claiming's over with."

On that less-than-comforting note, he left, and Asha wondered for the hundredth time what on Earth she'd gotten herself into.

"Well, let's get you cleaned up, sugar," Lana said to her, wrinkling her nose. "Because no offence, but you reek."

"A couple weeks wandering the wilderness will do that," Asha replied, resigned. She followed Lana as she led her down a hallway. "Are you the madam here, then?"

Lana frowned. "The madam?"

"It means a woman who's in charge of a brothel."

She giggled. "Never heard that before. I guess it applies, though I do a lot more than that. As do the other girls."

Other young women filtered in and out of the rooms in the hallway, talking and laughing. They shot Asha curious glances when they spotted her, but if they had questions, they kept them to themselves. Asha guessed that, like her, they'd learned that questions only invited unwanted attention.

Lana turned right near the end of the corridor, into what was once the clubhouse's public washroom. The tile was dirty and cracked, and there was a narrow, glassless window that had been boarded up. The stalls and toilets had been gutted, but surprisingly, the sinks had been left intact. It seemed that without indoor plumbing, the women had converted them into washbasins, like something out of a period movie. A water barrel stood in one corner, confirming Asha's suspicion. In place of the toilets, someone had put in an old metal stock tank, which she could only assume they used as a bathtub. It was currently empty.

"You can wash up here," Lana said as she opened a small cupboard built into the wall. From there, she offered Asha a thin washcloth and a metal bucket. "Most of us fill the bucket from the water barrel, then stand in the tub to wash. If you need to pee, the door at the end of the hall leads to the yard. The latrines are at the very back, farthest from the door."

Asha nodded. "Thanks."

"I nearly forgot." Lana briefly left into the room across the hall, then returned holding a pile of clothing. "Every new girl here gets a set of basic clothes to wear. These are free, but anything extra, you'll have to either earn yourself or have Cade gift to you."

Asha didn't bother asking how she'd *earn* such things. "Okay."

"Oh, and just so you know—Angel doesn't allow women to cut their hair," Lana added, as though this were a minor addition rather than a massive violation, just like everything else in this place. "Even attached ones have to keep their hair long."

With that, Lana left her alone, but there was little privacy. Whether the washroom door had been removed on purpose or had simply succumbed to the sands of time, there was nothing to stop anyone from walking in at any time. Still, she had to admit that Lana was right: she fucking *stank,* and she'd do just about anything to remove the gross, sweaty film of grime that clung to her skin.

She visited the latrine first, and the stench felt as though it might sear her eyebrows off. She finished as quickly as she could, then took Lana's advice and washed up in the tub, mindful of the open doorway. Thankfully, no one walked by. She then dressed in a simple white t-shirt and black pants from the pile of clothing she'd been given. Wearing clean clothing felt like a revelation in itself after so many days of wandering.

After she was done, she peered down the corridor, looking for Lana. A moment later, she emerged from a closed door and waved Asha over. The door led to a small, simple bedroom, with a double bed that looked far plusher than the bunk beds in the women's dormitory. Each side had a wooden nightstand. One side was neat, with only a few personal effects: a hairbrush, a tarnished silver locket, and an assortment of what seemed to be crudely-made cosmetics. The opposite side was messy and had children's toys, crayons, and a one-eyed, raggedy teddy bear.

"This is your room?" Asha asked, and Lana nodded.

"A privilege of my status," she replied. "I live here with my little sister, Cassie. It's the safest place we've lived."

Asha carefully kept her face neutral, not letting herself consider what Lana's previous homes must've been like if she considered this the best one.

"So, you and the other women all live here together?"

"Yep," Lana said, cleaning under her fingernails. "All the unattached women, anyway. A few of the men have claimed women, and they live with their men. But the rest of us live here, and we serve the single men."

"Serve...how?" Asha asked carefully.

Lana shrugged. "How ever they need, really. We cook, wash clothing and linens, sort the packages that come from the Settlements."

"The Settlements?"

"Where we get the things we need—food rations, clothes, and such," Lana replied, sounding surprised. "Where did you think it came from? Someone's gotta grow and make that stuff."

Asha frowned. "What do you trade for it, then? I haven't seen anything that—"

Lana's tinkly laugh contained a note of disbelief.

"Where'd you say you came from, sweetheart?" she asked, then moved on without waiting for an answer. "We don't trade. None of the big gangs like us do. The Settlements give us stuff in exchange for protection."

Like the mafia in an Old World movie. I should've guessed.

"So, when you say you *serve* the men," Asha continued slowly, "do you—"

"Fuck them?" Lana asked, sounding amused. "Geez, you don't have to be so precious about it. Yeah, it's part of the arrangement. Unattached men can ask for a girl for a night. Usually, they give gifts to their favourites."

Asha couldn't help but make a face. "Gross."

"Nothing gross about it," Lana said sharply, and Asha could practically hear her eyeroll in her voice. "Don't know where you lived that made you so judgy, but there are worse lives than this, sugar. The girls who live here have a community of women around them. They never go to bed hungry, and they're safer than anywhere else they could be. For many of them, opening their legs is a small price to pay for that."

"I didn't mean *you're* gross," Asha replied, a little stung. "It's just...it's barbaric that the men here expect that of you. Treat you like slaves."

Lana chuckled. "And just where are the men that expect any different? If they exist, I don't know them. It's only by accepting how they are that I got to be in the spot I'm in now."

"What spot is that?"

She flipped her strawberry blonde hair over her shoulder. "In charge of the women and children. I help make sure they have what they need. And I'm Angel's first choice, which has its privileges."

Must be why she's the best dressed one here.

Still, Asha only just managed to avoid wrinkling her nose. Being *that* man's favourite didn't seem like much of a prize to her...but then, she didn't know what Lana's options before this had been. Maybe there were people even worse than him.

"There are kids here?" she asked instead, mildly appalled.

"Of course," Lana replied, as though it were a silly question. "We do our best, but sometimes pregnancy happens to unclaimed women. The kids live here with their mothers."

She gestured for Asha to follow her, and in a small room across from the dormitory, there was a children's room. They had the same bunk beds as the women's dorm, but there were small wooden toys here and there, and childish drawings on the cracked concrete walls. It all looked a bit forlorn—worn and torn by the hands of time, put together as an afterthought for these accidental children.

It struck Asha as a depressing place for a child to grow up, but unfortunately, sad childhoods were not the exclusive province of extreme poverty. As she knew from personal experience, nothing impoverished a child quite like a lack of love.

"It's not so bad," Lana said quietly, watching Asha survey the room. "At least they're with their mothers. That's more than I had, growing up."

Asha bowed her head. "Sorry to hear that."

Lana brushed her off. "It's fine; I'm over it. But it helps to remember that things can always be worse."

"Fair enough. Thank you for showing me around, and giving me the clothes."

"You're welcome," Lana said with a smile, and then her tone turned playful. "It's like anywhere else here, you know. You just gotta figure out how to work the system, sweetness. You want food and nice things? Fuck a man. You want to get off? Fuck a woman."

Asha couldn't help it; she laughed. "I'll keep that in mind."

Chapter 5

The meeting took place in a large courtyard on the west side of the clubhouse. It must've once been the patio of the ruined restaurant that now served as a mess hall. Most of the people who lived at the Nest seemed to be assembled there, chatting and laughing around a massive bonfire. Flames shot toward the darkening sky, illuminating the party with an orange light. The men largely stood or sat in small groups while the women brought food or drink to them. A small gaggle of children with dirt-streaked faces played together in a corner, largely unsupervised.

At the far end, a small wooden platform had been constructed, and Asha's eyes widened at the sight of Angel sitting there on what was unmistakably a throne. A throne made of scrap metal and decaying old tires, but a throne nonetheless. On his left side, an enormous bald man with crude tattoos and multiple facial piercings stood. He was evidently some kind of bodyguard.

Cade sat in a plain wooden chair next to Angel, his arms folded, his expression impassive. He was one of the only men who looked like he wasn't enjoying himself. Lana tugged on Asha's hand and led her to the foot of the platform, presenting her with a nod to Angel. Angel gave her a nod in return, and she retreated back with the other women to help with serving food.

"Welcome," Angel said to Asha, but there was no warmth in his voice. "We'll start the claiming in a minute."

He wore the same filthy clothes as earlier, including the crude circlet. His dark eyes were cold and unfeeling as he appraised her—there was nothing behind them. The corner of his mouth was upturned in a self-satisfied smirk, which sparked unease in her belly.

To distract herself, she looked at Cade instead. His gaze was much warmer, though he maintained an aura of aloofness. He inclined his head in the tiniest acknowledgment of her, as if to tell her, *I'll keep my word.*

Asha had to hope that was what he was communicating, because seeing Angel again reminded her that he scared the shit out of her. There was something about him that seemed innately cruel and eager to cause pain. He still stared her down, and her heart jumped uncomfortably when his smirk broadened.

Angel lifted his dirty fingers to his mouth and whistled, calling everyone to attention. Instantly, every conversation fell silent, and all eyes were on him. It would've been impressive if it hadn't been so frightening. They were so *deferential* to him by default.

"We have a guest," Angel said in a loud voice. "In Little River, we picked up a stray. A damn fine-looking stray she is, too."

Asha flushed, embarrassed. She didn't like the way all the men were looking at her now, with an obvious curiosity and hunger. They were hoping he'd announce it was a free-for-all—she could feel it. She forced herself to focus on Cade, but his expression hadn't moved an inch. Still, he was the only possible source of comfort she had.

"Cade wants to claim her," Angel continued with a chuckle. "Never thought my boy would take a woman. He's been living like a priest or some shit."

There was collective laughter, and Cade's eyes narrowed, but he otherwise showed no reaction.

"But are there any other takers?" Angel asked the crowd, raising his eyebrows. "Fair's fair. Raise your hands."

Asha's heart started pounding. *Other takers?* Cade had said nothing about this. What would it mean if someone else wanted her?

She cast around her, but to her immense relief, not a single hand raised. The men's eyes were on Cade, who stared them down with complete confidence...and a palpable air of menace. Nobody wanted to challenge him, Asha realized.

What, were they just gonna brawl over me otherwise? she thought, disbelieving. But her answer came immediately when Angel goaded the crowd: "What, no one wants to take on our fearless Blackguard leader? Cowards."

Yes, they very much would have brawled over me. And what does it say that not a single man here dares to challenge the guy who wants me?

She didn't want to examine that thought too closely.

"Alright, spoil my fun," Angel said, rolling his eyes. "Cade, you claiming her, then?"

"Yes." Cade spoke for the first time as he got to his feet. He stepped down from the platform and approached Asha. From the sheath at his hip, he drew out a long knife, and Asha instinctively recoiled.

Angel snorted, mocking her fear, and Asha gritted her teeth. But Cade didn't pay him any mind; his eyes were fixed on her.

"Give me your hand, darling," he said. "It'll only take a second."

His voice was a soft caress, a soothing balm on her anxiety. He was trying hard not to scare her even more. Asha hesitated, unsure of his intent. Her pause caused speculative murmurs to begin among the crowd.

"Trust me," Cade whispered, low enough so that only she could hear.

His grey eyes pled with her, and in the end, what choice did she have anyway? She reluctantly offered him her hand. He took it gently in his, and in one quick, precise motion, opened a small, clean slit across her palm with his knife. Asha gasped in pain, and blood immediately oozed out onto her brown skin, reflecting orange rays of firelight in the dark crimson droplets.

Quick as a cat, Cade sliced through his own palm as well, and took her bloodied hand in his, pressing them together. His eyes met hers with the same intensity she'd felt when she'd first seen him. Like he *saw* her. Like he already knew her.

"My blood runs in her veins," he announced to everyone else, though he didn't tear his eyes away from Asha's. She trembled slightly, though not with fear. She didn't understand the connection she felt with this man when he looked at her. "She's claimed. Mine. Now. Always."

Mine. The word sent a shiver down Asha's spine, part-horror, part something else she was ashamed of. She hated the idea of him owning her, but at the same time, when he looked at her like that, she found herself wondering if maybe it wouldn't be such a bad thing to be owned by *this* man.

You're the worst feminist ever, Asha. Seriously, what the fuck.

She flinched as Cade's other hand came up to touch her face, and he murmured, again only for her, "Sorry. It's part of it."

"Okay," she breathed, trying to regain her sense of equilibrium.

Well, as long as he apologizes *for the barbaric blood ritual, that makes it okay,* she scolded herself. *He's still participating in this system. Never forget it.*

Then he stepped back, looking at Angel, who appeared darkly amused. She didn't like the look in Angel's eye, like a hawk surveying prey. An uneasy pause stretched out for several seconds, and Angel's expression didn't change.

"There's just one problem," the gang leader finally said, the corners of his lips twitching. "Payment."

Cade frowned. "We agreed—"

"Yeah, on you taking Rockland for me, like you keep promising," Angel cut in sharply. "So, here's what we're gonna do."

He snapped his fingers, and in an instant, three men emerged from the crowd, surrounding Asha. She gasped in pain and surprise as one of them kicked her feet out from under her. Cade reached out for her automatically, but they shoved her away from him. Before she could react, the largest man sat on her back, and she felt cold, hard metal pressed to the back of her head. A gun.

She froze, her eyes wide.

"What the fuck is this?" Cade snapped at Angel. "We had a fucking deal, Angel. We even did your stupid fucking ritual."

Asha squirmed instinctively, which only earned her a blow to the back of the head that made her see stars. Meanwhile, Angel's expression didn't shift an inch. His smile was haunting. He was *enjoying* this.

"So, our deal's changed," Angel said simply. "You get me Rockland, and you get your girl back. Don't get it to me, and she's my new pet. I'll put a collar on her and walk her like a dog through the streets."

"Fuck *you*," Asha spat at him, unable to contain herself. "I'd rather die."

Angel's cruel laughter pierced her ears. "I like the girls with spirit, you know. It's more satisfying to break them, in the end."

Cade's jaw worked, and when he spoke, his voice was laced with fury.

"Let her go," he ordered, with all the authority and coldness of a hardened military commander. "We can settle this some other way. But she's off limits."

Asha noticed that Leo and Dom had suddenly appeared behind Cade, emerging silently like shadows. Both of them looked resigned, but determined. They'd follow their friend into a fight, if it came to it.

The only thing that kept Asha from succumbing to her terror was her refusal to let Angel see her fear. It was the kind of thing he'd get off on, seeing a woman afraid of him.

Pathetic.

"No other way to settle it," Angel replied, grinning, though it looked more like he was baring his teeth. "You've been dragging your feet on Rockland long enough, man. So, here's the next part of the deal: you have two weeks. If you don't get back here before then, she's mine. Forever."

Cade paled. "Two weeks is fucking impossible and you know it."

Angel shrugged. "That's your problem, *Captain.*" His disdain on the last word was unmistakable. He nodded at the three men around Asha. "Lock her up."

Asha cried out as they started to drag her back toward the clubhouse. She clawed at the dirt in desperation, but only succeeded in breaking two of her fingernails. More of Angel's men coalesced around her, preventing escape.

She locked eyes with Cade before they blocked him from view, and for the first time since she'd met him, he looked away.

Asha's new home was a tiny concrete box of a room with nothing in it except a ragged straw pallet on the floor. There was a narrow window near the ceiling in one corner—far too small to crawl out of. Even if it had been large enough, however, steel bars had been installed over it.

They threw her in, then bolted a heavy steel door behind her. Night had fallen now, and the room was completely dark, as there were no candles present. Only moonlight filtered in through the barred window.

Asha collapsed on top of the straw pallet, shivering from the draft. It was March, and the nights were still cold. She'd wisely worn the warmer clothes that Lana had given her, but they weren't enough. She curled up under a thin blanket that'd been left on top of the pallet, desperate to get warm. It was musty and stank like stale urine, but it was better than nothing.

She stared up into the dark. She'd heard Cade shouting some more at Angel while she was being dragged away, and more raised voices in return, but she had no idea what they'd ultimately decided. In the end, it probably didn't matter. The game was clearly rigged against Cade from the start, and by extension, against her, too.

It was stupid of her to put such faith in Cade's promise. But he'd been decent to her, and he'd seemed so sure of himself that she'd believed him. She wondered what had made Angel decide to move against Cade so decisively, since it had seemed like Cade was trusted to protect Angel personally.

Asha shivered again, but the cold wasn't as bad as before. She wondered how long they'd leave her here, or indeed, if they'd ever come back for her. Her imprisonment was clearly intended more as a punishment for Cade than for her, but that didn't mean they cared about her. If anything, it only proved she was merely a pawn to them in whatever stupid power games they were playing.

Chattel, she thought again dully. *Nothing more than chattel.*

Her question was answered half an hour later, when the door opened. She shot up on her pallet, and Cade walked in, carrying a candelabra for light. He was followed by Leo, and Angel's enormous bodyguard. While the former two entered, the bodyguard merely waited by the doorway, his arms crossed and a permanent frown etched between his eyebrows.

"I'm sorry," Cade burst out, crouching beside her. "That wasn't supposed to happen."

"Yeah, no shit," Asha replied acridly. "What the hell happened back there?"

"Power play," Leo supplied as he set down a large medical bag. "Are you injured, Asha?"

She sighed. "Cuts and scrapes, but otherwise okay, I think."

"Let me take a look at that hand."

Surprised, she allowed Leo to examine the hand that Cade had cut during the claiming, and he began to clean it with supplies from his kit.

"Angel does loyalty tests from time to time," Cade said wearily, not looking at her. "The Blackguard has grown recently, and my guess is he sees me as a threat. So yeah, it's a power play. A way to put me in my place. Rockland's a settlement that's been on his radar for months, and I've been planning a takeover for just as long. It takes time to gain sources on the inside, and turn them to our side...but it hasn't been happening fast enough for him."

Asha gasped at the sting of alcohol on her hand as Leo cleansed the laceration. He shot her an apologetic glance.

"So, what now?" Asha demanded, piercing Cade with a look. "Am I Angel's pet? Because if so, do me a kindness and shoot me in the head right now."

"You're not his pet," Cade replied sharply. "You never will be. I'm going to take Rockland, and I'm going to come back for you."

"You said it's impossible to do it in two weeks," she said, and when he opened his mouth to reply, she added fiercely, "Don't lie to me."

Cade held up his hands in surrender. "I'll never lie to you, Asha. It doesn't look good." When she made a sound of disbelief, he continued, "But I'll do it."

"How?"

He winced. "I don't know yet, darling. I've laid the groundwork, but it'll be a challenge. I'm leaving immediately, though. Leo will stay here with you."

Leo started as he wrapped Asha's hand in clean bandages.

"But if there's going to be a battle..."

"You're staying," Cade replied pointedly. "We'll bring one of the women to act as a medic. I need you to stay here and keep an eye on Asha. Make sure she's okay."

"But—"

"That's an order," he snapped back, and Asha was surprised when Leo shut his mouth and nodded in response.

"Time's up," the bodyguard said from the door, startling her. She'd forgotten he was there. "Better get a move on, Captain, or I might ask Angel for a turn with your girl."

"Fuck off, Dax," Cade snarled. He reached for Asha's good hand and squeezed it gently. "I'll see you in two weeks. I promise."

With a final squeeze and a single backward glance, he and Leo left, and Asha was again entombed in the tiny room.

The first day following Cade's departure started out better than expected.

Asha awoke at dawn, the sun streaming into the small room through the barred window. She sat up and stretched, silently lamenting how uncomfortable the straw pallet was. Her stomach grumbled, and she wondered whether they intended to feed her at all in the next two weeks.

An hour later, the door swung open. Asha was unenthused by Dax's return, but thankfully, he was followed by Lana. Her strawberry blonde hair was braided down her back, and she wore a heavier jacket against the morning chill. She gave Asha a look of what seemed like genuine concern.

"I've come to get you for breakfast," Lana said in a rush. "I figured you must be hungry."

"Starving," Asha admitted as she got to her feet. She followed Lana out of her cell. Dax watched her carefully, and she didn't like the way he leered at her.

"You can go, Dax," Lana said to him in an overly cheerful way. "I've got this under control. Breakfast will be ready soon, so you should go relax before it's time."

Dax grunted. "Fine. Don't let her out of your sight. Angel's orders."

"I'm well aware," Lana replied brightly. "Don't trouble yourself about it. There's a good boy."

Asha could've sworn she actually saw the hulking man flush. Then again, she herself wasn't immune to the charms of the tall, voluptuous beauty next to her. Dax merely grunted again in goodbye, then took off in the direction of the mess hall.

Lana let out a breath. "I thought he might not leave. That makes our lives easier."

"What do we do now?"

She raised her eyebrows. "We serve breakfast, of course."

Lana led Asha into the ruined restaurant, where the women had set up in the old kitchens. Naturally, none of the old stoves worked, so they'd been replaced by fire barrels. Women chatted back and forth as they grilled eggs and some kind of meat over the flames. A teenage girl stirred a large pot of what looked like some approximation of porridge; another was mixing dried fruit into a salad. Lana walked Asha through the various cooking tasks and introduced her to the women and girls. They seemed friendly enough, though they looked at her with wariness.

Guess I can't blame them.

All the while, Asha's stomach protested loudly at its emptiness. But, Lana told her sternly, the women weren't allowed to eat until the men had, and it was the women's job to serve them their meals first.

"You work, you get fed," Lana said definitively. "You don't, and you go hungry. Simple as that."

That's how they keep the women in line, Asha thought bitterly. *Serve us, or starve.*

As a result, she found herself serving eggs and wild turkey to the very men who were keeping her here. They laughed and jeered at her, and she had to bite her tongue to keep going. She hated every second, but she just about managed to get through it without spitting at them.

"It gets easier, sugar," Lana said afterwards, when they ate their breakfast in the kitchen. "And when Cade gets back, you'll only have to do this for him. Claimed women only have to serve their own men."

That is, Asha thought with some dread, *if he gets back at all.*

Chapter 6

The rest of the day passed in a blur of chores. Lana walked Asha through the women's daily work, from prepping food to sorting supplies to cleaning laundry on old-fashioned washboards and hanging it to dry. She also helped tend to a small vegetable garden that they kept in a fenced-off yard near the clubhouse. In the early spring, they'd only just begun planting, which meant hours kneeling and digging in the dirt.

It was all backbreaking labour. Asha had never worked so hard in her life, and she had a newfound respect for the women and girls who lived there. Meanwhile, the men did things like guard duty, strategy meetings, and patrol. It struck her as a rather charmed existence, even if it did theoretically carry more risk than washing a pile of laundry.

"You've done really good for your first day," Lana said, giving her a sweet smile. "And I've got good news! I talked Angel into letting you stay in the dormitory with the rest of us until Cade comes back. I have a bunk ready for you, so you'll have a real bed tonight."

It didn't seem like much, but when Asha thought again of the straw pallet on the floor, it was the best news she'd gotten in some time. As afternoon slipped into early evening and it was nearly time to prepare dinner, she found herself exhausted and irritable. She was grateful when Leo appeared to rescue her, looking vaguely apologetic.

"Sorry I didn't check on you sooner," he said, running a hand through his short blonde hair. "There were more patients than I expected today, and then I ran out of alcohol, so...anyway, how're you holding up?"

"It's fine," Asha replied with a shrug. "Hard work, but if they do it every day, so can I. What do you mean about patients? Do people go see you regularly?"

"Oh, yeah. I've converted one of the rooms on the west side of the clubhouse into a clinic. I'll show you."

Relieved to take a break from domestic duties, Asha followed him to the west wing of the clubhouse. She'd never been in that area before, but she noticed it was considerably less shabby than the east wing, where the women were housed. More structures were intact, there were fewer cracks in the concrete walls and floors, and overall, it looked as though it had perhaps been minimally maintained. However, the west wing was far smaller, with just a few doors to choose from. All of them except for one were closed, and at the end of the corridor, there was a set of double doors that were painted in vibrant navy blue, which stood out against the bland grey and beige of everything else.

Curiously, in front of the colourful doors, Dax stood with his arms folded, staring ahead into space. It looked like he was guarding something.

"Angel's Wing," Leo said, catching her looking. "He has a few doormen, but he seems to have a special fondness for Dax for some reason. Best to keep your distance."

Asha nodded, though she wondered about what Angel did all day. Did he simply lounge around in his quarters, being waited on? He hadn't appeared for meals in the mess hall, and when she'd asked, Lana had told her that she brought his meals to him personally. Supposedly, it was an honour, an acknowledgement of her as his favourite, because it meant he trusted her not to poison him.

Lana needs to take one for the team, Asha thought bitterly as Leo led her through the single open door.

Leo's clinic was far more impressive than she'd have expected, given their limited resources and the fact that he had no formal training. It wasn't a large room, but he'd packed in a long metal table for exams that he'd somehow managed to polish to a sheen, as well as a single cot in the far corner with a privacy curtain connected to the ceiling by small hooks. On the table lay an array of metal surgical tools and syringes, along with clean bandages, and a large bottle of alcohol. Most impressively, there was a new-looking cabinet on the wall behind the table with a glass window, through which Asha could see various pill bottles and other medicines.

"How did you manage all this?" Asha asked in wonder. "The rest of the place looks like it's about to fall apart."

Leo smiled. "With some help. Most of the fixtures were made in the Settlements. Angel—and everybody else—benefits from a doctor having the right tools."

She frowned. "But where'd all the medicine come from? I can't imagine they can make much of that in the Settlements. Not if they're anything like Little River."

"Little River's in worse shape than our settlements," Leo replied, "but no, a lot of it is scavenged. Or grown by Dom."

"Dom?" Asha asked, more surprised by that than even the medicine. "He grows things?"

"Oh, yeah. He's a big gardener. I'm lucky he helps me out."

Asha couldn't help herself; she giggled. Her limited experience with Dom made clear that he was a man of few words, and usually grumpy. The image of him kneeling in the dirt, fussing over delicate flowers, was too much.

But another question niggled at her, and she raised an eyebrow. "Isn't scavenged medicine long since expired?"

Leo shrugged and looked away. "Sure, but we make do with what we have."

His too-casual tone gave him away. She couldn't imagine why, but Asha was certain that he was lying.

Before she could interrogate him further, however, he changed the subject. "I should bring you back to the mess hall. Wouldn't want them to think you're missing at dinner." He paused briefly, staring at his exam table. "But...if you need help at any time, come find me." He pointed at a door behind the exam table. "I live in the back room. I'm always here."

Asha nodded slowly, trying not to think of why she might need his help. "I just hope Cade..."

She trailed off, not sure how to express herself, but Leo seemed to understand.

"He'll find a way, Asha," he said gently, touching her shoulder. "He's the most determined man I've ever met. If it's at all possible, he'll do it."

She smiled in spite of herself, cheered a little by his kindness. "Thanks, Leo."

A week passed in hard domestic labour and little else. Each night, Asha fell into bed exhausted and slept like a baby. Besides the hard work and constant leering from the men, however, she had few complaints. Lana and the other women were decent company, and Leo checked up on her often.

She hadn't actually seen Angel since the night of the claiming. He rarely seemed to leave Angel's Wing during the day, and in the evenings, it seemed like Lana mostly kept him entertained. Still, there was that nagging worry at the back of her mind that Cade wouldn't make it back in time.

On the eighth night since Cade's departure, Asha was sound asleep in her bunk, much like the other dozen women who shared the dormitory with her. All candles had been extinguished, and the room was pitch black.

She was abruptly awoken by a cold hand wrapped around her throat. Alarmed, she tried to scream, but the man tightened his grip, strangling the sound.

"Don't scream," a voice she recognized as Dax's demanded. "Stay quiet and I'll let you go."

Asha nodded slowly, terrified. Dax forced her to her feet and directed her out of the dormitory and into the corridor wearing nothing but the standard-issued nightdress that all the women wore. At least out here, there was a single torch burning on the wall, illuminating the way.

Dax pushed her down the hallway, stopping in front of Lana's door. The silence of the night was split by his hard knock on the wood. Asha heard movement within before a bewildered-looking Lana appeared.

"Find something for her to wear," Dax ordered. "Angel wants her."

Lana's confusion turned to alarm. "Why?"

"No business of yours, is it? The boss wants what he wants."

"If he wants entertainment, I can—" Lana began, but Dax growled at her.

"Shut the hell up," he spat. "He wants the new girl, and that's what he'll get. Got it?"

Lana nodded mutely, her eyes wide. She gestured for Asha to come into the room, and closed the door behind them. Lana's young sister, Cassie, appeared to still be asleep on her side of the bed.

"What's happening?" Asha asked in a low voice, and she hated that her fear had crept into her voice. "What does he mean?"

Lana's mouth hardened into a thin line. "I think you know, Asha."

Panic flooded Asha's system at her words. She'd expected Lana to give her some kind of comfort, or an alternate explanation. Instead, she was left with only the horrible truth: she had no control over what happened to her next.

After that, they spoke only occasionally. Lana went into her closet and found a skintight black dress that was a little short on Asha and barely covered her ass, which was probably the point. She sprayed Asha with rosewater to make her smell good, and applied some approximation of lipstick to her lips.

"What now?" Asha asked, her voice cracking.

Lana sighed, her expression weary, like she'd seen a thousand nights just like this one. Like she was tired, not just of this, but of everything—of living.

"Now, you do your best to forget, sugar."

Half an hour later, Asha stood in front of the colourful doors to Angel's Wing, where Dax the doorman was waiting. He gave a low whistle on seeing her, and it made her want to peel her skin off.

"Hot piece of ass. No wonder the boss couldn't wait any longer."

For a moment, Asha was frozen, unable to make her legs move. She couldn't think about what that man would do to her. She took a deep breath and tried to think of what Lana had said just before she left: *just close your eyes and let him have his way. Pretend you're somewhere lovely. I like to think of a beach I went to when I was a little girl.*

But Asha had never been anywhere lovely. She'd lived inside concrete walls for the entirety of her twenty-six years, with the same sights, the same people, the same stifling job and the indifferent husband that saw her as an object. Her parents had been absent her whole life; it was why Claire had always come to her house when they were teenagers, to escape her crazy mother. She'd never had many friends besides that, and her childhood was something she'd rather forget. What good was it to escape to those lonely times?

Still, she'd been safe back then, hadn't she? Eric may have been an irritating sex pest, but he'd never forced himself on her. Her job as a science teacher hadn't been exciting, but it'd been...stable. Her living quarters had been small, but comfortable. She'd had decent food, clean water, and the knowledge that there was an order to things. The only real threat of violence was for those who disobeyed the regime; if you kept your head down and followed the rules, you could enjoy a tightly controlled—but otherwise safe—existence.

"Get a move on, whore," Dax sneered, jolting her out of her dissociation. He grabbed her arm, wrenched one of the blue doors open, and practically tossed her inside. Her heart dropped at the loud *thud* as it slammed shut behind her.

Asha found herself standing in a corridor. At the opposite end, it forked into three doors, all of which were surprisingly intact. She made herself take two steps forward, her heart hammering in her ears as she took in her surroundings, illuminated by burning torches on the walls.

Angel's Wing was about as immaculate as a place could be, thirty years after the Fall. Unlike the rest of the Nest, which was sparsely furnished, inevitably dirty, and in various stages of disrepair, Angel's Wing was obviously cleaned regularly. A long, threadbare rug stretched down the length of the hallway, and the windows had glass—the only ones she'd ever seen in that condition—and were framed by heavy velvet curtains. Cracks in the walls were filled in with clay, and the walls had artwork on them, which surprised her, as no other room she'd seen had any.

Hard to care about art when you're barely making it, she thought grimly. *But if you're the king of the Wasteland, you get special privileges.*

There was an odd painting of a duck, and a faded photo montage of old buildings behind a plastic screen. On the opposite wall, someone had painted a large mural of black angel wings, stretching outwards. The torches on the walls made it feel like a dungeon, a thought that filled her with an even deeper sense of foreboding.

Asha was startled out of her thoughts by the door at the end of the corridor opening. Angel appeared, outlined by the dim candlelight. He was shirtless and barefoot, wearing only a pair of loose black pants. Across his chest, black angel wings spread out, crudely tattooed by an untrained hand. Those heavy dark circles under his eyes stood out in the firelight, giving him a haunted look that Asha didn't like.

"Come in," he said, with a small smirk. "Let's get started."

A horrible shiver went down her spine, and every instinct inside her screamed at her to run, even though there was nowhere to go. She took several involuntary steps backward, toward the colourful doors.

"Come on, Asha," Angel said, a mocking softness to his tone. "It won't be so bad. I'll even warn you when I'm gonna nut, like a real gentleman."

Bile rose in Asha's throat, burning it with her fear and revulsion. Flashbacks danced in front of her eyes, disorienting her. All at once, she relived a furtive hand snaking up her eight-year-old thigh and the murmur of an old friend's voice: *don't you want to know how mommies and daddies make babies?*

Her brief dissociation cost her precious seconds. Angel had moved toward her slowly, like a cat cornering a mouse. She backed up again, but hit the double doors. She could hear Dax, still right outside, trapping her in.

"You're even prettier close up," Angel said, his putrid breath falling over her face as he moved in. He touched her face, and Asha recoiled. "There's no point in fighting it, sweet pea. Just give in. You might like it."

Asha didn't think as his hand migrated south; she merely reacted. Her knee shot up in a flash, making contact with his groin. Angel let out a low groan of pain and doubled over, and Asha ran.

Of course, with nowhere else to go, she ran right into Angel's bedroom. But perhaps there was a window, or *something* she could—

The room was large and dimly lit with several candelabra. A massive bed sat at its centre, covered in animal furs. Asha stopped in front of it, casting around the room for an escape route. The two windows on the far wall contained glass too, preventing her flight. And a second later, Angel appeared in the doorway, his expression murderous.

"We're not done," he snarled. "I was gonna be nice and let you just lie there and take it. But bitches like you need to be taught a fucking lesson."

"Fuck off," Asha spat, but her voice shook with fear.

He was too fast, too strong. Before she understood what was happening, he'd thrown her down onto the mattress. She hit the bed hard, the breath knocked out of her, and had no time to react to Angel throwing himself on top of her. She pushed herself up towards the top of the bed with her feet, trying to slide out from under him, but he pinned her, panting furiously, his knee coming up to force her legs apart.

"You think you can just do whatever you want, say whatever you want?" he growled as Asha struggled against him. "Well, you're about to find out that you fucking can't. You want to act like an uppity little whore? You'll get fucked like one."

Asha fought back as hard as she could, but he was too heavy for her to lift. She squirmed helplessly like an eel trapped underneath a rock, her hands flailing wildly. He smelled like stale sweat and alcohol, and the stench invaded her nostrils, overpowering everything else. And in an instant, his hand closed around her throat.

She tried to gasp, but couldn't. She felt like she was drowning as her vision darkened at the edges, desperately trying to kick her way to the surface, even as the light faded above her. His grip loosened and blood rushed to her face, and all she could see was Angel's malicious little smile, enjoying every second of her struggle.

"Think he'll still want you after this?" he asked with a little laugh that made Asha's skin crawl. "Well, Cade's in for a nasty surprise when he fucks you and feels me still inside you, sticking to your insides. You think he'll still take you when you're nothing but my leftovers?"

He reached down and pulled up the hem of Asha's night gown, and she shrieked, exposed from the waist down. She considered giving up for a moment, afraid of how he might hurt her even worse if she continued resisting, but her body simply wouldn't allow it. When he attempted to shove his filthy fingers into her mouth, she bit down hard, making him scream and smack her furiously across the face to make her let go...but briefly, he released her.

Panting and aching, she flailed her arms out toward the bedside table, and her hand closed around a glass ashtray. In a split second, she'd smashed it into Angel's face, shattering it. Blood poured from his nose, and he howled in pain and staggered backwards off of her.

"You fucking bitch," he growled. "You almost got glass in my fucking eye."

"Good," Asha retorted, her breath heavy.

For a moment, she thought she'd won. She thought he might genuinely give up and return her to her bunk, seeing that she couldn't be bullied into fucking him.

She was very wrong.

Angel went from seething to laughing in the space of a minute. It was the kind of cold, cruel laughter that could make one's hair curl. He grabbed an empty glass bottle from a nearby end table, holding it by the bottleneck, and smashed the opposite end. Asha eyed the sharp, jagged edges with alarm.

"I like a challenge," he said, his face contorting with a terrifying combination of amusement and rage. "You wanna fight dirty, sweetheart? Fine by me. You're gonna scream so loud, the whole Nest's gonna hear you."

Unfortunately, he was right.

Chapter 7

Asha hacked a dry, painful cough. Her head was pounding, and her whole body ached. The rough, uncomfortable cot she was lying on didn't help. Straws poked up out of the mattress, and the rough bedsheet was irritating on her damaged skin. Covered in scrapes and bruises, she couldn't get comfortable in any position.

"More water," Leo demanded, holding a cup to her lips. "Just a few more sips."

"You're gonna waterboard me," Asha complained, but even to her, she sounded like death; her throat was raw from screaming. She realized too late that Wastelanders likely wouldn't understand the reference.

Regardless, Leo gave a half-hearted chuckle. "I promise I'll give you a hit of the good stuff if you drink."

She reluctantly took another few sips, her swollen lips impeding her. At least it washed the coppery taste of blood out of her mouth. Several long candles were lit by her bedside—the best light that one could get at this late hour—and briefly questioned the wisdom of performing medical procedures by candlelight.

Not that we have much choice.

"That molar has to come out, I'm afraid," Leo said critically as he took the cup back from her. "It's broken, and leaving it will invite infection. Consider yourself lucky that I'm giving you painkillers before I pull it out. I've pulled a lot of teeth here, and most have to do it raw."

"Is that what you'd call me, Leo?" Asha asked weakly, closing her eyes. "Lucky?"

His expression darkened briefly. "No. Sorry."

He busied himself with examining her battered left wrist, which was mottled purple. She hissed in pain as Leo gently tested its mobility, and he frowned.

"Minor muscle strain and bad bruising," he said. "You'll need to rest it."

He retrieved bandages from his medical bag and began to wrap her wrist. Asha winced as he pulled the bindings tight, but didn't complain. She wasn't going to jeopardize her chance of getting that sweet painkiller he promised. Leo started sanitizing forceps with a small bottle of alcohol that he'd told her he made himself. *Not as pure as I'd like,* he'd said, *but better than nothing.*

He'd subjected her to an invasive physical exam when she came in, as he had for the last four nights that she'd gone to Angel's Wing. She hated lying back on the exam table, letting him look and touch between her legs. To Leo's credit, he was nothing but detached and professional throughout the process, but it still deepened her feelings of humiliation.

There's some bleeding, he'd said again tonight. *Still mostly superficial tears, but...I worry about them getting worse if you keep fighting him, Asha.*

Tears pricked her eyes, and she wanted to hide her bruised face in the pillow. She hadn't told him the extent to which Angel had tortured her. But how could she not fight back in that situation? How was she expected to lie still and let him torment her, over and over?

She refused to gift him her silence. If he was going to break her, he would suffer for every damn second of it. It hadn't even been a conscious decision on her part; it was her kneejerk reaction to his regime of torture. Perhaps, if she'd been a different—*smarter,* she added ruefully—sort of person, she could've simply locked herself away, like Lana had suggested. She could've just lain there, spaced out, and walked away a little less black and blue than she had for the last week. It was what everyone had told her to do, before and since: *just lie still and let him get it over with.* Maybe they were right. Maybe if she'd had something to lose or someone to survive for, she'd have been able to.

But she didn't. The only person who'd tried to help her had also put her in this mess. And then there was still that voice of rage inside her, that little girl angry at a world that had failed her so miserably, that said, *you won't break me. You won't.*

So, each night since that first one, she had been forced to return to Angel's Wing, fought for her life, and left beaten and bruised, but not broken. Never broken.

As promised, Leo injected her with a powerful painkiller, and Asha soon felt her eyelids fluttering. She barely reacted to Leo yanking out the remains of her broken molar; it had been hanging by a thread anyway. The two tiny stitches he made in her gums bothered her more, oddly enough. She hated the way the needle poked at her, but she was in no condition to complain.

"All done," Leo said a moment later. He gathered his instruments for cleaning. "Rest now. You need it."

She sighed and closed her eyes. "He's going to kill me, Leo. Before Cade gets back."

A long pause. "Yes, that's what I'm afraid of."

He sounded genuinely concerned for her, which she found strangely touching, considering he hadn't known her long.

"You should stay here overnight," Leo said after a moment. "For observation. Want to make sure there aren't any adverse reactions to the medication."

Asha made a noise that was supposed to be assent, but just sounded like a weak groan. She rolled onto her side, sleepy and finally free of pain. As her consciousness faded away, she felt the weight of a blanket being placed over her, cocooning her against the chilly evening air.

Asha's mind was a strange swirl of dreams. She dreamt that she held a bluebird in the palm of her hand, feeding it seeds and petting its head. It twittered happily and accepted the food. But as it tried to take flight, her fingers closed around it, squeezing, and squeezing, and squeezing, until its feeble cries for escape were silenced. A moment later, she looked upon its mangled, broken body, and lifted it to her lips to feast on its flesh.

The price of freedom is death. Cade's words came back to her again, repeating over and over, like an echo in an empty hallway. They were familiar. Where had she heard them before? Who had said them?

Suddenly, the voice of a documentary she'd once watched came back: *"The price of freedom is death," a quote attributed to the civil rights advocate, Malcolm X...*

He was an Old World civil rights advocate. How would a Waste-lander with no real education know about him? So much of that knowledge had died with the Fall. He wouldn't know, unless...

Something suddenly clicked into place. *Unless he's not a Waste-lander at all.*

"Who fucking did this to her?"

Cade's voice, low and furious, cut through Asha's dreams. Still, the drug Leo had given her kept her drowsy, on the edge of wakefulness.

"You know who it was," Leo replied ruefully. "And it doesn't change anything. We're not ready."

"She's *one of us,* Leo," Cade shot back. "You know it as well as I do."

"Sure. But it doesn't matter. There's nothing you can do right now except play nice so you can get her away from him."

"I'm not good at playing nice."

Leo scoffed. "You think I don't know that? But that's not going to help her."

She heard Cade pacing the room. "He's sending a message that I shouldn't get any ideas about doing what I want—having what I want."

"Probably," Leo said. "But if you go after him, she becomes collateral damage. Bide your time. Don't be as stupid as he is."

Cade let out a long breath. "Fine."

"Did you manage to capture Rockland?"

"Yeah," Cade replied more calmly. "It went easier than I thought, thanks to the prep work we did. No casualties on our side, and only a few on theirs. They manufacture plenty of weapons, so we should be able to set up a supply chain."

"Good."

"I'll be back in the morning to pick her up," Cade continued, resigned. "In the meantime, if Angel wants to send a message...I'll give him a reply he'll never forget."

Asha heard him start to walk out, but Leo said, "Wait."

"What?"

There was a brief pause, but Leo pressed on: "I don't know what your plan with Asha was before all this...but she's in no condition to be doing anything strenuous."

Another, longer silence descended.

"Who do you think I am, Leo?" Cade snapped. "Have the last couple years really changed me that much?"

"Okay, okay," Leo replied, conciliatory. "I just wanted you to make sure you knew. He beat her worse than any of the other girls. Probably because she fought him."

"Is that why he looks like hell, too?" Cade said, and he sounded different now—amusement mixed with his fury. "Good. She gave him a taste of what he deserves. We'll need that."

He left the infirmary, and Asha pretended to be asleep when Leo came to check on her. She couldn't pretend, however, to be relieved at Cade's return. Whatever curiosity she'd had about him was gone, and she wished nothing more than for all of them to simply go away.

Sunlight seared Asha's eyes as she awoke the next morning. The painkiller Leo had given her had worn off overnight, and now her body was screaming at her. She shifted in bed, trying to find a comfortable position, but it didn't exist.

"Good morning," Leo said amiably as he pulled the curtains around her bed aside. He set down a tray with two steaming mugs of herbal tea. "How are we feeling?"

His sunny greeting grated on her in her wounded state, but she took the mug he offered her. The tea was peppermint, and its crisp, fresh flavour was surprisingly comforting.

"Like death warmed over," she replied, still sounding like she'd swallowed gravel.

"I can imagine," Leo said, withdrawing a small burlap package from his pocket. "Here. Something to help with the pain."

He handed her the packet, and she unwrapped it to reveal a bundle of green, six-pronged leaves.

"Cannabis?" she asked, eyebrows raised. In the compound, unauthorized drug use was banned, and the supply was tightly controlled enough that there were few addicts. She always found it odd that they had no problem letting residents drink themselves to death, but drugs were a hard limit.

"It's a good natural painkiller," Leo said with a shrug. "We work with what we can get, and it's easy for Dom to grow it in his garden. Chew a few leaves when you need pain relief, but start slow. Too much at once will make you sick to your stomach."

"Isn't this just going to make me stoned?"

Leo chuckled. "Maybe a small high, but Dom tries to grow CBD-rich strains, which are low in THC. Or that's what he tells me, anyway."

"How would he know?" Asha asked, wondering if Leo would tell the truth.

Leo broke eye contact before saying, "He's our amateur botanist, I suppose. Learned everything from his grandmother, who raised him."

Asha wrinkled her nose. How had she not noticed it before? No Wastelander knew a word like *botanist*. Leo spoke like an educated professional...because he was one. He was a legitimate, went-to-medical-school doctor. It explained all the tools he had, his store of advanced medicine, his obvious knowledgeability—everything. She was sure of it, and there was only one way it was possible, given that he was far too young to have trained before the Fall.

"Or from the school he went to, in the compound you're from?" Asha asked casually, sipping again from her mug.

Leo choked on his tea.

"Surprised it took you this long to get it," Cade said conversationally, leaning against the doorframe. "I knew you were one of us from the second I saw you."

Asha eyes darted over to him. He wasn't in his uniform anymore, though he still wore all black, even when dressed casually in a t-shirt and long pants. Without the bulk of the tactical outfit, she could more clearly see that he wasn't just in good shape—he was absolutely *shredded*. The sleeves of his t-shirt strained against his biceps, and he crossed his muscular forearms over a *very* well-developed chest, which she noted, she told herself, with nothing but irritation. The April morning was probably too chilly for short sleeves, but if he noticed, he didn't seem to care...and she was glad, because it allowed her to admire his full sleeve of black tattoos on each arm.

A black snake was coiled all the way down his left arm, with intricate designs in between, and his right arm was covered in vines, with leaves stretching upward into his shirt. In spite of everything, Asha found herself wondering where they ended, and what other tattoos he might have in hidden places. Unlike Angel's tattoos, which were crudely drawn, these were clearly done by a professional.

Cade strolled into the room like he owned it, and Asha had to admit that it was a little embarrassing that she *hadn't* gotten it sooner, watching him. His skin was perfectly smooth, free of scars or marks, and his light skin didn't have any signs of a tan, even though he probably spent a lot of time outdoors. He looked more youthful than any of the other men, even the ones who were clearly younger than him. When they'd walked through that swampy bit of forest with the gnats, the other men had complained of being bitten, but the bugs hadn't bothered Cade, Leo, or Dom. Their physiques, though not impossible for regular men, were surely easier to achieve with the cocktail of vitamins, hormones, and whatever else they put into the compound implants to chemically enhance their people. They had the same implant that she did, and it should've been obvious.

Shockingly, when you're constantly scared that you're about to die, survival is all you can think about, even when a perfect, unfairly beautiful man abruptly enters your life.

"That's why you helped me," Asha murmured in sudden understanding.

Cade nodded. "Wondered how a girl like you ended up in a place like that."

He didn't pose it as a question, but he clearly wanted an answer, because he paused briefly, watching her. But she wasn't about to offer him anything when she didn't know anything about his past either. When she stayed quiet, he cleared his throat.

"She cleared to go?" Cade asked, nodding at Leo.

"If she feels ready," Leo replied, turning to Asha. "Do you need anything else?" When she shook her head, he gave instructions to keep her sprained wrist bandaged for the next week, and otherwise to rest as much as possible, to give her bruises and internal tears time to heal.

"Time to go home, then," Cade said, and Asha's heart sped up, pounding unpleasantly in her ears. *Home.* His, maybe. She didn't think she'd ever consider this wretched place—where she'd been bled, and tortured, and raped—home. Home wasn't the place that haunted you.

"I'd get my things, but I have none," Asha deadpanned as she got up and walked toward Cade.

She was going for levity, but it just sounded hollow and pathetic. Fitting, since that was exactly how she felt.

Cade raised an eyebrow, but otherwise didn't comment as they left the infirmary. He led her through the hallways of the clubhouse, where the women were already bustling about, preparing breakfast for Angel's inner circle. Asha was glad she didn't have to join them.

"You don't need things," Cade said as they walked out into the sunshine. "Not now, I mean. We...we can get you things of your own, in time. But I have enough for both of us for now."

She said nothing. What was she supposed to do? Thank him? She couldn't summon much gratitude at the moment—for him, or even for her own existence. Dying at the compound with everything she knew suddenly didn't seem like such a bad end. At least she wouldn't be living here, with these people who lived hand-to-mouth and thought nothing of slavery and torture.

"My place is near the back of the settlement," Cade continued, sounding cagier than she'd ever heard him. He spoke carefully, as though weighing each word. "There's a fenced-in backyard, and it's pretty overgrown, so it's more secluded than the other houses. There's...privacy."

Asha frowned, wondering why on Earth it mattered. Her dignity was in pieces already. She kept her face as hard as marble: cold and unbreakable, even as she was collapsing inside.

Cade swallowed hard at her expression, and he gave up any further attempts at conversation as they walked to his home. After about twenty minutes, they reached the edge of the gated community, and one lone condominium at the end of what was once a cul-de-sac. Ivy covered the worn brown brick, all but camouflaging the house in the greenery behind it. If Asha hadn't spotted the sun-bleached grey door, she might've missed it altogether.

The window frames were glassless and covered by thick, dark curtains. The roof looked sunken with age, but surprisingly intact. A brick chimney snaked up the side, leaning precariously. The porch was tiny, its concrete cracked in half a dozen places...but all things considered, Asha thought, it could've been much worse. At least it was decent shelter from the elements.

Cade hopped up the steps to the door and held it open for her. It was heavy, solid wood, probably expensive in its day, and Asha took a small amount of comfort from the fact that it wouldn't be easy to break down.

This is my life now, she thought bitterly. *I think of all the ways someone can hurt me, so that when it happens, at least it's less surprising.*

The interior of the house was small and dark, with all the curtains drawn over the windows. It was an open concept floor plan with the kitchen and living room as one space, and a well-worn door on the opposite wall that led to a small backyard. A short hallway in the far corner led to what Asha assumed was a bedroom. The discoloured kitchen cabinets and small island had no doors on them, and only held a couple of iron pots and wooden dishes. The old appliances were scratched to hell and rusted—nothing more than giant bricks at this point. There was an old metal table and a couple of metal chairs for a dining area. In what was once the living room, there was a fire barrel with a metal grate laid over it to create a makeshift grill. Otherwise, there were only a few small end tables, strewn with Cade's various belongings: old maps, compasses, and a few books. The rest of the space was bare and unfurnished, with no place to sit other than at the dining table. The wood floor, which flowed throughout the house, was worn down to almost nothing.

It was one of the most depressing-looking dwellings Asha had ever visited. Dark, drafty, and utterly devoid of personality or homey touches. Her house back at the Cave was more lovingly decorated, and it had largely been a sterile, prefabbed box.

The best thing she could say about it was that it was cleaner than the clubhouse, at least. Granted, compared to the Cave, it was still a dirty hovel, but unlike the other living spaces Asha had seen in Angel's Nest, it at least looked like it saw a broom every once in a while.

Cade must've read her expression, because he said, a little sheepishly, "I'm not usually home that much. When I am, I spend most of my time in the yard."

"Why?" Asha couldn't help asking.

"Training," he replied. "There's gym equipment out back. I work out in the morning, and then I usually do training drills with the guys in the afternoons. But that's out on the field—we have a setup."

Asha didn't say anything. She felt strangely detached, as though she were watching her life instead of living it. Reality felt distorted, like a bad dream that wouldn't end even after she realized she was dreaming. She couldn't have known, those mornings when she delayed getting up for a job she didn't enjoy, that she'd one day long to wake up in her bed at the Cave. She'd even welcome seeing a classroom full of bored teenagers if it meant escaping this place.

Asha realized too late that Cade was staring at her, clearly trying to parse what the hell was wrong with her. Her glassy-eyed stare was probably starting to unnerve him. She cast her gaze at the floor; his piercing grey eyes penetrated her defences in a way she didn't like.

"Make yourself at home," he said after a moment, walking into the kitchen area. "You hungry?"

"No," Asha replied, even though she was. She looked around the sparsely furnished room, trying to figure out where, exactly, she was supposed to make herself at home. She settled for sitting at the dining table.

"Is that your standard response when someone asks if you need anything?" Cade asked, a sliver of impatience in his voice. "It's not a trick question, darling."

She recalled him sharing his meagre meal with her when they traveled to the Nest. She'd said no then, too, and he'd shared anyway. She'd found that surprising and even sweet. Now, she felt nothing. His kindness had only lured her into a false sense of security. If he'd been brutal from the start, maybe it would be less confusing as to how a man who'd only been kind to her could stand to live in a place like this, to serve a gang leader like Angel. There was nothing more repugnant than a man who cloaked his depravity in a thin veneer of civility. It was the kind of cruelty that the compound's regime had excelled at.

"What will happen to me now?" Asha asked in a hollow voice.

Cade cocked an eyebrow. "What do you mean?"

"Living with you. What will my duties be?"

He fetched a bag from under the kitchen island. "For now, your only job is healing. We can talk more about it when you're feeling better."

"I want to talk about it now." She hoped she sounded firm, despite how she felt.

Cade pulled two chunks of red meat out of the bag before walking over to the fire barrel. He didn't say anything as he lit the fire and began to grill the meat on top of the metal grate. He used a metal rod to flip them, and Asha hated to admit it, but the smell made her mouth water. She hadn't had anything except Leo's peppermint tea since the night before, and her daily rations had hardly been enough.

That Cade was cooking for himself struck her as peculiar; Angel certainly never did. He had far too many of his women available to trouble himself with that, and besides, it was beneath him.

After another few minutes of stilted silence, Cade grabbed a nearby aluminum tray and scooped the meat onto it. He held it out to Asha and said simply, "Eat."

She took a hesitant bite as Cade sat across from her. The fat melted in her mouth, and she sighed. It felt like so long since she'd eaten anything more substantial than gruel or soup. Hunger took over and she ate with abandon until the meat was gone and her belly was full for the first time in weeks.

Cade finished his portion, then walked back to the kitchen. He pulled out a knife and began sharpening it on a stone. Asha froze, her hands shaking. She remembered the knife that Angel had heated over a flame, then pressed against her back.

Cade clearly noticed her reaction, because he promptly tucked the knife away in a backpack at his feet.

"Just sharpening it," he said. "It's used for hunting."

Not for torture seemed to be the unspoken message. A heavy silence hung between them that Asha didn't know how to break. She'd told him what she wanted, and he'd ignored her—a likely harbinger of things to come.

"Where are you from?" Asha finally asked. "You're from a compound, but clearly not mine."

He folded his arms over his chest. "A question for a question: where are *you* from, and how the hell did you end up out here?"

"I asked you first," she replied testily, "and you *still* haven't told me what my duties here will be now that you're here. If you expect me to get on my knees for you and suck you off every day, then I'd at least like some warning."

He gave a dark chuckle. "You really do think I'm a monster, huh?"

"You work for Angel," Asha said, unflinching. "You may come from a compound, but clearly, the life of a Wastelander suits you just fine."

"I'm not like Angel," he replied coldly. "I would never do what he did to you."

Asha didn't know when she'd clenched her hand into a fist, but it ached now, as did the rest of her battered body.

"Don't act innocent," she gritted out. "You may not do it yourself, but you allow it to happen to others. If you think that *not* being a rapist and torturer absolves you of that, think again. You're still a monster, and a hypocrite."

Another tense silence descended, and Asha wondered if this was it: the moment when he'd explode, show his true colours, and rip away the mask to reveal a man every bit as soulless as his master.

So, she was downright shocked when the corner of Cade's mouth ticked upward.

"You're right."

She wasn't sure she'd heard him correctly.

"What?"

He shrugged. "You're right. So, what're you gonna do about it? So far, the whole spitfire routine you have going on isn't doing much for you."

Asha balked. "Oh, I'm sorry, how am I *supposed to* react when a bunch of brutal Wastelanders kidnap and rape me? Fuck you. I don't need your judgment."

He raised his eyebrows. "Just stating a fact. I like a woman who takes no shit. But you need friends if you want to survive here, and so far, it doesn't seem like you have anybody on your side except me. I'm no prince, darling, but I'm what you've got."

She exhaled sharply. She hated everything about this moment...but he had a point. He wasn't the hero she would've chosen. Far from it. But he was also the only one who'd done anything to help her besides Leo, and Leo had only done it on Cade's orders.

"I do what I have to do to survive," Cade continued. "Your problem is that you're still in denial. You think of this as a temporary setback rather than your permanent situation. Your compound is gone. Your old life is over. Now, you adapt or die, and you won't find anyone who understands that better than I do."

Asha sighed, rubbing her eyes. She felt exhausted, even though she hadn't been up for long. Her body was still terribly sore, and she didn't have it in her to argue more.

"Fine," she said wearily. "I take your point. But if I'm going to live here with you, I'd at least like to know a bit about you."

He nodded. "Fair enough." He paused, as though considering his words carefully. "I'm from the Delta. It's a compound up in the northern part of the province. Quite isolated. I was assigned as a captain in the military. Leo and Dom were on my squad."

He leaned over the island counter. "Now, you tell me: where did you come from? We'll trade an answer for an answer."

She couldn't pretend that that wasn't fair.

"I'm from the Cave," Asha said. "It's maybe a day or two's walk from here. I was assigned to be a high school science teacher. A terrible disappointment for my parents. They were high-ranking officials, but they weren't in charge of the career assignments, so that's what I got."

Cade's lips twisted with amusement.

"What?" she asked sharply.

"Can't picture you as a teacher, frankly," he said with a chuckle. "Aren't you supposed to be nurturing and all that bullshit?"

She couldn't help but smile. "Yeah. I was never very good at that part. I did an adequate job...but not much more. Claire was always the better teacher."

Her name was out of Asha's mouth before she could think better of it.

Cade's brow wrinkled. "Who's Claire?"

"No one," Asha said too quickly, and he scoffed. "Fine: she was my best friend. But you owe me an answer now: how did you end up outside the Delta?"

"We're coming back to that," Cade warned, but then continued: "We left. Deserted on patrol, a couple years back. There was a lot happening in our compound at the time. There'd been an uprising, and some unrest. Then something...unfortunate happened, and I decided to leave rather than be kicked out. Leo and Dom agreed to go with me. Maybe someday, I'll tell you the story."

The closed look on his face told her that there was definitely more to it than he let on, but also that he didn't trust her with it. In a strange way, Asha respected that, if only because his distrust was relatable.

"How did you end up outside the…Cave, was it?" he asked, drumming his fingers on the old stone countertop. "I can't imagine how a civilian would've gotten out."

She took a deep breath, bracing herself for the images that would inevitably resurface in her brain.

"I didn't leave," Asha confirmed. "A faction of our own people attacked. They seized control of the compound and killed everyone who wasn't in their group. They wore strange masks with gold eyes painted on them."

Cade shot her a bewildered look. "The military didn't fight back?"

"No," she replied with a sigh. "I don't know why. I can only assume that enough of them were part of the attack that whoever was left couldn't put up much of a fight. There were no alarms, no fire-fights…nothing, as far as I could tell."

"Very strange." *Can't say I disagree.*

"I only escaped because I made it to Claire's house."

"What was so special about her place?" Cade asked, leaning back against the counter.

"Nothing, except that her sister was one of the attackers, and she decided to spare Claire's life and get her out of the compound. When I got to her house, Claire insisted that I be allowed to go with her to the outside. So, her sister escorted us out into the Wasteland, and we never went back."

"So, everyone else…" he trailed off.

"Dead," Asha said with a short nod. "My husband. Her husband. My family. As far as I know, I'm the only survivor."

"The only survivor?" he said, stroking his chin. "So, what happened to your friend?"

She tried to take another breath, but found herself holding it instead. Pain rose up inside her chest, and she covered her hand with her mouth in a desperate bid to hold it in.

"Look," Cade said, clearly seeing her distress, "it's okay if you—"

"No," Asha murmured. "It's not okay. I did something…bad."

Chapter 8

ade frowned. "We've all done bad things. If it's my judgment you're worried about, I don't have much of a leg to stand on. You said it yourself."

The images of her last days with Claire flashed through Asha's mind. The fear they both felt, cast into a wilderness that nothing in their lives had ever prepared them for. The shock and ache at the loss of everything and everyone they knew, and the knowledge that they had no time to grieve. Survival wouldn't allow it.

It was enough to make her shudder and avert her eyes from Cade's. She couldn't tell him the story if she saw him looking at her with that piercing stare of his.

"At first, we were just scared out of our minds," Asha said haltingly. "We had no food, no water, nothing to really help us survive beyond a flashlight and some blankets that Claire brought. I had nothing but the clothes on my back. Then, hunger and thirst set in. We drank from a stream that made us sick. We didn't know to boil the water."

Out of the corner of her eye, she saw Cade nod. His expression was unreadable.

"We holed up in an old barn," she continued. "For a couple days, we were so sick that we couldn't move. On the third day, we felt well enough to walk. I think we both knew that if we didn't, we'd die there."

She took a hard swallow. "We found this old, abandoned factory. At least, it *looked* abandoned. We were desperate for supplies, so we stopped. All went to hell in a matter of minutes, though."

Asha bit her bottom lip and took a sharp inhale as more images resurfaced: a horde of young men. Dirty and dressed in rags, carrying clubs and bats. Fierce, angry, and worse—*hungry.*

"But it wasn't abandoned, right?" Cade eventually prompted, and she shook her head to clear it.

"No," she replied. "There were...strange men there. They looked something like Old World depictions of cavemen. One of them—seemed like the leader—was wearing this weird necklace. All these small, off-white beads, lined up in a row. Took me a minute to realize they were human teeth."

She heard Cade inhale sharply before he said, "Cannibals."

"You know about them?" Asha asked, hating how her voice shook.

He nodded. "Had some run-ins with them. They attack settlements from time to time. From what I gather, they move in packs and breed like rabbits. Wouldn't have thought that people would go feral so quickly after the end, but a lot of them were born into it and never knew anything else. I always wondered if maybe the powers-that-be might've...tipped the scales towards them never recovering."

Asha frowned. "What do you mean? Powers-that-be?"

"Whoever runs the Delta," he answered, like it was nothing. "They keep civilians in the dark about it, but they always had some new science experiment going on. I only knew a little more because of my position, but it doesn't take much imagination to think they may've had something to do with it."

Unsure how to process that information, Asha filed it away for later.

"Anyway, they chased us, and we ran for our lives," she continued, trying to take deep breaths. "I barely even remember that part because I just...panicked. Never been so scared. I couldn't think clearly, so I picked a direction and ran as fast and as far as I could. I was almost to the chain-link fence around the property before I even realized that Claire wasn't with me, and that the cannibals had stopped chasing me."

Cade's eyes had softened, and she hated how damn *understanding* he looked. She didn't deserve it.

"They caught her," he said quietly.

Asha hugged herself, shaking like a leaf. "Yeah. I doubled back and saw them grab her. She tried to get away, but there were too many. They dragged her by her hair, and…"

She was quiet for long enough that Cade said, "Did they kill her?"

"Definitely," Asha replied, her chest swelling with shame. "I didn't see it, though, because I left her there."

There it was: the awful truth that she'd been trying too hard to suppress. She was a coward, and she hadn't lifted a finger to help her friend.

"Even now, I don't totally understand why I did it," she continued, her lips trembling. "And why I spit in the face of a man who tried to sell me, when just days earlier, I choked at the most crucial moment. All I can come up with is…ordinary men, I can handle. They weren't ordinary men. They were like animals, and I didn't know what to do, and—"

"You did exactly what you should've done," Cade broke in crisply. "For a civilian compound woman with no training and no weapons, you did the only thing that made sense for your survival. The only thing you'd have achieved by helping her is your death."

"*You* wouldn't have done it, though," she said, a little brokenly. "You wouldn't have frozen up like that and abandoned Leo, or Dom."

He folded his arms over his chest, straightened to his full height, and fixed her with a steel grey stare.

"I'm a soldier, darling. I was assigned at eighteen and served for a decade before I left the Delta. It's my job to run *towards* the danger. That's not something I was born with; it's years of training that you don't have. Leo and Dom have the same training. We're not a fair comparison."

There was a long, tense moment where Asha wasn't sure what to say. Whatever she'd expected, it hadn't been this. She'd thought he would scoff at her, tell her she was a silly girl who wasn't prepared to face the realities of this world. She wasn't sure how to interpret mercy coming from a man who lived in a place like this.

"Why do you live here, with these people?" she burst out. "You obviously know how to survive. Why would you settle here with Angel, if you're…not like him?"

Cade considered her for a moment before answering. "It wasn't my first choice, but it became the logical one. At first, when we left the

Delta, we were just trying to get by. We moved around a lot, hunting and trapping for food and sleeping under the stars. But winter was coming, and we needed somewhere to settle. We eventually found Ashburn."

"Ashburn?"

"An abandoned fishing village," he answered. "It was secluded, out in the middle of nowhere, and had a bunch of cabins that were in decent condition. It was on a lake, and the fish meant we wouldn't go hungry. We fortified it, planted a garden, and even recruited a couple dozen residents from the Post that spring—people who could help us built it into a proper settlement. It wasn't much, but it was a good enough home."

"The Post?" Asha asked, frowning.

"It's a Wastelander settlement up north," Cade said. "Only a hundred-and-fifty kilometres or so from the Delta. It's independent, not owned by gangs. Some good people there. But it didn't matter, because the winter after that, there was a plague that wiped them all out."

Asha gave a small gasp. "All of them?"

"Yeah. I don't know why me, Leo, and Dom didn't get sick. Only thing I can figure is that, coming from the compound, we must've been immune somehow, or just damn lucky. But nobody else was. It was...grim, for a long time."

She softened. "I can imagine. Do you think...I mean, I don't know if it's possible, but...that it was *the* virus that caused the Fall? I know they told us it's extinct, but they also told us that there were no Wastelander settlements."

Cade's brow furrowed. "I guess I don't know. They didn't have the classic neurological symptoms, but then again, none of us ever saw someone afflicted with it before. It's possible, I suppose, that through our implants, we're immune somehow. But..."

"But they always said there was no vaccine and no cure," Asha finished. It was an unsettling thing, to realize everything you knew was questionably true. Sorting through propaganda was never an easy exercise.

"Yeah. Hard to know the truth."

"So...what happened after that?"

"None of us wanted to stay after that," Cade continued. "Probably stupid in retrospect, but at the time, we were demoralized. We'd worked hard to build a decent life on the outside, and it was torn apart so quickly. We decided to be nomadic again—move from place to place, seeing where we ended up. We traveled south because we knew there were more settlements here, especially near the old capital."

"And that's when you met Angel?"

"Yeah," Cade said bitterly. "About eight months ago, we ended up in a skirmish with some of the members of a rival gang. Angel was there and saw what the three of us were capable of. So, he made us an offer: become his special forces group, and we'd have a decent place to settle, food to eat, and more. We weren't starving, but winter was coming, and we knew how quickly that could change."

His lips twitched. "He dubbed us the Blackguard because of our black military uniforms, and because he wanted us to sound intimidating. He let me pick out some of his better fighters, and we trained them as best we could. We've been here ever since."

Asha let out a breath. "Not your best decision, was it, soldier?"

Cade shrugged. "Not my worst, either. My job is to make the calls that keep my guys alive. I did what I had to do at the time."

There was an uncomfortable silence where Asha wasn't sure what to say. Cade was hard to pin down. She wanted to villainize him, to write him off as a willing participant in the horrors in this awful place. At the same time, however, he was the only reason she wasn't either dead or servicing every man in the Nest. He'd admitted he found her desirable, and he certainly could've taken advantage of her in her weakened state, but he hadn't made a move. If anything, he'd tried to put her at ease as much as possible.

But it was also his fault that she'd ever been in a position to be raped by Angel. He'd miscalculated how much Angel would enjoy cuckolding him, holding something over his head, because Angel wasn't a rational man who would negotiate in good faith. He was an amoral psychopath who saw his power as an opportunity to inflict cruelty with impunity. He *enjoyed* it. Cruelty wasn't a side-effect of his reign; it was the whole fucking point.

"So, what makes you think Angel's going to let you have me this time?" she said acerbically. "What's stopping him from holding me over your head again as a prize for whatever stupid thing he wants you to do next?"

Cade's expression darkened. "I'll handle it. There's supposed to be a welcoming party tomorrow night…and I plan to give him a gift he won't forget."

"Well, I wish that made me feel better," Asha said with a sigh.

His expression softened slightly. "I wish it did, too."

The tension between them didn't lift, and for a moment, they stared at each other in silence. What a fragile thing trust was, Asha thought. Even its beginnings could be shattered in a single second.

Cade was the first to break the staring contest, clearing his throat awkwardly. She followed the black snake on his arm with her eyes as he unfolded his arms.

"So…you had a husband, back at the Cave?"

"Yeah," Asha replied, not keen to discuss Eric. "Not like we had much choice, right? I'm guessing you had a wife, too?"

"Eventually," he said with a small, rueful smile. "In the military, you can apply for delays on spouse assignment. I always figured they allowed it because when you've got less to lose, you're not as worried about dying on the job."

For some reason, the thought of Cade having a wife at home bothered her. She pictured him going home after a long day on patrol to a kiss and dinner on the table with the perfect wife—her exact opposite. *Ugh.*

"Why are you making that face?"

Asha rearranged her features carefully. "I'm not making any face."

"You wrinkled your nose," he said, amused. "Interesting."

"I wrinkle my nose all the time," she insisted, irritable. "Ever considered that you repulse me?"

"Nope," Cade said with a grin, and she rolled her eyes, which just made him laugh. He really was the most irritating man she'd ever met.

"Tell me about this wife you abandoned, then," Asha said, folding her arms. "Did you think of her before you decided to run off?"

Cade sobered. "That would've been a waste of time, since she'd been dead for weeks by that point."

I really do have a terminal case of foot-in-mouth disease, don't I? she thought helplessly.

"I'm sorry," she said, gentling her tone. "I shouldn't have assumed. What…happened to her?"

He hummed, as if trying to sort out what to tell her and what to keep to himself.

"I said there was an uprising at the Delta," he said. "My wife—Janie—was part of it. I didn't know at the time. I only found out because it was my job to help put down the rebellion. Violently."

He looked at the floor, suddenly seeming distant. "She was shot by someone on my squad. We didn't know it was her until later. We'd only been married a year."

"That's awful," Asha murmured. "Did you love her?"

You care about this way more than you should, she told herself, but there was no heat behind it. She felt bad for him, put in a position where he might have to fire on his own wife without even knowing it. *That's what compound life is like. No constant conflict, but everyone is still pitted against everyone in the end.* A single report could get someone sent to "re-education", from which nobody returned un-scathed—physically or emotionally.

Cade gave a sad smile. "'Love' is a tough word in a govern-ment-arranged marriage. We got along, and she was good to me. Most of the time, though, neither of us were home enough to do much more than fuck and go back to work. Granted, we both liked that just fine." He chuckled at Asha's wrinkled nose. "You're doing it again."

"I am not," she argued, even though she was. "You're even worse than my husband. He, too, was an annoying ass who didn't know when to quit...for different reasons."

Cade's amusement didn't fade. "I hope to live up to his legacy, then. Big shoes to fill."

Asha gave him the most irritated look she could muster, but some-thing about the humorous glint in his eye made mysterious warmth stir in her belly, the way that sunshine did after a long bout of rain.

Chapter 9

Eventually, Asha had to admit that she was still injured and exhausted. Cade led her down the short hallway by the kitchen, which led to a small bathroom with a dry toilet and cracked bathtub, a small bedroom with dumbbells and a homemade punching bag hanging from the ceiling, and a larger master bedroom with a big, squishy-looking bed, covered in animal furs.

Asha balked. "There's...only one bed?"

Cade chuckled. "Considering I lived alone until a couple hours ago, yeah. That a problem, darling?"

She bit her lip. It *was* a problem, but she wouldn't give him the satisfaction of knowing how uncomfortable it made her. She was nothing if not stubborn.

"No," she replied, tossing her head. "Not at all. Hope you like loud snoring, though, because that's all I do all night, every night."

He laughed. "Looking forward to it. It'll be a nice break from the sound, peaceful sleep I usually get."

There was obvious irony in his tone, making her wonder if he rarely slept. It wouldn't surprise her; he always seemed hyper-aware of everything happening around him, those grey eyes always surveying. That level of vigilance would keep anyone awake.

Cade had briefly shown her the backyard, which contained more dumbbells and weights, as well as a small archery range with a homemade target and two arrows sticking out of it, both in the bullseye position. There was also a workbench in the corner with what looked like more arrows, in various stages of the creation process. Most impressive, however, was the makeshift obstacle course set up in a circle around the yard, using random everyday objects.

"For training," Cade said, catching her staring at it. "We have a better course at the training yard, but I like to have my own, too."

"And the arrows?" she asked, raising an eyebrow.

He shrugged. "Can't waste valuable ammo on hunting, so we use bows. Ammo is for conflict only."

She wasn't sure why he'd hunt for himself, seeing that the gang had its own team of hunters. When she asked, he smiled.

"I'm sure you've noticed that the rations are nothing to write home about," he answered, "and maintaining *this* physique for combat—" he gestured at his muscular form, "—requires a lot more protein and calories than our rations provide. Same for the rest of the Blackguard. So, we hunt to meet our needs."

Asha's eyes flicked over that high-maintenance physique one more time, unable to help herself. His body was like a feat of engineering; it was so precisely built. He wasn't like the bodybuilders of the Old World. He probably didn't have a six-pack, or muscles so well-defined that you could see every quiver they made. But he was big, and solid, and his every movement exuded the strength, power, and sheer effortlessness that only came from years of daily training.

Thinking about how disciplined he must be shouldn't have made her admire him, but damn it, it did. He was a smartass when he wanted to be, but he was also always completely in control, and it was hotter than she wanted to admit.

Eager to distract herself from her confusing feelings, she asked, probably more aggressively than necessary, "So, how does this work, day to day? Am I your prisoner now, instead of Angel's? Are there going to be shackles? Chains? Or will you just force me to do your laundry?"

Cade rolled his eyes, but he looked like he was holding in a laugh. "You're free to come and go as you like, but I wouldn't recommend roaming the Nest alone. I don't trust any of the men beyond Leo and Dom, and neither should you."

"Mission accomplished, I hate all of you," Asha replied blithely, and this time, he did laugh. She liked the sound of it—deep, full, and gravelly—though she'd never admit it. "So, I should stay at the house? What do you do with your days?"

"Training, in between missions," he replied, moving to the workbench and picking up a half-finished arrow. "When I'm on a mission, I'm usually gone for a few days to a few weeks at a time. During that time, you'll be free to do what you want, but some chores would be—"

"You'll just leave me here?" she said, panic seeping into her voice.

He stopped short, frowning. His gaze pierced through her again in that revealing way she didn't like, and he made a *hmph* sound.

"I thought you'd be pleased," Cade said with a shrug. "A minute ago, you said you hated us all. You'll be provided for, the same as before, with gang rations. You can spend time with Lana, or the other women. You seem to like them more."

Did she imagine it, or was there the tiniest hint of hurt in his voice? *Fuck your feelings. This is about survival.*

"You can't leave me here," Asha spat out, folding her arms. Anger was her veneer over the terror that now pulsed hideously in every part of her body. "You just got back, and what happened while you were gone? I'll give you a hint: Angel raped me with a broken bottle, and I nearly passed out on the infirmary doorstep before Leo even knew I was there."

Cade flinched as if she'd struck him. His jaw clenched, and his whole body seemed suddenly tense.

"I've claimed you now," he answered tightly. "He'll leave you alone."

She laughed bitterly. "If you believe that, you're more naïve than I thought. Angel has no moral code, even within his own ranks. If he wants me, and you're not here as a deterrent, he won't care."

She took a step towards him, trying to look braver than she felt. "You got me into this. You can't just abandon me now."

Cade glowered at her. "If I wanted to abandon you, I wouldn't have bothered speaking up for you at the slave market."

She could tell he was irritated now, but she wouldn't back down.

"You could've let me go," she gritted out. "We had a bargain. I give you my body, and you give me your protection. Leaving me here is *not* protection, Cade."

"So, what am I supposed to do?" he burst out, throwing down the unfinished arrow on the table. "Take you with me into dangerous situations, with half the Wasteland's most wanted? That's not protection either, but those are my only options."

Asha walked right up to him, lifting herself to her full height. He was still a head taller than her, but she didn't care. Their faces an inch apart, she stared directly into his intense, perceptive eyes, arms folded, and murmured, low and menacing, "Not my problem, soldier. Figure it the fuck out."

His eyes lit up at her challenge. They stared at each other, neither willing to break eye contact. A moment passed between them, then two. She could feel tension emanating off him in waves, could feel his warm breath tickle her face. There was a strange pull between them, and she hated how good it felt.

Finally, Cade said, in a near-whisper, "I'll handle it. But you may not like my solution, darling."

The tension broke, and he moved back to his workbench, deliberately turning away from her. She let out a long breath, wondering at the sudden heat between them.

"Rest now," he commanded. "I'll wake you when it's time for the meeting tonight."

Asha napped fitfully in Cade's bed that afternoon. The fur blankets were warm, but the worn linen sheets smelled like him, and it made her uncomfortable.

Uncomfortable? Is that what we're calling it? she needled herself. *You're just mad that the guy you supposedly hate for trapping you here is fucking hot.*

When Cade came to wake her, the light outside had dimmed, and the evening air was chilly on her skin. She shivered as she got up, and he wordlessly offered her a jacket from his closet.

"Oh," she said, surprised. "Thank you."

She slipped her arms into the sleeves, which were black wool and very warm.

"Where did you get this?" she asked.

"Made in the Settlements," Cade replied, sounding distracted. "Like most of what we have at the Nest."

He carried a black bag beside him. She could hear something rolling around inside when he moved.

"What's in the bag?"

Cade smiled, but it didn't reach his eyes. "A message."

She frowned. "What do you mean? What kind of message?"

"The only kind of message a guy like Angel understands," he answered, and her blood chilled. "Don't worry about it."

That definitely means you should worry about it. Just so we're clear.

"Are you ready?" he asked, heading for the door. "It's time to go."

She nodded nervously, pulling his jacket tighter around herself as she followed him out of the house and back toward the clubhouse. As usual, the party was in the courtyard, and she bit her lip to keep flashbacks of the last meeting they'd had here. The horror she'd felt, knowing Cade would leave her to the wolves that roamed this place. The pain and humiliation she'd suffered in the aftermath.

She was afraid of what Angel might do.

The bonfire reached sky-high just as before, and there was music and dancing already in progress when they arrived. Angel sat indulgently on his ugly throne, surveying his subjects with all the interest of a cat watching flies. There was always something predatory in his gaze, no matter who he was looking at.

For a moment, she thought they would slip in unnoticed, and that Angel would ignore their presence. Instead, he slowly turned his head, and upon seeing them, his mouth curled into a small, sick little smile that turned Asha's stomach.

As if Cade sensed her unease, he wrapped a hand around her elbow.

"Cade!" Angel boomed, his tone jubilant. "You made it back. And from what I hear, Rockland is mine now. That true?"

Cade tensed, and Asha tried to look anywhere but at Angel. The party fell silent.

"It's true," Cade finally replied. He sounded like the words caused him physical pain. "We took Rockland. We have a new weapons supplier, and a new source for product."

Lana had informed her that *product* meant *drugs.* Asha grimaced. Filling the Settlements with drugs was probably one of the ways they kept them under control, if she had to guess.

"Impressive," Angel said, eyebrows raised. "And you did it in the two-week timeframe. I guess Asha's yours now...if you still want her."

He looked to the men of his inner circle and gave a cruel laugh. "Now that she's been rode hard and put back dirty."

Asha cheeks flamed with a shame she knew she shouldn't feel, but it crept up on her nonetheless, like the ivy that slowly but surely infiltrated the exposed nooks and crannies of every building in this place. It got into the soft, vulnerable parts of her that she didn't know how to protect.

Cade froze, every muscle in his body taut. His jaw worked as he reached into his black bag and withdrew the object inside. In one smooth motion, he tossed it in a tall, wide arc. It landed just shy of Angel's feet and bounced, then rolled until it just kissed the toe of Angel's boot.

"She's mine now," Cade said, his voice smooth as silk, yet somehow more menacing than if he'd yelled. "Here's a reminder of what happens to those who take what belongs to me. Consider it next time you want to come after her. Goodnight."

He pulled on Asha's elbow, leading her away from the spectacle, but not before she caught a glimpse of Angel's face. He looked dumbfounded as his eyes traveled downward toward the thing at his feet. As he nudged it with his toe, there was a collective gasp.

On the shrivelled grass at Angel's feet, there lay a severed head, its mouth hanging open uselessly, and its eyes half-closed. Yet even death could not erase the look of shock from the corpse's features; its facial muscles were lax, yet somehow still frozen in alarm. A chill went down Asha's spine.

The head belonged to Dax, Angel's doorman.

Chapter 10

That night, a thunderstorm blew in. Lightning splintered the pitch-black sky, and rain fell in fat droplets as thunder rumbled in the distance. Despite her predicament, Asha was thankful to be inside Cade's small house, even if the roof leaked a little. She sat on the edge of the bed in her nightgown, two candles burning on a squat bedside table while Cade impatiently shoved a metal bucket under the small leak in the far corner of the room.

"Have to get that fixed," he muttered, more to himself than to Asha. "Place is a shithole as it is without adding water damage into the mix."

Asha almost laughed, but the image of Dax's severed head still lingered in her mind. Cade had shown off his mettle and his capacity for brutality today. But he had done it with the intent of keeping her safe from Angel. In a strange, fucked up sort of way, it was touching.

That didn't make sharing a bed with him that night any less nerve-wracking. She was still injured and sore from her ordeal, particularly in the genital area. She wouldn't be able to fuck him without screaming in pain.

You'll just have to blow him, she told herself, resigned. *He probably won't be bothered after that anyway.*

That was how she'd handled her husband, Eric. She'd only let him fuck her a few times, and then after that, she'd appeased him with blowjobs. It didn't stop his simmering resentment, but it did stop him from forcing himself on her, so she'd considered it a win. She'd also had a pushy girlfriend in her teen years that was similarly appeased, so Asha was used to it by now. She wouldn't enjoy it much, but she'd get through it with Cade as many times as he wanted if it meant she never had to deal with Angel again. Just the thought of his name was enough to make her shiver.

Cade busied himself in the bathroom. Though they had no running water, he kept a jug of water on the cracked vanity for washing up, using the sink as a basin like they did in old, period piece movies. Asha had washed up just before and was surprised when he kept his distance, giving her privacy. Then again, he'd done the same when they'd first met.

Still, sharing a bed was another thing altogether. She slid under the furs, snug and warm, and silently waited. Cade entered the room a moment later, carrying a candle with him to light his way. He'd changed into a pair of loose linen shorts, with no shirt. The candlelight danced over his well-defined chest, shoulders, and arms, highlighting the beautiful, sharp angles of his body. The dark ink of his sleeve tattoos only looked lovelier in the soft lighting, and Asha wondered what they meant to him, why he'd gotten them. She definitely shouldn't have been staring so hard at his hard, carefully sculpted body, and his dark, pensive stare and easy, smartass sense of humour should've made her roll her eyes.

She got the sense that maybe sex with him wouldn't have been so bad, before what happened with Angel. Still, there was a pit in her stomach when she thought about servicing him, and a terrifying desire to flee, to run off into the wilderness and take her chances with the predators and the perils of nature. At least bears didn't take pleasure in toying with their prey.

As Cade turned to set down his candle, she briefly spotted another, larger tattoo on his back. She wondered what it was, but he took a deep breath and blew out the candles, plunging them into total darkness.

Asha felt his weight as he got into bed next to her. She waited for several minutes, but Cade didn't speak. As her eyes adjusted to the darkness, she could just make out his outline. He was lying on his back under the blanket, staring at the ceiling. The light of his eyes told her that he was awake, yet he made no move toward her, staying solidly on his side of the bed.

She suddenly felt awkward. She didn't know how to broach the subject of fulfilling her side of their bargain. She thought he would do it, because he was the one who'd made it in the first place. He clearly wasn't shy, and nobody she'd been with before had hesitated when taking what they wanted from her.

"So..." she said quietly, into the blackness. "How are you?"

'How are you'? What the fuck is that, Asha?

Predictably, Cade gave a low chuckle, but he sounded concerned when he said, "Fine. How about you, darling? I know you rested earlier, but Leo said you were pretty banged up."

Caught off guard, she replied, "Uh, yeah. I'm still pretty sore." She swallowed hard, telling herself to stop being such a coward. She rolled onto her side, toward him, steeling herself to make an offer she had no desire to fulfill. "I'm probably not up for sex. But I can satisfy you other ways...if you want."

The offer hung there awkwardly in the silence of the night, and Asha cringed at her amateur-hour delivery and at the mortification of being in a situation where sex was her only currency.

"You think I want that?" Cade said quietly. "For you to get on your knees, reluctantly, and pretend to be somewhere else while I get off?"

"I wouldn't—" She cut off her own denial. That was exactly what she'd thought he wanted, if only because that was what they *all* wanted, in her experience.

"And then what?" he continued with casual disgust. "I roll over while you try to cry quietly enough into your pillow that I won't notice? Is that what you think of me, Asha?"

She didn't know what to say. Finally, she managed, "I didn't mean to offend—"

"The only thing that offends me," he cut in, "is that someone, somewhere, did that to you often enough that it's all you expect. Even in an arrangement like ours."

"But that *is* what I agreed to," Asha objected, hardly believing she was arguing with him over this. "You provide the protection; I provide the blowjobs."

Cade's low, ironic laugh danced deliciously over her skin. "I think we can agree that I haven't exactly delivered. When I manage to do that, maybe we can talk more about it."

She shifted uncomfortably. She should've been relieved that he didn't want her to service him mechanically, hating herself the entire time. But it left her to wonder what he wanted instead. Sex was a transaction; it was something she did because she had to, not because she wanted to. Either because it was her obligation as Eric's assigned wife, or, in the case of Shelly, because that was the price of having a relationship.

"So...you *don't* want me to blow you?" Asha clarified, a little in disbelief.

"I didn't say I didn't *want* to," Cade replied, and she could hear his smile. "But when I take you to bed, Asha, it'll be because *you* want me to. Because you begged me to. And when you do, you'll taste even sweeter to me, knowing I brought such a brave woman to her knees with desire."

His words conjured images that made Asha squeeze her thighs together. He thought she was brave? Why? And what would it be like, she wondered, to want someone the way he described? Despite her obvious attraction to him, she didn't want him quite like that...but his silken, self-assured tone made her *want* to want him like that.

But she couldn't tell him that, so instead, she forced a painful chuckle.

"Don't hold your breath waiting for that. You'll die."

The words were out before she could consider them. She hadn't intended for them to be a biting insult—they were simply a kneejerk reaction to her discomfort—but she wouldn't have blamed him for taking it as a ruthless rejection. Or for being angry with her.

But Cade simply laughed, his voice rich with humour.

"And she brings me back to Earth," he said, thoroughly amused.

He seemed to like her best when she was insulting him. *What a strange man.*

A scream split the air of the night, startling Asha awake. She bolted upright in bed, saturated with cold sweat, her heart pounding a painful rhythm against her ribs. It took her a moment to understand that it'd been her screaming, that her nightmare had clawed its way out of her into the real world.

His hands on her throat. His malicious little whisper in her ear. His disgusting, unwashed body against hers, the violation of him invading her most private places. The burn of his cigarettes on her skin, and the bottle inside her. All the shame and the pain and the humiliation she'd suffered those four nights when she'd been *his* to toy with.

She was still screaming when Cade's hands found her in the darkness, gently shaking her, and it took her a minute to understand what he was saying.

"What is it? Are you in pain? Do you need me to get Leo?"

His voice was concerned but calm, and somehow, that steadied her. She closed her mouth, her throat raw, and lay back against her pillow.

"Nightmare," she whispered into the blackness. "Horrible nightmare."

Cade's grip on her relaxed, and he withdrew his hands. She ached with the loss of his comforting touch, and with it, the knowledge that she wasn't alone, that she'd only been dreaming and that it was alright.

But it wasn't alright. It could never be alright again, because she hadn't woken up in her bed in the Cave, and Angel's abuse hadn't been merely a dream.

"Sorry for waking you," Asha whispered, her shame threatening to engulf her.

"You didn't," Cade replied mildly. "I was already awake." Then he gave a sad sigh. "I'm sorry, darling. If it helps...I have them, too."

Asha shifted, surprised. "You do?"

"Oh, yeah," he replied with a humourless snort. "Haven't slept well in about a decade. That's why I was awake. I don't get the screaming night terrors as much anymore, but that's only been in the last year or so."

That surprised her, if only because Cade was so often cool and collected. She couldn't imagine him panicking, drenched in sweat like she was.

"What do you dream of?" she asked without thinking, then thought better of it. "Sorry, I didn't mean—"

"It's fine," Cade replied with another sigh. "I was a soldier for a long time. Most of the time, when you're on patrol, it's just boring. Those are the good days. On the bad days, we'd have Wastelander attacks. Mostly they were just desperate people who were willing to try anything to get food or supplies. And it was my job to kill them, stop them from ever reaching the compound."

Asha lay in silence, contemplating that. "That's really hard."

Cade's shrug jostled the bed. "Yeah. So sometimes, I dream of their faces. There's a kid I dream about often. I got reprimanded because I refused to shoot him."

"God," Asha whispered in horror. "They wanted you to kill a kid?"

"Yeah," he said, as though stating the obvious. "They were Wastelanders, and they were on our territory. In their minds, they were all the same—didn't matter how old they were. They couldn't be allowed to live, because what if they rallied up more Wastelanders to attack us? That was their logic."

"But it's not like it would've mattered, would it?" she asked. "The Cave had more guns, more firepower, than anyone here. Easily."

"Yeah, the Delta was the same. Occasionally, though, we'd have a casualty here or there. A buddy of mine stepped on an IED that a gang planted in the patrol zone. Probably just left as a 'fuck you' to us, hoarding all those resources in our fortified castle—that wasn't uncommon."

Cade took a breath, as though steeling himself. "Blew both his legs off instantly. I radioed Leo, and Dom and I tried to tourniquet Gavin's legs, but he was bleeding out too fast. By the time we got him to the hospital, he was DOA. Sometimes, I dream about washing his blood and bits of burnt flesh off in the shower, after my shift."

Asha shivered. "I'm so sorry."

Those words were always inadequate and empty in these situations. She wished she had something better to say, but it was all that came to mind.

"It's alright," Cade said, and she started a little when she felt his hand brush hers under the covers. "I just wanted you to know...you're not alone, you know? We've been through different things, but I know how it feels to wonder how you'll ever sleep again, or to wonder how you'll ever find life worth living again."

His voice was soft and sincere. Asha could feel body heat radiating from him, warming the bed between them, and along with his words, it brought her some small comfort.

"I just...I don't know how to keep going," she heard herself say, a tremor in her voice. "How do you feel normal again?"

"Not an easy question," Cade replied with a sigh. "Have you tried crying?"

"Crying?" Asha repeated, in disbelief. "What good would that do?"

He made a sound of amusement. "It helps sometimes, believe it or not. My mom always used to say that it was like a pressure valve. It doesn't feel good while you're doing it, but it keeps you from erupting down the line."

"My mom used to say that crying was for people without real solutions," Asha said doubtfully. "And my dad would say that it promoted a losing attitude."

Cade scoffed. "There are things in life that have no real solutions. If it was that easy, why would you be struggling so hard? It's because you're hurting in a way that nobody can fully heal."

Asha couldn't reply; she felt as though her throat had closed up. She hadn't expected his compassion for her, and she wasn't sure how to respond.

"Do you cry?" she asked eventually. She couldn't picture a soldier—especially one as fierce as Cade—weeping uncontrollably.

"Sure," he answered easily. "Cried like a baby when I first left the Delta. When I buried my friends at Ashburn. When I had to identify my wife's body, and know that one of my guys had killed her."

He paused for so long that Asha began, "I'm sorry—"

"Don't be," Cade cut in with a sigh. "It's maybe something I'm not supposed to admit...but then, keeping it all to myself never seemed to help, either. Just made me explode later when it all got to be too much."

Her heart softened at the thought of Cade's tears. The image of him being inconsolable made her ache inside. It made him feel like a kindred spirit somehow, and she was touched by his open vulnerability with her.

"If crying's out," Cade continued with a hint of humour, "have you tried talking?"

"Talking?" Asha chewed her lip, suddenly nervous.

"Yeah," he said, his voice gentling. "It's just me and the dark, darling. We'll keep your secrets."

She considered his offer quietly, in a kind of wonder. The abuse she'd suffered at Angel's hands felt deeply personal somehow, something that her instincts told her to bury, to box away in her mind and never look at again. That was how she'd managed her whole life: compartmentalize and forget.

But it had become so heavy. So burdensome. So hard to carry alone.

That was how she found herself whispering some of her deepest secrets to Cade, the darkness acting as her protection. She didn't have to read his expression, see his pity, or be deterred by his reactions. For his part, he remained completely silent as she unloaded.

She told him almost everything, from the beginning: how she grew up; the suffocating expectations of her government-official parents; their utter disappointment in her; Shelly, her high school bully-turned-girlfriend, who she'd had to break up with when she received her marriage assignment to Eric; their doomed marriage.

Broken and disjointed, she detailed Angel's assaults on her. He raped her repeatedly. Burned her with cigarettes and hot knives. Punched her in the mouth, cracking her tooth. Smacked her head against the bedpost. And at each turn, she'd fought him violently, ferociously, like a wildcat. All for naught.

Asha relayed all of this matter-of-factly, with all the enthusiasm of recalling a weekly shopping list. It was the only way to keep enough distance from it, to keep her head above water. Only now did she sense more of a reaction from Cade. He remained silent, but she heard his little intakes of breath, and felt the tension in his body through the mattress.

When she'd finally finished, she lay back against her pillow, exhausted. They lay there in silence for a long time—not talking, not touching. She'd nearly dozed off again when she suddenly felt Cade's warm hand cover hers, holding it on the mattress between them. He squeezed lightly, sending tingles up her arm.

"I'm proud of you," he murmured, and in spite of what she'd said earlier, she nearly burst into tears. She couldn't remember the last time she'd heard those words, and she choked on the lump in her throat.

Thankfully, Cade didn't seem to require a reply. He kept holding her hand until she'd slipped back into sleep.

Chapter 11

A week passed, and in contrast to her first two weeks at the Nest, Asha's days were quiet and uneventful. Cade went for a jog in the early morning hours, then worked out in the yard. He was gone in the afternoons, training with the Blackguard in the south end of the Nest, and returned for dinner each day.

He made no demands of Asha, other than that she rest up and heal from her injuries. When she asked him about the problem of leaving her alone with Angel, he merely answered, "When you're better, we'll figure it out."

By the end of the week, Asha was feeling much better physically, but she couldn't wait anymore. They hadn't talked about what she'd told him since that night in bed, but surely, he could understand her anxiety? She had to know what to expect.

After dinner, she watched him go out into the backyard, where he seemed to be preparing for something. He'd rested a backpack against the outside wall of the house, and he looked up at her when she walked out.

"Good, you're here," Cade said briskly. "I want to try something. Throw a punch."

Asha balked. "What?"

"You heard me. Throw a punch at me."

"Why?"

"The sooner you do it, the sooner you'll find out."

She scoffed. "No."

Cade's mouth curved into a small, confrontational smile. "You scared there, darling? What happened? I've always thought of you like a little viper—always ready to strike."

Asha rolled her eyes, but much to her annoyance, the taunt was working on her.

"Not scared. Just bored."

He closed the gap between them, his face inches from hers. She took a sharp inhale at his nearness. She could feel the heat of his body.

"So, it should be easy, then, to take me down," Cade said in a low, intimate tone. "You gonna show me what you got, or what?"

Asha shot him a glare. "Fuck off."

To her further annoyance, he laughed. "This should be good. Show me a little bit of what you gave Angel, huh?"

The mention of her tormentor finally made Asha snap. She threw a punch, but he caught her fist in his hand and twisted her arm behind her back. His other arm wrapped around her throat, holding her firmly in place. He wasn't hurting her, but she wasn't going anywhere.

"Lesson one," he said by her ear. "Uncontrolled rage makes you sloppy. Sloppy fighters make stupid mistakes."

Cade released her, and she lashed out at him again. He blocked each of her blows almost lazily, like it was too easy. That only heightened her frustration, and she struck out at him again, only to have him step out of her reach. She paused, panting, and was vexed when she realized that he looked entirely unbothered. He didn't even look winded.

"As a woman of average size, you're at a disadvantage against most male combatants," he said matter-of-factly. "Weapons even the odds, but your best weapon is your brain."

"Did your *sensei* teach you that?" Asha said sardonically, and he laughed again. She hated how much she liked the sound of his laugh, and the way it lit up and softened his intense, serious features.

"No. But it's what I've known to be true, in battle after battle. The ability to stay calm, think clearly, and make good decisions in extreme situations is what keeps you alive."

"And you're saying that I haven't made good decisions," she shot back.

"On the contrary," Cade replied, catching her fist in his hand as she threw another punch. "I think you've done the best anyone could do without any training. It's not something we naturally know how to do. Panic is our default."

He walked over to his pack, which leaned against the outside wall of the condo. He fished inside, then withdrew two long strips of fabric, plus what looked like crudely fashioned kneepads. They were like tiny cushions, clumsily made by wrapping burlap around some kind of stuffing.

"What the hell are those?" Asha said, bewildered.

Cade smiled. "Padding. Give me your hands for a minute."

She hesitated. No one had touched her since the attack except for Leo, when he'd tended to her. She thought of the last week, when they'd shared a bed and Cade had been careful to stick to his side, putting as much distance between them as possible. How she'd both wanted it and hated it, and how she'd hated herself for wanting it.

"I'm not gonna hurt you," Cade murmured, breaking through her thoughts. "Haven't I proven that, at least?"

His grey eyes were focused, but softer than usual, entreating. They asked for her trust. She didn't know if she could give it, but they made her want to. She sighed and held out her hands.

Cade unraveled the strips of fabric and wound them around each of her palms, then up her fingers, his touch featherlight and careful. She knew he was trying not to frighten her, and paradoxically, that angered her. She hated being so fragile that he had to walk on eggshells around her. She needed to be better, stronger.

"Alright," Cade said once her hands were wrapped. He tied the odd-looking kneepads around his own hands with ribbons sewn onto the sides. They looked bizarre, and Asha had to suppress a snort as he held up his hands. "Now, punch me as hard as you can."

She did snort at that. "Anywhere, or?"

He rolled his eyes. "You know what I mean. Quit stalling."

Asha took in a breath, then struck out at him again, hitting his left hand.

"Terrible," Cade remarked. "That can't be how hard you hit Angel. Guy had a black eye and a fat lip."

She hit him again, this time on the right. "So what if it's not?"

"So what?" he repeated, raising an eyebrow. "So maybe what really happened was an accident, huh? Maybe you and him got a little kinky, and things just got out of hand?"

Flashbacks came, fast and furious. Hitting Angel in the face with the ashtray; him screaming; her screaming as he burned her with cigarettes; stumbling out of his room, blood oozing between her thighs.

"Fuck you," Asha bit out, striking his hand harder. "Fuck you and every man here who protects him. You're all guilty."

"Seems if we were guilty, you'd be hitting harder," Cade replied nonchalantly. "You've never killed anyone, have you? You gotta mean it, or it'll be your head on the pike instead."

An image of the severed heads on the gate flooded her brain, followed by more of the torture she'd suffered at Angel's hands. The deep well of rage inside of her, that part that refused to be broken, resurfaced, and she was glad. It was her reservoir of survival. It made her keep going even when she saw no reason to try.

Her blows grew stronger, faster, until she was no longer seeing anything but the blur of motion, no longer feeling anything except a swell of humiliation and fury that threatened to swallow her whole.

"You think I wanted that?" Asha said, and she realized distantly that she was screaming at him. "That I wanted that motherfucker to rape me and beat me? That I wanted to be burned, and bled, and broken?"

Cade didn't reply, didn't react, and she couldn't see him anymore anyway. All that existed was the swirling torrent of shame in her gut, and the feeling of her fists hitting the pads. The impacts were satisfying, even as they made her more desperate for a reprieve from all the pain inside her.

"That I wanted my safe home to be destroyed? That I wanted to leave my best friend to be eaten by cannibals? That I wanted to lose everything—*everything*?"

She was getting tired, panting and sweating, but he needed to hear the truth.

"And it's your fault!" she burst out, and she hated that she heard tears in her voice. "You were supposed to protect me. I s-said yes to your stupid bargain, offered you my body, because you were supposed to protect me from him!"

All the strength went out of her at once, and she dropped to her knees, gasping for breath. To her horror, she was shaking like a leaf. Tears blurred her vision, but she didn't allow them to fall.

She didn't register Cade dropping to his knees across from her, but the next thing she knew, his arms slowly wrapped around her, drawing her against him. Her instinct told her to resist, to pull away, but she was startled by how gentle he was. He held her loosely, allowing her to easily escape if she wanted to, but somehow, she didn't.

It had been a long time since someone's touch had felt good to her, and his was oddly comforting. She buried her face in his shoulder.

"I know," Cade said, and to her surprise, he didn't sound angry. He sounded crestfallen. "He's a monster. And maybe I am, too. But let me use my skills to sharpen those fangs of yours, little viper. To help you never need anyone to come to your rescue. You have a fire burning in you that I saw the moment you spit on that asshole at Little River. Use it."

"I don't know how," Asha blubbered. "I just...maybe the fire's still there, like you said, but I can't feel it. Like he snuffed it out, and all I feel now is this darkness inside of me. And I don't know how to turn the light back on."

"That's what this world does." He patted her back. "We all feel it. The trick is to realize that the only way to survive the darkness is to become its mistress, darling."

She considered that as she let him hold onto her for another moment, inhaling his scent and grounding herself. When she finally pulled back, he wore a small, sad smile.

"You said that rage makes sloppy fighters," Asha said, and he gave a low chuckle.

"Yes, *uncontrolled* rage," he replied. "I'll teach you to use that beautiful anger wisely. To give you focus, and to inflict pain on your enemies." He swallowed and looked away. "To become a Blackguard."

"There are no women in the Blackguard."

"That's true," Cade said as he helped her to her feet. "But there's a first for everything. It'll take years of training before you're on a similar level to me, Leo, and Dom; we're soldiers. Professionals. But that doesn't mean you can't keep yourself safe in the meantime."

Asha fidgeted uncomfortably. "But the others won't accept me."

Cade shrugged. "They'll follow my orders, even if they don't like them. And we won't introduce you to the others anyway until I know you're ready to prove yourself in the field."

"In the field?" she asked, her stomach churning. "Like...on your raids? On scavenging missions?"

"Yeah, that's part of the job."

Asha swallowed hard. "And if I say no?"

"You don't want to say no," Cade said with a knowing smile. "But nothing would change. You'd spend your days with the other women, doing their chores, and your nights here. You can choose that life, if you want...become a servant. But it seems to me that you've already proven that you're nobody's maid."

His voice was tinged with amusement, and Asha managed a weak smile. She'd never thought about being a soldier. It wasn't an option that ever would've been possible for her in the Cave. But Cade was right that she didn't want to serve in the roles assigned to women there. She hadn't enjoyed being a wife in the compound either, and that had been much more palatable than anything she could do in this place.

She was nervous at the prospect of learning to fight, but it also excited and comforted her. Never again would she have to rely entirely on someone else to rescue her. She could rise out of the learned helplessness that'd been drilled into her in the compound, that she'd always been desperate to escape, even if she hadn't realized it until this moment.

"Alright," she said to Cade. "I want in."

He smiled at her with real warmth, and chucked her chin.

"You're a *brave* little viper," he said. "I hate that you've had to be...but there aren't many women—hell, many *people*—who would've stood up to Angel the way you did. Right now, you're afraid of your own darkness, but one day, you'll learn to embrace it. You'll use it to survive impossible odds. That's real power."

Cade stood and pulled her to her feet.

"Now, the real work begins."

He didn't lie. The next four weeks were the hardest, most exhausting weeks of Asha's life, and for a woman who'd been sold into slavery and endured Angel's wrath, that was saying something.

Cade took her training seriously, and he put her through a brutal, crash-course bootcamp that left her falling into bed in the evenings, asleep before she hit the mattress. She still woke every night from terrifying nightmares, but at least he was there to hold her hand, fetch her some water, and talk to her until she fell back asleep. He told her more stories about his time in the military at the Delta, and about his mother, who he'd obviously loved dearly. Asha knew she was dead, but Cade clearly hadn't wanted to talk about it, so she let him be. Still, she wondered if her death had influenced his decision to leave.

Every morning now, he woke her at the crack of dawn and had her run laps, followed by intense strength training in the backyard. He joined in, completing his own daily training tasks, but otherwise he mostly acted like the worst motivational speaker ever as Asha tried to force her body to accomplish things she'd never thought possible. He even put Dom in charge of the usual training drills with the men so that he could focus solely on grinding Asha's bones into dust, or at least, that was how it felt to her.

"You can do five more reps," Cade said sternly to Asha, who lay on her stomach in the grass, having just completed so many push-ups that she'd lost count.

"Fuck you," she gasped out. "I *can't.*"

"Make it ten, then," he replied, his tone razor-sharp.

She wanted to cry, but she wasn't convinced that he wouldn't increase it to fifteen if she did. This was a side of Cade she'd only seen glimpses of: intensely focused, insanely disciplined, and utterly ruthless. During training, she learned, he had absolutely zero sense of humour, and was far less tolerant of her snark than he was outside of their sessions.

He was every inch the military commander during that time. As much as she might hate him during the moments of intense pain during training, she had to admit that there was something hot about that amount of discipline. And she was indeed growing stronger by the day, especially since Cade fed her a steady diet of almost exclusively protein—meat from the hunts that he and the Blackguard went on every few days. He brought her on her first hunt after a couple of weeks, and was pleased when she shot a deer on her first try.

After lunch each day, Cade taught her weapons training, knife skills, and hand-to-hand combat. He introduced her to using a rifle and a pistol, and taught her to shoot.

"Your first thought should always be your weapon," Cade said, adjusting her shooting posture. "Like I said before: you're at a physical disadvantage against most male combatants. Guns even the odds significantly."

He'd set up makeshift targets at the opposite end of the backyard to start with—much closer than the targets at the training yard everyone else used, he told her. Asha worked harder at target practice than at anything else, determined to master this one thing that would even the odds between her and someone like Angel.

"You're actually a pretty decent shot," Cade said during their fourth week, a rare bit of warmth in his voice.

Nonetheless, Asha beamed with pride. She didn't know what to make of the fact that training as a soldier—painful though it was—came to her more easily than anything she'd done before. Perhaps because she *wanted* this. She'd *chosen* this. She reveled in her new strength, and in the combat skills she was learning. For the first time, she felt powerful.

She mimed clapping her hand over her mouth in shock at Cade's praise.

"So, you're saying I'm actually doing something *right*?"

"You're doing plenty right," he replied with a shrug. "Better than most. But it's not my job to pat you on the back. It's my job to make you into a soldier, in the very limited time we've got."

She turned to look at him, surprised by the last bit. "Time?"

"I've gotten word from Angel," Cade said, and she forced herself not to flinch at the name. "We're due to collect the rents from the Settlements, starting in a month."

"The rents?"

"Payment for our protection," he answered, and Asha tried not to make a face. "They provide us with goods, and Angel offers them a full-time security team to protect them. The Blackguard visits a couple times a year to collect payment and to consult on the security side of things."

"And you're taking me with you on this trip," she said, her voice quavering. "Right?"

Cade nodded. "I'll be introducing you to the men next week. After that, you'll train with all of us."

"You really think I'm ready?" Asha asked, a little doubtfully.

"I think you'll handle it," he replied, neatly avoiding a direct answer. She rolled her eyes. "We may take you on a couple smaller missions in the meantime, to get you some experience. We'll also have to get you a uniform."

The first week in May, Asha stood in the larger training yard where the rest of the Blackguard trained. There was a small shooting range, as well as a makeshift obstacle course, with rope ladders and wooden platforms for climbing. A mishmash of workout equipment and weights were reserved for the far corner.

Asha swallowed back her nerves as a dozen Blackguard soldiers filed into the yard, with Leo, Dom, and Cade bringing up the rear. She'd braided her long black hair out of her face, and Cade had gotten Lana and the other women to alter a spare black tactical uniform for her, but it still didn't fit her perfectly. She felt like an imposter wearing it, and she shifted uncomfortably from foot to foot.

Most of the soldiers eyed her with a mix of confusion and curiosity, though a few of them didn't bother to hide their distaste for her wearing their uniform. A large, redheaded man rolled his eyes and gave a sarcastic chuckle, while another man with a mop of curly hair shot her a look of disgust.

But as soon as Cade stood by her side in front of them, arms crossed with a commanding expression on his face, they immediately stood at attention, single-file, emptying their expressions. The instant effect on them was remarkable.

"We have a new recruit," Cade announced, looking down the line at each man's face. "Asha will be joining the Blackguard on all future missions. She's done a few weeks of basic training, but as a rookie, she'll need your help to find her place with us."

A long pause ensued, where the men couldn't help glancing at each other awkwardly. The redheaded man scoffed quietly.

"Do you have something to share with the group, Garett?" Cade demanded, fixing him with that piercing, grey-eyed stare that Asha had found both so unsettling and compelling.

Garett shook his head. "No, sir, it's just—"

"Do tell," Cade cut in. "I'm interested."

His tone was frosty, and Asha was glad to not be on the receiving end of it. He'd never spoken that way to her, even during training.

Garett scoffed again. "You really gonna make me say it, Cap? She's a woman!"

"And?" Cade lifted his eyebrows.

"We don't allow women to join," the curly-haired man said with a shrug. "You can't just bring your girlfriend here and expect us to take her seriously."

Asha chewed her lip. "I've been working hard on—"

"Women don't belong here unless they're spreading their legs," Garett interrupted, shooting her a glare.

"That's enough," Cade snapped. "Garett, you'll be spending *your* afternoon cleaning out the latrines instead of training. Same with you, Tom."

Both men opened their mouths to protest, but Cade talked over them.

"And if you can't shape up before tomorrow, don't fucking bother coming back. You can settle for guard duty at the gate, or whatever useless busywork Angel sees fit to assign you. Closed-minded dipshits do not belong in the Blackguard."

Amid much muttering and cursing, Garett and Tom left, staring daggers at Asha on their way out. She couldn't help but gulp.

"This applies to the rest of you as well," Cade continued, looking back to the rest of the men. "I expect that every person here will treat Asha with the basic respect you give to all your fellow soldiers. Is that understood?"

The general chorus of *yes, sir* surprised Asha again. The rest of the men may not have cared for Asha, but it was clear that they respected Cade and his authority. They seemed somewhat doubtful but willing to give her a shot, and that was the best she could've hoped for.

They went down the line, introducing themselves to her. A tall, pale, lanky man in the middle identified himself as Raph, their chief navigator on missions, and a shorter, playful-looking man with copper skin and honey-coloured eyes told her his name was Davy. He looked like the youngest of the group, barely out of his teens.

"We'll start with our usual drills," Cade said. "You know what to do."

The men, including Dom and Leo, headed for the equipment. Cade nodded at Davy and beckoned him over.

"Davy's our former rookie before you," Cade said to Asha, in the same businesslike way he spoke to the others. She supposed she had to appreciate that he was treating her the same as anyone else there. "He'll help you figure out the drills. Understood?"

"Yes," Asha said, nervous but eager to prove herself.

"Yes, *sir*," Cade corrected. "When you're here with the others, you'll refer to me by *sir*, like everyone else."

Asha nearly laughed at him, but caught herself just in time. She couldn't imagine referring to him as sir. It was too formal and so unlike him.

"I'm not gonna call you that," she said with a wry smile.

"Oh yes, you will," he replied firmly. "Or there'll be...consequences."

Asha was briefly tempted to ask exactly what kind of consequences, but his steely glare convinced her that she didn't want to die that day. Still, there was an undeniable spark of amusement in his eye.

She gave a single nod. "Fine. Can I get to work now?"

"Fine, *sir*."

She rolled her eyes, and Davy stared at the ground, looking vaguely uncomfortable.

"Fine, *sir*," she parroted, not bothering to hide her sarcasm.

"Very good," Cade said silkily. "She can be taught."

He walked away, taking a position to supervise the climbing drills the others were doing.

"Dickhead," Asha breathed, and to her delight, Davy laughed. She turned to him with what she hoped was a winning smile. "Could you show me the ropes? I'd appreciate it."

Davy had a lovable grin. "Train with the same fierceness you give the Captain, and we've got no problem here."

Chapter 12

The next few weeks were hard, but Asha had built up enough strength that she was able to finish the drills, something she wouldn't have accomplished just a month or so before. True to his orders, Davy helped her through demonstration, and although the two of them were always last to finish, she felt like they were making significant progress.

Garett and Tom still hated her—they seemed to hold her responsible for their punishment and for the downgrade in respect they now enjoyed among the others—but other than that, most of the men seemed to tentatively accept her presence, even if they still didn't entirely understand it.

At the start of June, they took her on her first scavenging mission, which was a strange experience for Asha. They sought out a far-flung, long-abandoned hamlet, some way from the city. They stayed on high alert for cannibals and for other gangs, but the village was so small and pitiful that Asha doubted there were any that would be interested in the place. It was totally derelict, with nothing but old, empty buildings slowly crumbling into dust.

Cade was patient with her throughout, showing her how to search for things that others may have overlooked, like metal scraps, ammunition, and other weapons like knives or baseball bats. The others chimed in when they could, though Garett still refused to speak to Asha directly.

Whatever, asshole.

Seeing the ruins of civilization made Asha understand why they'd called it the Wasteland at home. Searching the husks of old houses and businesses somehow felt like sorting through corpses. There was an enormous, overwhelming sense of loss that she felt to her bones, and she wished that there was a way to return to that fragile world of glass that had once existed here, so peaceful compared to the desecrated carcass it had left behind.

"It's sad," she said to Cade, in a quiet moment. "I wish I'd lived back then. That I hadn't lived to see this time."

He considered. "The world always had problems. I'm not convinced that the choices they had back then were much better—or even that different—to the ones we have now. Swim against the current, fight to survive in a hellscape populated mostly by dicks who don't care about anything but themselves. Sounds the same to me."

Asha snorted. "I wouldn't hate going back to hot showers, though."

"You got me there," he replied with a small smile.

The sun had dropped lower in the sky, and the golden rays softened his sharp features, making him look gentler, less severe. Asha admired him, though she tried to hide it. He was still somewhat mysterious to her, his past incomplete, but he'd given her so much in such a short time.

Such an odd thought to have about a man who'd literally purchased her, yet it was true.

"I haven't been too tough on you, have I?"

"What?" Asha said, surprised by the question.

"I know I've been demanding, these last few weeks," Cade replied, a little regretfully. "Especially since you're a civilian. It's just that we've had so little time to prepare, and I couldn't think of another way to keep you away from Angel—"

"It's fine," she cut in. "I'm used to your massive ego by now."

He chuckled and moved closer to her, into her space, so they were barely a foot apart. She looked up into his eyes, and there was a strange, new affection in them.

"And I'm used to your big mouth," he murmured, but it didn't sound like an insult when he said it with that kind of warmth. He leaned closer, and for a wild second, Asha thought he might kiss her.

But then she panicked. She turned away and cleared her throat, saying, "Thanks for training me. You were tough, but not cruel."

Cade gave a little sigh and looked off toward the horizon, probably judging that it was time to leave.

"I think that's the closest you've ever come to giving me a compliment, darling."

They didn't recover much from the buildings on that trip, but on the way back, Asha discovered an empty campsite with a tent, sleeping bags, and a small cache of ammunition, hidden beneath the leaves of a shrub.

"Aren't we stealing from someone who might need this stuff?" Asha asked after they'd left with the loot, wringing her hands. "The camp didn't look that old."

"It was unattended," Cade replied, and his indifference struck her. "Out here, that means it's ours."

"But what if they need the sleeping bag to keep warm? Or—"

"Asha," he said, short and irritated. "It's survival. That's it. There's nothing personal about it. You need to learn that there are some things you can't change."

She fell silent, upset by his tone. She wasn't used to him speaking to her like that, and the comment about *things you can't change* sounded too close to a rebuke for the way she'd been disgusted by the social hierarchy at the Nest.

Well, I'm not going to accept it, Asha thought angrily. *Not forever, anyway.*

After they got back to the Nest, she decided to distance herself from Cade for the evening. She instead asked Leo if she could help him prep medicines for their journey to Hillside, the first settlement they were to visit. He let her tag along on his trip to Dom's house, where he would collect medicinal plants for his kit.

"You can help harvest, if you like," Leo said with a small smile. "Dom might have something for you to eat, too."

"Eat?" Asha asked, raising an eyebrow.

"He maintains a vegetable garden."

Asha wasn't prepared for the sheer amount of greenery that practically engulfed Dom's small, modest home. He had carefully maintained flowerbeds that wrapped around the entire building. The shrubbery was impeccably trimmed, and the ivy that crawled up the walls was artfully arranged. Leo had told her he was an avid gardener, but she still hadn't been able to picture stoic, grumpy Dom as the type to fuss over delicate daffodils.

He answered the door exactly as she expected: with a short, clipped greeting, before stepping aside to admit them. He led them out the back door and into the yard, where Asha was once again floored by the sheer number of plants. He tended a large vegetable garden, but he also had a separate garden for what she assumed were the herbs and medicinal plants that Leo was after.

"You planted all this?" Asha dared to ask Dom, awestruck.

He grunted, then rubbed the back of his neck. "Yep."

After a moment, it became clear that that was all she was going to get from him, so she knelt in the dirt next to Leo, who was examining various plants in the herb garden. Dom watched for a minute, then retreated back into the house.

"He likes plants more than people," Leo confided in a low, confidential tone, his amusement palpable.

"I couldn't tell," Asha replied wryly. "He's seriously talented. I couldn't do all this."

"I know. Best not to tell him, though. He'll get all awkward about it."

She giggled, forgetting all about her earlier annoyance with Cade. Leo opened his medical bag, and Asha recognized it as the basic kit that paramedics used at the compound. The top had holders for syringes, scissors, surgical tools, a small flashlight, a blood pressure cuff, and a stethoscope. The rest was filled with typical supplies like bandages, as well as various jars and bottles of medicine. What made Asha stop dead, however, was a small, red-labeled auto-injector of clear liquid strapped to the top of the bag.

"Is that Regenerex?" she asked in wonder.

"It is," Leo replied as he trimmed peppermint leaves off the plant.

Her brow furrowed. She'd only seen the distinctive packaging once before: in the nurse's office at the school where she worked. It had incredibly rapid regenerative healing abilities and was capable of healing even serious wounds in hours. A teenage boy had had a bad fall in the early days of her working there, and the drug had saved his life.

"It's standard in every military doctor's kit," Leo continued, stashing leaves in a pouch from his pack. "Just the one shot, though. It's not easy to manufacture, so we'd use it only for cases that'd be truly terminal otherwise."

"I'm surprised you still have it, with everything."

He shrugged. "I wouldn't use it on just anyone, frankly. It's pretty much irreplaceable now, so I'd save it for Cade, Dom, or myself."

At Cade's name, Asha flinched. She was beginning to regret how she'd left things with him. Her anger may have been disproportionate, but it came from what she realized was a real need to tell him something important: that she wasn't willing to put up with gang life forever.

She spotted some of the other medicines Leo had: long-life antibiotics, morphine, and a cluster of other drugs that she didn't know the use for.

"You have so much compound medicine left," Asha said. "How?"

"Why do you think we're harvesting plants right now?" Leo replied, as though it were obvious. "I use herbal medicine for minor to moderate complaints. I save the good stuff for situations where it's truly needed."

"Like when Angel..." She trailed off, but he nodded solemnly. It explained why having her tooth pulled hadn't hurt nearly as much as expected. She felt oddly touched that he'd given her a hit from his precious supply of morphine.

She finished helping Leo with the plants, said an awkward goodbye to Dom, and returned home. Night had fallen by then, and the house was dark except for flickering light coming from the bedroom.

Cade was lying on the bed, fully clothed, reading a book by candlelight. He looked up when she entered, and she flopped down next to him, suddenly very tired.

"Are you still mad at me?" he asked, his tone careful.

Asha sighed. "I guess not. I probably overreacted. I just..."

He waited patiently, setting his book aside.

"You said that I need to accept the things I can't change, but I don't want to live this way forever," she managed to get out. "I don't want to live in this gang forever. I don't want to be technically someone's property forever. I want...more than this, you know? Maybe you'll say I'm being spoiled, but—"

"No," Cade said softly. "I get it. The compound's far from perfect, but not worrying about basic survival every day is a major perk."

"But it's different for you," she continued, a little frustrated. "You're a man in this world. Not only do you have the physical advantage, but you have all the power in this place, too. If you wanted to, you could kill me on a whim and who would do anything about it?"

He was silent. Then, "I would never hurt you."

"That's not the point, Cade. The point is that you *could,* and because of who you are and because, let's face it, they see me as little more than your whore—an accessory that you can put on and take off whenever you like—there would be zero consequences. So, my entire well-being hinges on my own ability to fight off someone bigger, stronger, and inherently more powerful than I am. My only value comes in my attachment to *you.* You don't understand how powerless that makes me feel."

"But I do," he said, and he enveloped her hand in his. "It's why I wanted to offer you something more with the Blackguard. Give you the tools to defend yourself."

"I know, but sometimes...sometimes, we have to change the things we can't accept. For now, I accept that this is my new home, but one day...I'll be done with this place. I hope when that day comes..."

She paused, swallowing back what she was afraid to say, fidgeting with the furs on the bed. Cade waited again, but when it became clear she wouldn't continue, he prompted her with, "What?"

Asha took a deep breath and finally replied, "That you'll come with me."

His expression softened, and before she knew what was happening, he'd pulled her into his arms. Unsure what to do, Asha rested her cheek against his chest and listened to the slow, reassuring thump of his heartbeat. She was surprised that her instinct was to sink into him, that his warmth was comforting.

"You'd really want me to go with you?" Cade murmured into her hair.

"I have no one else," she said without thinking about how it sounded.

Nonetheless, he chuckled. "Just when I think we're about to have a moment, darling."

She laughed too. "I didn't mean it like that. I just mean...I..."

She felt suddenly unbearably awkward. She was bad at this. She still didn't know exactly how she felt about Cade, other than that she preferred him to anyone else here.

Luckily, he didn't seem to require her to sort through it.

"It's alright, little viper," he teased, giving her a squeeze before releasing her. "And even though right now, I think we're best served by staying here... when the day to leave comes, I'll go with you. I'm not going to leave you twisting in the wind."

Asha smiled. "Thank you." A thought occurred to her. "Have you ever thought about going back to Ashburn one day?"

Cade's smile faltered, and he looked serious again. "I don't know. It's a long way, and it'd need some significant TLC after being empty for—"

"I know all that. I just mean...one day, I'd like to think we could do that. Have a place where we can make our own rules. Where I could...have a say."

He touched her cheek. "Maybe one day."

Sensing that was all she was going to get for now, Asha got ready for bed.

Chapter 13

Summer 2097

The following week, they departed on their trip to Hillside, the first settlement on their list. The plan was to visit two settlements to the west of Angel's Nest on this trip, return home and rest, then visit the second two settlements to the east before autumn arrived.

The journey was rough on Asha, who'd never traveled so far on foot before. They brought the horse-drawn wagon with them, but it was strictly for carrying cargo. Outfitted in her uniform and carrying a backpack of basic supplies, a rifle, and a pistol at her hip was more weight than she was used to carrying over long distances. Thank God she'd spent the last month and a half in bootcamp.

They followed the crumbling remains of an old highway, with Raph using a hand-drawn map and compass as a guide. Asha had no idea how accurate they were, but Cade had made the trip more than once, so she only hoped she wouldn't get lost in the dense forest that surrounded the road. She stuck close to Cade.

He estimated it would take a couple of days to arrive at Hillside, so when it got dark, they pitched their tents in a forest clearing, away from the road to minimize the chance of discovery by others. A couple men were appointed to be on nighttime watch while the rest of them slept. Asha shared a tent with Cade, and she was so tired from the day of travel that she was asleep before he even retired to bed.

The moon was high in the sky when Asha awoke again. It wasn't strange for her to wake up in the night, but for once, it wasn't nightmares that troubled her. Her bladder was uncomfortably full, aching and nagging at her. She didn't want to leave her tent and go out into the night, so for a while, she lay there, delaying her decision.

Cade was fast asleep in his own sleeping bag next to her, lightly snoring, which made her smile involuntarily. She tried to go back to sleep, but eventually, her problem couldn't be ignored. She considered waking him, but she didn't want to bother him. Eric would've yelled at her for something like that. Besides, wasn't that why she'd been training so hard, these last few weeks? To stop being such a scared mouse?

With a yawn, she stood and pulled her boots on. She wore nothing but the thin nightgown that Lana had given her. On her way out, however, she picked up her holstered pistol and strapped it around her thigh, concealed by her skirt.

Just in case.

She thought about lighting her lantern, but decided against it. It'd be a glowing beacon that'd only draw attention. Luckily, the moon was almost full, and silver moonlight bathed the camp in shadows, layered with light fog. Shivering slightly in the cool spring air, she walked across the camp towards a copse of trees that would provide decent cover, away from that creep, Garrett, who was on the night watch. With the chirp of crickets in her ears, she entered the brush and went far enough that Garett wouldn't be able to spy on her.

After she peed, she silently made her way back toward the clearing. The mist had thickened considerably, obscuring her path, and after a couple of wrong turns, Asha had to admit that she was lost. She couldn't see more than a few feet in front of her.

Fear shot through her, but she took a deep breath. Panicking wouldn't help. Rather than get herself even more lost than she already was, it was best to sit and wait for the fog to lift, or for morning to come, if it came down to it. Pushing down the urge to run, she found the nearest tree trunk that was mostly clear at its base and sat beneath it, leaning back against the bark.

Asha waited for what felt like a long time, but the mist didn't disperse. She did her best to stay calm, but every minute that passed, that became harder. Her heart leapt when she heard footsteps nearby, crunching through the brush. She prayed that it was Cade coming to look for her, but she had no way of knowing who it was.

The footsteps abruptly stopped, and a faint light became visible through the fog.

"Asha?"

Ugh, it's Garrett, she thought with a grimace. *Better than nothing, I guess.*

"I'm here," she called softly. "I got lost."

"Yeah. Saw you go off on your own. Keep talking and I'll find you."

She did, trying to keep her voice low to avoid attracting predators or people. Eventually, the big, ginger-haired man came into view, holding up his lantern. At the sight of her, his lips curved into a lascivious smile, and Asha shifted uncomfortably. He offered his hand to help her stand.

"I'm fine, thanks," she said stiffly, moving to get up.

It happened in a fraction of a second: Garrett dropped the lantern and shoved her backward. She landed in the dirt with an *oof,* and then he practically threw himself on top of her. He was so massive that his weight knocked the breath out of her, temporarily stunning her.

"If Cade thinks he can bring a woman on board without sharing her," Garrett panted, "he's got another thing coming. Open your legs, sweetie."

"Fuck you," Asha gasped. "Get *off* me!"

He laughed at her, struggling under him. "Some soldier you turned out to be, huh?"

She managed to inhale deeply enough to scream—as loudly and shrilly as she could manage—right before Garrett fist closed around her throat.

"This doesn't have to be so hard," he said through gritted teeth. "Open your legs and I'll let you live."

This isn't happening to me again, Asha thought frantically. *I'll fucking die first.*

Cade's voice came to her: *your first thought should always be your weapon.*

In one smooth motion, she drew her pistol and jammed the barrel against Garett's gut. It took a split second for him to register what she'd done. Fear and rage coloured his features rapidly.

"Let me go and I'll let *you* live, asshole," Asha snarled in his face.

Perhaps reflexively, his grip on her throat tightened, and she squeezed the trigger. Once, twice, three times in quick succession.

Three loud bangs that made her ears immediately start ringing. Garett's eyes blew wide open in shock. He tried to speak, but blood bubbled out of his mouth, and then he went dead weight on top of her. His eyes were blank, staring at her without seeing. She started shivering.

"Asha? Asha!"

Relief surged through her. It was Cade's voice.

He arrived a minute later, his rifle locked and loaded.

"Help," was all she could manage, crushed beneath Garett's corpse. Cade rushed to her side and threw the body off of her like it weighed nothing.

"What the hell happened?" he demanded. "Garett…"

His eyes trailed over to the body, seeming to register for the first time that it was indeed Garett's. He swore loudly.

"He attacked me," Asha said, hugging herself in an attempt to stop the shaking. "I got up to pee, and he…saw an opportunity, I guess. I got lost, and he followed me, and he was on top of me, and I wasn't going to let him do that to me, Cade, not again, I couldn't—"

"Okay, okay," Cade said soothingly, slinging the strap of his rifle over his shoulder. He crouched in front of her and took her hands in his. "It's alright, darling."

"Captain?" Leo's voice called, and several sets of footsteps approached. Thankfully, the fog was finally beginning to lift. "We heard shots. What's going on?"

Cade shot Asha a meaningful look. "Let me handle this."

Still shaking like a leaf, she nodded. She didn't know how to tell the men that she'd just murdered one of their own, even in self-defence.

What if they don't believe me? she thought, horrified. What if they turned on her for killing their comrade?

"I'll tell you what happened," Cade growled, sounding entirely different to just a second earlier. No longer soft and soothing, he sounded murderous—terrifying. "This piece of shit attacked Asha. Got up to take a piss and saw it happen, so I shot him."

More relief surged through her, and she wanted to burst into tears. He was taking the fall for her. Protecting her from his own men. She was immensely grateful; she didn't know what she'd have done if they'd all started in on her.

Leo and Dom came into view, along with a couple other men. Their eyes widened as they took in the scene, and the blood rapidly pooling underneath Garrett's body.

"Leo and Dom, you're on disposal," Cade ordered. "String him up. The rest of you, go back to camp and tell the others we're not under attack. We'll be having a meeting at dawn."

"Cade—" Asha began, but he shook his head at her.

"You're coming with me," he said, clipped.

He offered Asha his hand, but she couldn't take it. Not after what'd happened. Cade clucked his tongue and lifted her onto her feet, and despite his manhandling, Asha was grateful. She wasn't sure she could've stood on her own.

He linked arms with her, holding her up since her knees kept wobbling, and walked her back to camp. The other men were peering out of their own tents, obviously curious, but they stayed where they were when told they weren't under attack. Cade led her to the far end of the camp, out of earshot of the other soldiers.

"Are you injured?" he asked sharply. "Does anything hurt?"

Asha shook her head. She was still trembling, though not as hard.

Cade examined her critically with his flashlight, focusing on her throat where Garrett had briefly choked her.

"Just a little bruising," he said, clicking off the light. "Not serious. Now, let's get you out of that nightgown."

Asha started, unsure of his meaning, but when she looked down, a dark, round stain soaked through the fabric. Garrett's blood.

Bile scorched her throat, and she scrambled several steps away. As she doubled over and puked her guts out, she felt Cade's hands gently holding back her hair. When she finished, he offered her his water flask, and she took a long drink.

She wiped her mouth on the back of her hand and looked back to Cade. He was silent, arms folded over his chest, and there was tension in his entire body. His face was marble, unmoving and unreadable.

"Why didn't you wake me?"

His voice was a low growl, and it took Asha a moment to recognize that he was angry. Furious, even. She'd never heard him sound quite like that. He was usually so carefully contained, with his soldier's discipline.

"I don't know." Her voice was almost a whisper, and her shoulders shook.

"You do know," he shot back, pacing back and forth. "Tell me. Right fucking now."

He had a frantic energy about him that frightened her. She was ashamed to admit that her usually sharp tongue failed her. All she felt was a deep fear that he blamed her for what had happened.

"I guess...I d-didn't want to bother you," Asha managed to say.

"Bother me," Cade repeated tightly, as though the words offended him. "So, rather than *bother* me, you'd rather get yourself killed. Is that it?"

"No," she said, hurt. "That's not—I didn't want to be an inconvenience. I wanted to prove that I was fine on my own."

He squeezed his eyes shut, as though in pain. "You didn't trust me. You thought I'd be annoyed, or dismissive, and not help you."

It's so fucking stupid when he lays it out like that...but he's right. Years of being treated as little more than a nuisance had trained her to avoid asking for help at all costs. When she'd looked to him at the slave market and mouthed *help me,* it'd been the first time she'd ever entreated anyone to come to her aid, and it'd been born of sheer desperation. If she'd had any other options at the time, she wouldn't have done it. She'd have muddled through it on her own, because that was the only way she'd ever done anything.

"Yes," Asha admitted in a small voice.

A muscle ticked in Cade's jaw. "And you put yourself, your *life,* at risk," he said, almost shouting now. Asha gasped as he suddenly grabbed her face in his hands. She recoiled in fear, but he held fast, forcing her to look at him.

"You don't do that!" he burst out. "You don't *ever* fucking do that! Nothing is more important than your survival. Nothing! Do you understand me?"

His steely eyes demanded an answer. She swallowed hard. She felt on the verge of tears, but for a very different reason.

"Yes," Asha said again, trembling. "I'm sorry."

The façade of Cade's anger cracked. He made a choked sound in his throat and pressed a hard, desperate kiss against her forehead.

"Don't be sorry, darling," he said, his lips still against her skin, his voice suddenly a whisper. "God, don't be sorry. You did what I taught you. You survived."

He pulled back, and his hands moved to her upper arms, holding her.

"But you can't doubt me again," he said, much gentler now. "If you being one of us is going to work, you have to trust me. We have to be able to rely on each other, work together. For my part, I promise to take you seriously any time you come to me, and to protect you any way I can. Can you do that?"

"I think so," Asha replied softly, strangely moved by the depth of his concern. "I never had anybody I wanted to trust before. Not really. So, I don't really know how."

Cade exhaled slowly. "I understand. But we made a deal—a bargain. And I've already failed once to hold up my end."

Asha made a noise of protest. "You didn't really fail. I know I was mad at you before, but...you couldn't have stopped Angel. You did what ultimately *did* protect me by meeting his stupid deadline, even when he thought it was impossible."

"Even so," he replied roughly, "I won't fail you again, Asha."

She knew by the intensity in those mysterious grey eyes that he meant it. Something deep inside her calmed. For the first time, she felt like he was truly on her side, like they were a team.

"What do we do now?" she asked, glancing over his shoulder toward the trees.

Cade sighed wearily and released her. "What we have to."

"This is what happens," Cade said, his voice booming and dangerous as he looked on the Blackguard soldiers, "when you betray your comrades."

Golden rays of dawn fell over Garett's pale, lifeless complexion. He stared straight ahead at nothing, strung up between two tall trees. He dangled precariously, ropes creaking as he hung there. They'd stripped off his shirt, and his waxen skin seemed to glisten in the early morning light.

Asha shivered as Cade unsheathed his knife, and she flinched as he carved a long, deliberate line down the corpse's bare chest. He finished with a second line that struck through the first, cutting through the flesh like butter and forming the letter *T.*

Traitor.

"No one who attacks one of their own deserves a soldier's death," Cade continued, cold as ice. "He'll be left for the crows as a reminder to everyone: an attack on one of us is an attack on all of us. Is this what you want for yourselves?"

The chorus of *no, sir* was so immediate and sonorous that it was almost comical. Asha watched Cade closely: his tight body language, commanding tone, and unapologetic bloodthirstiness. She realized now, as she hadn't at the bonfire, that it was mostly an act. He had a dark side, to be sure, but he didn't relish brutality. He saw it as a necessity, like hunting or daily chores, to keep his troops in line. He understood that the Wasteland was brutal, and that that was all they'd ever known. When he was like this, it was as though he was speaking their language. Violence was a message they all understood.

Is it wrong that I find his bloodthirstiness...kind of hot now? Asha wondered, and then decided she didn't want an answer. But she had to admit that he cut a striking figure in his black tactical uniform, his eyes so stormy and serious. The tight control he had, the command he took of any given situation...there was something intensely attractive about that. She found herself wondering what it might be like to witness that control suddenly snap.

"Good," Cade said in response to the soldiers, his eyes flicking briefly to Asha before gesturing ahead. "Let's move out."

They set out again on their journey, leaving Garett's corpse twisting in the wind. Asha shivered as a crow abruptly landed on his head. It had already begun.

As she walked by Cade's side, she reflected on how sad it was that these Wastelanders actually respected him more for this kind of stunt. Not because she felt disgust for him anymore, but because he was so much more than this. So much smarter, and kinder, and funnier than his act suggested. Perhaps the Wasteland had forced him to act like a brute, but underneath that, he was still a man. One that mystified and fascinated her in equal measure. He held so much darkness and so much light inside of him, a duality that he wielded to his advantage in any given situation.

In a world where nothing was promised and tomorrow was never certain, her growing attachment to him was perilous...yet she couldn't find it in herself to reject him now. He may have been the only person she'd ever gotten this close to trusting.

Chapter 14

Hillside was a farming community more than a single settlement. There was a central, fortified village where the marketplace was housed, and where some of the farm workers lived, but it was otherwise made up of small farms that dotted the area around the base of a high, steep hill. Some had small flocks of livestock, while others held fields of crops. These were humble operations, farmed by hand, the way Asha had seen in old movies at the Cave. A thin river snaked through the landscape, and a few of the farms had waterwheels to power their mills.

Asha appreciated the soft, rolling hills and the hustle and bustle of the people, all hard at work. Every so often, however, she saw those who clearly did not belong: men with feather tattoos, carrying weapons of various kinds: clubs, bats, and a few with guns. Angel's men.

"Grunts don't get guns," Cade explained when she asked. "There aren't enough to go around, so only higher-ranking Guardians get them."

He led her and the rest of the Blackguard into the village, which was surrounded by stone walls, with feather-tattooed guards posted at the entrance. While the village itself was populated by regular folks, it was clear that Angel's men were the ones who controlled and ran the place.

The guard waved them in, though he gave Asha a second, curious glance. But he knew Cade, and he didn't question it. Asha was used to people deferring to Cade by now, but it still surprised her a little.

The village was small, but the market was bustling with busy stalls that sold a variety of goods: mostly food, drugs, and weapons. Asha was shocked by how openly drugs were advertised and sold, and the wide range of people who bartered for them; recreational drugs were so tightly controlled back at home. Some looked like regular folks, but a large contingent were rail-thin and desperate-looking.

"Why does Angel allow drugs here?" Asha asked Cade in a low voice. "Surely that can't be good for...for anyone."

Cade shrugged. "If they didn't get it here, they'd get it somewhere else. It also makes it easier to get them to work, if you promise them their fix in exchange."

He said this as though it were entirely normal to use addiction against an entire population to get them to perform slave labour.

Asha shot him an appalled look. "That's barbaric."

"I don't disagree, but that's not why we're here," he replied dismissively, then raised his voice: "Blackguard, assemble! Let's get set up."

They got to work setting up a table in the marketplace where residents could come to drop off their rent payments. These mostly came in the form of food, tools, and clothing. Cade also had a list of supplies that had been requested by people back at the Nest, and residents could fulfill their rents by supplying these items. A handful of the Blackguard stayed by the table, guarding their horse-drawn wagon, which they filled with the supplies, while others patrolled the market. Cade had Asha sit with him at the table, though he handled the transactions with residents.

She watched Cade closely throughout the day, surprised by the two sides of him that once again emerged. He was stern and commandeering to residents who gave him a hard time, especially if he judged that they were well-fed and simply complaining about paying their share. But to those who were clearly struggling—with poor harvests, family deaths, or something else—he was a different man altogether.

"It's fine, Archie," Cade said, reassuring an older man who looked about to burst into tears over his crop failing that season. "We'll figure it out. Shit happens."

Archie fumbled with the buttons on the threadbare knitted shirt he wore. "You...you won't tell A-Angel?"

Asha tried not to show her disgust at how much Angel obviously petrified every person who lived here. She couldn't imagine what he'd done to make them so.

"He'll never know," Cade replied gently. "You keep whatever you have for your family. I'll make up the difference somewhere else."

Archie thanked him profusely, so enthusiastically that it turned Asha's stomach a little. *He shouldn't have to beg for mercy over a fucking bushel of vegetables,* she thought, anger resurfacing from the constantly-simmering well of emotion under her skin.

"I need a break," she snapped at Cade, then strode away before he could respond. He didn't follow her immediately, and she was glad. She needed some alone time after being stuck with a bunch of men for over a week.

Asha walked through the rest of the market, which—relative to the size of the village—was large and full of interesting wares. A man shouted at her about farm-fresh produce; another advertised his fine selection of weapons outside what appeared to be a blacksmith shop; and a little girl offered to sell her flowers. At the end of one of the aisles, there was a woman selling human-hair wigs. Asha didn't want to know how she'd obtained the hair, but she had to admit that whoever made them knew their craft well.

At the back of the market, towards the stone wall, there was a flat wooden platform that looked all too familiar. A small crowd of men gathered around, and perhaps a dozen terrified-looking young women stood above them, hands bound, their wide eyes on the ground. A short, chubby bald man carrying a large black whip stood to the side, calling out numbers like an auction.

It was a slave market. Like the one she'd been rescued from.

Hot, putrid bile rose in Asha's throat, which somehow also felt as though it was closing up. She was suddenly burning hot all over, as though she'd been dipped into a cauldron of boiling water. Her mouth was dry as sawdust, and she could hear nothing more, as a loud ringing began in her ears that shut out all sound. She tried to speak, but no words would form.

All she could do was grapple at her side for her pistol. Somehow, getting it out of its holster was proving impossible; her hands were shaking too badly.

I'm going to shoot him, she thought, looking toward the trafficker with the whip, even as her vision blurred with rage and something else far more potent. *I'm going to kill him. I don't care.*

"Stand down!" Cade's order was frantic behind her, but she didn't care. She'd finally managed to retrieve her gun. "I said *stand down, soldier!*"

Half a second later, she was tackled to the ground by his mass of muscle and military gear. She didn't fight him because she didn't quite understand what'd happened, or what she was doing. The last few moments felt like she'd been sleepwalking.

Breathing heavily, Cade barked in a harsh whisper, "What the fuck are you doing? I turn my back on you for five minutes—"

"They're selling women." Asha's voice was low and hollow. She lay back on the hard ground and stared blankly at the sky.

"I ordered you to stand down, and you disobeyed—"

"They're selling women, Cade," she repeated, in the same tone, as though she hadn't heard him. "Aren't they?"

For the first time, he softened a little. "Yes. But unless you want to get yourself killed, and me right after you, you have to stop. This isn't the way."

"What is the way?" she asked blankly, staring past his shoulder at the sky, listless. "If this can happen to any of us, and no one says a thing, what's the point, Captain?"

People were starting to stare at them, in a heap on the ground. Cade ignored her question, took her gun, and helped her to her feet. He took a moment to reassure the bystanders that all was well, trying to pass it off as a 'training exercise,' which Asha doubted anyone would believe, but she didn't really care. She didn't care about anything right now; everything felt as though it was being filtered through a haze of brutal despair, unlike she'd ever felt before.

She didn't know how something could make her feel so numb and so terrified at the same time.

Cade led her through the streets towards two houses near the gate. One was a small, white-washed cottage, while the other was a larger building with its door open. Inside, a bunch of bunk beds were visible, and one of the Blackguard—Raph—was fiddling with one of them.

"Where the men stay," Cade explained, then nodded at the cottage. "This is the Captain's quarters. There's one at every settlement."

He brought Asha inside the one-room house, which was sparsely furnished with a large double bed, a dresser, a closet, and a washstand with a cracked mirror above it. The walls and floor were bare stone. It was clearly a fairly new structure, since it didn't suffer from the decay that was obvious in Old World buildings.

"Sit," Cade ordered, gesturing at the bed, which had been made up by someone.

Probably one of the many slaves that live here, Asha thought, her disgust and shame threatening to engulf her.

Nonetheless, she obeyed, perching on the edge of the mattress, her arms hanging uselessly beside her. She felt emptied out, as though someone had scooped out every bit of hope she'd begun to build.

"Look at me," Cade said firmly, his arms folded, and she forced herself to look up. "You *cannot* do this again. There will be more slave markets at the other settlements, and there's nothing you or I can do about it. We're here to do a job. That's the end of it."

Right now, he wasn't the soft, understanding man he'd been when he comforted her after her nightmares, or when he'd held her in his arms and told her he wanted to train her to defend herself. Now, he was every inch the military commander—her superior—and he was giving her another order.

"Promise me that you will *not* endanger yourself or the rest of us again like that," he demanded. "Or I'll have to confine you to the captain's quarters at every settlement, and post a guard to make sure you stay put."

A spider crack of outrage made its way over the smooth, featureless glass of Asha's numbness.

"You'd *imprison* me," she said slowly, "to stop me from interfering with the process of human trafficking."

Cade raised an eyebrow. "I would. For your own safety, as well as mine. You have to know that if you had attacked them, and anyone had retaliated, I'd have gone down with you."

If that was supposed to make her feel supported, it didn't. Instead, despair creeped back in. This was her life now. She was part of facilitating this horrible system of pain and misery and torture.

"You can't do anything about this, Asha," Cade said, his jaw tightening. "It's how it is. Do we like it? No, but we have to live with it to survive out here."

She took a shaky inhale, staring at the floor again. She couldn't look at him.

"Before I came along, Angel used to do these trips himself," he continued. "It's why everyone is scared of him. Every time he showed up, there was mass chaos—looting, pillaging, rape. It's why I volunteered to take over with a team of soldiers I selected and trained myself. I know my men won't cause trouble, bully the residents, or hurt anyone without a direct order. It's one way that I tried to make things better for the people here. Sometimes change happens slowly."

"It's not enough," Asha replied, still avoiding his gaze.

He gave a weary sigh. "That may be true. But it doesn't change anything. If I tried to unilaterally free everyone here, I'd succeed in nothing but ensuring my own death, plus yours and everyone I'm responsible for. Angel wouldn't think twice."

Asha knew that was certainly true. Yet it still wasn't enough. He stared at her for a long time, evidently hoping for her to say more, but she wouldn't.

"Can I trust you to stay here for the rest of the day, until I finish my work?" Cade finally asked.

She nodded mutely. She didn't think she could muster the energy to leave anyway, in her current state. She felt hollow, like she'd felt after Angel raped her.

With a searching look, Cade left the cottage, and Asha crawled under the covers on the bed, cocooning herself.

It was dark outside before he finally returned at the end of the day. Asha had done nothing all afternoon but stare straight ahead at the wall. She wondered if she'd even had any thoughts in that time.

Cade carried a lantern with a candle inside, and he did a quick washup before undressing and climbing into bed beside her. He blew out the flame and moved closer to her. She instinctively scooted back toward the edge of the bed, away from him.

"Asha," he murmured, much gentler than hours earlier.

She didn't reply. A moment later, his hand found hers under the covers.

"You're clammy," he said softly, and he held her arm against his chest. "I'm sorry. I really am."

"Nothing to be sorry for," Asha finally answered. "You said it before: it's how it is. I have to accept that I'm nothing more than property. Chattel."

He rubbed her hand between his, massaging her fingers, which had been clenched tightly into a fist. He knew there was no point in denying her statement, even though his silence told her that he didn't agree.

"I know you're angry," he sighed eventually. "You're right to be. It's just me and the dark again, darling."

The sincerity in his voice told her that he wanted to hear it, and the darkness provided the cover she needed to whisper her ugly truth: that she wanted every man at that slave market dead, and that nothing but the blood of all those like them would sate her thirst for vengeance.

Chapter 15

A day later, with the rents collected from Hillside, they departed for Silver Creek, the second settlement on their journey. They followed another derelict highway back into the woods, and Asha hoped the trip would be a little less taxing than the first one.

The forest was quiet, and they walked in silence for a long time. Eventually, the flat terrain transformed into a rockier, more treacherous region, and the brush thickened around the old, overgrown highway. Trees had grown right up to the road, effectively encasing it in wilderness. Soon, even this highway—this small, battered sign of what the world used to be—would crumble into dust, reclaimed by time and nature.

Asha was a little unnerved by the wildness of their surroundings, but the others seemed untroubled; they'd been this way before.

"How long until we reach Silver Creek?" she asked Cade.

He looked at Raph, who replied, "At least a few hours."

She suppressed a groan of impatience. Her feet were hurting more than usual.

"You throwing in the towel, darling?" Cade asked with a small smile. "I thought you were made of tougher stuff than that."

She bristled, pulling herself up to her full height. "I'm just fine, for your information. I was asking for..." Her eyes scanned the group and landed on the youngest recruit's face, who looked a bit peaky. "...Davy's sake. He looks like shit."

Several of the men laughed, including Cade, and Davy flipped her off with a grin on his face. They started taunting him about tapping out before the only *girl* in the group, and Asha rolled her eyes.

"Children," she said to Cade, who continued to look amused.

They came to a section of woods where the path forward was surrounded by hills, and that was when Cade gave the order to stop.

"Good spot for an ambush," he said to the troops, but he was looking at Asha with wariness. "Let's go slow and tread carefully now, guys."

There was murmured agreement through the group, and they did their best to step lightly as they crossed the passage. Asha sucked in a breath, letting Cade get ahead of her as she watched the ground with every step to avoid tripping on rocks and errant tree roots. With the highway so overgrown, leaves covered much of the disintegrating concrete, making it difficult to see obstacles until she was on top of them.

Was it her, or had the woods gone oddly quiet? A few moments before, she'd heard birdsong. Now, there was only the gentle breeze through the trees, and the blowing leaves suddenly seemed ominous rather than peaceful. As she set her foot down on a small pile of leaves that covered the road beside a large tree, she felt a sharp, painful jolt on her ankle.

Asha screamed as the ground fell away underneath her. Rough, vine-like ropes closed in around her, forming a net around her as she hung upside down from a high tree branch. At the same time, she heard Davy's shout from the other side of the road, and then a cacophony of shrill, animalistic shrieks from the hills.

Her blood ran cold. She recognized the calls. The last time she'd heard them, she'd left her best friend behind. *Cannibals.*

Three dozen filthy, primitively dressed men descended on them, still shrieking wildly. Some carried crudely formed handheld weapons like spears, clubs, and bats, while others had bows and arrows, which they immediately began firing at the soldiers. Vastly outnumbered and caught by surprise, the Blackguard scattered.

"Asha!" Cade's frantic voice carried over the din, but he was too far ahead to reach her.

Asha struggled furiously against the ropes as all the blood rushed to her head, but it was futile. She couldn't reach the snare around her ankle, and the netting around her was thick, woven by practiced hands.

Chaos surrounded her. No one was close enough to cut her down, and the cannibals were attempting to box the entire squad into the narrow space between the hills. Arrows rained down from the hills on either side of the road; there were more of them up there. She thought she would go deaf from the explosion of sound: the crack of gunshots as the Blackguard returned fire, Cade shouting orders over the havoc, and the continued shrieks of the cannibals as they attacked.

Across the road, an enormous man dressed in furs, sporting a distinct-looking half mask, gave a furious warrior cry and brought his club down hard on Raph, who fell like a sack of potatoes. He locked eyes with Asha, hanging helplessly, and her heart stopped as a small smile spread across his features. He started to run in her direction. As he drew closer, she saw that what she'd assumed was a mask was actually the top half of a human skull.

"Cade!" she screamed as loud as she could, but she knew he was too far away to make it to her before Skullface did.

She did the only thing she could think of: she threw her weight as hard as she could in the opposite direction. Her head spinning, her ankle aching, she swung as hard as she could, effectively catapulting herself directly at Skullface. As the net swung back the way she'd come, she braced herself. She collided hard with the big man, knocking him off his feet. Pain exploded in her body.

A half-second later, a gunshot sprayed Skullface's brains on the road, spattering her with blood. A scream of shock escaped her lungs, but relief surged through her at the sudden appearance of Cade and Dom. Cade lowered his rifle and reached for the knife he held between his teeth. He moved behind her, and Dom covered him as he began to saw at the net.

"It's alright, darling," Cade said as the first rope came free. "I have you."

Rings kind of hollow when there's a bunch of cannibals about to feast on your flesh.

Cade made quick work of the net. He freed her, but she was still suspended, upside down. The rope around her ankle was too high. Dom fired on several cannibals who rushed them. An arrow whooshed past Cade's ear as he struggled to reach Asha's ankle rope, and he cursed loudly.

On the opposite side of the road, Asha spotted Davy surrounded by three cannibals. The rookie was struggling to reload his rifle as they descended on him. As if by instinct, Asha reached for her pistol, aimed haphazardly, and fired on them. Upside down, her aim was atrocious, but it didn't matter. The cannibals dispersed in alarm, buying Davy precious seconds. He managed to reload and return fire.

A second later, the rope gave way, and Asha squeaked as she fell from the tree. Cade caught her, righting her in his arms as quickly as he could. Thankfully, the Blackguard had largely regained control of the situation, and the road was littered with cannibal corpses. The few that remained were retreating into the woods, snarling and spitting. They knew when they were beaten.

Cade barked an order for everyone to assemble and carried Asha toward the middle of the road. They briefly regrouped. Leo moved through the squad, treating minor injuries, and they all took a breather. When he reached Asha, Cade carefully lowered her to the ground. She winced as Leo assessed her ankle, which was swollen and purple.

"Minor sprain," he said matter-of-factly. He wrapped it tightly with bandages to hold it as still as possible, but it hurt like hell to put weight on it.

Still, they had a settlement to get to. They all agreed that remaining in this area after dark was a bad idea, so they set out once more to reach Silver Creek before nightfall.

"You did incredibly well," Cade said to Asha as they set out again.

"By ending up caught in a net?" she replied skeptically, through teeth gritted with pain. "I don't think that's what you taught me in training."

"Maybe not," he conceded, "but I *did* teach you to think on your feet and defend yourself vigorously, and you did. You didn't freeze."

"You saved my life," Davy piped up from just behind them. "Would've been a goner if you hadn't fired on those guys when you did. To do it in that situation makes it more impressive."

Asha flushed. Pride was an unfamiliar feeling for her, but their praise warmed her heart. She had a purpose now, and it felt strangely good. Better than she'd expected.

"See, even the rookie thinks so," Cade teased, and the corners of her mouth lifted. "Speaking of...take this, rookie."

He handed his pack to Davy, who scowled at him. Cade ignored him, however, and Asha squeaked as he scooped her back up into his arms again.

"What are you doing?" she asked as he resumed moving forward, carrying her with one arm at her back and the other under her knees.

He smiled. "You looked like your ankle was hurting you. It can't be good to keep walking on it."

Before this trip, she would've objected. She would've been suspicious of his help, and loath to accept it. But she trusted now that his desire to help her was genuine. He cared about her. There really was nothing more to it than that...and yet it was everything.

Besides, her ankle really was hurting.

"This doesn't mean I like you any better, you know," Asha said, but she couldn't help smiling.

"Of course not," Cade replied, amused. "Wouldn't have it any other way. There's nothing that keeps me honest quite like being bullied by a beautiful woman."

She couldn't help snorting. They fell into silence as they kept walking. Eventually, Asha felt her eyes fluttering shut despite her best efforts. The letdown from adrenaline was no joke. She wondered how Cade handled it and decided he must be used to it after years of practice.

"You can lean on me, darling," he murmured, evidently noting her fatigue. "If you want to."

The words felt like they contained a double meaning, but for once, instead of questioning them, Asha simply lay her head against his shoulder and shut her eyes.

"Thank you, soldier."

Chapter 16

Despite their best efforts, they didn't make it to Silver Creek that night. They were all exhausted, and Cade made the decision to make camp. They found a quiet, secluded clearing by a small stream where they pitched their tents, and Asha was grateful to rest her aching ankle.

She awoke with the first rays of dawn the next morning. It was easy to rise with the sun these days, following its natural rhythm. It made her realize how much of her life had been dominated by the clock in the past. Everything was rushed, and every ounce of productivity was squeezed out of every single second. In the Wasteland, they'd reverted to a time when people accepted that things took time. It was a slower pace of life that she was growing to like, much to her surprise.

Usually, Cade was up before her; he'd been a soldier for too long to sleep in. Today, however, he lay in his sleeping bag with his arm draped over his eyes. Asha would've thought he was still asleep, except that his jaw was working, his teeth gritted. Just looking at him, she could sense something was wrong.

Sudden worry gripped her. She sat up and scooted over to his side.

"What's wrong?" she asked softly. "Are you hurt?"

"Fine," Cade exhaled, but his voice was saturated with pain. "I'm fine."

His reassurance only alarmed her more.

"Please," she pleaded, and, hesitating, she reached out and placed her hand on his arm. The simple contact sent an electric current through her, even as she feared for his well-being. Too much had happened between them for her to feel neutral while touching him. "Let me help."

Cade gave an uncharacteristic groan of pain. "Get Leo."

Panic shot through her, but Asha nodded and leapt to her feet. Her injured ankle twinged in protest, but she ignored it. She dressed in a rush and hurried outside. She ran to Leo's tent and, without thinking, threw back the flaps.

"Leo," she gasped, "Cade's hurt—"

She froze. Leo was lying on top of his sleeping bag, and in response to the summer heat, he didn't have a stitch on. Naked as the day he was born, he made a sound of surprise and sat up. Asha yelped and shielded her eyes, but not before she got an eyeful of his lean, muscular form.

"Good fucking grief, Asha," he bit out. "You couldn't have given me some warning before barging in? It's the crack of dawn, literally!"

Asha burst into peals of helpless laughter. She was worried about Cade, knew she had to get back to him, but she couldn't help it.

"Well, I'm glad one of us finds this amusing," Leo said acridly as he stood and got dressed. "Now, what's wrong with Cade?"

Immediately, she regained her composure. "He's in pain. I'm not sure why; he just told me to get you."

Leo made a sound of acknowledgement. "Probably a migraine. He's a chronic sufferer."

"He is?" Asha asked, frowning. "What does he usually do?"

He shrugged. "Whatever he can. Back at home, he got periodic injections that prevented them, but we don't have that anymore."

On that ominous note, they went to Cade's side. When Asha entered the tent, she was hit with the pungent smell of vomit. There was a smear of it on the grass next to Cade. He lay in the same spot as before, still with his eyes covered, his whole body tensed.

"You're having a bad time of it, huh?" Leo said sympathetically. "I'm sorry that I don't have much to give you except cannabis. Unless you want me to—"

"No," Cade croaked. "Save the good stuff. This is nothing."

Asha wrinkled her nose. "It sure doesn't look like nothing, soldier."

He groaned. "Go away, Asha. You shouldn't see me like this."

She frowned. "Why the hell not?"

He didn't answer, just groaned again.

"You seeing auras?" Leo asked as he snapped open his medical bag and knelt beside Cade.

"Yeah. Can't open my fucking eyes without seeing flashing lights."

"Auras?" Asha asked, looking to Leo.

"Visual disturbances," Leo replied distractedly as he held open one of Cade's eyes, examining the pupil. Cade made a sharp sound of pain. "He sees flashing lights, but there can be other kinds. Light and sound cause him pain, too."

"Will he be alright?" she asked, worry creeping back in.

Leo took a moment to respond as he examined Cade.

"He should be," he finally said. "I'll give him some cannabis to chew, which may take the edge off the pain, but probably won't resolve his symptoms. The only thing that will is time, I'm afraid."

Poor Cade, Asha found herself thinking, then wondered what was wrong with her. She'd never thought such a thing in her life. *Sympathy and empathy are dangerous weaknesses,* her father's voice whispered in her ear. *They allow a drowning person to drag you down with them.*

But she cared for Cade. Somehow, this battered soldier had shown her more humanity than her administrator father ever had. So, while Leo continued his physical exam, she gathered up one of the wash-cloths they used for bathing and cleaned up Cade's vomit from the floor of the tent. She went out to the stream and washed it, then hung it up on a tree branch. The Blackguard were mostly awake now, and there were mutters through the camp that Asha interpreted as wondering about their Captain's condition.

When she returned, Leo said to her, "I've done what I can. He's taken the cannabis; he just needs to rest now. Maybe you should go—"

"No," Cade mumbled from under his arm. "Stay, Asha. Sit with me."

Five minutes ago, he was sending her away, and now he was ordering her to stay? Asha huffed, but she couldn't suppress a small smile.

"I'm fine to stay with him," she said to Leo, trying to sound nonchalant. "You can go back to...whatever you were doing."

There was a smothered giggle at the end of her sentence, and Leo shot her a censorious look before leaving, telling her to call him if something changed.

"This is very dramatic," Asha said casually, sitting next to Cade. "The men probably think you're dying."

"Thanks for your concern," Cade replied sarcastically, and Asha saw him flinch with pain again. "You definitely missed your calling as a doctor. That bedside manner? Ten out of ten."

She couldn't help laughing, but...she *was* concerned about him. More than she ever thought she would be.

"How bad is it?" she asked, fidgeting with her hands. "What's it feel like?"

He made a huffing sound. "Like my head is being crushed by a military truck that keeps running over it, and every time I try to open my eyes, it has little daggers on the wheels that stab into my eye sockets, just for fun."

Asha winced. "Well, that's vivid."

She hesitated before kneeling beside his head.

"Are you sure you don't want me to go?" she asked, gentling her tone. "Leo said you're sensitive to sound, so maybe it's better to leave you alone."

"No," he gritted out. "I don't want to be alone. I...like the sound of your voice, darling. Even when it hurts."

Oddly touched by that, Asha said, "We should at least try to make you more comfortable, then."

She retrieved another washcloth from her bag and went to soak it in the stream. In the blazing heat of July, the water wasn't cold, but it was better than nothing. When she returned to Cade's side, she rolled up the cloth, and before he could protest, lifted his arm off his eyes. She placed the cool cloth over his eyelids and his arm at his side.

He gave a shallow sigh, the smallest sign of relief, and thanked her. Asha relaxed a little; she hadn't realized her shoulders had been up near her ears. She wanted to ease more of his pain if she could. Before she could question the wisdom of such a thing, she scooted closer to him and lifted his head into her lap.

"What're you doing?" he asked in surprise.

"Shut up," she replied nervously, and he laughed, but didn't pull away.

Asha took a breath and laid her hands on his head. His hair, cropped so short, was prickly against her skin. He was warmer and softer than she would've imagined, for some reason. Maybe because he always *looked* so intense, and his frown and his tattoos gave him a hard look. But his skin was smooth and pliable, and as clear and un-marked as her own.

With the tips of her fingers, she tentatively began to knead his temples. His long groan told her that it brought him additional relief...and stirred something between her legs. She bit her lip and chose to ignore the flutters in her stomach.

"Is that good?" she asked as she kneaded lower, onto his jaw. "You're clenched up as tight as I always imagined your asshole was during drills."

Cade laughed again, relaxing into her lap. "All that tells me is that you've been thinking about my asshole, darling."

Asha clucked her tongue in disapproval. "You know, for a soldier, you're surprisingly undisciplined, *Captain*."

"Only with you, it seems," he said with a small smile. She could feel his muscles slackening under her touch, which she took as a good sign. "The only time I've ever impulsively rushed a slave market was when I saw you there."

A strange warmth bloomed in her chest. She couldn't think of a less romantic setting for a first meeting, yet the fact that he'd met her eye and really *saw* her there, as a human being rather than as an object, was something she'd remember for the rest of her life. It was as if he'd seen into her soul.

"That look you gave me," she said quietly. "It was like you knew me. Like you'd been looking for me, even. But you'd never met me."

He took a few moments to answer, sighing as she continued to press on painful points on his head and neck.

"I did feel like I knew you," he finally said in a low voice. "Not directly, but I knew you were from the same place as me, from the same people I was supposed to protect, back when I was in the line of duty. You reminded me that I used to have a purpose."

Her heart tugged uncomfortably. She hadn't realized that that moment had had as much meaning for him as it had for her.

Asha frowned. "We're not from the same place."

"We might as well be. They're all controlled by the same people."

She stopped kneading. "What are? The compounds?"

"Yeah," he replied. "Not something civilians are supposed to know, but I figure it can't hurt to tell you now."

"So...the Cave and the Delta are controlled by the same owners? Who are they?"

Cade tried to shrug, but gave up halfway through. "Above my pay grade. That's one of the big secrets that nobody but those at the very top know for sure."

They were both quiet for a while after that. She resumed the head massage, and eventually, she felt Cade's body grow looser and heavier, his breathing deepening.

"You getting sleepy?" she asked.

He yawned. "Guess so. Feels good."

She smiled and continued, moving down onto his neck and shoulders. She thought he'd fallen asleep, but he mumbled, "You're my angel, Asha."

She froze. "Why would you call me that? After everything he—"

Her voice cut off. She only associated that name with pain and torture and death. Even now, they were only on this mission because of that asshole.

The corners of Cade's mouth lifted. "Because to me, you are. You're sweet, and—"

"I am *not* sweet," Asha protested. "You know I'm not. Don't lie."

He gave what looked like a painful chuckle.

"Alright," he admitted, amused. "Not sweet. You may not be *an* angel, but you're *my* angel, appearing in that slave market to remind me of what I'd lost. That's what I care about."

Asha bit her lip. That was probably the kindest thing anyone had ever said to her.

"You're stoned, soldier," she quipped, and he laughed again. "Out of your mind."

"Maybe," he allowed. "But also, Angel shouldn't get a monopoly on the name, considering he only uses it ironically. I'm reclaiming it."

"Is it not his given name, then?" Asha asked, interest piqued.

"No. It's Hoyt."

She burst into laughter. "No, it's not. You're fucking with me."

Cade grinned, eyes still covered. "I'm not. He told me once when he was plastered. Made me swear not to tell afterwards."

Asha dissolved into more giggles. "Oh my God."

"Don't tell anyone," he said playfully. "We have a reputation to protect."

"I won't," she replied, swiping at her eyes. She couldn't remember the last time she'd laughed so hard. "Thank you for telling me. That was the best thing I've heard in ages."

"Glad to be of service."

He grunted when she pressed on a particularly painful spot at the back of his head.

"I have a funny story to trade," Asha said, trying to distract him. "When I went to get Leo, he was stark fucking naked. You should've seen how he jumped—"

"Leo exposed himself to you?" Cade cut in, his voice suddenly cold as ice. He struggled to sit up, ripping the washcloth off his eyes and wincing at the light.

"No, no," she hurried to say as she gently pushed him back down. "Nothing like that. It was an accident. I was worried about you, so I barged into his tent. He just...happened to be naked at the time."

Cade relaxed a little, though he didn't seem to find it funny like she'd thought. There was an awkward pause.

"See anything you liked?" he asked after a moment. His tone was carefully neutral.

"What?" Asha asked, taken aback. "Why?"

"I mean, he's a good guy," Cade continued, though he now sounded a touch resentful. "Brilliant doctor, good-looking...a woman could do worse, I guess."

She frowned. *What is he on about?* Then it dawned on her, and more laughter bubbled to the surface.

"Oh my God. You're actually jealous."

"No," he protested, but it was a pathetic attempt. "It's my job to know what my troops are—"

"You are so fucking jealous, soldier," she said, deeply amused.

"Fine," he growled. "But you agreed to be *my* woman, darling, and I'm not about to share you with the doc. I don't care how great his dick is."

She laughed some more. "I didn't get a good enough look to judge."

His grumble told her that didn't make him feel much better, but she was enjoying him like this. She liked that he cared enough to want to keep her to himself; she'd never had that before. Nothing physical had happened between them, yet she felt closer to him than she'd felt to anyone. Their connection wasn't one that followed conventional rules; instead, it'd been solidified in a single glance, a single moment of mutual need. They'd needed each other in that slave market to remember who they once were, and to give one another a spark of hope for a better tomorrow.

"I like Leo a lot," Asha continued, and she rolled her eyes as he grumbled again. "He's always been nice to me, and he's a good doctor. But there's nothing between us. He's a friend to me in the same way he is to you."

Cade relaxed fully. "Okay." He reached up and took her hand. "Because you're *my* angel. Not his, or anyone else's."

Despite her earlier protest, she felt tingly all over when he called her *my angel*.

"You like that, huh?" he said, amused.

"No," Asha replied primly, returning to her ministrations on his scalp. "I'm just thinking about how huge your head is. It's a miracle I can even massage it. A miracle it even fits in my lap."

"Sure, my angel." He wore a smug smile that made her huff. "I know the truth: you feel some sort of way about me, and you don't know what to do with that."

He was right, but she covered her discomfort by rolling her eyes at him again.

"The smugness is really unattractive."

He wouldn't let up. "If you say so, my angel."

Cade grimaced, blinking rapidly, and Asha realized that his eyes were hurting him again.

"Auras?" she asked, and he nodded. She frowned and adopted a scolding tone. "Relax. Don't undo all my hard work. Close your eyes."

For once, he listened, and they eventually lapsed back into comfortable silence. This time, Cade did fall asleep with his head on her lap. Asha smiled, tracing along his jaw with a finger as he breathed slowly in and out. Her touch must've brought him comfort, because he leaned into it, even in sleep. That same unfamiliar warmth from earlier radiated even stronger from her chest, and she sat quietly with him, stroking his head, until it was time for Leo to check on him again.

Chapter 17

S ilver Creek was smaller than Hillside, but otherwise similar. As Asha walked through the fortified gate, she noted that there seemed to be a lot of sheep grazing in small pens, and outside the walls, fields of flax blew gently in the breeze on small farms.

"It's where most of our textiles come from," Cade confirmed. "Mostly wool and linen, but some others too. They grow some food as well, though not as much as Hillside."

And just like at Hillside, Asha knew, the gang took a large cut of everything that this settlement produced. She still didn't feel good about it, but she was learning that given enough time, you could get used to anything. Even injustice. Especially when survival was on the line.

The villagers seemed to respect Cade, just as the Hillside residents had, even though they still treated the Blackguard with the same deference and wariness. Asha couldn't blame them. Though no one seemed to be starving here, Silver Creek showed the same signs of poverty as Hillside: everyone was thin and weary-looking, missing teeth and hair, and drug use was open and rampant. Flophouses were openly advertised on one of the main streets, and there was a woman behind a stall that allowed one to barter their hair for food, medicine, and supplies.

They had a smaller market square than Hillside, and Asha spotted the platform where the slave market usually took place. Mercifully, it was empty. She didn't know how she'd handle seeing another one full. Cade caught her looking at it and enveloped her hand with his, leading her away. Likely to distract her, he took her to a fruit cart, where a smiling man—one of the only genuinely happy-looking people she'd seen—offered her a fresh peach.

"A gift for the lady," he insisted, pressing it into Asha's hand.

The first bite was so sweet and refreshing that Asha wanted to cry. It'd been a long time since she'd had fresh fruit, and the peach was so perfectly ripe that juice dripped down her chin. She relished eating it, and Cade watched her with amusement, though there was also something like heat in his eyes. She pretended not to notice.

Cade showed her to the captain's quarters, which was a small, one-room cottage similar to the one in Hillside. Inside, there was a double bed, a bookcase, a washstand, and a fireplace. There was a small yard out back, and predictably, Cade had set it up with targets for practice and a pull-up bar. *This man cares more about fitness than I've cared about anything, ever.*

Asha flopped onto the bed, grateful to get off her ankle, which still ached.

"Rest that ankle," Cade said, echoing her thoughts. He walked to the bookcase, which was mostly empty except for a handful of slim volumes. He gathered the books and dropped them onto the bed beside her. "I keep a few books here to pass the time." He headed back toward the door. "I have to take care of the rents. Will you be alright here until I get back? The door locks, and I won't go far."

She nodded. "Hurry back."

His grin was a little too smug. "I will. Don't miss me too much."

"Don't worry," she said breezily. "I'll just ask Leo to come *entertain* me in the meantime."

"Like hell, you will," he growled, but he was smiling. "I'll throw you over my shoulder, caveman-style, if it comes to that."

Asha gave him a token eyeroll, refusing to admit how much she liked that image at the moment. After he left, she curled up on the bed and fell asleep, even though it was only early evening. Nonetheless, the trip had been tiring, and she was under Leo's orders to rest her ankle now that they'd arrived.

When she awoke, the sun was low in the sky, and Cade had still not returned. She stretched, yawning, and decided to go into the yard. She couldn't believe she was going to work out without Cade pushing her to, but there wasn't much else to do, and she hadn't had a proper workout in a few days. She did some basic exercises, then moved onto Cade's pull-up bar. She was curious about how many chin-ups she could do—if she could do any at all.

Asha managed the first one with difficulty, then a second, and a third. By the end of that one, she was huffing and puffing and cursing the man who no doubt invented this torture.

"Good work. I usually do five sets of twelve. So...get at it."

She whirled around to see Cade leaning casually against the wall of the cottage, smirking.

"Five sets of twelve?" she burst out, wiping sweat from her brow. The air was still warm, even as the sun had begun to set. "Are you trying to kill me?"

He chuckled. "No. But...while we're out here, we should brush up on your hand-to-hand combat skills."

Asha rolled her eyes as she walked over to him. "Is that really necessary?"

"You worried?" he asked with a smirk, standing up straight.

"No," she replied, and threw a punch.

Cade caught her wrist and tried to pull her into a hold, but Asha twisted away, out of his grip. Unfortunately, that meant her back was toward the cottage wall, putting her in an unfavourable position. She managed to dodge his next strike, countering with a blow of her own. He grunted as she hit his shoulder, pushing him off-balance. To counterbalance, he threw his weight forward, toward her. Asha retreated instinctively, but there was nowhere to go; she was backed against the cottage wall. His low, intimate chuckle at her predicament turned her insides molten, but it also challenged her to fight back. She caught his wrist and twisted it away from her, executing a hold he'd taught her. One good twist and it'd fracture. He couldn't move without risking the same outcome.

They were an inch apart now, both breathing heavily. Asha was painfully aware of his big, impossibly muscular body, and the heat that radiated from it, creating little sparks along every one of her nerve endings. There was an unbearable tension unspooling between them, pulled tight like a cord that connected their bodies. Cade rested his free hand against the wall beside her head.

"Go ahead and break my wrist, little viper," he breathed, low and husky, his grey eyes boring into hers. "I'll still kiss you."

The pleasure of his lips on hers startled her, filled her with an unrecognizable need. He kissed her slowly at first, and she melted against him, dropping his wrist and closing the gap between them. He pressed her mouth more firmly against his, and when she made a small sound of pleasure, he grew wilder, more passionate. He stroked his tongue over her lips, and she allowed him in, tangling her tongue with his.

Cade groaned and pushed her against the wall again, grabbing her face between his hands and kissing her still deeper, harder. Asha felt wondrously, deliriously out of control—something she never thought she'd enjoy. But she'd never been kissed quite like this, and certainly not by someone she cared for as much as she cared for him. It added a sweet dimension to the passion that surprised her. It gave it purpose. It made her *want* him in a way she'd never wanted anyone before, as if she'd die without his touch.

In a move that surprised her most of all, Asha clung to him, looping her arms around his neck and rubbing herself against him. Another deep groan from Cade, and he pressed between her legs, nipping her bottom lip. She gave a small yelp, clawing at his back, and he lifted her easily off her feet. Her legs automatically curled around his hips, and he carried her to the back door of the cottage, only pausing his kisses to open it and bring her inside.

Once in the house, Cade pinned her against the wall next to the door, grinding against her as his mouth plundered hers. She felt his erection through their clothes, and for the first time, stone-cold fear shot through her, as if she'd been doused with freezing water. She broke away from his lips and squirmed against him, panting.

Cade, ever attuned to her mood, paused. Spreading kisses across her jaw, he asked softly, "What is it?"

"It's just...I know where this is going," Asha replied, and she hated how afraid she sounded.

"It can go wherever you want, darling," he said, but his tone was different now: gentler, more careful, more like it'd been at the beginning of their time together. She instantly mourned the loss of his wilder, more passionate side. That part of him was new and already addictive.

But still...the memories of her past violation were hard to shake. Even before Angel had raped her, she'd never enjoyed having sex. She'd only ever brought herself to orgasm, and even then, she didn't masturbate often. She could close her eyes, pretend to be somewhere else, and mindlessly pleasure her husband, but her own pleasure made her feel dirty.

"But you want sex," Asha said flatly. "And I…"

She couldn't continue, mostly because Cade had discovered a particularly pleasurable spot just underneath her ear and was now kissing her there. She sighed.

"You want it, too," he said in her ear, sending pleasant shivers down her spine. "Don't you?"

Yes. It was the immediate answer of her body, but her mind was still mired in her fears. In some ways, there was more at stake because she cared about him. She *trusted* him, which was a minor miracle. If he hurt or humiliated her, it would be more painful than she could bear. At least when it was someone she hated or resented, it didn't destroy the only fragile trust she'd ever managed to cultivate. It could ruin everything.

"I'm afraid," she blurted out, and her heart started pounding in her ears. This was far more vulnerability than she would've ever shown anyone else. "I'm scared that…that you'll hurt me. And I don't think I could recover if you did. I'd just…break."

"Ah, darling," Cade sighed sadly, and he carefully set her on her feet again. His hand came up to caress her cheek, and she shuddered under his gentle touch. She squeezed her eyes shut, and a single tear cascaded down her face. He caught it with his thumb and wiped it away.

"Look at me," he said, and she forced herself to meet his solemn eyes. "I'd never do anything you didn't want me to, my angel. I promised you my protection, and that includes from myself."

Asha swallowed hard, nodding.

"But hear me now: there is no one, and nothing, that can break your spirit so completely that you wouldn't recover. *I* could never break you, because you're always at your strongest when your survival is threatened. I've seen it."

His words were a balm on her still-healing wounds. She pulled him down to her and kissed him again, more tenderly than she knew she was capable of.

"Thank you," she whispered, their noses touching. "I…I think you were right. I do want it. But…" Asha gulped, her nerves at the surface. "I've never had sex that I liked before. Never had sex that didn't hurt me or wasn't forced on me. I...I don't know if I can do this. I don't know how."

"I'll show you," Cade replied, sounding much surer than she felt. "Give yourself to me, and I'll show you how good it can be."

He was so close that she could feel the heat of his body, the warmth of his breath on her face. She could still taste his lips on hers, and desire burned inside of her in a way that both alarmed and tantalized her.

At the same time, she felt exposed and vulnerable like never before. Cade's stormy grey eyes bore into hers, as if he could see through her. It felt like he could smell her fear.

"I used to just...submit," she mumbled, casting her eyes to the floor. "Lock myself away to a secret place in my mind. And wait for it to be over."

He caught her chin in his hand, tilting her face up to his. His gaze was softer now, yet every bit as intense.

"Submission can be a gift," he said, his voice a deliciously low timbre. "When willingly given, it can make you feel freer than you ever have before. Safer, too."

She frowned. "I don't see how giving up control would make me feel free *or* safe."

He smiled. "The control is always yours to give and to take back. If you want me to stop, you only have to say so."

"How do I know you'll listen?" Asha asked, looking away from his eyes again. They disarmed her in their earnestness.

She flinched as he leaned toward her, but he only lowered his lips to her ear.

"Any coward can brutalize a woman to take what he wants," Cade said in a coarse whisper, his voice raising goosebumps on her skin. "It takes skill to bring her to her knees willingly. To make her beg you for it, over and over, until she barely knows her own name. Until she offers you her complete surrender, in exchange for what she craves most."

Asha shuddered, and he pressed his lips softly against her, just below her ear. Even now, with only his breath in her ear and his mouth on her neck, she was suffused with pleasure from head to toe. The ache between her thighs wouldn't abate. She wanted him now more than she was afraid of him.

"Okay," she exhaled. "But...I don't want pain."

Cade kissed slowly down her neck. "Pain is only ever a tool to enhance your pleasure. But I'll never use it unless you ask, my angel. Tonight is about trust. About what I can give to you."

Asha took a shaky breath. "What do I do now?"

He took her clammy hands in his warm ones, giving them a reassuring squeeze.

"Do you trust me?" he asked, and she nodded nervously. "Alright. Then get on the bed."

She immediately tensed, familiar with this particular order. Seeing her distress, he pulled her close, kissing her again with his tongue in her mouth until the angles of her body softened—until she was panting and aching again with need. He carefully guided her toward the bed and eased her down, so she was seated on the edge.

"There's a good girl," he said, and the praise made her scalp tingle with pleasure, to the point she was almost annoyed with herself. "One more thing, then."

Cade went to the wardrobe on the opposite wall and rummaged inside for a moment before withdrawing a long, thin strip of fabric. He approached her with it outstretched and motioned as if to cover her eyes. His gaze sought her permission.

"You want to blindfold me?" Asha said with an incredulous giggle. "Why?"

"Trust," he replied. "And I want you to focus on how you feel. Without your sight, you'd be surprised how much other senses take over."

Fear bubbled in her gut, but so did a sense of intrigue. How would it feel, to trust him that much? In the past, she'd never have considered it. But hadn't Cade proven himself to her? He'd saved her life. He'd protected her from Angel and even from his own men.

It was exhausting being constantly vigilant. For once, she wanted to listen to her desire instead of her fear.

So again, she said, "Okay."

The corner of Cade's mouth quirked up. "My angel's brave."

Asha flushed a little, but if he noticed, he didn't comment. Instead, he covered her eyes with the blindfold and secured it. Her vision was plunged into darkness, and she inhaled sharply, anxiety rising in her chest.

"Take a deep breath," Cade coaxed, and she did. "Good. Before we start, I want you to know that you can say no to anything, anytime, and I'll hear you. For now...keep your hands at your sides. Stay perfectly still for me. If you move, I'll stop."

A bolt of lust surged through her, unbridled and inexplicable. She let out yet another shaky breath as he moved his mouth back to her neck, where he spread long, languid kisses. Deprived of her sight, the warmth of his hands was grounding, and she sighed at the goosebumps that rose on her flesh as he kissed onto her collarbone.

He was right that she felt him more acutely without her eyesight. Every touch sent a tremor through her that, far from dissuading her from continuing, made her ache for more. She'd never thought she could want someone as much as she wanted him.

Cade took his time, kissing her until she couldn't help it—she squirmed. As promised, he stopped, and she let out a small, involuntary whine that embarrassed her.

Cade chuckled darkly. "You'll have to learn to be still if you want more. Can you do that?"

Asha took another deep breath. "Yes. I can."

"Alright. Let's try again."

He ramped up her torment by spreading open-mouthed kisses over her chest and caressing her over her clothes, his hands finding her breasts and her inner thighs, teasing her. Her nipples pebbled at his soft, intimate touch, and the heat in her body was maddening—unbearable.

"Please," she finally whispered. "I want more."

"Ah," Cade said knowingly. "Good. She knows how to beg."

She let out a tiny whimper, and he eased the straps of her worn tank top over her shoulders. She moved to lift her arms but then remembered his order.

"Oh, very good," he said, a note of wonder in his voice. "Better than I expected, even. You can lift them."

She hastened to obey, surprised at how much she was enjoying this. Cade lifted the shirt over her head, then removed her pants and underwear. When she was finally naked, she shuddered, unsure if what she felt was fear or arousal. The two blended together in a way that seemed to sharpen her senses even further.

Cade's scent mingled with hers, and his mouth seemed to send tiny electric shocks over her skin, giving life to new desire that she didn't know what to do with. She liked hearing his breath, steady and heavy, breathing her in. Not being able to see him added a new, unexpected dimension to her pleasure; she delighted in the surprise of his lips and tongue touching her in sensitive places.

"Has anyone ever told you how beautiful you are?" Cade asked, trailing kisses down her bare chest towards her breasts.

"No," Asha replied, a little discomfited by the question.

"Hmm," he murmured against her breast, and she gasped as his tongue lightly flicked over her nipple. "Their loss, then. Because you're gorgeous. A goddess among women."

Asha huffed a disbelieving laugh. "You're laying it on a little thick."

He chuckled. "You like it, though."

Silly as it was, she did. His tone was playful but sincere, and it didn't feel like he was mocking her. Nor did it seem like he was objectifying her, the way she was used to; rather, he was admiring her, cherishing her. The thought was as frightening as it was exciting.

She shivered as he continued to lick slow, deliberate strokes over her nipple. When he took it into his mouth and sucked, so slow and deep, she couldn't help herself: she moaned. Her cheeks stained red with embarrassment. She wasn't used to expressing pleasure.

Evidently reading her reaction, Cade moved back up to kiss her lips, then said, "Don't be shy, my angel. I want to hear you. Want you to feel so good that you can't help yourself. Want to know what you like, what makes you shiver with pleasure."

It was always uncanny, how he seemed to simply know what she was thinking, and equally strange how simply he was able to put her at ease.

"What I like?" Asha asked in wonder. "I...don't know what I like."

"Then let me find out."

His tone was commanding and self-assured. She thought she might've hated that, that it would've brought up her past viola-tion...but it didn't. Instead, he was lifting a burden from her. He would take care of her; she didn't have to worry or overanalyze. She could, for the first time, let go.

Cade drew her nipple back into his mouth, then gently pinched the opposite nipple between his fingers. Asha fought the urge to moan again as he alternated between them, sucking and licking, but eventually, she couldn't help herself.

"Good girl," he encouraged, and she flushed with more embarrassed pleasure. "You're doing so well, showing me what you want."

The cleft between her thighs was slick with arousal, and she shuddered once more as Cade licked a lazy line down to her navel. The ancient floorboards groaned in protest as he knelt, taking his tongue lower, and lower...

She jumped at the shock of his mouth between her thighs.

"Mm," he murmured, inhaling deeply. "You're gorgeous here, too." She gasped as he gave her clitoris a long, indulgent lick. "And the taste of your pretty pussy...I could get used to that."

He spread her knees farther apart, settling between them, and then his tongue was on her again. Asha tensed, more moans escaping from deep in her throat. She was all desire and ache, grasping for something just out of reach.

"This is good, hmm? You're getting close now, aren't you?"

Asha made a face beneath the blindfold. "You're enjoying this too much."

Cade chuckled. "Why wouldn't I enjoy pleasuring you?"

It wasn't supposed to be a trick question, but she thought of her teenage girlfriend, and then her husband, and then that old memory, the one she rarely dared to look at...and none of them had ever troubled themselves with what she got out of their time together. Despite his clear preference for dominance during sex, Cade did care that she enjoyed it. And though she was submitting to him, it was his plain desire to please her, to be worthy of her submission, that granted her a feeling of control, of ownership.

She hadn't known that submission and pleasure could co-exist...or that submission could *add* to this pleasure, that it could make her feel powerful in a way she'd never felt before.

As though he sensed her distraction, Cade murmured, "Stay with me, darling. Feel me giving you what you need. Lose control and let yourself fall. I'll catch you."

Asha's lips trembled with emotion. His reassurance was almost too much, but she swallowed hard and nodded. He started again, relaxing her once more with gentle, patient touch before licking her pussy in slow, sensual strokes.

This time, Asha made an effort to let go. She leaned into her lack of sight and simply *felt* the rising sensations as Cade's tongue swirled over her clit. He made a noise of approval before carefully sliding a finger inside her, then two. Asha gave a soft gasp at the intrusion, but she was relaxed and wet enough that the penetration wasn't painful. As he slowly pumped his fingers, she sighed with pleasure.

"That's it, my angel. Just let this happen. It's going to feel so good, I promise."

His voice was pitched low, but there was a tenderness to his tone that pulled at all the jagged edges inside her. She gave into the feelings he coaxed from her body, and at last, she teetered on the edge of bliss.

"You're right there, hmm?" Cade crooned. "You want to come?"

"Yes," Asha said breathlessly.

His tone darkened. "Then beg, Asha. Beg me for it, and I'll give it to you."

She didn't think. "Please. Please, I need it so bad. I need—"

She made a sound of desperation, and he grunted before she felt his mouth on her clit, sucking her gently, and she was lost.

Asha's sense of time and place was obliterated by the euphoria of her release. The delicious spasms that rocked her body left her panting and shaking, filling her with satisfaction and exhaustion. Her climax sated some deep hunger she'd perhaps never known she had.

When she'd come back to Earth, Cade lifted the blindfold from her eyes and kissed her, a sly, pleased look in his grey eyes.

"Thank you," Asha whispered, starry-eyed. She felt like she'd been hit by a truck and didn't know what else to say.

Cade laughed softly. "My pleasure."

She pressed her lips back to his, and the kiss morphed into something more, something desperate trying to claw its way out of her. She clutched at him, and he kissed her back, though not with the same fervour.

She felt the need to repay him. She owed him a favour in return, didn't she? He'd put in more of an effort than anyone else she'd been with. She felt out of control, ready to melt and combust at the same time, her body on fire.

"Cade, I—" she gasped out, fumbling with his belt. "I need—"

He stayed her hand with his and pecked her lips.

"Another time," he said, and his voice was so gentle. "Tonight was a lot for you."

At this, Asha trembled, overwhelmed by emotion she didn't fully understand. She felt like she could cry, which was absurd. She hadn't cried when her parents had expressed their crushing disappointment at her assignment as a teacher. Or during her teenage breakup, or when she was told she had to marry Eric. Or even when Angel raped and tortured her. Her tears were nowhere to be found at the cruelest, most unjust moments in her life.

But there was something about Cade's kindness that made her feel things she'd never thought she could. She hadn't trusted it in the beginning, but somehow, this literal gang member had treated her better than anyone she'd ever known.

"But I—you didn't get to—"

"You owe me nothing," Cade said firmly. "Like I said: it was *my* pleasure."

She bit her shaking lip, hugging herself tightly. He knew again what she'd been thinking. And he was telling her, in no uncertain terms, that he expected nothing in return. She wasn't used to sex as anything but a transaction or an obligation. Her bottom lip trembled.

"Can I touch you?" Cade asked. His hands hovered in front of her, but not in a way that demanded anything of her. It was a promise of giving, not taking.

"Y-yes," she stammered.

He pulled his t-shirt over his head, baring his beautifully built chest and dark tattoos, then lay back on the bed and pulled her with him. She felt stiff and awkward, unsure of his intent, until he tucked her against his body, his arm around her.

He's holding me.

That thought shouldn't have been shocking to her, yet it was. Who had held her since she was a small child? No one that she could remember.

Cade was warm and as solid as a brick house. His breath was slow, even, and relaxed. He seemed content as he rested his cheek against her head and slowly rubbed her back.

Asha stayed frozen, uncertain, but Cade didn't seem to mind. He kept rubbing for several minutes in comfortable silence, and as tears spilled onto her cheeks, Asha felt ridiculous. How pathetic was it that an orgasm and a few minutes of positive attention from a man could undo her so completely?

Suddenly, she felt her lack of positive human touch like an open wound. How was it that she'd never felt deprived until now? Was it because she never knew it could be quite like this?

Her weakness was off-putting, and Cade was sure to see it as such. There was no room for this kind of weak, womanish weeping in the Wasteland. She tried to delicately swipe at her face, hoping he wouldn't notice.

"Even your tears are beautiful," Cade said, pressing a kiss against her head. He lifted his hand to her face, catching a couple tears on his fingertips.

She took a long, shuddering breath, and to her horror, a small sob escaped.

"I don't know what's wrong with me," she blubbered, hiding her face against his chest. "Sorry. This is probably not what you hoped for from me."

She heard his frown in his voice. "This isn't a service you're providing me, Asha. If I just wanted a woman to warm my bed, I could've had it anytime. You're here because I want *you*."

After another minute of pathetic sniffling, she finally looked up at him, and there was a softness to his expression that she couldn't define. She felt like she could tell him anything, and he'd simply nod as though he already knew all her darkest secrets.

"I was molested as a kid."

She didn't know what made her say it. It came up like word vomit, with the urge to make him *understand*.

To his credit, he didn't flinch. Instead, he tucked her hair behind her ear and kept rubbing her back. She struggled with her next words; she'd never told anyone about this since it happened. She'd done her best to forget it, and most of the time, she had.

"That was my first experience," she finally managed. "With sex. He was a family friend. He was supposed to babysit me, and, well..."

She swallowed hard, uncomfortable with the way that Cade was simply looking at her. He was watching her, studying her expression, as though he really wanted to know her, which was disarming.

More disarming still: she wanted him to.

"Anyway," she pressed on, "I was eight. I told my mom after, because it made me feel...icky."

Asha let out a long breath, and still, Cade said nothing, as though knowing that his interruption would render her incapable of finishing the story.

"My parents were well-connected, since they both worked for the government. The family friend was another important official. Powerful. My mom told me it'd be better for everyone if we just forgot about it. We couldn't afford to confront him."

Cade's brow creased. "Shit. That's the best she could come up with?"

Asha gave a watery laugh. "Yeah. Honestly, she and my dad were barely in my life, even at that age. Too busy being involved in important things. He watched me a few more times before my parents got a nanny."

"Wait, they let him keep having access to you?" Cade's outrage was palpable, and despite the seriousness of the situation, Asha laughed.

It had never occurred to her how bad that might've looked to an outsider. She'd always just accepted it as something that happened inevitably, like lightning or a tornado. Of course they kept letting him have access; they wouldn't have wanted to offend him by accusing him of being a pervert.

Think of how that would look for us, Asha's father had said to her. *How badly that would damage our careers. We applied for a nanny, and you ought to be grateful; they're in short supply in the compound. It's only because of our positions that we can apply at all.*

"Only for a little while," she replied. "The nanny that came after was alright, but she thought I was a difficult kid. To be fair, I probably was."

"No wonder, you practically raised yourself," he said angrily. "Fuck them. I'm glad they're fucking dead."

She laughed again in spite of herself, then grew thoughtful. "Does it make me a horrible daughter if I am, too?"

Cade clucked his tongue and caressed her cheek so softly, so gently, her heart wanted to break.

"No, my angel," he replied. "Makes me like you even more. I admire a woman with a little wrath in her. Kind of a turn-on, to tell you the truth."

That elicited a helpless giggle from her, and he grinned before turning serious again.

"Didn't you have anyone who cared for you?" he murmured. "What about that friend you mentioned—Claire? Was she good to you, when she was around?"

"She had her own problems," Asha replied reluctantly. She didn't like talking about Claire. "Her dad died, and her mom was a nightmare. I never told her about any of it. I didn't want to burden her, and I didn't think she'd understand. Plus...I was ashamed."

The admission brought unwelcome heat to her face, and she glared at Cade, because she saw the sympathy in his eyes and couldn't bear it.

"Stop feeling sorry for me," she snapped.

He chuckled, much to her annoyance. "I don't feel sorry for you, darling. I admire you. All those years, being so strong when you shouldn't have had to. But you survived."

She balked. She hadn't expected that.

"It's why I wanted to help you to begin with," he continued.

"I thought it was because you knew I was from a compound."

"Sure," he said with a nod. "But...I liked your fight. Even when you thought the worst would happen to you, you fought back. You spat in the face of the man who tried to sell you. And you didn't hesitate to let Angel know exactly what you thought of him. It's that much more incredible now, knowing what you've been through."

Asha was quiet for a moment. Then, "I didn't want to be the kind of person I grew up with...someone who just goes along to get along."

Cade smiled, and she marvelled at the spark of real respect in his eyes.

"I said it before: you're a brave little viper," he said, and she rolled her eyes, but couldn't help smiling back. "You fight for yourself. You have real courage, to call out the bastards who subjugate you. Even when it hurts to do it."

Asha felt a strong surge of affection for him. He offered her something beautiful and dangerous: true, unconditional acceptance. It was the first time she'd thought that someone was capable of liking her for who she was, not who he wanted her to be.

She pressed herself into him and whispered, "Thank you."

Cade simply held her tighter, and she let herself believe for the first time that he wouldn't let her go.

Chapter 18

The following day was torture. When Asha woke up, Cade had already left, likely to attend to his inspections of the settlement. With nothing in particular to do, she ate and dressed, then lay back on the bed with her sore ankle elevated on a cushion. She started reading one of Cade's books, titled *Navigation for Dummies,* which had lessons about using a compass, reading maps, and more modern innovations like GPS. It wasn't terribly interesting, but it was useful, at least.

Hours ticked by slowly, and Asha grew restless. Her desire for Cade was like a fire under her skin, heated and burning, and as unfamiliar as it felt, she relished it. She thought of what they'd done the night before, the way he'd touched and pleasured her, and heat pooled between her thighs. She tried to push away the tantalizing images of his head between them, but they danced behind her eyelids every time she blinked. He'd awakened her hunger, and now she was starving.

At the back of her mind, he'd also awakened her curiosity. She was curious about all that he'd promised the night before, when he'd said he would show her how good it could be, and how pain could bring her more pleasure. It seemed inherently contradictory, yet she couldn't stop thinking about it. About him, and what it might be like to see him naked and let him inside her body—something she'd never relished the thought of before, but now craved in a way that was nearly painful.

So, when Cade finally came through the door of the cottage, Asha practically pounced on him. Before he could say a word, she pulled him into a kiss that felt most unlike her—not cautious, not dubious, but happy and grateful and so very hungry. His body softened against her, and he kissed her back with the same level of need. They explored back and forth with their tongues until they had to surface for breath.

"That's a welcome I won't soon forget," Cade said wryly.

Asha bit her lip, suddenly shy. It was an odd feeling, to put her affection for him on display like that. But more surprising, it felt good, and not just physically. It fed something deep in her soul, to have someone, at long last, to trust.

"I missed you," she admitted, feeling foolish and exhilarated at the same time.

Cade's sweet smile was worth it. "That doesn't sound like my Asha. She'd tell me to go jump in a lake."

My Asha. She felt like an idiot with how giddy that made her.

"I haven't ruled it out," she replied with a snort.

Cade smiled wider, then kissed her some more. She got lost in his lips, and a thrill went through her when he pushed her back onto the bed and climbed on top of her, deepening their kiss. She loved the feel of him, powerful and strong, against her.

Powerful, but never cruel.

Still, a nagging voice in her head castigated her for enjoying her submission to him as much as she had. *What is wrong with you? You call yourself a rape victim, then you go and do this? Beg for it?*

Cade must've felt her stiffen, because he abruptly stopped kissing her and fixed her with that piercing grey gaze that she both loved and hated. It meant he was analyzing her.

"What is it?" he asked, hushed. "Did I do something wrong?"

"No, no," Asha replied in a rush. "I just..."

When she didn't continue, he said, "You're going to have to help me out here, darling. Talk to me."

"It's just...last night," she managed after a moment. "I feel...guilty. For submitting to you. I've spent my whole life seeing sex as submission, and it was humiliating and horrible. But then, last night, I let you..."

She faltered, not sure how to properly express herself. Cade's eyes, however, softened with understanding. Somehow, he'd listened to that muddled mess and knew what she was telling him. She loved that about him.

"Did you enjoy submitting to me?" he asked, gently caressing her jaw.

Asha swallowed hard. "So much."

Her cheeks flamed. She felt a sense of shame about just how *much* she'd liked submitting to him. It felt like a betrayal of her past experiences with submission, which had been at best uncomfortable, at worst violating. He must've read it in her expression because he bent and kissed her—so gently, so patiently.

"It doesn't invalidate any of what's happened to you before, my angel," Cade murmured. "It's different now. When you submit to me, it's a game we're playing together that gives both of us pleasure. Trust is sexy, darling."

She quirked an eyebrow. "Trust is sexy?"

He nodded. "I can't tell you how hard I got last night when you just let go of control...let me blindfold you, let me eat your pussy. When you followed my orders without question. Your submission is...intoxicating. Especially because in your day-to-day, I doubt anyone would describe you that way."

He grinned, and she acknowledged his point with a sheepish giggle.

"So, your submission is just for me," he continued, with a suggestive smile. "And that feels pretty special."

Her flush deepened, but this time with pleasure. It felt special to her, too, to share herself with him in a way she hadn't with anyone else before. To let go of her inhibitions and seek pleasure for herself.

"I'm...curious about something," Asha said awkwardly, hesitating. Cade lifted her hand to his lips, kissing along her palm. "You said last night that...that pain could be a tool to enhance pleasure."

"Mm," he replied, his lips moving down her hand. "When used the right way, pain can make your pleasure stronger—more potent."

She shuddered as the tip of his tongue grazed the soft underside of her wrist.

"Did you want to explore that?"

He was right about submission making me feel freer. She was choosing to trust that he'd be right about this, too.

She hesitated again, but ultimately answered, "Yes."

His pupils dilated with arousal, but he exhaled slowly. "Are you sure, darling? You don't think it'll bring up...bad memories? I don't want you to do it because you think it's what I want. I'm happy to have you in whatever way I can."

His words touched her heart. He really cared.

"I'm sure," Asha said. "I want this with you."

Cade lips curved into a small smile that felt equal parts seductive and dangerous.

"I'll start slow," he murmured against her skin. "If you need me to stop, use the safeword 'red.' Everything stops when you use it, no matter what. Understood?"

Asha nodded, desire blooming deep in her core. Cade kissed her again, deeper this time, and the effect it had on her was drugging. She clung to him, pressing herself against his warm, hard body. His arms closed around her, and one hand twisted into her dark hair. He gave it a harsh tug, pulling her head back, and she gave a small gasp at the slight sting as his mouth moved to her neck.

"Ah, you're so soft," Cade breathed against the delicate skin of her throat. "So beautiful. So ready to submit to me, hmm?"

He spread open-mouthed kisses down her neck, and his tongue darted out, teasing her skin, distracting her. His quick, sharp bite made her squeal in surprise more than pain, but the dull sting still managed to set every nerve in her body on fire.

"When I ask you a question, I expect you to answer, my angel," Cade growled. "Now, tell me you're ready to submit to me. To give yourself over to me. To put me in charge of your pleasure...and your pain."

"Yes, sir," she gasped out without thinking, the way she did during drills, and she felt his grin against her neck.

"*Sir*," he repeated with quiet delight. "Hmm. I do like that. Now, strip."

"What?" Asha asked, still in a haze of desire. How was it possible for a few kisses and a bite to make her want him so badly?

"You heard me. Strip. Quickly. Or we'll be introducing you to pain faster than I planned."

His voice brimmed with both threat and dark promise. A shiver of anticipation and fear rippled down Asha's spine. She stood and grappled with her clothes, shedding them faster than she ever had before. Somehow, her fear didn't activate that impulse to fight that she usually felt. Instead, it imbued her with a small, intensely pleasurable shot of adrenaline that made her pussy wet.

When she stood before him, naked as the day she was born, Cade exhaled in appreciation. Asha had never been especially self-conscious about her body, but she'd also never thought of it as anything but average. She may have been beautiful compared to most Wastelanders, who endured such hard living, but among the women of the Cave, she was just another pretty face in a sea of them.

The way Cade's eyes scanned every inch of her skin, however, made her feel like she was the rarest, loveliest woman on the face of the Earth. Though she'd giggled at his compliments the night before, there could be no doubt from the look on his face that he'd meant them.

"All of you belongs to me," he said, his voice a soft, menacing caress. His hands cupped her breasts, kneading at her soft, brown nipples with his thumbs. She moaned, arching up into his touch, and he gave her what she wanted. Her pussy ached from his attention, as though an invisible cord were tugging at it, attached to her nipples.

Cade stood and walked behind her, surveying every inch of her.

"Why don't you bend over the bed, darling?"

She scoffed as she obeyed him. "I thought you were supposed to be ordering, not asking, *sir*."

She couldn't help mocking him. He made it too easy, even in bed.

Smack. She cried out at the profound sting of his hand hitting her left ass cheek, hard. He hadn't used his full strength, yet it still hurt enough to make her squeeze her thighs together.

"Now, I get back at you for every barb you've sent my way," Cade said, amused. "Keep it up, little viper. I'll leave your ass bright red and aching. Not even your tears will stop me."

The brief pain had morphed into a delicious warmth that somehow stoked her desire higher. She sighed.

"As if I'd cry from a couple of spanks."

His soft, intimate laugh sent more heat through her. "We'll see. What's your safeword again, darling?"

"Red," she said, and he made a sound of approval before parting her thighs with his hand.

Asha gasped as he penetrated her with two fingers. She'd expected more of a tease based on the night before, but he wasted no time, pumping into her with precise, even thrusts. His other hand reached around her front, finding her clit. His careful, clever fingers circled it in rhythm that made her legs turn to jelly—gentle, but with a pressure that was impossible to resist. At the same time, he pressed hard against a soft, ridged spot inside of her that made her jaw clench.

"That's it," Cade crooned, and she mewled as he pressed even harder inside her. "You can take it. You can take anything I give you, my brave girl."

Once again, his praise made her preen foolishly. She soaked in his approval as though it were precious, and as much as she loved to tease him, to match her wit against his, she loved pleasing him even more. There was still that resistance within her that told her not to trust this feeling, but she was finally able to silence that voice and enjoy being his. Giving up control now didn't mean giving it up forever; he'd shown her that.

Cade continued until Asha was shaking with pleasure, moaning wantonly in his arms. She was so close, so very—

"Don't come," he warned. "Not until I give you permission."

"What?" she burst out. "Are you—"

"If you come, you'll be punished. Show me that you have at least *some* self-control, that you aren't just a desperate little slut."

The degradation hit her like another spank; she hadn't been expecting it. Yet somehow, it didn't *feel* degrading...possibly because the way Cade said it made no secret of his desire for exactly that outcome.

She opened her mouth to retort, but his fingers sped up inside her, and she gave a helpless moan. Her teeth gritted, she desperately tried to resist the rising sensations, but it was a lost cause.

"Gonna come," she gasped. "Oh God, Cade, I'm gonna come, I can't—"

She fell over the edge and cried out as pleasure surged through her whole body, filling her with warmth and sating the raw hunger inside her.

"Fuck, it's beautiful to watch you come," Cade murmured as he withdrew his fingers. "To get what you've deserved, all these years. But still...you disobeyed me."

"Like I could help it!" Asha protested, still breathing heavy. "With your fingers in my pussy, what did you expect, genius?"

He laughed with real humour. "Well, I didn't say it would be easy. That doesn't matter; you obey me anyway."

"Oh, fuck you," she sneered. "You set me up to fail."

He jerked her head back by her hair, and she squeaked. "What was that?"

His voice was a low snarl. But either because she was still woozy from orgasm or because she had a secret death wish, Asha replied, slowly enunciating each syllable, "Fuck you. *Sir.*"

She was provoking him on purpose now, though she didn't quite know why. Maybe she was just curious to see how far he'd go, or how much she could push him before he snapped.

She let out a breath as Cade disappeared into the closet for a moment. She stayed where she was, uncertain what to do.

When he returned holding a spare leather belt, she knew she'd gone too far.

"What...what's that for?" she asked, her mouth suddenly dry as sawdust.

"You wanted to explore pain?" he growled. "You got your wish, darling. Stay where you are, and you tell me when I've whipped some manners into you."

Oh, fuck. Her heart raced, and she thought about using her safeword, but she didn't want to chicken out before she'd even gotten a taste. Her hallmark stubbornness also meant that she wanted to show him that she could take it.

The first crack of the belt across her ass was easy; the sting retreated almost as quickly as it had come. Asha pressed her lips together, determined not to make a sound, but it was futile effort after three or four strikes. A whimper escaped her as the pain increased, but she didn't want him to stop. A coil of arousal was tightening again inside her, against all her natural instincts.

She lost track of the number of strikes, but her ass burned as though it was on fire, and she whimpered again, louder this time.

"Ah, my angel, I know it hurts," Cade said, his voice softening. "Should I make it just a little easier for you? Show you what I meant when I said the pain would enhance your pleasure?"

His hand moved between her thighs, and she moaned as he penetrated her with his fingers again. He established a steady rhythm that made Asha squeeze fistfuls of the blanket, panting as he sped up. A second later, the belt made contact with her ass again, and she made a choked sound. The pain shot through her as before, but the pleasure of Cade's ministrations seemed to somehow soften it. More than that, as her pussy tightened around his fingers in response, her pleasure bounded to the forefront, blending with and eclipsing the ache in her backside.

She just wanted more—more of everything. Her need to come again barreled into her, and suddenly nothing else mattered more.

"Please." The word just slipped out, unbidden, and she felt no shame. Just hunger.

She let out a small scream as the belt came down again, harder than before.

"Greedy girl. You already came once. Why should I let you come again? What will you give me?"

Crack. She was making desperate little sounds now, tears pricking the corners of her eyes. She didn't let them fall, but it was a close call.

Cade lowered his lips to her ear, tickling her deliciously with his whisper. "How about this? I let you come again, and you ride my cock for me, as long and as deep as I want."

She couldn't refuse him. She needed release too badly.

"Please, sir," she begged, her own voice sounding foreign to her with its neediness. She didn't even say *sir* in a mocking way; she was too far gone. "Please let me come. I'll give you whatever you want."

His slow exhale told her that she'd said the right thing. "Fuck. Nothing is sexier than reducing you to a begging mess like this. My brave, feisty girl, giving me everything because she's so desperate. My dick's never been harder."

Asha moaned as he pressed his erection against her aching ass, teasing her. Without another word, he thrust his fingers into her, hard and fast, and she gasped. He gave her a brief reprieve from the belt, instead allowing her to grow closer to what she craved with every cell in her body.

She reached the precipice of her release, and right as she was about to tip over the edge, Cade brought the belt down again. She screamed as her orgasm broke, and the pain of the belt melded with it, so intense that her vision whited out. When she came back to herself, she was lying face down on the bed, limp and boneless. Her cheeks were wet with tears, and she touched them with an odd curiosity.

They weren't tears of sadness, or even of pain. They were a natural reaction to the intensity of her experience, and she somehow liked them. They were a symptom of all the incredible new emotions and experiences she'd had with this man in such a short time.

"Are you alright, darling?" Cade asked, stroking over her hair.

"Yeah," Asha sighed. "I want more."

"What a good girl you are," he murmured, and her heart swelled with pride and affection. "You took your punishment so well, like I knew you would. But now it's time for you to deliver on your promise."

He pulled her upright and kissed her, hot and heavy, aching with his own unsatisfied desire. She slipped her tongue past his lips, and he groaned, low and rough in his throat. Catching the hem of his t-shirt, she broke away and met his grey eyes, clouded with arousal.

"Can I...?" she asked, a little shyly. He'd already witnessed her during her most intimate, private moments...yet she'd still never seen him naked, or watched him come. She was suddenly overcome with the need to rectify that.

"Yes." His answer was low and husky. "You can touch me how you want. Whatever feels right to you."

Permission granted, Asha lifted his shirt over his head, baring his gorgeous chest and shoulders. She caressed each line and curve of his body with her fingertips, and he shuddered under her touch. His jaw flexed, and she realized how much restraint he'd been practicing this whole time. He'd delayed his own gratification for hers.

Determined to return some of the favour, she made it her mission to kiss every muscle in his upper body. His erection was a hard, very visible bulge in the front of his pants.

"You're killing me," he panted.

She made innocent eyes at him. "I thought you'd enjoy being worshipped."

He choked on a laugh. "Worship later. I need to fuck you, my angel. I've waited long enough."

He really had, so Asha quit her game and finished undressing him. With his cock finally free, she wrapped a hand around his shaft, exploring him. He was thick and hot in her hand, and he groaned as if in pain when she gave him a shallow pump.

Cade pulled her hand away and kissed it, then led her back over to the bed. He lay back against the headboard and tapped his lap with a grin, his erection curving up over his belly.

Asha quirked a brow. "This doesn't seem very dominant, if I'm on top."

It was part-tease, part-challenge, and her arousal was stoked again by the flash of wicked amusement in his eyes. *Challenge accepted.*

"We'll just have to fix that then, won't we?"

He retrieved his belt, which he'd dropped at the end of the bed, then beckoned her to straddle him again. She cautiously obeyed, eyeing the belt. She wasn't sure she wanted more of *that* tonight. Her ass was already sore as hell.

However, her thoughts were obliterated by Cade's cock notching at her entrance.

"You gonna take all of me?" he murmured, touching her cheek. "Let me feel that incredible pussy. I've been dying for it."

He guided her hips down, sheathing him snugly, and Asha gasped at the fullness. He felt big, but not painfully so, and she relished how pleasurable it was when she was wet enough. He'd taken such care with her.

Cade let out a sound between a moan and a gasp, and his hands tightened around her hips.

"Oh, Asha," he sighed, and her heart tugged at the tender way he said her name. "You feel perfect."

"Really?" she asked playfully, tightening her pussy around him, making him groan. "How perfect?"

"So perfect I don't know what I've done to deserve it," he managed to say with difficulty. He guided her hands behind her back and wrapped the belt around them tightly, securing them there. "Is this alright?"

With her hands bound behind her, Asha couldn't move on her own without losing her balance. As Cade's hands moved back to her hips, she realized he now had complete control over her movements. *Well played.*

"It'll do," she said dismissively, and he chuckled before eliciting a yelp from her as he moved her hips. She was taking all of him now, as deep as she could, and her head fell back in a helpless moan.

Her hands being bound added another layer of desire. It allowed her to once again let go and experience the exhilaration of being out of control without the shame and abuse she'd always associated with that state. He was teaching her how to be at peace with herself and her own pleasure, and she was becoming an eager student.

Cade set the rhythm, urging her to ride him as hard as she could without toppling over. He'd kept such tight control over his emotions, his desires ...but now, at last, he let loose. He cupped her ass tightly, his fingers digging into her skin, and he groaned with abandon.

"That's right, darling," he growled. "You're gonna ride me till I come. Keep going."

He was surprisingly vocal as he grew closer to climax, and his eyes were glued to her, traveling from her eyes to her bouncing breasts to the place where they were joined. But it was the low, husky sweet nothings he said to her that eventually tipped her over the edge one last time.

"You're magnificent, Asha," Cade murmured. "Your face, your body, your beautiful pussy. You're a vision, submitting to me. When you're ready for it, my angel, I'll gag that hot little mouth and come listening to you make those slutty moans around it."

The image was too much. Her wrists strained against the belt as she cried out, and the dull ache only made her climax larger, longer, more intense. He followed her with a bellow, and she felt him fill her. It was incredible to watch him, to know that she'd given him that kind of pleasure. She instantly wanted to give it to him again, as many times as she could. He deserved everything she could offer him.

Somewhere deep within her, the cracks in her psyche were filled with molten gold, and she felt remade.

Chapter 19

Cade was as meticulous about aftercare as he was about training.

After they'd finished, he'd lit a candle, helped Asha out of bed, and cleaned both of them up at the washstand. He'd then tucked her back in and brought her water and some strips of jerky that she'd happily swallowed down. He rubbed arnica ointment into the sensitized flesh of her backside despite her protests, probably because it was starting to lightly bruise. He insisted on rubbing her wrists, her shoulders, her hands—anywhere that may have lingering aches from his treatment. All the while, he spoke to her in hushed tones, soothing and sweet and *loving.* There was no other word for it. She may not have known how to process that, but she enjoyed the comfort and safety he was providing. He'd become more precious to her than she was ready to admit.

When Cade settled next to her in bed and held her close, she felt as close to perfect as she ever had. He splayed out on his back, his formidable chest bared to the warm evening air, his arms curled around her in an affectionate, protective curve.

"How are you feeling?"

With the words came no judgment, no pressure, no expectation to say any particular thing. But Asha knew the answer without thinking.

"I'm so good," she murmured, still feeling a little drunk on him, and she felt his smile against her hair as he pressed a kiss there. "How do you feel?"

His deep chuckle reverberated in her chest. "Like a fucking god."

She burst into laughter. "A god?"

"Yes," he said, smirking at her. "You're a tough nut to crack, Asha Agarwal. Not the trusting type. So yeah, you submitting to me and letting me touch you and discipline you and fuck you...it makes me feel like a fucking god, and I won't apologize for it."

She giggled some more, feeling lighter and sillier than she ever had before. She'd never have imagined that she could make a man feel that way, and it gave her a strange sense of power that she treasured.

They lay together in peaceful silence. Asha lazily traced over Cade's sleeves of tattoos. She'd never had the chance to look at them properly before, up close.

"Do your tattoos mean anything?" she asked, following the line of long, black vines up his right arm.

"Sure," Cade replied indulgently. "That one, I got because it was cool-looking."

She clucked her tongue. "You know what I meant."

He turned onto his side, giving her a better view of his broad, muscled back. The vines connected to a sprawling tree, with branches that spread out up his shoulder blades like fingers, reaching heavenward. Small, delicate leaves decorated the branches, with a few pictured mid-fall toward the ground.

"It's beautiful," she murmured, leaning forward to kiss the tree trunk. He gave a small, addictive shudder at the touch of her lips, and so she kept kissing down his spine.

"The Tree of Life," Cade said eventually, after he'd rolled onto his back and gathered her close again. "I got it back when I was more of an idealist." He adopted a mocking tone. "*Life is sacred, deserves protecting,* blah blah blah. Back then, it was supposed to represent what I was protecting as a soldier: the lives of everyone in the compound." He huffed. "I'm less precious on my views these days."

"You don't think life is sacred anymore?"

He shrugged. "If it was, it wouldn't be so easy to destroy it."

Asha considered that for a moment before moving on, next tracing the fat, black snake that coiled up his left arm, from his wrist to his shoulder. "What about this one?"

"The snake represents the Delta. Or, maybe more accurately, the people that ran it. The more control they asserted over our lives, the more I saw them as the real enemy—the snake in the grass."

"Why?" She sat up to look at him. "I know that a lot of the rules were bullshit, but they kept us safe. *You* kept us safe, soldier."

He pulled her back down to kiss her, and she got lost in his lips for a while before he answered her question.

"Might be true," he replied. "But it came to a point where I wondered if I was keeping dangers out...or keeping people in. We had no real freedom, and no recourse if things went to shit. They controlled every part of our lives: our jobs, who we married, when or if we had kids, where we got to live and who got to know anything about the inner workings of our little society."

Asha was quiet. Everything he said was, of course, true for her as well. She'd never known anything else...but she had long since understood that much of the misery in her life could've been avoided if she'd only had another choice.

"There's no guarantee that our choices would've made us happier," she said, but it sounded hollow even to her own ears.

"That's true," Cade conceded, "but at least we wouldn't have been stuck. That's how I felt so much of the time: stuck, and there was nothing I could do about it."

Asha snuggled closer to him. She knew the feeling.

"It's only recently that I've felt...unstuck," she admitted. "A lot is still out of my control. But with you...you make me feel like I have agency."

He stroked her hair. "I'm glad."

They lay together quietly for a few minutes before Asha worked up the courage to ask, "Is that why you left?"

"Left?"

"The Delta. Did you just get sick of it? Were Leo and Dom sick of it, too?"

He sighed. "It's not a pretty story, darling. I'd rather—"

Asha lifted herself up on her elbows to fix him with a stare. "Do you trust me or not, soldier? We had sex last night, and I told you a secret. Now, I think it's time for you to return the favour."

Cade made a sound of amusement. "Sex and secrets, is that it?"

"Yes," she replied in a definitive tone. "Every time we fuck, one of us owes the other a secret. Now, tell me yours."

He laughed and kissed her. "Alright, I guess."

He paused, but she sensed it wasn't to stall. He seemed to be trying to determine how to begin. Asha stared at him, waiting. He'd never broached the subject again since she'd first asked, but she was more curious than ever as to how a man like Cade—a man who clearly excelled at what he did and was a natural leader—ended up in the Wasteland, especially if his compound still existed.

"You said before that they would've kicked you out anyway," she prompted, trying to help him.

Cade chuckled softly. "More like they would've put a bullet in my head, really. I was—or would've been—wanted for a crime."

"What did you do?"

His smile turned into more of a grimace. "Murder."

"Did you do it?" Asha knew that people sometimes were blamed for crimes in the compound for reasons other than their guilt. Anyone who asked too many questions had a habit of being charged with crimes or simply disappearing without explanation.

"Yep," Cade replied, with a glibness that she didn't buy for a second. "Murdered my old man in cold blood."

She frowned. "Why?"

He looked away, uncomfortable for the first time. "He killed my mother."

Asha stayed silent, watching him and offering him the same quiet witness to his pain he'd given to her.

Cade swallowed hard, then continued: "He was always a dickhead, even when I was a kid. Liked to smack her around. He was a soldier too, in the Old World and at the Delta...and he didn't keep his shit together very well."

"Did he hit you?" Asha asked.

"Not often," Cade answered, with a shake of his head. "Mom always protected me, and he was a coward. As soon as I was big enough to hit back, he rarely wanted anything to do with me anymore. But he started treating her even worse when I got drafted and left home."

He paused again, letting out a breath filled with tension. Asha found herself holding him tighter, stroking his chest in soothing circles.

"Anyway, I was trying to get her out," Cade said after a moment. "Trying to get her to report him. But she wouldn't. She really loved that asshole, God only knows why. Had every excuse in the book for him."

"How did you find out what he did?"

"Went over to their house before my patrol shift. I always said bye to my mom before I went, because you never know. I get there, he's standing over her in the kitchen, and she's bleeding out on the floor with her head busted open."

Asha winced. "Oh my God."

Cade ground his teeth. "My *father*—" he spit the word out like it was poison, "claimed that she fell and hit her head on the counter."

"But he pushed her?"

He shook his head in disgust. "No. He always thought I was an idiot, see—that's why he lied. But even an idiot can see blood on a heavy marble rolling pin and put two and two together."

Asha grimaced. "He got what he deserved, then."

"I'd say so," Cade said with a mirthless smile. "Beat him to death with his own weapon. Never lost my temper quite like that before...or since. But then I had a problem, obviously."

"So, how did you get out?" she asked, intrigued. She didn't know how one would escape a functioning compound; they were heavily fortified. If the Cave hadn't been destroyed, she'd never have been able to leave, even if she wanted to.

"Figured that it'd take at least a day for them to even notice my parents were missing, and that gave me time to plan. Told Leo and Dom what happened, and that I planned to desert. I gave them the option to stay home, but they didn't. Like I told you, there'd been an uprising recently, and they had their own reasons to leave...plus they're just the best fucking friends a guy could ask for."

Asha couldn't help smiling a little at his tone.

"When we went on patrol the next day, we all deserted together."

"And then you went to Ashburn?"

"Not right away. Our main concern initially was getting out of range of our tracking beacons."

Asha frowned. "Tracking beacons?"

"Oh, right," Cade said, as though remembering something important. "I guess you wouldn't know, as a civilian. Your implant—and mine—has a tracking beacon on it. Allows them to track you up to 300 kilometres from the compound. All soldiers carry a PID—that's a Personal Identification Device—that we use to sign in and off shift. Among other things, it also allowed us to track people. Didn't happen often, but sometimes people would try to escape, so…"

"Wait, *what?*" She asked in alarm.

"Yeah. They billed the tracking as a safety feature, because it also enabled protection from the guns on top of the Walls. If the AI can track you, it can identify you, so the guns won't accidentally fire on soldiers and other personnel. But realistically…it was surveillance, like most of what they did."

Asha tried to swallow her panic. "If they can track me, I'm not safe here. The compound isn't that far away."

Cade pulled her back down into his arms and kissed the top of her head.

"Darling," he said gently, "if they were going to do something about it, they would have by now. It's been months." He stroked her hair away from her face. "And I'll protect you. No matter what happens, or who comes knocking, or what it costs. I promised you."

She relaxed a little against him. "You better. Because I'm fulfilling my end of the bargain *pretty* well lately."

He laughed. "I'll give you that. Anyway, we didn't find Ashburn right away. We put as much distance between us and the Delta as we could first. And despite what came after, I've never regretted leaving. Or killing my father."

"You don't miss running water and central heating?" Asha mused, tracing over his snake tattoo again.

"Sure. But out here, I'm free. Not just a chess piece in the game of people whose identities I'm not even allowed to know."

"Free to die of starvation," she countered. "Free to be sold into slavery. Free to be shot by a gang member. Free to be eaten by a bear. Is it freedom if even your basic needs are a daily struggle?"

Cade's small, ironic smile was back. "I never said I was a philosopher, my angel. Just a man trying to determine his own destiny. What I always tell you is true for me too: we do what we have to do to survive. Whatever we have to. Whatever it leaves us with."

Chapter 20

C ade declared the next day a day off to allow Asha to rest her ankle before they headed back to the Nest. They spent the day in bed together, cycling through sex, napping, and chatting, and Asha thought it was the best day she'd had in a long time...possibly ever. She'd never been able to completely relax with another person before, but Cade made it easy somehow. He didn't expect her to be anything other than what she was, to contort herself to fit his expectations. He teased her, laughed with her, and held her like she was precious to him. He gave her space to let her guard down.

He's also fucking amazing in bed, which doesn't hurt.

"Sex and secrets time," Cade insisted after their first round that day, a sly smile on his lips. "It's your turn."

"Give me a minute," Asha replied breathlessly, flopping on top of her pillow as he chuckled. He'd folded her nearly in half on the bed and fucked her hard with her ankles on his shoulders until she'd come twice, helpless against him, before sating his own need for release and collapsing on top of her.

This is how good it can be, he'd whispered in her ear, still inside her. *This is how it always should've been for you.*

"I have no more secrets. You know them all."

"That's not true. When's your birthday?"

Asha rolled her eyes. "I'd hardly call that a secret."

"Then tell me."

"No."

"See, it qualifies." His smile was annoyingly infectious.

"August tenth. Not that it matters, because I have no idea what day it is."

The conversation flowed from there, with each of them revealing more of their 'secrets' in turns. Asha learned that Cade had turned thirty-two in January; he'd been into spy movies back at home; and his favourite colour was black (Asha argued it wasn't a colour, and then he picked grey, to which she also objected).

Then she took his cock in her mouth and slowly, torturously, got him off. Cade had been worried that it might be triggering for her, but Asha was beyond that now. She liked being in control of his pleasure for a change, and she was pretty good at blowjobs, if she did say so herself.

"Shit, Asha," he gritted out as she caressed his balls. "You're way better at this than is fair."

He dropped out of her mouth as she laughed, pleased by his approval. He groaned and added, "No. Keep going. Please."

"Who's begging now?" she teased, and he shot her a dark look.

"You will be, if you keep up the backtalk. Now, be a good girl and finish sucking *sir's* cock. I want to coat that pretty throat with my cum."

With a sardonic raise of her eyebrows, Asha wrapped her lips around him again and continued sucking him, slow and measured, until he came in her mouth with a groan, and she swallowed him down.

"You owe me a secret," Asha asked playfully a few minutes later, safely snuggled against him again. "What's your biggest fear?"

She expected him to tease her, or say something unserious like *spiders* or *heights*.

Instead, after a long, thoughtful pause, he answered sadly, "Becoming my father."

Asha looked up at him, and his eyes were surprisingly pensive, his mood changed.

"Why would you become your father?" she asked quietly, reaching out to stroke his cheek. "You're nothing like you've described him."

He sighed. "Sure, most of the time. But I have his temper. Most of the time, I have a decent handle on it, but every so often...it explodes, like his did."

"How do you mean?"

He kissed her forehead before responding. "I've had episodes of blackout rage before. Mostly when I was younger ...before I became a soldier and learned more discipline. When I was fifteen, I put my fists through a wall at school because of a fight with a friend. Got suspended for that one, and my dad beat the crap out of me before my mom could intervene. One of the few times he hit me after I got into my teens."

He blew out a breath. "And when they ordered me to shoot that Wastelander boy, and I refused. When my CO brought me in for a lecture, I lost it. Screamed at him and threw his desk lamp against the wall. Got in pretty big trouble for that one. If I hadn't been good at my job otherwise, I'd probably have gotten discharged."

Asha stroked his chest, comforting, and Cade pressed a kiss against her hair.

"Most of the time," he eventually continued, "I channel my anger into training, or working out. But sometimes, I still feel it there, under the surface."

He looked worried about admitting this, as though he thought she might pull away. But Asha was touched, as ever, by his willingness to make himself vulnerable for her. In the beginning, he'd done it to make her comfortable with him...but now, she felt for the first time that maybe he needed her tenderness as much as she needed his.

She kissed him, then held his gaze with hers. "It's okay. I like a man with a little wrath in him."

Cade chuckled and pulled her in for another kiss. "Well, that's a relief, because I have plenty. But why am I the one spilling all my secrets? I haven't heard you say anything in a while."

She arched an eyebrow. "When you make me come again, maybe I will. If you're capable of that, anyway."

"Is that a challenge?" he growled, and before she knew what was happening, he'd playfully tackled her and pinned her to the bed. "When I'm done with you, you'll be begging me for mercy."

"You sure about that?" Asha taunted, a combative smile curving her lips. "I don't know. I think you're all talk."

His eyes darkened. "Keep talking, and I'll whip your ass so hard you won't sit right for a week."

Pushing him gave Asha a masochistic kind of thrill.

"Prove it, then."

Soon after, she found herself on all fours, her wrists bound to the headboard, crying out as Cade alternated between eating her pussy from behind and bringing his belt down, over and over, on her ass.

She came once, then twice, then lost count, screaming as the pleasure and pain melded into something new altogether. And in the end, she did beg—helplessly, desperately, gratefully, for the one man who could make falling to her knees for him feel like strength instead of weakness.

When they'd finished, Cade retrieved something from his pack and settled back into bed with her. He held a couple of metal tags on a long chain that he draped around Asha's neck.

"Your dog tags?" Asha asked, and he nodded, giving her a fond smile.

"They're yours now, darling."

He spooned her as she fell asleep, and she drifted off with his name pressed against her heart.

They set off again the following day for the Nest. The wagon was full, and they had to drop off the goods they'd collected before heading to the other settlements. They went back the way they'd come, but it all felt different to Asha now. She couldn't take her eyes off Cade, to the point that he commented on it.

"Eyes on the road, soldier," he teased her. "Be vigilant. You don't know what could be around the bend."

He wasn't wrong, but all she could feel was his dog tags that she still wore under her clothes. After walking most of the morning, Asha spotted a rising spiral of black smoke in the distance. Cade gave the order to stop, frowning up at it.

"What is it?" Asha asked, wondering if this was usual on these trips.

"Don't know," Cade replied, still staring at the smoke. "But it looks like it's coming from Applegate."

"Applegate?"

"It's a settlement occupied by the Skulls."

There was a murmur among the Blackguard, who followed behind them.

"What should we do, Cap?" Raph asked after a moment. "Check it out?"

Cade was quiet for a moment, but then answered, "No. Move out."

The men hastened to obey his order. Only Asha stopped short.

"Wait, what?" she blurted out. "What if they need help? The Skulls aren't our enemies."

"Not our problem. We have a schedule to stick to, and we don't know what might be waiting there. It's not worth the risk."

She glowered at him. "But—"

"I gave you an order," he interjected coldly. "Defy me again and see what happens."

Stupid, stupid man. He should've known by that point that that was just challenging her, *daring* her to defy him.

"Guess I will," Asha said with a too-casual shrug. "Because I'm going. Whether you come or not is your decision."

She turned on her heel and walked toward the smoke, drawing her pistol.

"That's not going to work, Asha."

She ignored him and kept walking. A few minutes later, she heard a string of curses, and the collective footsteps of the men following behind her. Satisfaction bloomed in her chest.

It was short-lived. As they moved toward the smoke, a small village loomed in the distance. And it was on fire.

Flames licked several roofs of derelict houses, and though the fortified fence around the settlement was still standing, the gate was not. It looked as if it'd been blown open by some explosive force. There were bodies lying around, broken and forlorn, strewn across the wreckage of what had once been a hub of activity. Of *life*.

"Hold up," Cade ordered, and this time, Asha obeyed. She waited for him, and he accompanied her into the carnage, the Blackguard at their backs.

"What caused this?" Asha asked, hushed, as they walked across a ruined courtyard littered with corpses. "Another gang?"

"Possible." Cade's assessment was cold and clinical, reminding her that he'd done this kind of thing before. Perhaps he'd even *left* a place in this state before.

She pushed the thought away and kept going. They came across a small village square, and this had clearly been the centre of whatever battle had taken place there. There were more dead people, and the dry, stone fountain in the middle of the square was cracked almost in half.

But it was the door of a nearby home that stopped Asha in her tracks. Over the weatherworn wood, someone had pinned a black mask painted with a large, golden eye opened wide, staring out at the ruined world.

The same mask worn by those who had destroyed the Cave. She'd seen it in her nightmares from time to time, if only because it was so distinct. As they walked farther, the corpses changed. No longer were they only of simple villagers. Instead, a few were dressed in all black, and they wore the black masks that covered their entire faces, all bearing that same emblem of the golden eye.

They had been here. They had ventured outside the compound.

All at once, Asha couldn't breathe. She clutched her chest uselessly, fighting for air. She felt like she was dying.

"Asha," Cade said, his voice containing a forced calm, masking the alarm underneath that only she could hear. "Are you alright? Talk to me."

She tried, but nothing came out. Instead, she sat on the ground, forcing herself to suck in short, desperate gasps.

"It's *them*," she managed to tell him when he crouched in front of her, a crease of worry between his brows. "The ones who attacked the Cave."

His eyebrows shot up. "Shit." He turned to the men. "Do a sweep. Find out if there are any survivors. If you find any masked ones alive, bring them to me."

The men hastened to obey, and Cade sat back on his heels across from her.

"Did you know they left the compound?"

"No," Asha shot back. "The last time I saw them, I was fleeing for my life." She buried her face in her hands. "What does this mean?"

A long pause. "I don't know, darling. But you're safe with us now. We won't let them hurt you."

Some time later, Davy announced, "No survivors, Captain, and the place is ransacked. Probably not even worth scavenging."

Asha bowed her head. A bizarre sense of shame set in; *her* people had caused this destruction, and undoubtedly would cause more.

These people, Wastelanders though they were, didn't deserve to die the way they had.

"I'm sorry, my angel," Cade murmured to her, touching her shoulder before standing again. "Alright. Nothing left to do here. Move out, guys."

He offered her his hand and pulled her to her feet.

"It's not your fault," he told her a few minutes later. "Not your fault that you survived and they didn't."

Asha loved and hated how well he read her. "I know that."

"Helps to hear it sometimes, though."

He had a point. She nodded reluctantly.

"What do you think it means?" she asked him.

Cade shrugged. "They've become a gang, just like the rest of us. So, it means the same thing it always means when a gang wipes out another settlement. More competition."

Asha's stomach dropped. "For what?"

"Survival, darling. Always survival."

Chapter 21

It took a few days to return to the Nest. They'd take a couple weeks' break before they headed onto the eastern Settlements, including the newly conquered Rockland. They emptied their wagon of supplies, with food going to the kitchens, clothes to Lana and the women to sort, and so on. The largest two wooden boxes were full of weapons.

"Dom will get those," Cade said to Asha when he noticed her staring at them. "He'll make sure they're stored safely."

"Why do we need so many?" she asked. "Most people in the Nest have guns, even if those outside don't."

"But there's always room for more, right?" Cade joked, but it didn't quite reach his eyes. Asha got the strange impression he wasn't being entirely honest.

He distracted her with a kiss that took her breath away, backing her up against the near-empty wagon.

"Now that we're home," he murmured in her ear, "I plan to use our bed to its full advantage. No more sleeping on the edge for me."

Asha laughed. "You're getting cocky, soldier."

He nuzzled his nose against hers in the sappiest gesture she'd ever seen him make, and that only made her laugh more.

"You're melting into a puddle right in front of me," she teased.

"I know," he said with a shrug. "I just don't care. I'm long since gone for you, my angel."

Is this what it's like to be happy? Asha wondered. Being with Cade like this made life far more bearable than it'd seemed otherwise.

When they got back into the house, Cade kissed her again, pressing her against the wall, and she moaned into his mouth. They both jumped at a knock on the door, and Asha groaned in protest when Cade moved to answer it. He grinned at her.

"Lana," he said in greeting, and stepped aside to admit her. "What a nice surprise."

Lana's strawberry blonde hair was up in a messy bun, and Asha liked how the stray pieces framed her pretty, peaches-and-cream complexion. She found it hard to look away from Lana's lush, full lips.

"Just came to see how the first trip was for Asha," Lana replied kindly, touching Cade's bicep. She was carrying a covered basket in her arms. "You look like you're doing well, Cade. Travel agrees with you."

"I agree," he replied, with a wry look in Asha's direction. "You look pretty good yourself, darling. You've got some colour on your skin."

Lana rolled her eyes. "Well, you always tease me about being so pale."

Darling. Asha bristled. She didn't like when he called anyone else that now, though it hadn't bothered her before. She'd seen him call women, children, and animals *darling* from the moment she met him. He probably barely even registered doing it.

But it felt special now. She didn't want him to think of anyone else like that.

What was wrong with her that she cared so much? It meant nothing.

But what if it means something? she couldn't help worrying anyway.

"You look good too, Asha," Lana said, putting her hand on Asha's shoulder and sending an electric current through her body. "Was it nice traveling to the Settlements? I've never been."

"Never?" Asha repeated, surprised.

"Women aren't allowed. Present company excluded," Lana replied with a sweet smile, and in a surreal moment, Asha realized that Lana actually admired her for breaking the mold. She probably saw Asha as *adventurous.* How strange.

"I thought I'd make us all dinner," Lana continued. "The other girls will be alright without me for one evening. I want to hear all about how the trip went."

"That's nice of you," Cade said with a smile, looking over at Asha. "Isn't it, Asha?"

Why did it seem like he was taunting her?

"Yes," Asha said slowly. "I'd like that."

Dinner turned out to be a lot of fun. They made a hearty stew with day-old bread from the kitchens, and everything was delicious. Lana was her usual sweet, affable self, and all in all, Asha enjoyed herself. If only she hadn't been analyzing the friendly looks between Lana and Cade the entire time.

Lana left shortly after, and there was an uneasy silence between them in her absence. Cade still sat across from Asha at the table, sipping on his water, looking utterly unaware of the brewing tension inside her. Finally, she couldn't stand it anymore.

"You and Lana seem close," Asha said, trying to sound casual. A strange, churning discomfort had started in her gut that she didn't understand. She'd never felt it before.

Cade shrugged. "She's a friend. I'm glad the two of you get along."

Asha kept her eyes down, but she could feel her features hardening. The thought of Lana in Cade's bed, her lips against his, her soft, pale thighs wrapped around his powerful body...

She was torn between the urge to bleach her brain and the unsettling desire to get herself off.

"What's up?" Cade asked, ending the fantasy. When she glanced up, he was looking at her with a raised eyebrow.

"Nothing," she huffed. "I'm fine."

He scoffed. "You're not. What's on your mind?"

A brief, tense pause. Then, "Have you slept with her?"

Cade frowned. "Is that what you're worried about?"

"You like her," Asha said, more accusatory than she intended.

He barked an incredulous laugh. "Green is a lovely colour on you, darling."

"I'm not jealous," she shot back, convincing no one. "And you didn't answer the question."

He shrugged. "We hooked up once, when I first came to the Nest. One night, just sex. We had fun, but nothing more came of it."

Asha felt another pang of jealousy, along with another painful bolt of heat that shot directly to her pussy. She was caught between hatred that Cade may have ever had feelings for Lana and keen, erotic curiosity about what they'd been like together. And what it might be like to be *with* them.

It was altogether very confusing, so her tone may have been sharper than she intended when she said, "Did you break up with her?"

"We were never together, so there was no need. What's got you all upset? You want me all to yourself?"

Yes, Asha thought, but then the image of Lana's big, soft thighs resurfaced. *And no.*

She stood up, unsure what to do with herself. "I just saw the way you look at her, that's all."

Cade's eyebrows shot up, and he sat back in his chair.

"And what about the way *you* look at her, huh?" he asked, his gaze darkening. "You thought I wouldn't notice how you watch her lips when she talks? Or the way you smiled when she touched your arm? How you like it when she flirts with you?"

Asha opened her mouth, but no words formed. She closed it, feeling suddenly parched.

"I don't know what you mean," she said, but her throat was so dry that it almost came out as a whisper.

His small smile was predatory. "Oh, I think you do. Tell me, how wet are you right now?"

He said it conversationally, as though asking about the weather. A wave of mortification swept over her.

"I'm not," Asha answered primly, smoothing her shirt.

She moved to walk past him, but he caught her wrist in a tight grip.

"Asha," he said, and his tone was the same commanding, clipped one he used to give orders, "you're going to show me. Right now."

Her nipples peaked as Cade pushed his chair away from the table. She couldn't help meeting his wicked gaze, filled with amusement and arousal. He stood with agonizing slowness, tormenting her.

"Bend over," he murmured, his hands curling around her hips. He eased her onto the table, face down. "Keep your hands at your sides."

His silky, authoritative tone sent shivers down Asha's spine, and as usual, it made her want to give him what he wanted. She breathed deeply through her nose as he took his time unfastening her pants and pushing them to her knees. Bare-assed and desperate for relief from the pulsing heat in her pussy, she whimpered as Cade sunk two thick fingers inside her.

"Oh, greedy girl, you're soaked," he crooned. "Lana gets you that worked up, huh? I don't know whether to be jealous or fucking hard. What do you think?"

He pumped his fingers, and Asha squeaked out, "Both. Oh God, both."

Cade's dark chuckle prickled her skin with awareness. "Is that you too, my angel? Jealous and sopping wet?"

"Yes," she croaked, and he rewarded her with a third finger. "Oh fuck, yes, sir. I hate the idea of you together, but I-I also..."

"You also what?" When she didn't respond, he stopped, and she let out an embarrassing whine. "Tell me, or I'll punish you by leaving you high and dry. Your choice."

Asha took a deep breath, then said in a rush, "I also want you both. So badly."

Cade made a sound of approval deep in his throat.

"Good girl, telling me what you want," he growled, and his fingers disappeared as she heard him fumble with his belt. A minute later, she moaned wantonly as he slid his rigid cock into her and started to fuck her.

He settled one hand on her hip, holding her steady, and the other squarely on her back, pressing her firmly against the table. She loved his gentle restraint, the way it paradoxically made her feel safe. He had her. He wouldn't let go unless she gave the word.

Pleasure surged through her as his hips sped up, and delicious pressure built at her core. The sloppy, erotic sound of their bodies slapping against the table stoked the flame of her desire ever higher.

"Can't help myself," Cade said between thrusts, suddenly sounding hoarse. "Thinking of you with her. I keep going back and forth between wanting to tell you that you belong to *me*, that nobody else can *ever* fucking touch you...and wanting to order you to eat her pussy while I watch."

Asha imagined Lana, legs splayed wide and head thrown back, as she licked her perfect pink clit...and knowing Cade stood over them, watching, stroking his substantial cock. The image was almost too much, and she mewled helplessly against the table, her pussy pulsing around him. She was so *close*.

"Oh, fuck," Cade grunted, feeling her tighten. "My little slut loves that thought, huh? Making her come with your mouth, all because I told you to?"

"Yeah, yeah," Asha babbled. "I love it. I want it."

"You want to come, my angel?"

"*Yes*," she sobbed. "So bad. Need to rub my clit. Please, sir."

"You have permission."

With another sob, she maneuvered her hand between her thighs. It was an awkward and uncomfortable position, her arm underneath her against the table, but it didn't matter. A few strokes were all it took to send her over the edge, crying out against the hard wood surface. Her whole body arched to meet the wave of euphoria head on, obliterating any sense of time or space. It was only in this moment of utter bliss that she felt no inhibition, no self-consciousness—only raw, primal pleasure, followed by a strange tranquility that she treasured.

"That's it, darling," Cade murmured roughly, and his approval brought a second wave of pleasure. "Shit, you look so perfect, coming on my cock. Do it again."

His demand increased the heat in her body, even after she'd already come. Despite her discomfort, she obediently began to rub her clit again, desperate for more. She gasped as he grabbed a handful of her hair, twisting it in his fist as he fucked her. The small pinpricks of pain in her scalp only enhanced her pleasure.

"Tell me what you want with me and Lana," Cade gritted out. "Now. Before I can't stop."

Asha took a sharp intake of breath and squeezed her eyes shut. The pressure of his thrusts was almost too much, right on the edge between pleasure and pain.

"I want to lick her pussy while you fuck me, just like this."

Her voice was a whimper, and she cried out as her pussy pulsed around him, her orgasm working through every muscle in her body. A second later, Cade groaned as he came, filling her in deep, hard surges.

"You really are something else, my angel," he breathed.

They took a moment to recover before Cade released her. She felt loose and boneless, barely able to move from her position on the table. He helped her sit in one of the metal dining chairs, then left to retrieve the water jug they kept for washing, and they cleaned up.

After, he massaged her scalp, soothing any discomfort from when he'd grabbed her hair, and she sighed. She liked the way he took care of her after sex, especially after their more intense encounters. He never said much during these quiet moments, but his small acts of care spoke louder than words.

She'd never thought she could feel like this about anyone, let alone a man who'd started out by buying her at a slave market. She treasured the sight of Cade's face when she woke up next to him. He made her believe in a better tomorrow just by existing—something she never would've dreamed possible.

"Are you alright?" Cade asked, without stopping the massage. "You look a little spacey."

"Yeah. Maybe for the first time, I really am."

She sealed her words with a kiss that held her whole heart within it, and he returned it—slowly, tenderly, sweetly.

"Maybe I am, too," he whispered a moment later, leaning his forehead against hers. "Was all that just dirty talk, darling, or would you like me to share you? Because...I might have unlocked a new kink there. One I didn't even know I had."

Asha laughed and kissed him again. "It wasn't just talk. Not if you don't want it to be."

He paused for a moment, staring in her eyes. "Not your heart, though. I don't want to share that. I've worked too hard to capture it for myself."

"Is that so?" she murmured, and she couldn't stop smiling. "Well...I don't think there's much chance of it escaping now, anyway."

Cade grinned in a way that warmed her all over, and Asha couldn't stop smiling.

Chapter 22

"Happy birthday, darling," Cade murmured in Asha's ear, the morning before they had to leave for the next phase of their trip with the Blackguard. They'd spent the last two weeks training during the day, and filling their nights with more of each other: more exploration of their limits; more pleasure; more pain; more submission. Asha was discovering a part of herself that she never knew existed, and she loved that it was with him.

The night before, he'd made good on his promise from weeks before and tied a clean rag around her mouth, gagging her while he teased and punished her in equal measure. He'd whipped her ass nearly raw, letting her scream herself almost hoarse through her gag. Asha was surprised once again by how much pain thrilled her in this context, with Cade's filthy mouth and his intoxicating touch.

"Don't speak, my angel," he'd murmured, stroking her abused skin as she whimpered. "I prefer your screams right now."

He licked up a tear that ran down her cheek, then made her come so hard she felt cross-eyed, moved almost to delirium with the pleasure and the pain, melding together into a symphony of intensity that she never wanted to end.

That morning, for the first time, Cade had allowed them to sleep in. They lay naked under the covers in bed, and Asha groaned as he spooned her and kissed along the back of her neck. She stretched like a cat under his touch, and he chuckled against her soft brown skin.

"It's not my birthday," Asha replied. "But if it means you'll keep doing that, I'll pretend it is."

He laughed again, his tattooed arms closing around her.

"Leo and I did our best to calculate the days. It's as close to your birthday as it can be, so I'm calling it that."

She rolled onto her back, looking up at him. "Does that mean I get a present, then?"

He smiled and kissed her, slow and deep. "You'll just have to see. But first, training drills." He gave her ass a playful spank and got up.

Asha hid her head under the covers. "That's my present? Training drills? You really are the worst."

Cade laughed and pulled the covers off her. "It's what I'm best at: being the worst. And whipping your ass into shape. In more ways than one."

She rolled her eyes and got out of bed at last. The day was filled with more tedious drills and a trip to the shooting range. To her surprise, Cade ducked out early, explaining that he had something to take care of. She gave him a suspicious stare; he hadn't said anything to her beforehand.

"Let me finish up," she told him, "and I'll go with you."

"Oh, no," Cade replied with a sly smile. "You still have a few runs to finish on the obstacle course. I'll see you at dinner."

He left her staring after him. *Tyrant.*

She finished her training a half hour later and decided to use the women's bathing room in the clubhouse since it was closer. She was planning to pounce on Cade when she got home. Soon, they'd be camping outdoors again with no privacy, so it was now or never.

When she returned to the house, she was surprised that Lana greeted her at the door. Her strawberry blonde hair was loose and flowing down her back, as usual looking so sleek and perfect that it defied logic, living in the Wasteland, where dirt and grime were ubiquitous. She wore a form-fitting off-white dress that hugged her luscious curves in a way that made Asha want to touch them, to feel the planes of her beautiful, voluptuous body and the velvet, alabaster skin that hid beneath the garment. *Ugh, how is she looking even better than usual?*

"A little birdy told me it was your birthday," Lana said with a wink. "So, I came for a visit."

Asha flushed like a schoolgirl, partly because she was remembering the interlude between her and Cade the last time Lana had visited. *He's so doing this to taunt me,* she thought with amusement and annoyance.

Desperate, horny annoyance. *And yet I'm still hoping for a repeat after she leaves.*

"Thank you," Asha replied brightly as she stepped inside. "It's not a big deal, really, but it's nice of you to stop by. Will you join us for dinner?"

She'd only taken a couple steps before she realized that Cade was seated at the dining table, leaning back in his chair and watching her with a catlike slyness in his eyes.

"Happy birthday again, my angel," he said, his voice low and husky. "I hope you like your present."

Asha frowned and turned back toward Lana, only to be met by Lana's soft, cushiony lips. Her scent was rosewater and strawberry—like heaven. She smelled so good that Asha wanted to cry, especially after spending months smelling sweaty, barely-washed men. The kiss was slow and sensuous, unassuming, but had a wantonness to it that left Asha breathless.

Asha broke away, a little alarmed. "What—"

"You're right, Cade," Lana said dreamily. "She does taste lovely."

He grinned wolfishly in response. Asha looked at him with bewilderment, and he walked to her and took her hands in his.

"It's up to you," he said, his voice gentling, "but I asked Lana if she might like to make one of your dreams come true for your birthday."

Asha looked back to Lana, who gave her a sweet smile. "Cade here told me you got a little crush on me, sugar. That true?"

Asha flushed even deeper before replying, in a small voice, "Yes." She ran her hands through her hair, unsure how to react. "So, you want...I mean...all three of us, together?"

"That's the idea," Cade murmured, arranging his arms around her middle and kissing her cheek. "You don't have to do anything, but..."

"What's Lana getting out of it?" Asha asked, her brow furrowing. "I mean, I don't want to make you do anything that you—"

Lana smiled wider. "You're not making me do anything. This is for *me*. Being Angel's favourite has its benefits, but getting off isn't usually one of them. I told you: if you want to get off, fuck a woman." She leaned in and pecked Asha's lips, making her heart pound. "So, I expect that you'll be a good girl and help me out."

"Oh, she will be," Cade said, nibbling on the shell of Asha's ear, sending shivers down her spine. "Asha's very...agreeable, when she wants to be. You just have to sweeten her up a little first."

Asha gasped as his lips moved to her neck and his hands to her breasts, gently kneading. Lana watched with rapt attention, drinking in the sight of them, before she moved close again and pressed her lips to Asha's. Sandwiched between them, Asha sighed and sunk into the kiss, allowing herself to be consumed by Cade's hard steel and Lana's pillowy softness. She felt a powerful tug of arousal at her core as Lana's hands moved into her hair, pulling her deeper, right as Cade's teeth dragged over the fragile skin of her throat.

It should be illegal for two people to be this hot. Holy fuck.

"Touch me, sugar," Lana urged in a sultry whisper between kisses. "You've wanted to, haven't you?"

"Yeah," Asha murmured breathlessly, then lifted her hand to Lana's hair, running her fingers through it. As expected, it was soft as spun silk, and Asha followed it to Lana's substantial breasts. Hesitantly, watching Lana's expression, she cupped one breast through the dress and found the nipple with her thumb. She stroked gently in circles.

To her delight, Lana gave a delicious moan, her head leaning back. She shimmied her dress down to reveal her breasts, full and supple, with dark pink nipples that pebbled under Asha's curious touch. Asha lifted both hands to rub the pink peaks, making Lana moan more and lean into her.

Asha gasped as Cade gently bit the delicate, sensitive spot between her neck and shoulder. His cock was like a brand against her lower back, stiff and unyielding.

"You can do better than that, my angel," he rumbled in her ear. "Make Lana's trip here worth her while, hmm? She came here just for you...the least you can do is let her use your mouth."

He fisted his large hand into Asha's hair, cupping the back of her head and guiding her face down to Lana's breast.

"That's it," Lana murmured as Asha tentatively swiped at her nipple with her tongue. "Open for me."

She held Asha's face in her hands, so gently that it touched Asha's heart. She opened her mouth, and Lana guided her to her breast, fitting the hard nipple between her lips. Asha suckled obediently, and

Lana's sharp gasp of pleasure sent shivers of arousal through her. She could already feel moisture leaking out onto her innermost thighs.

"Ah, you're the sweetest thing," Lana sighed, cradling Asha's head as she continued to suck. "Don't you think, Cade?"

Cade hummed his agreement. Asha could still feel his erection pressed against her ass as he slowly rubbed himself against her. She felt his gaze as Lana guided her head to the opposite breast, and he made a small sound—almost a tiny whimper—as she sucked the other nipple into her mouth.

Each pull into Asha's mouth made Lana sigh and tilt back, forcing more of her breast past Asha's lips. Asha moaned as her mouth was filled to capacity, and Lana stroked her hair affectionately. She longed to grind against Cade, against Lana, against both of them—anything to relieve the awful, pleasurable ache that engulfed her entire body, but the awkwardness of her position wouldn't allow it. Instead, she was left to mewl helplessly as Cade tugged her up by her hair and moved her back and forth between Lana's breasts, alternating sucking on each nipple. Being forced to pleasure Lana and neglect her own needs ignited a new spark of arousal and frustration inside her.

"There's a good girl, pleasing your friend," Cade purred. His approval sent an instant bolt of heat to Asha's pussy, and she groaned, her mouth full. "What else can we do to put that smart mouth to good use?"

There was a wicked undertone in Lana's voice as she said, "I can think of something. You want me to use your mouth some more, sweetness?"

She stroked Asha's cheek, and Asha made an eager sound, unable to help herself. Anything to end this, which was becoming less a pleasure and more a torture.

Cade chuckled. "See? She's a willing little slut once you soften her up."

More heat, more pressure at her core; the combination of Cade's harder, more direct brand of dominance and Lana's softer, sweeter version was tantalizing. Lana cupped her chin and lifted Asha off her breast, kissing her again before she and Cade led her back to the bedroom.

Once there, both of them had their hands all over her, and for a moment, it was simply a blur of hands and lips. Cade grabbed Asha's jaw in his hand, squeezing lightly as he pulled her into a hot, needy kiss, spearing his tongue past her lips. Lana's hands were on her breasts, fondling her nipples through her shirt, and she groaned into Cade's mouth.

They lay her out on the bed and stripped away her clothes, kissing and nibbling and sucking as her skin was exposed. They left her wearing nothing but Cade's dog tags, and her pussy fluttered as they each took a nipple, greedily suckling at her until she arched and moaned with abandon. Her body was on fire.

"Please," she mumbled, desperation leaking from every pore. "I need—"

"You don't need anything yet," Cade chided with a dark, cruel chuckle. "Don't be selfish now, Asha. You need to take care of your guest first."

"He's right," Lana purred. "But you're such a sweetheart, I bet you'll hold still for me, won't you?"

Asha swallowed hard and nodded, though her pussy burned. Lana undressed, and that body-skimming dress still hadn't done her justice. Her skin was peaches and cream all over, her ample hips curved and round, with a smattering of that same strawberry blonde hair over a perfect, dark pink pussy.

She's fucking beautiful.

"Like what you see?" Lana said with a knowing smile, and Asha nodded again, unable to form words. "I'm going to sit on your face, sugar. Lie back for me."

Asha gawked at her, and Lana giggled.

"Any objections?" Cade murmured by Asha's ear before kissing down her neck.

Asha's heart tugged. He was making sure she was okay, that she still wanted this. He knew they'd thrown a lot at her at once, and it'd been a surprise. Thankfully, she'd never wanted anything so much in her entire life.

"No," Asha replied softly. "I...want it."

"Good," he whispered with a small smile. "Tap her thigh three times if you need your safeword."

He moved to her lower half, out of Lana's way, then said slyly, "Give your guest your full attention."

Asha found herself between Lana's plush, generous thighs as she lowered herself over Asha's face. Her pretty clit was just an inch from Asha's lips, stirring a fierce need in her. Asha gave it a long lick, and the taste of Lana's pussy almost undid her right then and there.

"Yes," Lana sighed, her hips sinking deeper so that Asha's mouth was inevitably pressed against her pussy. She fisted her hands into Asha's long black hair, holding onto handfuls as she ground herself slowly against Asha's tongue. "Such a pretty darling. You gonna make me come?"

Asha moaned helplessly as Lana used her mouth, angling her this way and that. It took her a minute to find a rhythm, but Asha licked long strokes up and down, paying attention to Lana's sighs and moans, the way she sped up and rode her tongue harder with certain movements.

Just when she thought she was getting it right, that Lana was close, Asha gasped at the invasion of a tongue in her own pussy. Cade licked up through her folds, lazy and relaxed, and she quivered. He swirled his tongue in circles over her clit, bathing it with sensual attention, and her head felt fuzzy, and then...

Smack. Asha's scream was muffled against Lana as Cade gave her pussy a sharp slap.

"No coming yet," he growled. "For every other second that Lana hasn't come, you'll be getting a slap on this wet, eager pussy as punishment. So, I suggest you hurry it up."

Asha whimpered as he lowered his tongue to her clit again, repeating the motion that turned her legs to jelly. He wasn't going to make it easy for her—how could she focus with his mouth between her legs?

"You can do it, sweetness," Lana said, sounding hoarse. "I'm...almost there. Be a good girl and finish me off now."

Smack. Asha squealed again, white-hot sparks of pain fading into a hot, pleasurable ache that consumed her every thought. She forced herself to focus, to return to licking Lana enthusiastically as Lana rode her mouth.

Smack. Asha squeezed her eyes shut against the keen sting, letting Lana angle her the way she needed. *Smack.* Tears pricked her eyes, and she considered using her safety signal, but she didn't want this to end. The intensity, the contrast of pleasure and pain, was so profoundly wonderful that she couldn't get enough.

Smack. In a bid of desperation, Asha fastened her lips over Lana's clit and sucked hard, in and out, hollowing out her cheeks. Lana's back arched, and she came apart with a sharp cry, bucking her hips and coating Asha's tongue. Asha moaned helplessly beneath her, lapping at her pussy and swallowing her cum.

"Ah, sweet girl," Lana sighed as she carefully maneuvered off Asha. "Your mouth is heaven."

Asha's clit was still burning from Cade's slaps, and her only response was a whimper. She'd been teased past the point of reason, but Cade's crooked smile told her that he wasn't done being cruel just yet.

"Very good," he said in a low, dangerous tone. "But I don't think we've used you enough yet. What do you think, Lana?"

Lana practically purred in response. "Hmm. I think I could go for another. And she hasn't given you any yet. I'd like to see you come on her ass."

She held Asha's jaw in her hand, squeezing her cheeks.

"But—" Asha protested, though she knew it wouldn't matter.

"Don't be rude to our guest, Asha," Cade interjected, abruptly flipping her over. "Show her how *welcoming* you can be. Even when it's...inconvenient."

His amusement broke through on the last word, and Asha wanted to scream in frustration. He was so enjoying this little dance—dangling her fantasy in front of her, giving her a taste and then pulling back before she could be satisfied. He liked keeping her in this state of want and ache, because it meant she was always at his mercy.

Why did she like it so much?

Lana lay back on the bed, splaying her legs wide. Asha took an unsteady breath at her unvarnished beauty, perfectly displayed. Cade grabbed Asha's jaw, pulled her face to one side, and kissed her forcefully. She groaned as he squeezed her breast and plundered her mouth. She leaned into him automatically, realizing he was naked now, too. His rigid cock pressed sharply against her ass, and his muscular frame reminded her that he had a harder, rougher beauty all his own.

Cade released her and patted her cheek before saying in a low voice, "You're safe, darling. Same signal as before, okay?"

Again, Asha's heart warmed at his reminder. He so badly wanted this to be a great experience for her; she felt it. *Let me show you how good it can be,* he'd said on their first night together. He'd certainly made good on that promise.

She nodded, and he gave her one more kiss. "Then get on all fours, my angel. Make this easy for me."

It was embarrassing how eagerly she obeyed him, crawling between Lana's spread thighs on her hands and knees. Lana giggled and stroked her cheek, pulling her closer. Asha moaned as her tongue made contact with Lana's clit; she was so wet, so deliciously aroused. Right as she settled into a new rhythm, Asha gasped as Cade pressed the head of his cock into her slick pussy.

He paused briefly, letting her adjust, before pushing in farther, harder, until he was encased inside her. Asha moaned again at the snug fit, at the feel of him stretching her. She was so wet that any stimulation made her want to sob with relief.

"You're fucking soaked," Cade grunted, blowing out a breath. "Jesus, Asha. You're liking this so damn much."

Asha made a sound she hoped was assent. Her mouth was a little busy. She gave a small cry as Cade began to fuck her, thrusting into her hard and fast. He groaned and gasped as her pussy fluttered around him, and she ached for contact on her clit, but he wouldn't give it to her. She had to settle for the deep, pulsing rhythm of his cock, and the way Lana squirmed under her tongue.

"Fuck, Asha," Cade growled through gritted teeth. "How is your pussy this perfect?"

Soon, it was all too much, and Asha felt she would break into a million pieces if she didn't get relief soon. She sucked on Lana's clit, gently building the pressure until the other woman arched against her once more, coming with a string of moans. Half a second later, Cade pulled out with a wet gasp, and Asha felt the warm splash of his semen on her ass.

"She looks even prettier wearing your cum," Lana said breathlessly, and Asha thought she might spontaneously combust. They'd tortured her.

Cade retrieved a towel to clean her up, and even that light contact made Asha mewl in protest. He and Lana both chuckled.

"The poor thing," Lana said, clucking her tongue. "I don't think we have a choice but to put her out of her misery. She *has* been good."

"Couldn't agree more."

In a flash, Asha found herself on her back again. Cade caught her lips in a deep, drugging kiss, and his hand cupped her breast, pinching her nipple between his fingers. Lana spread languid kisses over her chest, heading south. Cade's hand followed her, settling between Asha's thighs.

Asha kissed him back hungrily, spreading her legs in eager anticipation. She sobbed with relief as two of his thick fingers sunk into her aching pussy. He pumped out a slow, steady rhythm that felt unbearably good. A second later, Asha moaned as Lana's tongue swept over her clit in quick, unrelenting strokes.

Together, they stoked her flame ever higher, until she was sobbing desperately, right at the brink. Then waves of euphoria crashed over her endlessly, bathing her in a restless, all-consuming pleasure that overwhelmed every other sensation. Her vision whited out, and she floated on a cloud of carnal bliss.

When her awareness returned, her body was loose and heavy, and she felt barely conscious. Her eyelids fluttered.

"Cade," she said softly, and she heard his low chuckle by her ear.

"I'm still here," he said, sounding amused, and he kissed her cheek. "You came so hard you went to another universe for a second there, hmm?"

Lana giggled. "Those are the best kind."

Asha was too tired to reply. She felt the mattress shift as Lana got up. She was gone for a few minutes, leaving Cade to pull Asha into his arms. He massaged her shoulders, then held her close to his body as she drifted.

"My sweet angel," he murmured against her hair. "You did so well. So responsive, so submissive. So beautiful and sexy. This was definitely one for the spank bank."

Despite her exhaustion, Asha couldn't help bursting into giggles. "Pardon me? Your *spank bank*?"

"I know you have one, too—I've been making sure of that this summer," Cade replied, but he was laughing too, in a low, sweet way that made Asha feel like he'd wrapped her in a warm blanket. She loved his humour, loved the way he held her so close and made her feel so safe in a world that was anything but. The way he'd broken down her walls not by barreling through them, but by patient, careful dismantlement.

I love him. The thought should've alarmed her, but it didn't. She was far too warm and relaxed for that. It just felt right, like the sky being blue or two plus two equaling four. He'd earned her love, and more importantly, her trust, at every awful, painstaking turn. He deserved her heart more than anyone she'd ever known.

"Did you enjoy yourself, darling?" Cade asked in an intimate whisper, pressing a kiss against her head. "You felt good? Safe?"

"Uh-huh," Asha mumbled sleepily. "So good. Thank you...for everything."

"My pleasure," he breathed, kissing her hair again. She snuggled close to his chest, perfectly content to let him cradle her.

"I'm gonna head out," Lana said in a stage-whisper. She must've cleaned up and fetched her clothes. "Thank you both for a lovely evening."

"Thank *you*," Cade replied, stroking Asha's hair. "Not to jump to conclusions, but...I think she liked the present."

Lana's soft, tinkly laugh was the last thing Asha remembered before she finally succumbed to exhaustion.

Chapter 23

The next few weeks on the road flew by with surprising swiftness. They passed through the remaining settlements to collect the rents, including a surprising number of weapons, but when Asha inquired about it, Cade merely shrugged and said that Angel had requested them. He wouldn't elaborate beyond that.

Their final stop was the recently conquered Rockland, and though she tried to prepare herself for what they'd encounter, Asha still wasn't ready. The settlement was largely intact, save for a few homes that'd been reduced to rubble. But it was the people—their furtive glances, simmering with resentment—that really bothered her. They didn't welcome the Blackguard the way the other settlements had.

Why would they? Asha thought to herself. *We're their conquerors.*

Cade conducted his business with ruthless efficiency, even in the face of the residents' icy demeanour. He ignored them, acted as though it didn't bother him one bit, and something about it disturbed Asha. She didn't like when he slipped from the warm, charming man she knew into this cold, calculated military commander. She knew that that was how he'd survived this long, and that he'd achieved his rank back at the Delta because he was good at it. Moreover, they'd deliberately hammered him into this blank, domineering shape, like soft metal.

But she still didn't like it. It put her on edge and made her feel like she didn't know him after all...especially because he wouldn't fuck her those nights that they stayed at Rockland. He'd been perfectly happy to oblige her on their other stops, but here, he remained brooding and unreachable, even to her. Something was on his mind.

Asha discovered what it was on their final day. They'd packed up the wagon again and were preparing to return to the Nest when Cade approached the wagon with three young women in tow.

All three had their hands loosely bound in front of them, and they glanced nervously at Asha before climbing aboard the wagon and sitting on top of wooden crates of goods as though they themselves were cargo. It took only a split second for the horrible truth to dawn on her.

They were from the local slave market, and they *were* cargo, for all intents and purposes. They now belonged to Angel.

Cade gave the signal to move out, and the horse set off, pulling the wagon. The Blackguard surrounded it to guard the cargo. Everyone was acting like what had just occurred was the height of normalcy.

Because it is, Asha thought desperately. *Because they do this every. Single. Time.*

She ran to Cade, who avoided her eyes and kept walking behind the cart.

"You can't be serious," Asha said in a low voice, trying not to let the girls in the wagon overhear. "You can't do this."

Cade fixed her with an impassive stare. "It's not my decision, Asha. I'm doing a job."

"Like *hell* it's not your decision," she shot back in a furious whisper. "You could refuse. You could resist. You could do anything besides what you're doing right now. Enabling this. Enabling *him.*"

"Sure, and I could also commit suicide," Cade replied, deadpan. "But I don't see how that would help either of us."

"Don't give me that glib garbage." She felt on the verge of tears. "At a certain point, you stop getting the benefit of the doubt, soldier. At a certain point, your inaction becomes an endorsement. You can't act like you're above all this, that you hate it, or that you care at all about me, when *this* is what you keep choosing. What you keep allowing to happen."

This finally seemed to affect him. His eyes softened with hurt, then hardened again with anger, and that only inflamed her temper further.

"Of course I care about you," Cade hissed. "I *don't* like this, darling...but this is part of survival out here."

The audacity of him acting wounded when he was literally *giving these girls to Angel* outraged her.

"Fuck you," Asha spat. "You and the rest of them."

She sped up to join the others and refused to look at him again for the rest of the trip.

Even when they arrived back at the Nest, things weren't the same between them. Asha refused to look at Cade, refused to speak to him. Unfortunately, the effectiveness of her freezeout was dimmed by the fact that he was never home in the evenings anymore. After training in the afternoons, he disappeared until bedtime and refused to explain where he was going or what he was doing.

She hated how much she missed him in spite of how angry she was with him. She hated that she was so hopelessly in love with a man who would save her from trafficking and then turn around and facilitate the same treatment for someone else.

Two of the women they'd brought with them went to live in the wider Guardian territory outside the Nest. Only one went to live with Lana and the other unattached women. Her name was April, and she was a pretty brunette with cute freckles and a sweet smile. Asha had seen her when she'd been visiting with Lana in the evenings.

"We're looking after her," Lana had said by way of reassurance. "She has a bed, and food, and a family now. That's better than what she had before, Asha. I know you don't think so—"

"It's not that I don't think so," Asha said with a sigh. "It's that I *cannot* accept that this is the best that any of you—or me—can hope for. That's all."

Lana gave her that soft, sympathetic look that she reserved for those moments when she thought Asha was being adorably naïve. Asha hated it.

Finally, a week after their return, Cade came home with her at dinnertime, and she resolved to confront him.

"You look like you're about to chew me out over there, darling," he said wearily.

"Of course I am," Asha snapped. "What—"

He held up a hand. "I'm sorry I've been gone so much. I—"

"Don't interrupt me. You being gone is the *least* of your crimes. We still haven't talked about the three girls you brought here a week ago."

Cade sighed. "I know. Trust me, I *know.*"

He sounded so defeated, and Asha hated the pang of sympathy it inspired in her. Because she saw, if she tried, how he, too, was trapped now, ensnared in Angel's web. Angel wasn't the sort of man to let anyone escape, or to tolerate disloyalty. He played mind games, and he pitted people against each other on purpose to dominate them.

It didn't absolve Cade. Not one bit. He had far more power than she did. But she could see how someone could get used to anything when they felt their survival was on the line.

"I just *hate* Angel so much," Asha said, her throat thick. "I hate that he can ask you to do these things. I hate that he can dictate so much of our lives, and that he still has so much power over me. It's not enough that he raped me, now he has to control my relationships, too."

Cade reached over and took her hand, and the look in his eyes was deeply empathetic—something she didn't expect.

"What if it wasn't up to him anymore?" Cade said, staring hard at her. "What if we could change things?"

Asha took a step back. "What do you mean?"

"Exactly what I said," he replied, sounding more determined. "Me, Leo, and Dom have been conspiring against Angel for months, darling. Gaining the loyalty of the people of the Settlements. They're ready for a change, and the Blackguard are all on board. That's what I've been working on these last couple months: getting the green light, and getting the supplies to pull it off."

He began to pace the room. "Now that we've collected what we need from the Settlements, we're ready to take them out—a coup d'état. We finally have the weapons we need."

Asha suddenly remembered the alarming number of weapons they'd collected from the Settlements. *That was what they were waiting for.*

"Once we take out Angel and his closest people, the rest will fall in line. But..."

He trailed off, then gave her a pointed look.

"What?" Asha said, a sick feeling beginning in her stomach.

"But we need someone who can get close to him without him suspecting that she's his assassin. Someone he perpetually underestimates. Someone he desires, who'll finally give him what he deserves."

His voice was quiet, and his words were calculated, but they hit her like a lead weight nonetheless.

"No," she said, clipped, and she stood up and turned away from him.

"Asha," Cade said—softer, sweeter, the way he spoke to her after they had sex. She hated that he would use it in this context, to wheedle her into doing this. "I know it's a lot to ask. It's personal. But that's why it has to be you."

"Why?" Asha demanded, whirling around. "Why the fuck would you put me through that? Having to face him again, alone? After what he did to me?" Her throat felt suddenly clogged, and her last words came out almost as a whisper: "After all those nights I shook in your arms, told you everything? How could you—"

Cade moved towards her cautiously, as though approaching an agitated tiger ready to pounce. He held up his hands, palms facing her, in a peace offering.

"Darling, I heard every word you said on those nights," he murmured. "I heard you, and I heard the space between what you wanted to say but didn't feel like you could: that you want this raping, pillaging, murdering asshole to face some justice. That you don't want him to ever be able to hurt anyone again. And that you wish you could see him suffer."

She trembled, hating herself for how emotional she still was about what had been done to her. But Cade had read her right—of course he had. He'd seen what was in her black heart. She didn't want to be the 'bigger person,' in the end. What good did that do? All her life, she'd let people abuse and take advantage of her, and she was done being a victim.

"I'm laying that justice at your feet," Cade said, low and determined. "It's not just that I'm asking a favour, Asha—I also *want* to give this to you. I want you to know, in your bones, that this piece of shit is dead, and that he will never, ever hurt you again."

He put his arms around her, drawing her against him. He rubbed her arms, soothing the shakes that still wracked her body.

"I know what it is to kill a man who took something from you that you can never get back," he continued, his touch gentle, his voice brutal and dark. "How it feels to watch the life leave the eyes of your tormentor. There's no peace quite like that, my angel. The people who ramble on about the morality of revenge never had anyone who destroyed their whole world in one fell swoop."

He lowered his lips to her ear, and there was something sickeningly seductive in his tone as he said, "This is where you use your fire to burn the world, darling, and unlike some, I won't resent you for it. Burn down this ugly world and we'll make a new one together. I'm handing you the match."

It was a pretty picture that he painted: Angel's downfall, the end of his exploitation and cruelty. She imagined him pleading for forgiveness, for mercy, begging her to spare him. The panicked, desperate glint in his eyes. Him feeling even a fraction of the pain and terror he'd inflicted on countless others. And then, his blood pooling under him, his mouth slack, his eyes open and unseeing. The knowledge that he was gone, and that even this post-apocalyptic hellscape was undoubtedly better off without him in it.

"What's your plan?" Asha asked, folding her arms over her chest.

Cade let out a breath. "It's simple. But it'll require some acting on your part."

"Will he suffer?"

He smirked. "Asking the important questions. I like it."

Chapter 24

A few evenings later, Asha left home at the agreed-upon time and headed toward the clubhouse. Despite the August heat, she wore a long, dark coat, buttoned in the front. It belonged to one of the clubhouse girls—a young woman called Nina who was in on the assassination plot. She'd been feeding information to Cade for months, and she loaned Asha her coat and the unusual outfit she wore underneath. Asha didn't want to think too closely about that, or she'd lose her nerve. With her, she carried a bag filled with her belongings...and everything else she needed to complete her mission.

When she arrived at the clubhouse, she sought out Lana, who looked dismayed by her predicament.

"I can't believe that Cade just...dumped you like that," she said with a shake of her head. "You two were so...when we were all together...ugh, I just can't *believe* that man. I thought he was one of the better ones. What the fuck?"

This would be the hardest part for Asha: deceiving Lana, who knew nothing of the plot because Cade had judged her as being too close to Angel. Lana benefited from Angel's rule as his favourite, he'd reasoned, and couldn't be trusted to turn against him, as unfair as that judgment seemed to Asha. She hated lying to her, especially after the incredible night they'd had together, but there was nothing else to be done now.

"There was a lot of stuff behind closed doors," Asha said, and it wasn't difficult for her to look crestfallen, since that was how she'd felt so often in the days after her old life had ended. "I just...I'll talk about it more when I'm ready. Right now, I just want to forget it."

"Of course, sugar," Lana replied, rubbing her upper arm sympathetically. "Let's get you a bunk, and then I'll see about getting Tara to bring you something to eat."

She led Asha to the dormitory and showed her to her old bunk, chattering away about how they'd look after Asha in the wake of Cade ditching her. Asha felt horrible by the end of it, but she had to stick to the plan.

"Do you think you could get me a visit with Angel tonight?" she asked Lana, trying her best to seem sorrowful but resigned.

Lana balked. "Why would you want that? Cade's already been to tell him your new situation, so I—"

"I want to try and smooth things over," Asha said, adding just the right amount of hesitation to her voice. "Things didn't go well with him before, with Cade. And now that I'm unattached, I...I need to appeal to him, don't I? I don't want him to get rid of me."

Lana bit her lip, and Asha knew her words rang true. Currying Angel's favour as an unattached woman was undeniably important in this hellhole, and Lana's silence told her that Angel getting rid of her in the wake of her new status was very much a possibility.

That fucking asshole, she raged, but she forced her mouth into a thin, hard line, suppressing her emotion. He wouldn't be in charge for much longer.

"I can try," Lana said after a moment. "He doesn't always agree to see every girl. Only ones he's interested in."

Asha—and Cade, for that matter—was confident that Angel would agree. The thought of Asha coming to him on bended knee, begging for his favour, would be too tempting a proposition for his sadistic side.

"If you could just ask, that'd be...well, I'd really appreciate it."

Lana kissed her cheek. "Of course. Anything you need, sugar."

She left Asha to get settled into her bunk, and Asha wondered if the bubbling cauldron of guilt in her gut would ever go away.

Lana returned only a half hour later, telling Asha that Angel would see her that night at approximately ten o'clock. She then led Asha to the kitchen to eat, since the evening meal had already been served and cleaned up. On a counter, exactly where Cade had told her it would be, Asha spotted a basket of red wine that they'd brought back from the Settlements.

"You really shouldn't take it too hard, girl," Tara was saying to her as she ladled soup into a bowl. She was a short blonde girl with a sweet disposition. "I always thought Cade seemed kinda stuck up, anyway. With his special soldiers, thinking he's better than everyone else."

Asha's stomach was doing flip-flops, but she merely nodded. Lana remained silent, looking as perturbed as she had earlier at Asha's situation. Asha only hoped she wasn't doubting the story too much.

She ate her soup in silence, sneaking furtive glances at the wine basket. When she finished eating, she went to pick up a bottle.

"Maybe I could bring this to Angel tonight?" she asked Lana, hoping the nervousness in her voice came off as appropriate. "As a peace offering?"

Her guilt returned with a vengeance when Lana gave her a gentle smile and said, "Of course. He likes to be served, and, well, you know his weakness for drink. It might make him a little less..."

"Violent?" Asha offered, unable to help herself.

Lana bit her lip. "Try to get him to drink a couple glasses before you offer yourself."

In no way would she ever offer herself to that man, but Asha nodded as though she appreciated the advice. She sat back at the table and waited for the kitchens to clear out as the women either went to bed or took a rare moment for themselves. Eventually, even Lana left to check on her little sister.

As soon as she was alone, Asha seized the wine bottle and un-corked it. From her bag, she withdrew a smaller bag loaded with a white powder.

"Odourless, tasteless, and invisible once dissolved," Leo had told her in a hushed voice. "It's a powerful sedative and poison, but it'll take some time to achieve full effect. You'll have to stall until then."

Asha took a deep breath. "Alright."

He pressed the bag into her palm and closed her fingers around it.

"Be careful, Asha," he said seriously before he released her. "Do *not* drink the wine. Not even a sip. I have no antidote."

On that ominous note, she'd kissed Cade goodbye.

"While you're with Angel, we'll take care of the rest," he'd said. "After we're done taking out Angel's inner circle, I'll come get you. Don't leave Angel's Wing until I do. Understood?"

She'd nodded, and now, looking around her to make sure there were no witnesses, she dumped the white powder into the wine and sloshed it around so it mixed well. She hadn't thought it would be so easy—that Lana would've asked more questions. But then, that was why Cade had chosen her for this mission: they underestimated her. As a woman in this brutal micro-society, her role was *victim*, not *threat*.

How wrong they would be. She re-corked the bottle with a tool Cade had given her, went to the dormitory, and waited on her bunk for the end of life as she knew it.

I experience way more of those moments than seems fair for one person.

As night fell, Lana made Asha up with her homemade cosmetics and teased her dark hair into a high, voluminous ponytail. Asha did her best to push down her nausea when she saw herself in the cracked mirror on the wall. She hated being painted and sent like a pig for slaughter, but there was no choice. She had to kill Angel before the real fight began. He would be dead before he could rally any of his allies, before he even knew what was happening.

When it was finally time to visit Angel, his new doorman—another mountain of a man who called himself Slade—came to fetch her.

"Get a move on," Slade grunted. "We don't got all night."

Asha was tempted to ask what else Angel had to do that was so important, but she bit her tongue. Instead, she shed the jacket she was wearing, letting it fall back on her bunk. The dress was more like lingerie than clothing: a bright red chemise that highlighted her cleavage and fell just past her ass, paired with black leather boots. What no one could see was the small, sheathed dagger strapped to her inner thigh.

Slade gave a crude whistle. "Lucky Angel. You got extra there for me, sweetie?"

"Yeah," Asha replied, showing him her middle finger. "Right here."

He laughed, she rolled her eyes, and he led her to Angel's Wing. As they stood in front of the blue doors, her heart was pounding in her ears, and the bottom of her stomach felt like it was about to fall out. She hadn't been anywhere near this place since Cade had returned to rescue her from Angel's clutches. She was struck with the urge to run.

But she had a job to do. A role to play.

So, she took a deep breath, pulled herself together, and walked through the door that Slade held open. And when it closed behind her with an ominous *thud,* she focused solely on carrying the wine bottle between her sweaty palms, taking care not to drop it.

Angel was in his bedroom, reclining lazily on the enormous bed. There were empty bottles and cups already strewn about the room, and the strong stench of stale alcohol. His eyes were already somewhat glazed, indicating he'd already been drinking.

"Asha," he said in greeting, a lascivious grin spreading across his horrible features. His eyes scanned her outfit, her body, and Asha immediately felt dirty.

"My favourite lay is back for another date."

It took all of Asha's energy not to react with rage and disgust.

Instead, she wet her lips and said, "It didn't seem like I was your favourite at the time. Isn't that Lana, anyway?"

He shrugged, still grinning. "Lana's good for when I just need a good, mindless fuck. Just a warm, wet hole that lies there and lets me do what I want. But when I want a real *challenge*...well, you gave me the fight of my life, sweet pea. Something real thrilling about that, isn't there?"

She was going to vomit, for Lana as much as herself. Lana, her friend, who was smart and sweet and so fucking sexy, and he described her like a blow-up doll. *Vile.*

"Well, given how things have gone with Cade," Asha said, "I wanted to know if there was anything I could do to...*improve* my situation."

She repeated the lines in just the way she'd rehearsed: a little playful, a little flirty, but not in a way that seemed unbelievable. She wanted to seem like she was *trying* to flatter him. That she was treating it as a transaction. It was what he would expect.

"Yeah, shame about Cade," Angel replied, sounding like he couldn't care less. "Can't imagine that guy fucking you like a real man. Probably says 'please' every time." He scoffed. "Pussy."

Asha elected not to point out that while Cade traveled around doing Angel's dirty work, Angel sat here in this glorified hovel drinking himself to death.

"Can I offer you a drink?" Asha asked in the same flirty way. "You know...before we get started."

She hated his laugh. It was a dry cackle.

"A woman who finally accepts that she's a whore and nothing more," he said, amused. "Willing to *serve.* Maybe I was wrong about Cade."

Asha took the opportunity to turn away from him so he couldn't see the hatred in her expression. She set the wine bottle on a small side table and retrieved one of the empty cups from the floor. As she poured the crimson liquid into the cup, she had to appreciate that Leo had been right: the drug was undetectable.

"Pour one for yourself," Angel said, slurring his words a little. "We're celebrating you getting fucked by a real man."

Asha gritted her teeth, but poured another cup for herself. She presented the glass to him, and he motioned for her to sit on the edge of the bed. Nervous sweat trickling down her spine, she did, fighting fiercely against the flashbacks of all the things that had been done to her the last time she was on this bed.

"To Asha, for finally knowing her place," Angel announced, and to her astonishment, he downed the glass in one swallow. "Another!"

This fucking idiot, Asha thought. She poured him another cupful of the tainted wine and sat down on the bed again. He babbled on for a couple minutes about some conquest he'd had with another woman the night before, and all the heads he'd mounted on his gate back in the day. Meanwhile, she pretended to sip at her wine but kept her lips firmly closed. Angel was either too drunk or too stupid to notice that her cup never emptied.

After another minute, he frowned. "I feel like shit."

Her heart skipped a beat. "Maybe you had too much to drink?"

"Nah, tha's not it," Angel slurred, though it definitely was. She may have drugged him, but he was also already drunk when she arrived. "I...I hold my liquor. Somethin' else."

He squinted at her, and Asha did her best to stare back at him impassively. But it didn't matter. The effects of the drug were gripping him: his jaw slackened, his eyelids drooped, and his eyes had trouble focusing. He knew.

"You...you *poisoned* me!" Angel hissed at her. "You stupid fucking bitch, I'm gonna kill—"

He lumbered toward her on the bed, barely able to keep his balance, but he was big and decently strong. Still, Asha was ready for him this time. She took hold of his hand, outstretched to grab her, and pulled him into an embrace. Her other hand wielded her knife, and in one smooth motion, she plunged the blade up under his ribs, cutting through the soft tissue like butter.

Time froze, and Angel choked on nothing, gasping for breath as she twisted the knife. The look of utter shock on his face—the bizarre look of almost *betrayal*—gave Asha a shot of sweet adrenaline. He didn't scream; Cade had told her that he wouldn't be able to. And that simple fact gave her incredible satisfaction.

Asha withdrew the knife for only half a second before stabbing Angel again, and then again. Hot, sticky blood coated her hands, and something in her relished it. Finally, she pushed him backwards, and he tumbled onto the bed on his back, choking on his own blood. He was incapable of calling out to Slade, or to anyone else, for that matter.

The air was scented with blood and booze, and she was going to let him die like this: bleeding out slowly, knowing before he slipped under the drug's spell that he would never, ever wake up again.

She stood and wiped the blood knife on her skirt, watching him writhe in agony.

"You stupid fucking bitch," Angel croaked again. "You killed us all. You and your boyfriend. You'll see."

Asha's brow furrowed. "What the fuck does that mean?"

"You gonna make a big speech now?" he gasped, ignoring her. "Just kill me. Make—make your boy proud."

The rage that she thought she'd buried surged forth once more, distracting her.

"You think you deserve *mercy*, asshole?" Asha snarled. "After what you've done?"

His weak chuckle sounded like a death rattle, and somehow that made her hate him even more, because she suddenly realized that he didn't consider it a mercy to not hear her grievances. On the contrary, the motherfucker was *bored* by them, and he was asking her to skip the lecture because he didn't care one single iota about what he'd done to her and never would.

The revelation hit her like a slap. Though she'd known, in some way, that Angel was a man who didn't exactly care who he hurt, she thought he'd do what abusers so often did: make excuses, distance himself, obfuscate. But no: this man was telling her, in no uncertain terms, that he saw what he had done, and it simply did not affect him.

Asha trembled with rage and a brokenness that frightened her. Her palms grew sweaty around the knife handle.

"He wants my place," Angel mumbled, his eyes glazed over. "Cade. Always wanted what I had. Power. Riches. Women."

Asha didn't bother to hide her disgust. "He's not like you. And when you're gone, nothing of value will be lost."

"He'll do what needs to be done, in the end. Just like me. Maybe he'll manage what I couldn't: knock you off—"

But he didn't finish, because Asha slit his throat. His eyes went wide in shock for a split second before his whole body slackened, and blood sprayed from him like a firehose.

The light left his eyes, and he was gone.

Asha was covered in his blood, slick with it. Her adrenaline abandoned her, and she fell to her knees on the floor, panting. She sat there for far too long, knowing that at that moment, the Blackguard had begun their bloody coup, killing off Angel's inner circle. She was supposed to wait for Cade to come and get her.

She felt immense relief, just like Cade had promised, that Angel was gone forever. That he could no longer torture her or others. And there was satisfaction, closure, in being the one who delivered what he ultimately deserved. There was satisfaction in the way he'd underestimated her and she'd proved him so very wrong.

However, a sickening dread at his last warning sat like a lead weight in her chest. When she finally stood and turned back toward the door, her heart stopped. She hadn't noticed it on her way in; she'd been too nervous. Now, all at once, she was terrified.

Because there, pinned to Angel's door, was a black mask emblazoned with the emblem of a golden eye.

Chapter 25

"**S**hit. Shit, shit, shit."

Cade paced the mess hall, where the Blackguard had gathered, bloodstained and battle-worn, to discuss next steps. His expression was stony and a little wild in a way that unnerved Asha. He'd looked like that since Asha showed him the mask nailed to Angel's door, similar to the way it'd been pinned to the door of that house in Applegate.

A message. A threat. A warning.

"Is there anything else you can tell us about them?" Leo pressed Asha again, not for the first time.

"No," Asha replied, frustrated. "I wasn't exactly taking down their names, okay? I was busy running for my fucking life. I don't know what they could've wanted from Angel."

Cade wouldn't stop pacing like an angry tiger. It was driving her crazy.

The Blackguard had sustained few injuries in the coup and no deaths, thanks to the element of surprise. Months of planning had made the operation a complete success; Angel's reign was over. It should've been a moment of celebration. Instead, it felt like they'd suffered a brutal defeat.

"It's nothing good," Cade said, clipped. "If they have control of the compound, they have access to advanced weapons and tech. Vehicles. Guns. Explosives. You name it."

Even though she already knew, Asha's heart sunk at his words.

"So, what do we do, Captain?" Davy asked, his deep skin marred by dried blood.

Cade pinched the bridge of his nose and took a moment before answering.

"Nothing we can do except be ready," he said at last. "First light, everyone here should go out into our territory and tell people to prepare for an assault. Send messengers to the Settlements with the same warning. We don't know where they might hit. In the meantime, if anyone sees anything like *this*—" he held up the mask with the gold eye, "you report to me immediately."

There was a general murmur of assent for this plan.

"For now," Cade continued, tossing the mask back on the table, "those of you on guard duty, report to your posts. The rest of you, go to bed. You were all incredible tonight, and you deserve rest. Good-night."

With that, Cade took Asha by the hand and led her back to their house, where he fucked her against the wall, hard and fast and silent except for their animalistic grunts. Both of them were still sweaty, bloody, and mostly clothed, but it felt like a necessity.

Like it might be their last time.

Two days later, at the crack of dawn, a military truck drove into Guardian territory and stopped at the Nest gate. A guard ran to get Cade, who was still at home with Asha.

The last couple of days had been a blur. They'd established Cade's new authority as leader, and though not everyone had been happy about it, they had enough support for the naysayers to accept it. But Asha had seen Lana crying, and she refused to talk to her. Being the gang leader's favourite and then having that leader dethroned introduced instability that Lana was struggling with. Asha's guilt was never going to go away; she was sure of that now.

"They say they just wanna talk," the guard said, with no small amount of confusion. "I told them you'd meet them in Angel's Wing."

Cade nodded, and Asha hovered nervously as they got ready to leave.

"It'll be okay," he whispered to her, then kissed her forehead. "Whatever they want, we'll figure it out. This is our show now. We make the rules."

Asha nodded, though she didn't for a second believe him. These were the people who murdered everyone she'd ever known, and left Applegate as a ruined husk. They didn't seem like the sort who'd be open to negotiations.

Fearing they may recognize her, Cade made Asha wear his clothes, including his jacket with the hood up. He arranged her hair so it hid most of her face. Wearing Cade's oversized clothes, she didn't look much like she had when she'd lived at the Cave, and to complete the picture, she smeared dirt on her face.

When they entered Angel's old rooms, they were met by Leo and Dom, along with three men in black tactical uniforms, not unlike the ones that the three Delta soldiers had. The key difference was that all three of them wore the black masks painted over with gold eyes. Their own eyes weren't visible, which made the effect that much stranger. They also wore utility belts with portable electronic devices—probably the PIDs that Cade had told her about. She hoped to God that they hadn't tracked her with them.

The man in the middle of the three also wore a black chest plate with gold painted designs that looked vaguely religious in nature. All three masked men were heavily armed with rifles and shotguns.

The air was tense. A shiver went down Asha's spine.

"Clyde Owens," the man with the chest plate said, holding out his hand to Cade, who frowned and didn't take it. "Chief General of the Order of Odessa. We'd been dealing with Angel, but your men tell me that he met a rather unfortunate end. Is that true, Captain?"

The Order of Odessa. Asha had never heard of them in the Cave before the attack. Whoever organized the insurgency, they'd clearly been able to keep it secret.

Cade bristled at the use of his rank, and Clyde laughed.

"Unclench, Captain, it's just what they called you at the gate," he said. "Congratulations on your success. Like Angel was, we hope you'll be...accommodating of the needs of the Prince of Pain."

Cade cocked an eyebrow. "The Prince of Pain? Never heard of him."

There was a hush, almost as though the three men were offended.

"What is it that this 'Prince' needs?" Cade asked, crossing his arms.

Clyde huffed, and Asha braced herself. She couldn't see his face, but she sensed that whatever was coming, it would be bad.

"Bodies," he answered simply. "We know that the Guardians, and all the other worthless gangs in these parts, have a robust slave trade. Angel agreed just days ago to supply us with as many able-bodied slaves as we could handle."

Asha made a sound of horror. This was a nightmare. Cade glanced at her, his eyes hard, silently ordering her to contain herself.

"In exchange for what?" he demanded, pinning Clyde with a look.

Clyde gave another harsh laugh. "For being allowed to exist. Obviously."

Asha's heart pounded hideously in her chest, and she covered her mouth with her hand to stop herself from speaking. Meanwhile, Dom's jaw had clenched and Leo's face had gone white.

"Surely, you know our capabilities, *Captain*," Clyde continued mockingly. "Yes, I know who you are, though I don't know what compound you're from. Can't be from ours—everyone who failed to bow to the Order is dead."

Cade's eyes flicked to Asha for the briefest of seconds before he deliberately looked elsewhere, and Asha had to resist the urge to run. It seemed as though they didn't know she'd survived, and she wanted to keep it that way.

"Since you're a compound military commander, you know the kind of weapons we can employ," Clyde said. "Weapons beyond anything these pitiful Wastelander gangs could dream of. Weapons of mass destruction, suffering, and death. If you choose not to assist the Prince of Pain in his goals, you will be signing your own death warrant, along with everyone else's. Angel—stupid but prudent man that he was—saw the wisdom in complying."

Cade was silent, his teeth gritted, and Asha's fear almost overcame her when she realized that he had no adequate response. How could he? He held the lives of every person here in his hands...yet surrendering so many slaves to Clyde and this strange Order was unthinkable. Everything they'd done up to this point to overthrow Angel's horrific rule would be for nothing. All their best laid plans for liberty and justice would be forfeit.

"Perhaps you need some persuasion," Clyde said, a nasty timbre to his voice, and turned to one of the other masked men. "Malcolm."

Before anyone could react, Malcolm raised a small gun, akin to a taser, and Asha gasped as her chest was pierced by a long needle. She had just enough time to look down and see small dart sticking out of her chest before she fell forward. The skin around the entry wound had already started to feel unnaturally numb, and the sensation was spreading outward.

Leo, to his credit, reacted faster than anyone else. He was at Asha's side in half a second, ripping her jacket open and surveying the damage. She cried out as he slowly worked on extricating the needle from her chest. Cade made a noise that sounded like something between rage and anguish.

"What. Did. You. Do. To. Her?" Cade demanded. She'd never heard him sound so murderous and out of control. "I'll kill you. I'll fucking kill you."

He made a move toward Clyde, but the masked man held up a hand.

"Careful, Captain," he crooned. "It's a fast-acting poison." He withdrew a small, loaded syringe from a pocket on his utility belt. "This is the antidote. I'd be happy to give it to her, if you keep your gang's agreement with us. If you don't, however, I'll be forced to crush this syringe, and she'll die a painful death."

The numbness had spread to Asha's whole body, and her teeth kept clenching involuntarily. Saliva pooled in her mouth and leaked out, and a second later, her body began seizing uncontrollably. Her sense of reality blurred, but she distantly felt Leo turning her onto her side, her mouth facing the floor. More shouting broke out between the two parties.

A moment later, she felt another stab in her left buttock, and heard Cade cursing profusely. She must've blacked out, because the next thing she knew, she was propped up against the wall, and Leo was carefully lifting her eyelids and shining his flashlight into them. Clyde and his friends were gone.

She drew back instinctively, coughing.

"Is she okay?" Cade asked, barely above a whisper. He sounded beside himself.

"She's conscious, which is a good sign," Leo replied, rummaging in his medical bag. "I have no idea what they gave her, but I'll monitor her overnight to determine if there's any lasting neurological damage from the seizure."

"Seemed like a chemical weapon," Dom commented, sounding detached as ever. "Designed to kill quick."

Asha still felt spacey and distant, even when Cade scooped her up into his arms and they headed for Leo's clinic. He held her close to his body, and she realized he was shaking. When they reached the cot in the clinic, he laid her down so gently, tucking her under the blankets with such care.

"Cade," Asha breathed, her vision still a little blurry. "I'm...I think I'm okay. I feel better."

It was true: the numbness in her limbs was slowly fading, and the drooling had stopped. She felt exhausted in the aftermath of the seizure, however.

"That's good," he murmured, low and tender, dropping a kiss on her forehead. "You scared me back there, my sweet angel."

There was a long pause while Leo listened to her heart and lungs and performed some other tests to ensure she was recovering. By the time he finished, Asha was falling asleep. Still, she remembered she had something important to tell Cade, something that couldn't wait.

"Cade?" she whispered, her eyes shut.

"What, darling?"

"Don't give them the slaves. Whatever...happens, don't."

Another pause, and when he didn't reply, she repeated it for emphasis. She was too sleepy for dread to grip her, and yet she felt certain, underneath her drowsiness, that something was terribly wrong. She felt a couple of wet drops hit her cheek, followed by more silence.

Finally, Cade kissed her, and she heard him get up and leave.

Chapter 26

"**Y**ou *promised* me!" Asha's voice was a howl of misery.

She'd awoken hours later in Leo's clinic and sought out Cade, only to find him in Angel's Wing...but it didn't look much like the rooms Angel had lived in anymore. The place had been trashed. The art had been torn from the walls and destroyed, anything remotely fragile shattered on the floor, and the bed was ripped to shreds.

He did this, Asha realized when she walked in, wide-eyed. *He was that angry.*

One look at Cade's face was enough to tell her why. What he'd done.

"You promised you'd end this. That's what the whole stupid assassination plot was for!"

Cade was unnaturally quiet, his eyes sharp and focused on her.

"I know," he said. He seemed outwardly calm, but there was a storm in his eyes. "But the game has changed. There are new players we didn't bank on. The goal is the same, though: survival. And right now, to survive, this is the price we pay."

"The price *we* pay?" she shot back furiously. "You mean the price that those young girls pay, for the rest of whatever's left of their lives. Meanwhile, we live here, in relative comfort at their expense."

He folded his arms. "That was always our position, long before now. You and I lived inside safe, fortified compounds with food and water and electricity, while the Wastelanders lived in poverty and ruin. This is no different, and this would be happening to those girls whether we were involved or not."

"That's a fucking copout and you know it," Asha snarled, and to her horror, hot, desperate tears formed at the corners of her eyes. How could he not understand what this meant to her? "Just because something evil is going to happen, it doesn't mean we actively participate in it. It doesn't mean we *help it along,* for God's sake. What the fuck is wrong with you?"

That, she noted with satisfaction, seemed to pierce the façade of calm he'd been maintaining. A crease appeared between his heavy brows.

"What's wrong with me?" Cade replied, with a shade of contempt she'd never heard from him before. "I'm sorry I'm not a stupid idealist pretending that there's a choice other than the one in front of me. I'm sorry I'm not willing to sacrifice you and me, and everyone else here, for a bunch of—"

"Of what?" Asha cut in sharply. "A bunch of whores? Slaves? I was one of those whores. Any one of those women could've been me."

His frown deepened. "You're not one of them, Asha."

She choked on something between a laugh and a sob.

"Not like the other girls, Cade?" she croaked. "Really? That's funny, because I seem to remember being sold at a slave market, and the only thing that kept me from being sold off to people like *that* was you. Had you not been there—or had you decided I wasn't worth saving—"

"You *are* worth saving," Cade interjected furiously. "That's why I'm doing this. Why I *have to* do this. Why can't you wrap your head around that?"

Asha recoiled as though he'd struck her.

"Don't you dare," she said, low and furious, "don't you fucking dare say that you're doing this for me. This is the opposite of everything I ever wanted, Cade!"

"What the fuck other choice do I have?" he growled. "They almost *killed* you, Asha! What was I supposed to do, say *thanks, but no thanks* and let you fucking die? You had a fucking *seizure* and you expect me to *negotiate* with these people, who'd kill my woman right in front of me? They have weapons that you can't imagine, but I can. We don't stand a chance if they decide to attack."

He threw another clay dish at the wall, shattering it into a million pieces.

"I'm not committing suicide on behalf of all of us just so I can say I was better than them in the end," Cade bellowed. "That doesn't fucking *matter* if we're dead!"

Asha paused, her stomach churning painfully. She swallowed back a wave of nausea.

"We could leave," she said quietly. "Together."

"That's your solution?" His disgust was palpable. "Run away? To where, exactly? Have you ever tried to survive in the wilderness alone? Oh wait, the last time you did, you ended up abandoning your friend to be eaten by cannibals and then captured."

His words twisted an invisible knife in her gut. He was using her past, her guilt, against her. Every bit of trust she'd so painstakingly built with him was crumbling faster than she'd ever thought possible.

"You know I'm fucking right. Leaving is suicide, and I've worked too hard for too long to throw our lives away on something so monumentally stupid."

Asha shook her head, over and over. "I can't do this. I can't be part of this."

"The price of freedom is death, darling, and it's us or them. That's what it always comes down to."

She laughed bitterly. "You know, soldier, I would've thought you'd understand that some things are worth dying for. I guess that was too much to hope for from a man who'd willingly associate with someone like Angel."

"Don't you dare compare me to that monster," he shouted, smashing another cup against the wall. "I've protected you as best I could, every step of the way. I've been patient and understanding with your many fucking *issues.* I've been better to you than I had any obligation to be, and this is how you fucking repay me?"

Every word hit her like a physical blow.

"I'm not a good man, darling," Cade continued. "You knew that from the start, and you fell in love with me. I'm never gonna sacrifice us on the altar of *goodness.* I refuse."

Fell in love. Because he seemed to always read her mind, he knew she loved him. And he was telling her, in no uncertain terms, that it didn't matter, didn't change his answer to their problem. If anything, he was weaponizing that love against her by implying she loved him *for* his darkness.

And, Asha had to admit, she did. But he was so much more than that, and she loved him more for being the man who'd held her, comforted her, made her feel safe and given her agency in a relationship that'd been stacked against her from the start.

"I'm not staying in this," she said in a low voice, with a shake of her head. "So, I guess you'll be happy to know that I don't intend to be an obligation to you anymore."

She turned to leave the room. She had no idea where she was going or what she would do when she got there. All she knew was that she needed to get away from the horrific betrayal that seared everything scarred and vulnerable inside her.

"We're not done, Asha," Cade commanded, in the same tone he gave military orders in. "Get back here."

She ignored him, didn't even look back. If she did, she thought she might be sick.

His footsteps followed her. He caught her wrist and spun her to face him again, fury etched into his features. His grip was just shy of painful, and the fire in his eyes was frightening.

"Don't fucking walk away from me," he gritted out, right in her face, his huge body looming over her. He looked like he could kill her. His eyes were glazed in a way she'd never seen before: unseeing except for blind rage.

It was the first time she'd ever been truly afraid of him.

"Let me—"

"Hear me now," Cade spat out. "There is nowhere on fucking earth you could go that I would not find you. I won't let you kill yourself and take away the one good thing I've ever had. I. Will. Not. Allow. It."

She struggled against his hold, but he tightened his grip on her wrist and crowded her against the wall. Terror struck her heart. Every breath between them felt like a small earthquake.

"You're made for me, Asha. Your darkness matches mine, and you know it."

She found her voice again. "Let me *go*, Cade. I mean it."

He didn't move, and that was when her own anger resurfaced, and her need to protect herself became greater than her desire to placate him.

"How fitting," Asha snarled back in his face. "Like father, like son."

And in perfect imitation of the moment he'd most admired her for, she spat in his face. The saliva hit his cheek and slid down, and for a second, she thought he might snap and commit physical violence.

But the second passed, and the fury went out of Cade's face like a candle being abruptly blown out. He blinked a couple times, as though waking from a strange dream, and stared at her like he'd never seen her before. Then he prickled with sudden awareness, and horror broke over his features like a wave. He dropped her wrist as though it had burned him and wiped his cheek, backing away from her immediately.

"I'm sorry," he croaked, staring at his wet hand. "Fuck, I—"

Asha just looked at him with contempt, her rage and despair dwarfing her.

"Thanks for proving my point," she spat. "I'm one of *those girls,* Cade. And you are definitely one of those fucking men. Enjoy whatever that brings you, but you'll do it without me."

She turned on her heel and left him there, along with the last shreds of her humanity and any hope for her future.

Nihilism descended like a dark curtain over everything as Asha threw things into her backpack. She didn't know where she was going. All she knew was that she couldn't stay here. The only person she'd ever trusted in her whole life lived here, and she could no longer stomach looking at his face and knowing what she'd lost.

In a way, Cade's betrayal was nothing. He was simply fulfilling the expectations she usually had of everyone. But for one precious moment in her life, she'd thought he would be better. He listened to her; he cared about what she had to say. He cared about *her,* and he didn't mind that she didn't really know how to be affectionate, or how to be in a real relationship. He liked her for the things that other people saw as flaws.

Now, she had nothing left—no hope for the future, no reason to keep going. She'd never be brave enough to put a gun in her mouth, but wandering into the wilderness alone seemed like it'd do the job anyway. Either she'd find somewhere else to be, or she'd die out there.

It was remarkable how little she cared, given all she'd done to survive.

She finished packing what little provisions she had, then holstered her sidearm at her hip. She took Cade's jacket, figuring that the least he could do would be to give it to her. His dog tags jingled together as she put it on, and she fingered them through her shirt. She considered leaving them behind, but in the end, she couldn't do it. Instead, she clasped them tighter to her, like a talisman of strength.

It was dark now, and Cade hadn't returned to the house, so he was likely still at the party. Silently, Asha made her way to the Nest's gate, where two bored guards waved her off without even asking any questions.

I guess when you're the chief pimp's whore, you can do what you want.

And just like that, she was gone.

Chapter 27

The woods were unforgiving at the best of times. In the three days since she'd left the Nest, she'd been exposed to poison ivy, had tripped and twisted her knee, and had eaten most of her food. Cade's jacket had caught on branches and shrubs and now sported several tears that felt like rips in her own heart. However, in her wandering, a new idea had come to her, and she'd taken out the compass she'd packed to navigate toward a new destination.

After another day of walking, Asha stood at the threshold of the Zone of Control. It was a one-kilometre area around the Cave where soldiers patrolled, and supplies were moved around, surrounded by a chain-link fence with warnings to Wastelanders to keep out. It separated the Cave from the Wasteland. Civilization from its ruin.

She'd decided to return to the Cave because of something she happened to remember the night before, as she lay on the ground, longing for a safe shelter: a small bunker underneath the school where she'd worked, with a keycode that only the teachers had known. Built to protect the school staff in an emergency, it held vital supplies like long-life food packets. It was possible that the Order had already raided it…but she doubted it. She hadn't seen any of her former colleagues among their ranks.

In any case, it didn't matter anymore. She had nothing to lose by checking it out, and if they caught her, she'd work up the courage to shoot herself. It seemed as good a plan as any, especially with starvation on her horizon. At the very least, she could resupply there while she contemplated her next move.

Asha watched carefully through the fence. The Order drove the large trucks that had once belonged to the Cave's military, ferrying supplies into the compound from who knew where. Probably gangs like hers, if their threat against the Guardians was anything to go by. She waited patiently, knowing from Cade that her implant would protect her from the guns on the Cave's high walls and help her avoid detection.

Eventually, opportunity arrived in the form of a truck that stopped in the middle of the Zone, down for a mechanical failure. As the agitated driver waited for techs to arrive, Asha slipped into the cargo hold unnoticed, as quick and silent as a cat.

Another life she'd lived was ending, and once she'd successfully hidden herself among a bunch of barrels in the back of the truck—where no one could see or hear—she finally allowed herself one small, broken sound of anguish.

Cade knew he'd fucked up the second Asha spit in his face.

He'd been in a fog of rage that hadn't descended since he discovered his mother dead on the kitchen floor. He'd always had a temper, but it took a lot to truly anger him. It had taken the threat of losing the one truly good thing he'd found in the Wasteland to unleash that particular fury.

He'd always known the darkness that lurked inside him, but he'd rationalized that he tried to use it for good. To protect people who deserved it. To bring justice and vengeance on people who did wrong, who hurt others. He didn't want to be his father, whose anger consumed everything it touched, like a wildfire that he fed with his own pain and despair. Whose rage on one ordinary afternoon had destroyed the only woman he'd ever professed to love.

He *was* his father, though. He was everything he'd hated his entire life.

But he still didn't think she'd actually leave.

Shame kept Cade from going after Asha immediately, from following her into the dark night and making sure she was alright, walking through the Nest alone. But he couldn't—not when *he* had been the one to threaten her. Not when *he* was the danger. More than that, he felt sure that she'd respond to him following her by pulling away that much harder. He knew her; she needed time away from him to feel safe again.

So, Cade went to the clubhouse courtyard and lingered for a couple of hours, staring vacantly into the fire. At various turns, the men tried to engage him, to bring him back to the present, but he batted them away. He could think of nothing but the absolute betrayal in Asha's eyes, and then, almost as quickly, the pure hatred in them.

She'd been a wounded soul from the moment he'd met her, though she'd never have described herself that way. But he'd seen it, in the way she expected less than nothing from everyone around her, and the way she'd offered herself to him that first night they lay in bed together, even when she was raw from rape and torture. Because she expected him, like everyone else, to take advantage of her. To use her up and throw her away.

The only time she'd ever wept was when he was kind to her. When he'd showed her tenderness instead of disgust or indifference. Mercy instead of cruelty.

"What's wrong with you?" Dom asked, in a rare moment of verbosity. Cade glanced up at his friend, usually so stoic and silent. He now looked vaguely concerned, which in a person who showed as little as Dom did, probably meant he was very worried indeed.

"Nothing," Cade mumbled back, but the lie was acrid on his tongue.

It was the thought of Asha's tears that made him finally push past his shame and disgust to seek her out. He assumed she'd gone home, and he fully expected to sleep on the floor that night. To spend weeks, or months, clawing his way back to the place he'd been. The place where she'd trusted him, when she'd never trusted anyone.

He didn't know what he'd do about the Order, or how he'd make Asha see that he loved her more than he'd ever loved anything. He loved her bravery, and her sass, and her secret soft side. He loved her submission and her strength.

But he hadn't cornered her, threatened her, because he loved her; he'd done it because he was terrified. Terrified of losing her like his mother, or Janie, or any of the countless men or women he'd seen die.

So terrified that he'd sacrifice *anything,* and even become a monster like Angel, to keep her safe.

Cade walked up the steps to the house, promising himself he'd be so patient with her, so attentive, for as long as she needed. He wouldn't push. He'd be happy with whatever she was willing to give, and in time, when he'd earned back some of her trust, he'd ask for her forgiveness. Whenever she gave it, he would make love to her—sweetly, tenderly. He'd be so gentle. He'd tell her, at last, that he loved her.

Instead, what he found was a dark, silent house. Worse, Asha's few belongings were gone. The jacket he'd given her was missing, along with a handful of supplies. She'd left no note, nothing that told him what had happened or where she'd gone.

Yet somehow, he knew, with absolute certainty, that she'd left him. Before he could object, before he could sway her with all the things he'd just been thinking of doing. She didn't want his apology; she knew how easily those could be taken back, or nullified with more ugly abuse.

Cade looked for her, of course. He grilled the guards at the gate over what they'd seen of her.

"She just left," one of the men said with a shrug that infuriated him. "Said she'd be back."

"When?" he asked shortly, though he knew the answer.

"She didn't say," the guard replied, running a hand through his greasy brown hair. "She said you'd sent her on a mission."

Cade ground his teeth. "I'd never send her alone."

The guard shrugged again. "If I'd known, boss, I woulda stopped her."

Cade tried to act rationally. He organized a search party. He tore apart the Nest looking for her, and then the wider Guardian territory in the city. No one reported seeing her besides the guard, which meant only one thing.

She'd retreated into the wilderness, and she could be anywhere by now.

As the sun rose on the horizon, Cade had to admit defeat. He was exhausted, and there was still no sign of Asha. His heart ached with the thought that she might be lost, afraid, or hungry. Or that she might die out there, all alone, and he'd never told her all the things he should have.

Eventually, Leo ordered him to get some sleep, but it was only after Dom promised to keep searching that he returned home.

Cade sat on his bed, lowered his face into his hands, and wept like he hadn't since he'd found his mother dead. He took short, stuttering breaths in staccato, shaking like a leaf, and remembered the way he'd relayed his mother's words to Asha: *tears are a pressure valve, a way to expel pain when it's too much.*

These released nothing, however. They only reminded him of how much he'd lost in the last three years, and of the precious little he had left. When he finished, he got up to wash his face at the basin, and as the cool water soothed his salty skin, he made a decision.

There were eyes and ears in all the Settlements. He would bide his time, stall the Order for as long as possible, and use all his new resources as leader to find her. However long it took. He expected that she'd have to stop at one of the Settlements at some point; she had little in the way of practical survival skills, and she would need to resupply.

There was still time.

Chapter 28

Autumn 2097

R *eunions never went quite the way you predicted*, Asha thought, as she watched the back of her once-best friend's head. It was the middle of the night, and the woods were pitch black, but the moon was full, lending a silvery glow to the brush. Claire walked ahead of her, her vibrant red hair flowing down her back, and glanced back at Asha every so often, as though she couldn't believe she was real.

Asha couldn't believe it, either. When she'd reached that little bunker under the school in the Cave, it had been untouched, as she expected. Shelves and shelves of long-life food and survival supplies meant that she could stay for weeks, if not months. She'd had no real plans beyond catching her breath and deciding her next move.

She certainly hadn't expected, on the third day of her stay, for her dead best friend to burst through the door of the bunker with a strange Wastelander in tow. Her *boyfriend,* she said. They were there to find a shot of Regenerex for a friend who'd been injured on their travels up north, towards a farm that the Wastelander claimed had electricity and water—a promise that was surely far too good to be true.

Since when do you consider Wastelanders fuckable, Claire? Asha wondered as she watched her friend carefully step over an errant tree root. *And since when are you so damn gullible?*

Claire had always been terrified of them, probably because she'd been required to teach the Cave's propaganda about outsiders. Asha had never believed the more outlandish claims—that Wastelanders were more animal than human, or that they all exclusively ate human flesh—because she'd gathered from her government-employed parents that they were exaggerated. Her parents rarely spoke of Wastelanders at all, contrary to the fearmongering that was encouraged in the public at large.

But Claire's own father had lost his life to Wastelanders. To see her hanging on the arm of a man who totally looked the part of a dangerous outsider was terribly strange.

Despite her misgivings, Asha left the Cave with them, sneaking out a breach in the wall that Claire had found. After all, she had nowhere to go now, and no one else to look after. They offered the most viable escape route.

"If you give us away or do something stupid, I'll kill you," the Wastelander said, pinning Asha with a hard look. "Understood?"

Asha spared a glance at Claire, who didn't even look sympathetic, before glowering at him. He didn't flinch, and grudgingly, she replied, "Understood."

From the moment Asha had set eyes on Claire's new *boyfriend,* she hadn't trusted him. He was white, tall and lean, with light brown eyes and dark brown hair that was shaved on the sides in an undercut, with the rest falling to his shoulders. He wore hiking boots, practical long pants, and a leather hunting jacket. A hunting rifle was strapped to his back, and he held a pistol in his hand. His physique was clearly fit and muscular, but it was the kind of body that came from hard labour rather than the gym. *John Madigan,* he'd introduced himself as, when they'd gotten clear of the compound.

As if this fucker has a last name, Asha snarked. No Wastelander she'd ever met had one; it was one of those things that died with civilization. *He looks like he walked right out of a cyberpunk comic, and he has the mouth of a sailor. No fucking way he has anything as civilized as that.*

She resolved to refer to him only as Madigan, if only to amuse herself with his lies. She believed none of what he said. After all, she'd met plenty of men like him, who gave women protection in exchange for their bodies. She mentally prepared herself to shoot him when he inevitably turned on Claire and her.

As soon as they'd left the compound, Madigan gave orders—not just to Claire, but to Asha, too. She clenched her jaw, irritated.

"We need to make good time," he said, his voice edged with impatience. "Kimmy's counting on us."

That was how they'd ended up hightailing it through the woods, away from the roads where bandits were most likely to roam. Asha knew the nearby highway was frequented by the Skulls, though she didn't share that with her companions.

When they stopped for a break, Madigan went to sleep at Claire's urging, and finally, Asha spoke to her alone. She hoped to speak some sense to her friend.

"Didn't think I'd ever see you with a Wastelander, much less be smitten with one," Asha said, trying for a laugh. "You really think that's a good idea out here?"

Claire looked confused. "What do you mean?"

Asha pinched the bridge of her nose. "The Wasteland's a ruthless place," she said frankly. "Every bit the hellhole we were told about. Didn't appreciate the warm bed and full belly I always had at the Cave, all because they matched me with someone I didn't want."

Asha shook her head. "Spent so much of my time whining about how tough we had it under tyranny, yet not a day's gone by that I don't wish I'd wake up in my bed back home. I'd marry that poor bastard a million times over again if I could just have that."

She hadn't put it in so many words to herself, but as the words escaped, Asha realized they were true. If she could erase Cade—even if it meant forgetting the best moments of her life—she would. Even thinking his name was searingly painful, like wilfully putting her hand on a hot stove. His betrayal left oozing blisters on her thoughts.

"I'm sorry," Claire said softly. "I don't know what must've happened to you to make you feel that way...but I'm sure it can't have been easy."

"You're saying that you don't agree," Asha replied, unable to hold back an ironic laugh. *Seriously, this guy must be* good *if he got to her like this.* "Come on, is Wild Man's dick that good?"

Claire frowned, and Asha briefly wondered if she'd offended her delicate sensibilities. Asha certainly couldn't imagine Claire making the sort of straightforward blowjobs-for-protection deal that she'd made with Cade. She'd undoubtedly clutch her pearls at the idea.

Asha had always been the more pragmatic one.

"John saved me, that day at the factory. From the cannibals. After you left me."

Asha's mouth opened in outrage, but her once-buried shame bubbled up to the surface. *You're a horrible person,* it whispered to her. *Worthless. Unlovable. Unworthy of—*

"I didn't leave you," she shot back at Claire. "We got split up, and by the time I got back to where I last saw you, you were gone."

Liar, her shame whispered again. *You could have fought. You could have saved her from him.*

Claire sighed wearily. "It doesn't matter. Fact is, he saved my life, and I've been with him since."

Of course she had been. What man in this brutal world wouldn't take advantage of an obviously desperate woman in need of assistance? Asha's anger got the better of her, and she couldn't help snapping, "How noble of him, to rescue a helpless woman to rape,"

Predictably, Claire looked even more offended. "That's not what happened."

Asha took a deep breath to collect herself. She had to be patient if she wanted to get through to her friend. Claire wouldn't see the truth right away; that was the nature of the kind of relationship she'd found herself in. Perhaps, though, she could chip away at it enough that Claire would eventually see the truth for herself.

"If he had, he'd be no different to any of the other Wastelander men I've met," Asha said, and she was pleased that she sounded much calmer. "Kinder, in fact, if he'd had the manners to ask first. They usually just take what they want—whatever they want."

Claire's expression shifted to something like horror. "Is that what happened to you, Asha?"

With a sigh, Asha began to tell her story, and wove a tale that was part-real, part-fiction. She told Claire that she'd been found by Angel and had made a deal with him for protection. She described the way the unattached women had been treated in her time with the Guardians as if it were her own experience, where they gave their labour and their bodies, and in return, they were fed and housed and protected from the worst of the Wasteland. She didn't like doing that, but it was the only way to entirely omit Cade from the story.

She had no desire to tell Claire, or anyone else, about him, or her time with the Blackguard. It was easier to pretend Cade hadn't existed than to admit she'd fallen in love with a man like him, that she'd been so easily duped by how good he'd been to her. Speaking of him would be too much to bear.

"I'm sorry for what you've been through, Asha," Claire said at the conclusion of her story, and her earnest eyes almost made Asha regret lying to her. "But I'm glad you got away, and that you're here now. I've missed you."

Asha doubted that was true, and when she finally rolled over to nap before they had to leave again, there was a leaden weight in her stomach. After all that time, to find Claire alive should've felt like a miracle, a blessing. But all things felt dulled to Asha's senses now, as though she'd died and her body just kept walking, oblivious. Perhaps if Claire had been as she remembered, it would've reawakened her, but this Claire had little in common with the friend she'd known.

She decided to follow them north to the farm Claire had mentioned. If it existed, which Asha doubted, she'd have a new place to live out whatever remained of her miserable life. If it didn't, well, at least it'd be satisfying to kill Madigan when his lies were found out.

Perhaps it should've disturbed her that the idea of slaughtering shitty, abusive men was one of the only happy thoughts she had these days. Then again, happiness was in such short supply these days that she'd take whatever she could get.

Madigan wasn't happy about Asha accompanying them to the family farm Claire had mentioned, called Summerhurst. It was located in a farming community in the far north they called the Valley, over a thousand kilometres on foot, and the journey—especially with winter looming—would be arduous. Asha figured it couldn't be any worse than whatever wandering she'd do on her own, however. Hardship wouldn't exactly be a shock for her.

The surprise instead came in the form of a short, dark-haired woman who Madigan claimed was his sister, though they looked nothing alike. She was clearly of East Asian descent, with pretty brown eyes and a smattering of freckles. She'd been deathly ill when they returned to the dilapidated cottage they'd been staying in, suffering from a horrific wound that'd gotten infected.

She recovered quickly after the shot of Regenerex, the same miracle drug that Asha had once seen in Leo's medical kit. Despite the wall of ice she'd built around herself, Asha had to admit to herself that Madigan's sister was cute—the sort of girl she might've been attracted to, at a different time.

"What's your name?" Asha asked her.

"Kimmy," she replied with a small, warm smile. "I know that you're Asha. Claire told me about you. I'm glad to see you're alive and well."

"*Well* might be stretching it," Asha replied with a snort. "Even *alive* might be."

To her surprise, Kimmy giggled. Her laugh was tinkly and sweet, exactly as she looked.

"It might be a stretch for me, too, after all this," Kimmy said amiably. "But maybe we can help each other."

Asha fixed Kimmy with a searching look, and to her surprise, Kimmy flushed a little in response and looked away.

She likes me, Asha thought, perplexed. *She's attracted to me.*

She had no idea what to do with that information. The sounds of a terse argument between Claire and Madigan carried into the cottage from outside. Asha's heart sped up in response. If they didn't let her come along, where would she go?

And at that moment, in her ear, a familiar voice whispered, *The only way to survive the darkness is to become its mistress, darling.*

Well, *he* may not want her along, Asha reflected, but maybe he wasn't the only one who could make that decision. Maybe there was another person—someone far less bossy and domineering and obnoxious—who could.

So, Asha gave Kimmy her most dazzling smile. "Yeah, maybe we can."

Chapter 29

Several weeks after Asha's departure, Cade found himself sitting in a derelict house in the same place he'd first met her—Little River—talking to a rat-like man named Waters, who represented the residents there. Little River was weaker than ever under the leadership of the Skulls, and taking it from them had been easier than he'd expected, given that they were totally incompetent.

"So let me get this straight," Cade said, murder in his eyes, "Asha was in Little River. And you let her go."

Waters gulped. "N-not exactly, sir. We *tried* to capture her. But she was with friends who were well-armed."

"Wait, you tried to *detain* her?" Cade shot back. A vein was popping in his temple; he was sure of it. "You attacked her?"

Waters backed up a step. "I'm...not sure what you wanted us to do differently, sir. We told her you were looking for her."

"And what was her response?"

Waters gulped again, looking more uncomfortable than ever. Cade rolled his eyes. He didn't have time for this weaselly little man.

"I...I believe her exact words were 'go fuck yourself', sir," Waters replied, looking at the floor.

Well, I had that coming, I guess.

Cade massaged his temples. He'd been getting more migraines ever since Asha left. It wasn't just losing her; it was the incredible stress of keeping the Order off his back, while trying to keep Angel's small empire intact. Seizing Little River from the Skulls had been a huge headache, but it'd been an effective delaying tactic to avoid sending slaves to the Order. He'd promised Clyde that after taking over Little River's slave market—which was larger than any of the markets in the Settlements—they'd be able to supply a higher volume of slaves to meet the Order's demands. Now that they'd taken it, however, Clyde was getting impatient.

"Where is she now?" he asked, dropping into a chair.

Waters gave him a confused look. "We don't know, sir. Her friends killed our men, and then took off."

Cade's eyes snapped wide. "You're telling me that two fucking yokels with hunting rifles took down six of your men without even blinking? How is that fucking possible? How the *fuck* did you all survive before I turned up?"

By this point, Waters was practically shaking in his well-worn boots. Cade took a deep breath, trying to calm down. He wasn't used to being so close to the end of his fuse all the time. Since Asha left, his temper had gotten worse. He'd flown off the handle again at Dom the other day over nothing. To Dom's credit, he didn't even speak; he merely turned on his heel and walked out, leaving Cade alone.

This is why she left you, he berated himself. *Get a fucking grip, soldier.*

Maybe that was the problem: he was a soldier, not a politician. Even though taking down Angel had been partly his idea, he'd really had no idea what he was getting himself into. The sheer logistical and ethical nightmare of dealing with five settlements and appeasing the Order's constant demand for more bodies was undoing him. Trying to fix it wasn't just difficult; it was proving impossible.

She was right, he thought miserably. *Of course she was right. And now she's gone.*

"It's fine," Cade managed to get out after a couple more deep breaths. "You did what you could, under the circumstances. Give the dead men's families extra rations for the next six months as compensation." *There. That wasn't so bad.*

Waters looked stunned. "Uh...okay, sir. Is there anything else I can do for you?"

"Sure," Cade said gamely, rubbing his eyes, which were now hurting in addition to his head. "You can get the hell out of here."

Waters left without another word, looking shellshocked. It took Cade a second to understand that the Skulls probably would've inflicted some dire punishment on Waters, or even the people of Little River at large, for their failure to capture a target. He smiled grimly as he leaned back in his chair.

That's the Wasteland for you: not one trace of humanity left.

He sat there for a long time, fighting his migraine as he tried to think. Asha naturally dominated his thoughts, and he wondered where she was, and what she was doing, and if her new friends were treating her right. He worried that she'd fallen in with someone even more dangerous than himself, someone she may not be able to escape from. He hated the thought that even now, someone like Angel might be hurting her, and he was once again failing to stop it from happening.

He'd failed her in every conceivable way, and he'd thought he could learn to live with that. Maybe it would be a good thing for her to get away from him and this mess he'd made for them. She'd been so disgusted by him during their last fight.

But the thought of her trapped in another situation where she was being violated made him realize he couldn't live with that. He had to find a way to track her down. Just to make sure she was okay. Not trapped. That she was safe, and warm, and fed. And then, hell, if she wanted him to leave, he would.

Cade rose to his feet, decided. This wasn't a frivolous mission. It was about her *safety,* and her *well-being,* and it had nothing—nothing whatsoever—to do with the deep, painful longing just to see her beautiful face again. Nothing to do with wanting to hold her, and tell her how wrong he'd been, and how sorry he was. He wasn't even going to do that, anyway. It was more like a wellness check than a visit. A wellness check over possibly hundreds of kilometres, sure, but still.

This was altruism in its purest form.

"So...if I have this right," Leo said, pacing Cade's meeting room, "you're going to leave *now* to search for Asha. You don't know where she is, or how far she's gone, or even what direction she's traveling. She's with a group of strangers that we know are armed, and she doesn't want to see you."

Cade sighed and rubbed his eyes. Trust good, old, ever-rational Leo to lay out how truly insane his plan was. The doc knew how to cut through the noise.

"I don't know where she is," he admitted, "but if I can take down Clyde during his next visit, get access to his PID...I can track her, if she's in range."

"From the Order, who we're trading slaves to, under threat of certain death," Dom said flatly. "Right?"

Cade winced. "Yeah. I didn't say it was my *best* plan."

Even Dom, usually so impassive, shot Cade a look of incredulity.

"Arguably," Leo continued, acting as if Cade hadn't spoken, "the entire power structure of the Guardians will collapse as soon as you leave, which means you'll never be able to come back. Everything we've worked for, all these months, was for nothing. And you want Dom and I to stay here, without you, because you somehow imagine you'll make it on your own in the Wasteland, even though we barely managed it before with the three of us? *And* we somehow have to ambush Clyde and take his PID?"

Cade sighed. "I know it's crazy. But I can't see a way for me to stay. I'm not cut out for this, and Asha might be in danger. You know I'm not doing well; you're the one who's been giving me the weed to manage my migraines, for God's sake."

That seemed to give Leo pause, but Dom broke in: "The Settlements are relying on you."

"Yeah, well, you know what, Dom?" Cade snapped. "I didn't sign up to traffic innocent people. If I remember right, the whole point of me taking over was to *end* that practice. And now, I'm becoming just like Angel."

"You're not," Leo said immediately, but Cade shook his head vigorously.

"No, it's the fucking truth," he growled. "That's what Asha was trying to tell me, and I didn't fucking listen. I can't be part of this anymore."

He blew out a breath. "You know, before Asha came along, I probably would've tried harder to make this work, because I was used to being unhappy. The idea of signing on for more years of unhappiness wouldn't have bothered me because I didn't know the damn difference."

It was him pacing now, as though trying to find a path out of this godforsaken place. His chest felt heavy with loss as he trained his eyes on the floor.

"I was happy with her," Cade croaked. "I'd never felt anything like that before, not with Janie, or with anyone. With her, I wasn't just...*surviving*. Getting through it. It felt like there was something...I don't know, purposeful? About it. Somehow. I just need to see her again—even if it's stupid and risky."

He glanced up to see Leo's piercing gaze. It was the stare he leveled at patients to get the truth out of them when they lied about drugs or pre-existing conditions. *I'm not here to get you in trouble,* Cade had heard him say a million times over to some young, plastered private. *I'm here to help.*

Dom looked largely unmoved, his arms folded over his chest, but then, he always looked like that, so Cade wasn't sure how to interpret it. There was a pregnant pause.

"So," Dom said, with his characteristic gravel, "when're we leaving?"

"Wait, what?" Cade stared at him, stunned.

"It's October," Leo said slowly, "so we should probably make a move now. Winter's coming, and being on the road won't be easy when it arrives. We'll have to dry as many of your plants as we can."

Dom gave a short nod. "There's lots to harvest."

"And," Leo continued thoughtfully, "I should restock my kit. I've still got the important things—antibiotics, painkillers, Regenerex—but some more bandages and alcohol couldn't hurt."

"Whoa, you guys aren't coming," Cade started, but all it earned him was an eyeroll from Dom. "You're needed here."

"So are you," Leo countered, "but that's not stopping you. Anyway, you'll die if we don't, Cap. So, that's our hands tied."

"So what?" Cade asked. "Just because I'm going on a suicide mission, doesn't mean you have to do it with me."

"If I remember right, we already deserted with you once, right after you murdered a man," Leo replied sardonically. "This seems tame in comparison."

"You're losing your touch," Dom said, with a rare half-smile.

Cade sighed. "Fine. What do we do about the women? If things are gonna collapse here, I'm not leaving Lana and the girls at the mercy of the men here, or to the Order."

The three of them fell silent, thinking hard. No matter what they did, there was no perfect solution that led to everyone being totally safe.

"We free the women," Cade said after a moment. "Give them a choice to stay or go, knowing that the Order is going to come down hard on this place. We give them time to evacuate. Then we hand the place over to Raph."

"Raph?" Leo asked, surprised. "Why?"

Cade shrugged. "He was one of the people most opposed to the deal with the Order. If we hand command to him, there's less chance he'll be willing to comply with their demands."

"But then everyone here is dead," Dom said, unconvinced.

"That's the same situation they're in now," Cade pointed out. "Once the women have made their choice, we can offer the men the same one: abandon this place, or stay and try to fight off the Order. My guess is that Raph will convince them to leave and settle elsewhere."

"And if he does?" Leo asked skeptically, his arms crossed.

"Then we send messengers to the Settlements and tell them the same thing," Cade replied wearily. "They can decide for themselves to leave or fight. I really hope for their sakes that they pick the first option, but we can't force them from their homes. And we all know that they can't take on the Order. That would be true whether we stayed or not."

A heavy silence descended before Leo said the thing that Cade didn't want to think about at all.

"What if we can't find her, Cap?" he asked sympathetically. "More than that, what will we do if we *do* find her? We need a new destination."

At least Cade had thought about the last part. "Ashburn."

"It's been two years," Dom said. "Not gonna be in great shape by now."

"We'll rebuild," Cade said with a shrug. "We did it once."

He hoped their second pause was indicative of assent, though he couldn't be sure. He knew the plan was holier than Swiss cheese.

"We have work to do, then," Dom sighed. "And not much time."

Cade nodded, and they set to work.

Taking down Clyde wasn't as difficult as he'd feared it might be. The man was terminally arrogant, and though he knew Cade was from a compound, he assumed the rest of them were basically unskilled, untrained troglodytes. He also assumed that Cade would be desperate enough to hold onto power that he'd do whatever he could to keep the Order happy.

But Cade knew now that assholes like Clyde were never satisfied, even when you gave them exactly what they wanted. They saw capitulation as weakness, and they'd exploit it over and over, asking for more and more, until there was nothing left to take. They were parasites, and the only way to handle them was to annihilate them.

"Clyde," Cade said in curt greeting, as the masked man approached the entrance to the clubhouse, flanked by two masked comrades.

"Captain," Clyde said with false warmth that grated on Cade. "It's rather quiet this time around. Where is everyone?"

"They've been told to shelter in place as a result of your visit."

It was a lie. They'd evacuated everyone days ago. Those who wanted to go off on their own were allowed to leave. Then Raph had taken control as planned and moved everyone to Silver Creek for the time being. It'd be the easiest settlement to fortify against attack and plan their next move.

"Ah," Clyde said. "A wise choice. But you have nothing to fear, assuming you've come to the right decision."

"I have," Cade replied, keeping his face impassive as small red lights appeared on each of the men's heads. He lifted his hand in the 'go' signal and retreated back through the door of the clubhouse before the men had time to react.

Bang. Three simultaneous sniper shots to the head, and all three men lay bleeding on the ground.

Cade dropped next to Clyde, drew his knife, and cut the PID from his belt. To his surprise, Clyde groaned in protest, even as blood pooled rapidly under his head.

"You," was all he could croak out.

"Me," Cade replied calmly as he aimed his pistol at Clyde's head and pulled the trigger.

Chapter 30

Winter 2097

I t was another day on the road to Summerhurst, and Asha was exhausted. She knew the others were, too, but it didn't stop her from snapping at them. Even Kimmy grew weary of her, and despite knowing she had to at least appease the one person ostensibly on her side, Asha found herself unable to hide her bitterness.

When they stopped to camp for the night, she was in an even worse mood. Hunger gnawed at her, as did the ever-present ache for a man she told herself she hated. The knowledge that he was looking for her had ripped her heart open anew, but it was too late now. He'd made his bed, and she wasn't going to be his tool to use ever again.

Around the campfire, Claire chatted amiably with Madigan, snuggled up beside him on a blanket. He had his arm around her, and Claire hung on his every word like it was gospel. Given the darkness of her thoughts, their cutesy flirting grated even more heavily on Asha. She tried to distract herself with cooking, helping Kimmy to roast pigeon on a spit over the fire.

"I do *not*," Claire exclaimed, "snore like a bear. I know that for a fact."

"No, more like a squirrel or something," Madigan replied, grinning. "The daintiest little snores I ever heard. It's cute, really."

Claire shook with giggles. "How does one snore *daintily*?"

"I don't know, but you do," he said with a chuckle. "Only when the air's especially dry, but it's funny."

Somehow, that obnoxious exchange led to a kiss, and Asha looked away in disgust. Kimmy, to her credit, was able to entirely ignore them as she turned the pigeon, like it was second nature. Asha wondered how she could stand it.

She's probably not hung up on her stupid gangster ex, a voice in her head needled her. *The one we're supposed to be forgetting about, remember?*

Asha dug her fingernails into her arm, grounding herself with the pain they brought. She and Kimmy had kissed for the first time earlier that day, during a break from traveling. Asha had hoped that it would make her forget the past, or at least make her feel *something*.

She felt nothing but numb in the aftermath. Kimmy, on the contrary, had been flushed and breathless, with stars in her eyes. For the first time, Asha knew what it felt like to see someone falling in love with you and not only not reciprocate their feelings, but feel repulsed by them. She'd seen this movie before, and she knew how it ended.

It wasn't fair, she knew, to string Kimmy along like this. However, Kimmy quite literally held Asha's life in her hands. They were far into the wilderness now, and abandoning Asha here after a nasty break-up would mean certain death.

Couple that situation with the fact that Claire and Madigan would *not* stop being obnoxiously happy together at every possible opportunity, despite Asha's dire warnings about him to her friend, and Asha almost wished she'd died back at the Cave like she was supposed to.

Mercifully, night fell. They had to sleep in shifts because they had only one tent, so she and Claire were due to sleep first before switching halfway through the night. Before turning in, Asha walked into the brush to relieve herself, leaving Madigan and Kimmy at the campfire. She wandered far enough to still see the light from the fire, but far enough that she finally felt truly alone for the first time in days. It was somehow a huge relief to be away from them, to not have to mask her pain with anger and irritation.

The darkness of the night was nearly absolute this far into the wilderness, so it was easy enough to follow the light of the campfire back towards camp. Relieved that she hadn't gotten lost, she stopped dead as Madigan appeared from the darkness, his outline illuminated by the dim light.

He leaned between two tree trunks, watching her. The ambient light was enough to just barely light up his features. His mouth was drawn into a hard line.

Asha's heart started to pound. Her instincts screamed at her that something was wrong, that she should turn around. But where would she go? It was dark, and they were in the middle of nowhere. She closed her fist around the knife in her pocket.

"Asha," Madigan said, folding his arms over his chest. "We need to chat."

"I don't think we do," she replied, keeping her tone haughty despite her fear. "Shouldn't you be jerking off somewhere right now?"

He clucked his tongue impatiently. "Let's cut through the bullshit, hmm?"

Madigan walked toward her casually, but she knew he was watching her every move. His stance was tense, and his eyes bore into her. She didn't like looking at him.

"Maybe you can pull the wool over Claire's eyes," he continued. "Maybe Kimmy's, too. They're both too soft for their own good. But I know better."

"You don't know shit," Asha scoffed, sounding much more confident than she felt. "Just like every other Wastelander man out there, you throw your weight around and intimidate people—mostly women—to get what you want."

Madigan smiled without humour. "You really are a piece of work, huh? You hitch your wagon to ours, and Claire takes you in out of the goodness of her heart, even after *you* left *her* for dead. And you're not even *grateful*. You treat her like trash. I'd ask what the hell's wrong with you, but I know I'd be wasting my breath."

Guilt settled in the pit of Asha's stomach—an unwelcome guest in the Wasteland. Guilt got you killed out here; guilt was an impulse that Cade had taught her to squash. It was also the reason she'd ended up on her own, without him, because she couldn't live with the weight of it. Guilt had nearly killed her.

It was of no practical use, so she buried it once more, under all the other things she no longer allowed herself to feel.

"Fine," Asha said, eager to be done with the conversation. "Let's just agree: you're a pig, I'm an ungrateful bitch, and be on our way."

So quickly she couldn't immediately process it, she found herself pinned against the nearest tree, Madigan's hands on either side of her head. He loomed over her, and the look in his golden-brown eyes could only be described as murderous. His expression was a mask of contempt. She couldn't help cowering a little, even as she hated herself for it.

"Don't fucking touch me," she spat.

"Trust me, I have zero desire to become the next guy whose balls you keep on a necklace somewhere."

His breath was hot, and half his face was shrouded in darkness, which somehow only made him that much more terrifying.

"If you ever hurt Claire or my sister," he said silkily, "I will fucking end you. You understand? I don't give a shit about your tragic back-story; I don't care who comes after me for it. I'll kill you and leave you for the crows."

Asha's breath came in frightened little gasps. "Kimmy would hate you."

He chuckled darkly. "Cute. You think this is my first time?" He adopted a mocking tone. "Such a *tragedy* that Asha stumbled off that cliff and broke every bone in her body. Or that she wandered off and was mauled by a bear. Or that she fell through that ice."

Madigan leaned in until their noses were almost touching, and Asha flattened herself against the tree trunk.

"There won't be a scene," he whispered. "You'll just disappear. And I won't say a fucking thing. Got it?"

She just wanted him out of her face, so she gritted out, "Yes."

To her relief, he finally backed away. As he walked back toward the camp, he turned and said, "And just to be clear, if you tell Kimmy or Claire about this...I'll deny every fucking word."

Madigan left her alone at last, and Asha let out the breath she'd been holding. She hated him with every fibre of her being. She hated the way he loved on Claire, buttered her up, when underneath it all, this was who he really was. This was who all the Wastelander men were, in the end.

Cade wasn't a Wastelander, that annoying voice in her head reminded her.

But he'd been forced to live among them, to adapt to their violent, brutal way of life. The Guardians left no room for him to be the softer, more caring man he was when they were alone. And like her, Claire had been forced to trade herself to a violent man for protection, because there were no other options for survival.

It didn't matter who they pretended to be when they needed to soften their women up for sex, or labour, or something else that they wanted. What mattered was who they were when the mask slipped, and sooner or later, Claire was going to discover that *her Wastelander*—as she called him—was nothing more than a brute, intent on using her up and discarding her when she no longer served him.

And it wasn't as though Asha stood in judgment of him because she thought she was better. She knew she wasn't. She thought of the girls at the slave market, still being sold because she'd stupidly believed a man's promise to free them. She'd killed for him, helped him get what he wanted, and then he let it keep happening to them. She'd fought by his side and helped the gang on its mission.

The thought made her sick to her stomach again, and a powerful wave of self-loathing washed over her. It was the same guilt and self-loathing that made her abandon Cade that night, even as her heart screamed at her to stay with him. It wasn't the kind of thing a person could live with indefinitely; it would eat her alive eventually.

It was then that she decided that she'd escape from this hellish existence in the Wasteland, one way or another. No matter what it cost her.

After all, she'd already bartered away her soul and crushed her own heart in a trembling hand. What more was there to lose?

Cold.

That was always Cade's first thought in the mornings now. They'd been on the road for several weeks, and it was mid-December, by his best guess. Snow had fallen in thick flakes the night before, and he was freezing his ass off every day now as they walked across a wilderness that seemed endless. They all were: him, Leo, Dom, and Lana and her little sister, Cassie.

That was a sticky point with him: he hadn't wanted to bring the girls. But Lana had had other ideas.

"You *owe* me this," she'd hissed at him when he'd told the women of their choice to stay or flee. "I had a fine life before you meddled and killed Angel! You and Asha are the reason my life is fucked now, asshole, and if you have a better place for me to be at this settlement of yours, you owe it to me to take me there."

Cade sighed. "You have a point, and I'm sorry. But it'll be dangerous, and it's a very long trip. We'll probably be on the road for months before we get to Ashburn. I don't know if that's the best idea for you and the kid."

Lana *tsk*ed at him. "That's what we'd be doing anyway: wandering, looking for a place to land. At least this way, Cassie and I will have a destination in mind, and decent men to protect us. But if you think I'm fucking you in exchange for that protection after all this, you have another thing coming."

He gave a dry laugh. "Wouldn't dream of it, darling. In any case, I only have one girl I'm interested in these days. Though I'm not sure she'll have me, after all this."

The PID hadn't failed, and Cade had successfully calibrated it to latch onto Asha's tracking beacon. Its solar battery meant that it could be recharged easily without electricity. That was where the good news had ended, however; she'd been so far ahead of them that he'd been worried she would move out of range in no time. After all, she had a few weeks' head start, even if she was mostly traveling on foot. As a result, they'd been hightailing it for weeks to keep her from vanishing off the tracker, and they were all exhausted.

Then it snowed for the first time a week ago, and things got even worse. Food was scarcer, the cold was biting, and they had to stop for more frequent breaks. *As Asha would say, fuck Canadian winter to death with a rusty chainsaw.*

Cade's temper had exploded again the other day when he'd gotten a migraine so painful that they were laid up for two days that they couldn't afford. That was when Leo had pulled him aside into a private copse of trees, wearing his ultra-serious, *I'm-a-fucking-doctor-so-listen-to-me* face.

"You can't keep going like this, Cap," Leo said firmly, in his no-nonsense tone, like when he told patients that they had to start taking their damn medication. "This blackout rage of yours...it's getting worse, and it's dangerous, for us and for you. You know I've offered—"

"I know," Cade snarled at him. "I don't need *therapy*, doc. I need to find Asha."

"Oh, and you think she's going to run back into your arms if you're spitting fire at her?" Leo shot back. "Funny, because from what you said, I thought that was why she left."

He almost blew up again. He really did.

"Deep breath, Cade," Leo said, his voice softer. "Do it with me."

Rather unwillingly, Cade followed him in a breath exercise. It made him feel stupid and ashamed. He should be able to control himself better. He shouldn't be having these bouts of anger. But he hated to admit that the breath work helped. A little.

"As I was saying," Leo continued after he'd calmed down, "I've offered you psych help before. I'm *not* a therapist, but I did receive more advanced psych training when they reassigned me from the civilian hospital to the military, because what you're feeling and how you're reacting isn't unusual for soldiers. It's extremely common."

Cade let out another long breath. "I don't like feeling out of control."

"I know," Leo replied emphatically. "And if you want to feel better, and you want Asha to come back to you, then you have to improve your mental health. I hate seeing you like this, and not just as a physician—as a friend. You deserve better than this, and I can at least teach you ways to help you manage things."

Touched, Cade paused for a moment. "Alright. But if you're gonna make me wear a daisy chain and hold my hand and make me sing kumbaya, I'm pushing you off the nearest cliff."

Leo grinned. "Deal."

Chapter 31

After two months trekking through the snow, ice, and general misery of winter, Asha discovered that the mythical Valley that Madigan had spoken of really existed. She had to admit that she was surprised, especially when the electricity and indoor plumbing also turned out to be real.

It was a sprawling farming community surrounded by largely impassable mountains. There was only one plausible way in and out, via a concealed mountain pass that still involved a lot more climbing than Asha preferred. Still, she got over the difficulty quickly, because to say that the residents did not welcome her there was a vast understatement.

From the moment she arrived, they treated her and Claire with suspicion and sometimes open hostility. Many refused to trade with them. Asha dealt with their stares every time she walked the dirt roads between their homesteads, no matter where she was going. A few times, children threw rocks at her. Worse, Zach Jameson—who seemed to be the Valley's asshole prodigal son—often wolf-whistled at her and made obscene gestures when he saw her on the road.

She often walked those roads to get in and out of the Valley, since she preferred to spend her time alone than in the company of people who either didn't understand her or treated her as an invading force. The Valley always needed people to scavenge in the Wasteland for materials, so she volunteered. She now spent far more time away and alone than she did at the Madigan farmstead, which was probably for the best...especially since Kimmy was starting to get ideas about their alleged romance and grumble about Asha's complete disinterest in commitment.

She wandered the frozen wilds alone, often aimlessly, stopping in abandoned towns and villages to scavenge supplies. She spent many a night in some derelict building, barely motivated enough to move. A deep despair and self-loathing had settled inside of her, and when she wasn't running away from it, it paralyzed her.

It was a few weeks before Asha came across a fenced-in village at the edge of what had once been a city. Madigan had mentioned that there was a trading post near the Valley, and she'd been determined to find it. Now, up to her shins in fresh snow, she stood outside the gate and read a hand-carved wooden sign that read *The Post.* The two guards at the gate eyed her warily.

The name struck a chord deep inside her. Where had she heard the name before?

Unprompted and unwelcome, Cade's voice whispered in her head: *It's a Wastelander settlement up north. Only a hundred-and-fifty kilometres or so from the Delta.*

So close to the compound, she thought with no small amount of longing. *There has to be a way to get there.*

But she knew getting there was only half the battle. Getting inside was another matter entirely, and it would require convincing them to take her in. She had no idea how to do that, but if she could find a way to contact them, she'd think of something. Anything. She needed to get out of this hell, and if it meant selling her soul a second time, she'd do it.

A guard at the gate made an impatient noise. "Lady, are you going in or what? You're blocking the road."

Asha jumped. Somehow, she'd lost touch with her surroundings. It seemed to happen a lot now. Her own thoughts consumed her whole.

"Yes," she finally decided. "I'm coming in."

"Fine. I never seen you here before, so the basic rules are: don't steal shit, don't instigate shit, and don't be an asshole. We got no problem dragging your ass out, or putting a bullet in the back of your head if you cause trouble. Got it?"

Asha nodded, and they permitted her entry into the little hamlet carved out of a city suburb. It was only a few streets, but it was cleaner and more orderly than any gang settlement she'd visited. The people looked relatively healthy, with meat on their bones indicating that they were decently fed. There were no beggars in the streets, and the aging buildings had been patched up and repaired; someone obviously maintained them regularly. All along the main street where she stood, there were stalls of wares, with merchants calling out to the few passersby.

She walked the strip somewhat nervously, but after a thorough search, she realized something remarkable: there was no slave market. No terrified young women or girls staring at their feet while some asshole bought them. Relief shot through her immediately, and she wondered how it might be to live in a place like this. Maybe she could live here, instead of the Valley? She had no idea what she might do here, except...

Asha stopped short in front of a stall that appeared to be selling, of all things, old radios—the kind that people used to talk to one another. Though the Guardians had never used radio, she'd heard since then that, although it was rare, it was pretty much the only long-distance form of communication left. In fact, she'd seen Madigan use one to talk to other Valley residents before.

If that's true, she mused, *then the Delta must have one, too.*

She approached the stall, where a grumpy-looking old man sat, surveying her with thinly veiled suspicion.

"Do these radios still work?" Asha asked, hoping she sounded friendly. She hadn't tried to sound friendly in so long.

The old man *pshed* at her. "Well, I wouldn't know now, would I? How am I supposed to test 'em, huh? No power out here. You buy 'em as-is, miss, and find your own power source. No refunds, no exchanges."

Asha raised an eyebrow. "So, you're selling merchandise that you don't even know if it works?"

He huffed again. "I told ya, didn't I? Buy 'em or make way for better customers. Makes no difference to me."

Asha suppressed an eyeroll, then walked away from the stall. *As if he has a line of customers just waiting to buy his Old World junk.*

She didn't have anything to trade at the moment, but they had alcohol back at the farm, which she knew was a hot commodity that could buy just about anything in the right amount. It was stored in the cellar, and surely Madigan wouldn't miss one bottle.

It wasn't exactly ethical, but then again, she'd once sold herself to a renegade soldier who murdered his own father, so in comparison, stealing a little whiskey seemed tame. Besides, since Madigan thoroughly hated her, he might ultimately be pleased if she up and disappeared one day, never to be seen again.

Asha walked back towards the gate, a new, dark hope brimming inside of her.

"This—piece—of—fucking—garbage!"

Asha slapped her new radio in disgust. She was in her bedroom at Summerhurst on a blustery winter morning, seated on the floor next to the outlet she'd plugged the stupid device into. To her surprise, the old machine had initially whirred to life when connected to power, despite its obvious age. The old man at the Post hadn't scammed her after all, which should've been cause for celebration.

Except that even after a half hour of fiddling with the knobs and controls, the damn thing had shitty reception. The only signals she could hear came from radios already inside the Valley. It definitely would never reach the Delta from there, but she knew of no other place where she could power it.

She paused, thinking hard. The radios inside the Valley were mostly handheld and battery-powered—unlike this one—and carried by what passed for first responders in this miserable place. Madigan had one, but he kept it on his person at all times, so it was unlikely she could steal it from him.

If there was a way to get one of those radios, she thought, *I could take it to the Post and try to get a signal from there. It's much closer to the Delta.*

It was an incredibly risky idea. No one would willingly give her such a thing, even if she had something valuable to trade. She had no idea how she would manage it.

Still, in the meantime, she'd envisioned an idea for how to persuade the Delta to take her in. There was a great deal of technology here in the Valley that didn't seem to exist anywhere besides the compounds, and she suspected that they would be very interested to learn of its location.

Of course, that meant that everyone here would be imperiled, but given that they treated Asha like trash, she didn't much care about any of them. She knew they'd likely see a community of Wastelanders with technology—*any* technology—as a threat that ought to be neutralized. But by the time that happened, it'd no longer be her problem.

The bonus would be rescuing Claire, as Asha didn't believe that they'd be willing to harm another compound person. Likely, they'd take her in as well, and things could perhaps go back to the way they were. If only Asha's attempts to persuade her friend of the danger of their situation worked, maybe Claire would even agree to go with her when the time arrived.

She recognized the darkness in her heart, and the secret horror of her plan. Some part of her screamed at the injustice of what she was doing. But Cade had been right about one thing, in the end: they did what they had to in order to survive. Whatever it cost. Whatever it left them with.

Safe. All I want is to feel safe again.

"Asha?" Claire called outside Asha's bedroom door.

Asha panicked, shoving the radio under the bed and hurrying to get the door.

"Morning," Claire said with a small smile. "Want to come milk the cows with me?"

Asha could hardly think of anything she wanted to do less—something about milking really disgusted her—but she nodded reluctantly and followed her friend out to the barn.

Claire thankfully handled most of the actual milking, but they were interrupted by the appearance of Zach Jameson, which instantly made Asha wary. He was a tall, lanky thing with a mop of brown hair, barely more than a boy—perhaps twenty at most. He still seemed to enjoy following her around the Valley whenever he spotted her, peppering her with various bits of sexual harassment. He was dumb as a box of rocks, and the only thing they had in common was how much they hated Madigan.

"You sure scare easy," he jeered at Claire. "Can't imagine what Madigan is thinking, bringing you here. You think you won't face far worse than a little spilled milk before we kick your ass out?"

Asha rolled her eyes as Claire made some retort that was far politer than she'd have been.

"Go home, Wastelander," Asha said to him, sneering. He was just another little man who thought he owned the place by virtue of existing in it. After Angel, he didn't scare her in the least.

I eat men like you for breakfast, little farm boy.

Eventually, Kimmy arrived, took one look at the scene in front of her, and her eyes turned to steel.

"Get off my land," she demanded. "Now."

Zach huffed and held up his hands. "Fine. I'm going."

He left, and as Asha stared after him, the wheels in her head began to turn. She thought back to her radio problem. Maybe *she* couldn't get her hands on one of the Valley's radios, but perhaps someone who had the inside track...

Someone stupid. Easily manipulated. Young, even. Inexperienced.

"I'll follow him to the gate," Asha said suddenly. "Make sure he leaves."

The other two accepted her explanation without suspicion, and she ran out of the barn after Zach. She followed him almost to the gate of the property to ensure they wouldn't be overheard. She had to make her next move very carefully.

"Hey!" Asha called after Zach. "Wait up."

Zach turned in surprise, but his expression instantly became wary.

"What do you want, outsider?" he asked curtly, crossing his arms.

"I just want to talk," Asha replied, keeping her tone casual. "Look, I know it's been a big adjustment, letting Claire and me live here."

"Let?" he sneered. "We haven't *let* you do anything yet."

She shrugged, forcing her temper down. This was too important.

"Regardless, I'm sorry we're in your space," she continued. "But you seem like a pretty important guy around here, and..."

Asha paused for effect, glancing at the ground in imitation of nerves. As if she'd ever be nervous talking to this worm. Regardless, Zach paused, leaning forward slightly toward her, and she knew this was going to work. If she could just find out what he wanted...

"Maybe we could help each other out," she said, fluttering her eyelashes ever so slightly, wondering if she was laying it on a bit thick as she leaned toward him. "You know a lot of important people, and...well, I'm sure there's lots of ways I could give you a hand, if you want."

Zach had been staring at her intently, and he suddenly cleared his throat.

"You offering to suck my dick, outsider?" he said, and Asha almost laughed. No one could say he didn't get right to the point, but if this was how he normally talked to girls, it was no wonder he was a virgin. And she could already tell that he definitely was.

Instead, Asha managed a demure, kittenish giggle that she'd never done in her life. Cade would've been incredulous that she could even produce such a sound. She regretted the thought of him, if only because he'd hate that she was doing this. But he was the reason she was in this mess, so he didn't have a right to object, even in her head.

"Maybe we could discuss it sometime soon," she replied, gently brushing over Zach's jacket with her hand. "Tell me where to meet you."

The stupid boy followed her hand with his eyes, and she could practically see all the blood in his body rushing to one particular place.

"Meet me at the gate to my family farm," Zach said shortly, though she could sense his excitement underneath his clipped tone. "Tomorrow. Noon."

"I'll be there," Asha said with a wink. "See you then."

She turned back toward the barn, feeling elated. Finally, fucking a guy would be to *her* advantage. It wouldn't be *her* exploitation, humiliation, or a betrayal so deep that it still reverberated inside her scarred soul. She wouldn't be the victim ever again. She wouldn't be used up and thrown away.

The only way to survive the darkness is to become its mistress, darling, he'd said to her what felt like a lifetime ago. Now, the darkness of this world would bend to *her* will, obey *her* command, help *her* survive.

Still, it felt, for the first time in a long time, like freedom.

Chapter 32

Spring 2098

T hank God it was spring.

Cade reveled in the warmer temperature as he walked beside the wagon he was guarding. It'd been a long fucking winter for all of them, trekking through the snow, and they all looked thin as a rail, except for the kid. They gave Cassie most of the food they managed to get, and the rest of them tried to grin and bear it.

Because Ashburn wouldn't be livable without major repairs, they'd decided to settle at the Post for a while. They needed supplies to rebuild, and they needed goods to trade for them, plus they needed a way to pay their way at the boarding house they were staying at.

As a result, Cade and Dom had taken on mercenary work, which was always needed at a trading post to protect shipments from bandits and gangs. Leo offered his medical services, which paid well because there were few legitimate medical practitioners available. Lana got work at the only tavern, a place called *Longfellow's* that sold shitty stale beer to travelers and residents alike.

"Dealing with drunk men is one of my skills," she'd said with a shrug, and for the first time in a long time, Cade had laughed out loud.

"It sure is, isn't it?"

The boarding house they were staying in was kind of crappy—lots of roaches—but at least there were no bedbugs. Lana and Cassie shared a room, and the three soldiers shared another. It was cramped, but they worked so much—both at their jobs and at Ashburn— that it didn't really matter.

The worst news was that Asha had disappeared off the tracker some time ago. Before Cade's sessions with Leo, that probably would have made him lose it again. But (at least according to Leo) he was making good progress, and he held it together. Even if he never saw her again, he had a new life he was building here. Even if he worried about her constantly.

The strange thing, however, was that she wasn't *always* off the tracker. She reappeared periodically, always in odd locations, and disappeared again before Cade could reach her. He'd taken to carrying the PID with him everywhere, checking it obsessively, but he was never near enough to meet up with her. It was infuriating.

"Eyes forward, recruit," the big, burly guy leading the mercenaries said to him.

Cade sighed. He'd never been good at taking orders.

Asha's relationship with Kimmy was becoming a problem.

Kimmy wanted more than Asha was willing to give, and Asha's traitorous heart was starting to care that she was hurting this lonely, clingy woman by stringing her along. She felt guilty now when she thought about the time she'd told Kimmy, in no uncertain terms, that Kimmy wasn't her girlfriend. The deep hurt—and even worse, the quiet resignation—in Kimmy's eyes made her feel sick.

Worse, Asha knew her guilt stemmed from the fact that she actually liked Kimmy...a lot. She was the sort of person who was easy to like: easygoing and funny, but passionate and principled. She was a nurse who was genuinely skilled and cared about the people she treated. She worked long, hard hours at the Valley's clinic, and then came home and worked hard on the farm at Summerhurst. She was pretty, smart, and well-liked by almost everyone in this overly snobby community of farmers, which made her commitment to Asha that much more baffling.

In contrast to Kimmy's warmth, Asha was quiet, withdrawn, and damaged. As if trying to lure a feral cat from its hiding spot, Kimmy kept patiently prodding the walls she'd put up, offering bits of affection as a reward. But it was never going to work.

Asha was never going to love Kimmy. How could she? She practiced the same detachment she'd learned from her short-lived marriage to Eric. She gave little pieces of herself—an affectionate look, an indulgent laugh, and of course, sex—to Kimmy, just enough to keep her interested and briefly satisfied. It was how she'd survived every relationship she'd had except for Cade.

Even thinking his name hurt, which was why she avoided it as much as possible. The well of agony inside her at his absence never ran dry. In her quieter moments, she clutched his dog tags to her heart and endured the hard, bone-shaking sobs that came to her as she wondered what he'd say now, if he could see what she'd become. Would he hate her? Would he be disgusted at how she'd fucked her way to survival? But then, wasn't that what she'd done with him, anyway? Wasn't that all she was good at?

Even though she'd once been able to be more herself with Claire, that time was long over. Claire didn't understand her anymore, which she guessed was fair, since Asha barely understood herself. *You're awful,* a small voice in her head kept telling her. *You're the worst thing that's ever happened to her and Kimmy. Madigan is right.*

Self-loathing was her default setting these days, however, and so her conscience could only have so much effect. She'd gotten used to being a disappointment at an early age, and her desperation and nihilism were the only things she had left. In a strange way, knowing that Madigan was right about her pushed her to continue with her plan. If she was already the worst thing that'd ever happened to Kimmy and Claire and everyone else she'd ever met, she might as well try to reach a place where she could live the rest of her miserable life in something like comfort.

Asha sighed, pushing away her thoughts, and sat in the soft spring grass just outside the Post. She reached into her pocket and pulled out the Valley radio she'd traded Zach a bunch of sloppy blowjobs for. He'd been way too easy to manipulate after that first rendezvous between them; he'd been practically giddy about stealing the radio for her, after she'd promised him that he could come with her to the Delta. The lure of adventure for a kid who'd grown up in an isolated farming community was too tempting.

It wasn't true, of course—they'd never take him in—but she didn't worry herself too much about that.

"Urgent message for the Delta compound," she said, slowly and clearly into the mouthpiece, depressing the talk button. "From a fellow compound resident. Over."

Nothing but static in reply, but she tried again. And again. For hours.

At last, she threw aside the radio in despair, tears choking her. She'd try again another day. It had to work.

It had to.

Cade was tired walking back toward the Post with Leo from a medical job. He'd gone with Leo to watch his back, since the patients weren't exactly upstanding citizens. Thankfully, there'd been no trouble. He couldn't wait to go back to their camp just outside the walls and pass out, even though it was mid-afternoon.

The good news was that his days as a mercenary were finally coming to an end. The last couple months had been productive, and they'd gotten Ashburn back to a livable state. The way he felt seeing it again, nestled in between the hills, with its small crystalline lake and fishing cabins, was indescribable. Waves of grief broke over him, but with it came a sense of hope.

A second chance. A new start.

He still missed Asha terribly, like a hole in his heart, and he worried about her constantly. She'd appeared more times on the PID, but again, he'd never been able to catch up to her before she disappeared again. He didn't know how she kept disappearing, but he lived for those moments when he saw her little red dot moving on the screen. Proof that she was still alive.

Dom had brought Lana and Cassie there the night before and gotten them set up in a cabin. They'd also started to convert one of the spare cabins into a medical clinic for Leo.

"All in all, not a bad day," Leo said briskly at his side.

"Yeah," Cade sighed. "Could've be worse."

Out of habit more than anything, he unclipped the PID from his belt and checked it wistfully. He didn't expect to see her, and he certainly didn't expect her little red dot to appear in the woods, just outside the Post. Maybe twenty minutes away. Less if he hurried.

He audibly gasped, and automatically started running.

"Cap?" Leo called after him, alarmed. "Hold on! What is it?"

Cade ignored him and kept sprinting. He heard a rare curse from Leo behind him, but he didn't care.

Only Asha mattered now.

All was dark, and there was a ringing in Asha's ears that wouldn't abate. The tall grass beneath her itched, and the crows wouldn't stop circling overhead, cawing incessantly. Soon, she thought idly, they'd have a feast.

She was bleeding. Her black tank top was soaked and sticky, and her vision kept blurring and doubling as she lay facedown in the grass. It was alright—there wasn't much to see besides the corpse of that idiot Jameson kid.

However much she hated Madigan, she somehow couldn't muster up enough animosity to blame him for killing her. He'd discovered her plan, had followed her and Zach into the woods by the Post, and after shooting Zach, he'd shot her, too. The bullet had burst through the flesh and sinew between her chest and shoulder, blowing her open. Then he'd left her there for dead. Worse, the Delta had never even replied to her radio calls. She was a failure.

She'd have done the same in Madigan's position, and if she was honest with herself, she wondered if this hadn't been her ultimate goal all along. If this entire mission had been some dark death wish, some sad, pathetic form of suicide for a person too cowardly to do it herself. She was a traitor, just like Cade. Just like every person who wanted to survive in this terrible world she'd discovered the day the Cave was destroyed.

As her life drained away, Asha couldn't help but be relieved that it was almost over. Dying was less than ideal, but at least she might finally know some peace. It was what she'd been desperately seeking all this time, after all, in her own twisted way. Her only regret was that she'd never see Cade's face ever again. No matter how much he'd hurt her, she still ached for him. For the foolish trust she'd once had in him.

She tried to imagine his voice—the soft, entreating one he'd used with her after sex. Soothing her, caring for her. She closed her eyes for what she was sure was the last time, trying to hold him in her mind as she met her end.

But then, something changed. Through the ringing in her ears, she heard frantic footsteps approaching, someone's heavy breathing.

"God fucking damn it, Asha," a familiar voice gritted out. "Who fucking did this to you?"

She groaned in pain as large hands turned her over in the grass, exposing the blood pooling on the ground beneath her. Her vision blurred again, but there seemed to be a man kneeling over her. Cade's voice was low and furious as he repeated his question.

"Dunno," she managed to murmur. It wasn't true, but she didn't want Cade to get himself killed for nothing. There was no saving her. She didn't even have the energy to wonder how on Earth he got there. But if he was the last person she ever got to see, she was glad of it. Even after everything that'd happened, his presence made her feel safe.

"We need to stop the bleeding," Leo's voice barked, calm and focused. "Apply pressure while I get my tools out."

Asha groaned loudly in pain as Cade pressed his hand hard into her bullet wound. Leo worked quickly, with a frantic energy, talking to her in a steady stream, but she couldn't understand his words. All she understood was that he was pulling her back from the place where she might find peace.

"No," she mumbled, pushing weakly against him. "Leave me."

She struggled against them. Cade swore loudly and grabbed her wrists.

"Stop, my angel," he ordered, in the same measured, calm way he'd once ordered her submission. That tone of his voice that arrested her senses and her ability to reason, that made her trust him implicitly.

As if her body knew its master, Asha stopped fighting him.

"She's bleeding out too quickly," Leo said, sounding hollow. "I...don't think this is fixable, Cap. Not here."

"*Here* is what we have, doc," Cade snarled. "*Save her.* Whatever it fucking takes. We did not come this far just to give up now!"

"Look—"

"No!" Cade bellowed, and he sounded almost crazed now, like a wounded animal. "This was not for *nothing*, Leo! It can't be. It...it can't..."

Asha realized distantly that he was crying, and that alarmed her more than anything else did at the moment. She'd never heard him sound so deeply distressed, and it hurt her heart, even after six months away from him.

"Alright," she heard Leo say definitively. "There's one last thing we can try. But we'll have to move her quickly after, back to the camp."

"Done." Cade voice broke on the word.

Through her blurry vision, Asha watched Leo bend over her with a syringe in hand, the red emergency label—*Regenerex*—on the side. A second later, she screamed in agony as he stabbed it into her wound and pushed the plunger down. The pain made darkness descend in her vision, and she barely registered Cade hoisting her into his arms and carrying her away from the forest clearing.

Chapter 33

Everything was burning.

Asha's skin felt ablaze, as though a fire was alive in her veins, but cool water brought no relief; it only sent her into uncontrollable shivers. When Cade placed a damp cloth on her forehead, she cursed him, her teeth chattering. Cade and Leo had traveled through the night to bring her back to Ashburn. They'd had to hightail it out of there because there'd been some attack at the Post; Cade suspected the Order.

Good to know they've moved this far north and are rapidly colonizing the province. Comforting.

As a result, Asha found herself lying in a bed in Cade's cabin, her hands bound to the bars of the bedframe. Bacteria were rapidly colonizing her blood, and again, she welcomed the arrival of peace, of an exit from this world where people fought one another over a meagre, brutal existence, and where she, too, had succumbed to its savagery. For safety, she had sacrificed *everything.* Even her once-best friend. Even the first real freedom she'd ever known.

"I don't...want your medicine," Asha repeated for the third time, through gritted teeth.

Cade refused to untie her, lest she move and reopen her wounds. He'd cut off her ruined clothes, so she lay naked under several layers of blankets. She was vulnerable in a way she didn't like, couldn't afford. Though she burned with fever, she'd bared her teeth at him and fought against her bindings when he attempted to inject her with a thin, silver syringe of clear liquid.

Antibiotics for her fever. The Regenerex had already almost closed her mortal wound, but it didn't stave off infection, and now Cade was trying to force her to live—something she'd never thought she'd be so opposed to, but peace had felt so damn *close*.

"I did *not* come this far for this shit," Cade shot back. He was far pricklier than he'd been yesterday. "Antibiotics are fucking liquid gold in these parts, darling."

"You think that I—" –she paused to shiver— "don't fucking know that?" Asha replied. "I still don't want it."

"If you don't take it now, you'll die," Cade said impatiently. "And that's not happening. Not on my watch."

Her teeth were chattering uncontrollably now, but she still somehow mustered the defiance that'd marked her since childhood as *difficult*.

"Why do you c-care?" she asked. "You let me go. I could've d-died anytime since then, and you d-didn't give a shit about me."

He paused briefly, then let out a long, tired sigh before replying, his voice low and urgent, "I regretted it from the minute you left my sight. And I've spent the last six months trying to find you. The least you can do is not fucking die on me, my angel."

"The l-least I can do? After everything you p-put me through, asshole, you have the n-nerve to lecture *me*—"

"I *know*, Asha," Cade burst out, cutting her off. "I know I was an asshole. I know I have no fucking right to you anymore. I just don't care. I'll do far worse than tie you to a bed to keep you—lie, cheat, steal, kill. And you love that about me, because you thrive in the dark as much as I do."

Somehow, that broke her open. He didn't know what she'd done, how much she'd given up just for the *chance* to be safe and accepted again.

"You don't know me anymore," she murmured, traitorous tears threatening. "I found my friend that I told you about—Claire. And I betrayed her. Lied to her, and more besides."

If this fazed Cade at all, he didn't show it; instead, he merely shrugged.

"If you did that, it was because you needed to survive," Cade said dismissively. "I told you: *nothing* is more important than surviving. There is nothing you can lose that's worth your life."

"I fucked someone else!" Asha burst out, unable to stop her-self—she needed to make him *see*, to *understand*, that he didn't want her anymore. That she was irredeemable and irreparably broken, that perhaps she always had been, and she didn't deserve his defence.

Unlike the first revelation, this one did give him pause. He looked down at the floor, and she could practically see the wheels in his head turning.

"Who?" he asked a moment later. "I need a name, so I can kill them."

"Fuck you," Asha spat back. "I'm not your property. I left you because I'm *no one's* property. And she was the best person I've ever been with."

A flash of pain went across Cade's features, quickly replaced by tightly reined anger.

"If that's true," he hissed, "where the fuck is she? Why isn't she here, fighting for you?"

Asha's tears fell, and she had to take a few deep gulps of air. This conversation was wearing her out in her feverish state, and it seemed Cade realized it, because he took a deep breath and looked skyward, as though praying for patience. It would've been funny if the situation had been less dire; she'd never seen him pray for anything.

"Because I betrayed her, too," Asha finally managed to croak. "I never wanted her like she wanted me. Just used her to keep myself safe."

She was choking on the truth of what she'd done, asphyxiating on the sour air of brutal, indifferent consequence. The bullet in her body had been the punishment, the retribution, she'd been seeking for herself. And now, Cade was trying to deny her what justice demanded.

"I don't deserve to live," Asha whispered. "Not after what I've done."

Cade bristled automatically. "Stop. I don't give a fuck what you've done. It's *my* fault. If I hadn't fucked up, you wouldn't have had to survive like this, on your own. We'd have been together, like we always should've been."

Cautiously, as though approaching a wounded animal, he leaned over the bed and brushed a kiss against her clammy forehead.

"Blame me, darling," he murmured in a low, intimate tone, stroking strands of dark, sweaty hair away from her face. "I've got so many sins of my own, I won't even notice taking on yours as well."

He kissed her then, and the hollow ache in Asha's chest that'd been there since she'd left him only intensified. His lips were familiar in their demand for her surrender, and she was so, so tired of fighting. She gave in to her weakness and kissed him back.

"Enough," he said when they broke apart. "Let me give you what you deserve, my angel."

Cade retrieved the syringe of penicillin, and she didn't even fight him when he carefully shifted her onto her side and lifted her blankets.

"Fuck you," she gasped out as he stabbed the needle into her left buttock and pressed down the plunger.

He chuckled darkly. "Curse me all you want. The devil knows I've done it every night since you left."

He removed the syringe and climbed onto the rickety bed with her.

As he put his arms around her, Asha muttered, "I'm gross and sweaty."

"Like I care," he growled. "Not letting you go again. Now, go to sleep. You need rest."

She let him cradle her, wrapped in a bundle of blankets, against his chest. His big body bracketed hers, making her feel secure. She rested her head, and though she didn't deserve his mercy, she thanked whatever silent force had brought him back to her.

For the first time in a long time, she slept soundly.

Asha's fever broke overnight, though she was still exhausted into the next day. Cade untied her bonds and let her sleep, curled up in her blankets, waking her only to offer water or urge her to eat a few bites of roasted fish. He remained gentle, stroking her hair away from her face or holding her hand on top of the blankets. He didn't kiss her again, but he sat by her bedside all day, fiddling with animal traps or washing foraged produce. He was always there when she awoke.

Nothing was settled between them. She should have been angrier with him, shouldn't have let him touch her. But after all she'd been through, all that she'd lost, his touch anchored her to something familiar: a rare time when she'd felt safe. The simple fact was that he was all she had left, and she no longer had the energy to guard her heart against him.

Try as she might, she'd never stopped thinking about him while they were apart. Shutting him out of her mind and fucking someone else hadn't stopped her from missing him.

As good as Kimmy had been to her, she wasn't Cade, and she didn't understand what Asha had needed. She was too good, too sweet, too pure. She lived with a mandate to heal people, to walk a path of light, and she couldn't understand the dark underworld that Asha now inhabited, and why she couldn't simply choose to leave it. *And,* Asha now acknowledged to herself, *I blamed Kimmy for it. For not being right for me. I blamed all of them for giving me a life I no longer wanted.*

Regret filled her. Kimmy hadn't deserved what she'd done. Neither had Claire, and she'd never be able to apologize. Even if she could, what good would it do? Some things couldn't be undone. Being haunted by her guilt, unable to dispatch it, would be her punishment. All things considered, she knew she'd gotten off lightly.

When she woke for the fourth time that day, the light outside was fading, and Cade was nowhere to be seen. However, there was a large metal tub beside her bed that hadn't been there before.

Asha yawned, too tired to care. Despite sleeping all day, she wasn't motivated to move from her nest of blankets. She dozed lightly on and off until she was awoken again by heavy footfalls entering the small cabin. Cade reappeared at her bedside, hauling two metal buckets full of water. Dominic followed him, carrying two more.

"Hello, Dom," Asha said sleepily. "Fancy meeting you here."

Dom shot her an incredulous look, and Cade suppressed a small smile. Both men set the buckets down beside the tub.

"Thanks," Cade said to Dom, who merely nodded and left without a word. His usual manner of departure, Asha supposed.

Cade dumped the buckets of water into the metal tub, then approached the bed.

"Come on, darling," he murmured, sliding his arms underneath her and hoisting her up, out of her pile of blankets. "You'll feel better after."

"I could've moved by myself," Asha said acerbically, and he grinned. "Now you don't have to."

He carried her the few steps to the tub and carefully lowered her into the water. The tub was old-fashioned, with a high back that allowed Asha to recline slightly. She couldn't help but sigh. The water was only lukewarm, but given the warm evening, she didn't mind. It rose to just under her breasts, ensuring that the fresh stitches between her chest and shoulder remained dry.

Cade retrieved a bar of soap and a washcloth from his pack, then knelt beside the tub. Asha watched him in disbelief as he started to bathe her, his touch gentle and tender. He touched her as if no time had passed between them, as if she'd only left him yesterday instead of six months before.

"Still gorgeous," he murmured as he lathered soap on her body.

Asha rolled her eyes, though she couldn't help but feel a prickle of pleasure at his approval. He was the only one who'd ever made her *feel* beautiful, with his words and his touch.

"I'm still mad at you, you know," she said defiantly, to remind herself as well as him.

She expected him to joke, to make light of it. But he didn't.

Instead, he sighed and said, resigned, "I know."

His expression was wounded, but hard-set. He clearly expected no reassurance from her—which was good, because he didn't deserve any, by her estimation. So why did she want to give it to him anyway?

"I know I hurt you badly," Cade continued. "It doesn't make any difference to say it, but...I'm sorry. So fucking sorry."

"For what, exactly? Setting me up to kill Angel for you? Forcing me to go along with the human trafficking scheme? Blowing up on me? Making me—" Asha stopped, a lump forming in her throat, before gasping out the rest, "—trust you?"

Pain flashed in those grey eyes she'd grown to know so well.

"For all of it," he replied, his voice thick. "I broke your trust and killed what we had. And I didn't even realize how much it meant to me until you left. Then I realized..."

He trailed off, uncertain.

"Realized what?" she said, exasperated. "That your little power play didn't make you happy, in the end? So, you came crawling back, because I wasn't there to wet your dick anymore and tell you—"

Cade's expression tightened, and his eyes turned steely.

"Shit, Asha, I'm trying to tell you that I love you," he burst out, tossing the soap into the water with a *plop*. "I didn't work this hard to find you just because I was sorry. I've done a lot of bad things in my life and have plenty to be sorry for. That sure as hell didn't make me risk my life, though."

He took a deep breath. "I risked it because I'm just...ridiculously in love with you, and after you left, I realized that I didn't fucking care about any of the things I'd worked so hard for, because you weren't there. I didn't care about taking down Angel, or being leader, because it didn't mean anything without you. Nothing did, and I couldn't live with myself, knowing I was going to put more people through what you went through. So, I evacuated everyone...and then I did everything I could to find you again."

Asha paused, hardly daring to believe him. She remembered the rage in his eyes, the way he'd frightened her, and forced herself back from the edge.

"Our last fight," she said quietly, and he flinched at the memory. "I thought you were going to hurt me."

"I could have," Cade admitted, and to her surprise, a tear escaped down his cheek. "But in the end, I remembered I'm *not* my father. You made me remember that I had a choice to be different, even if I didn't make it until I lost you. You were, and are, my purpose, Asha, and I could never harm you."

Asha took a sharp intake of breath. She didn't know how to respond, but that nagging lump in her throat surfaced again. He loved her, and as much as she'd tried so hard to forget him, to cut herself loose from his grip, she knew the truth: she'd never be free of him, because she didn't want to be. Her love for him was the only thing she still knew was real in the web of lies she'd spun for herself.

Silent tears flowed freely down her face, and the corners of Cade's mouth turned down.

"Is it not enough, darling?" he murmured, then sighed. "I know it's not. It's too late, and too long, and I didn't give you what you needed when you needed it...but I'm here now, and if you let me, I'll take care of you. Of us. My penance will be building you the life you want—whatever you want."

He sat back on his knees, his expression earnest.

"If you want to stay here at Ashburn, I'll rebuild it for you," he said. "We can settle here, try to bring it back to what it was. If you want to find a new group, we will. If you want to travel, I'll bring you where you want to go. I just...I want to be with you. I don't care about the rest. We can take it as slow as you want, between us. Just...please think about it. Please."

There was a desperate plea in his eyes that Asha had never seen before. Cade wasn't the begging type. But he was begging now—on his knees, no less. For her.

Asha wet her lips, overwhelmed. She still didn't trust him—not yet—but she believed him. And through all the pain she'd endured in the last year, he'd been the only guiding light. He'd saved her.

He'd made mistakes, done bad things to survive...but she knew something about that now. She knew regret, and she knew what it was to betray someone who trusted you for something you thought you wanted more than anything else.

We're fucked up, Asha thought. *But we're the same kind of fucked up.*

So, she gathered her courage and said, "I still don't trust you, but...I want to try."

Relief passed over Cade's face in a wave. He grabbed her hands and held them, then pressed his forehead to hers.

"You're still my brave little viper," he murmured. "I've always loved that."

For the first time in a long time, Asha smiled.

"Oh, Asha," Cade murmured, heartsick, and his grip on her tightened. "I'm so sorry, my angel. You've been walking wounded all this time, hmm? Since long before I met you. Since before you can even remember."

She couldn't reply with anything but a desperate wail. She'd never cried like this in her whole life. She would've been embarrassed if she'd had room for any emotion besides sheer anguish.

"I know, darling," he whispered, as though acknowledging something she'd said. "I can feel it. You've been carrying it all with you for so long."

"You said to master the darkness," Asha gasped out. "But I've *become* the darkness. There's nothing left of me."

"It's alright," Cade said simply, kissing her temple. "I've got you. You're right here with me, and I'm never, ever letting you go again."

It was what she needed to hear. He kept holding her until she'd finally exhausted herself. Then, at last, she began to tell him everything.

When she'd finished, Cade kissed her and said again, "I still love you."

Asha cringed. "I don't deserve it."

"Well, that's the thing about unconditional love, darling: deserving it isn't part of the equation."

Unconditional love. Something like awe filled her. She'd never been offered such a gift, and so freely. Immediately, however, she knew she felt it for him, too. Nothing he'd done had extinguished her love for him, even when she'd been at her most angry and betrayed.

"I'll love you until the sun burns out," Cade murmured against her hair. "Until we're all nothing but dust, and everything you've done is erased from living memory."

Summer stretched forward like an endless road before them. After Asha had recovered physically, she began to help the others with rebuilding Ashburn. Cade had already done a good job fixing up his own cabin, where she'd been staying, but the others needed more work. Leo took over the biggest one and was in the process of turning the main room into a makeshift clinic, so she spent a lot of time helping him organize supplies and scavenge for decent furniture.

Dom was spending all his time planting a new garden, full of new medicinal herbs and vegetables. To Asha's surprise, Lana and Cassie were eager to help him, even if Dom didn't seem to appreciate their presence. Then again, it was always hard to tell with him.

"It's good to see you again," Asha had said to Lana one warm afternoon in the garden, feeling a little awkward. "I'm sorry it's under these circumstances, but—"

Lana scoffed. "You should've told me about everything *before* you ran off, Asha. I would've helped you. You should've trusted me."

Asha nodded. "Yeah, I know. That's a tough one for me. But...for what it's worth, I'm glad you're here. I'm glad you're safe. And I missed you."

Lana still gave her a severe look, but her eyes softened a little. "Alright. But you're still on thin ice with me."

"Understood," Asha replied with a small smile.

A week after arriving at Ashburn, she awoke alone in bed, which was unusual. Cade typically woke her when he got up, but sunlight was streaming in through the window, and he wasn't home.

Irrational panic squeezed Asha's chest like a vise. She jumped out of bed. *He's gone, he's gone, he's—*

Sitting on the grass outside. What?

It was true: in the early morning sun, visible from the front window, Cade sat cross-legged on a patch of soft grass. His back was to her, but his palms lay open, facing skyward, on top of his knees. Curiosity overtook her fear, so she got dressed and headed outside to meet him.

He was still just sitting there, and when Asha approached him, she realized his eyes were closed. His breath was slow and deep, and he looked...calm. Relaxed. Maybe more than she'd ever seen him before.

It was only once she dropped in the grass beside him that Cade opened his eyes and looked at her, and his gaze was so full of soft affection that it made her flush a little.

"What are you doing?" she asked, reaching over to take his hand.

"Meditating," Cade replied with a touch of dry humour. "I do it a lot now. Even if it still feels a bit hokey sometimes."

Asha was surprised. "I never saw you do it before."

"That's because I never did before I left the Nest. When we were on the road, Leo talked to me about some things. Helped me learn to manage my temper. He tried to offer me psych help before, but I never took him up on it till then."

He paused, seeming to consider his next words carefully. "Even though I told you to talk about it before—about your trauma—I never took my own advice much, except with you. Then when I decided to search for you, I knew I wanted to be better. Not just for you, but for me, too. So, I've been...working on things."

Asha was seized by sudden tenderness. She didn't quite know what to say, except, "I'm proud of you."

Cade smiled warmly at her, like her praise really meant something to him. "You should join me, darling. You might be surprised by how much it helps, over time."

So, she did. Every morning over the next few weeks, they meditated together for an hour. Like Cade said, it sometimes felt a little hokey, but she was surprised by how much she started to look forward to it. Something about focusing all her energy on breathing, on the sounds of nature, on the sunbeams warming her face felt healing. And in the dark of the night, she still whispered her secrets to him, told him her nightmares, and let him comfort her.

That felt like healing, too.

After that, they spent a lot of days hunting and fishing, since it was now their main source of food. The quiet of the wilderness was peaceful in a way she'd never found it before, until she understood that it was being with Cade that brought her peace.

He still didn't press her for anything more. He did, however, start planning little outings for them. A long walk in the woods, or a picnic by the lake. A trip to the Post for supplies or just for fun. A candlelit dinner in the cabin.

It was different. He was different.

"Since when are you Mr. Romantic?" Asha asked one evening, with a small giggle.

"Since I lost the one good thing that walked into my life," Cade answered with complete sincerity. "And...we didn't get to have a normal relationship before. The way things started between us wasn't how I would've wanted. We never went on a date, or did anything that wasn't just part of survival. We didn't have the space to enjoy more of the good things in life. Now, I want to give you all that."

She couldn't help herself; she walked around the small dining table and bent to kiss him full on the mouth. He jolted briefly in surprise, but quickly settled into it, his hands coming up to hold her in place.

Asha moved to straddle his lap, and their kisses soon grew wilder, more passionate. Cade's hands moved into her long, black hair and stayed there, pulling her in. Before long, she felt him growing hard against her, and she sighed with pleasure. It'd been so long since she'd felt him like this.

Lingering doubt still clung in the dark recesses of her mind. She loved him, but hadn't said it to him yet. Though Cade gave no indication that he minded, she wanted to test the strength of the trust that they were slowly rebuilding before she gave him the final gift of her forgiveness.

Since she was now aching with arousal, grinding against him and kissing him with fervour, there seemed to be one obvious way to do that.

"Asha," Cade murmured when she pulled back, his eyes glazed with desire, "we don't have to do this yet. If you're not ready…it's fine. I'm in no rush."

She kissed down his neck, making him shudder. She liked the way his breath was coming out in small pants, simply in reaction to her touch.

"How much do you trust me?"

Cade frowned in confusion, and Asha giggled, feeling most unlike herself. She felt more like the person she used to be, in bed with him. Freer. Sweeter.

"I want to take the lead tonight," she said, kissing along his jaw. "Would that be okay with you?"

He chuckled. "More than okay. I trust you."

She stood. "Good. Then I want you to kneel, soldier."

"What?"

"You heard me. Kneel."

Cade shot her another look—more curiosity than confusion now—and bit his lip in a way that made her want to bite it for him. Slowly and deliberately, he got on his knees, never breaking eye contact with her. The sight of him there, so vulnerable and handsome, made Asha's pussy ache with need.

"Give me your belt."

He arched an eyebrow, but unbuckled it and handed it to her. She used it to secure his hands behind his back, then moved back in front of him. His grey eyes stared at her with a mix of dry amusement and a new, fervent intensity that made her weak at the knees.

"Tonight, you're going to be *mine*," Asha said wryly, and the corner of Cade's mouth ticked upward. "And you're going to do as you're told. Follow orders. Like a good soldier. Right?"

When he offered no reply, she grabbed his chin in her hand and forced him to look up at her. "Aren't you going to do as you're ordered? Be a good boy?"

He let out a breath that sounded shakier than she'd expected. *This is turning him on.* The thought was titillating.

"For you, yes," he breathed.

"Good."

Asha took her time undressing in front of him, teasing him. His sharp intakes of breath told her that he was getting more aroused with every moment. When she finally wore nothing but Cade's dog tags around her neck, she palmed her breasts, sighing as she flicked over her nipples with her thumbs.

"Not fair," Cade said breathlessly. "God, you're beautiful, Asha. I need to touch you."

"You'll get your turn," Asha replied, and she saw him swallow hard, watching her. "Until then, you'll suffer."

He made a small sound of protest, but Asha ignored him. She was enjoying herself. She continued her own ministrations, caressing her breasts and the rest of her body. Cade's eyes never strayed from her; his attention was rapt. He watched her as though she was the most fascinating, arousing thing he'd ever seen.

Asha sighed and kept going until he was practically quivering with desire, a desperate glint in his eye. He looked damn good on his knees for her.

"Something you want?" she asked, teasing, but her pussy tightened and got wetter with each brazen look he gave her.

His Adam's apple bobbed. "To feast on your gorgeous pussy. This is cruel and unusual punishment after being away from you for so long."

Pleasure bloomed inside her, and a desire for more of his surrender.

"Then beg," she murmured, in imitation of what he'd once said to her. "Beg me for it, and I'll give it to you."

Cade make a choked noise, and then, to her surprise and delight, he did what he was told.

"Please," he croaked. "Please let me lick you. Touch you. Serve you. Worship you."

His hushed tone sent a pleasurable shiver down Asha's spine. She wasn't quite done toying with him, however. She pulled a chair from the table and placed it in front of Cade, then lifted her right leg to plant her foot on the seat, exposing her pussy to him. He inhaled sharply and gave her a look of what could only be described as reverence.

"Only your tongue," Asha instructed, not that he could move his bound wrists. "No other contact."

Cade nodded, and she guided his mouth to her pussy. Immediately, he worked her with his tongue, fast and eager and *ravenous*. A long sigh escaped him, and the tension in his shoulders eased slightly as he devoured her. Unable to use his hands, he simply leaned harder into her for balance, applying an exquisite pressure to his strokes. An orgasm coiled tight at Asha's core, and it didn't take long for her to topple over the edge, gasping and murmuring his name.

"More," Cade panted. "I need more. I'm starving for you."

Another wave of arousal passed over her, and she allowed him to make her come a second and third time using only his tongue, until she was nearly spent. When she looked down at Cade, his face was both smug male satisfaction and sheer misery. She could see his erection straining painfully against his pants.

"Please, my angel," Cade gritted out, and she loved his desperation for her most of all. "Please let me fuck you now. Make love to you. Tell you that I've never seen a woman so beautiful, and that I'll spend the rest of my life making up for the ways I've hurt you. I want you. So fucking much. Please."

Poor guy, she thought with amusement. *I think I broke him.*

She stroked his cheek, and he shuddered under even that slight touch.

"Such a good boy you've been," Asha whispered to him. "Alright. Prove it to me."

She freed him at last, and he practically pounced on her. He scooped her up into his arms and dumped her onto the bed, smothering her giggle with a kiss. A moment later, his clothes were on the floor, and his warm, naked body was pressed against hers. Asha spread her legs beneath him, and they both gasped as he pushed his cock inside her.

"Yes," Cade groaned. "Oh, fuck, yes. I've waited so long for this, darling. For you. I don't care where we are or what you've done...you're still mine, and I'm yours. I'll always be yours."

Asha shuddered with pleasure at his powerful thrusts, so deep inside her, giving her everything she needed. He covered her mouth with his in a kiss that felt brutal and tender at the same time, filled with months of longing. His hips sped up, making her moan, and then he was coming, calling her name and filling her up with a low groan. She arched to meet him, taking in every movement he made, every sound of his pleasure.

Cade collapsed on top of her, panting. "Sorry. I didn't mean for it to be over that quickly. It's just...it's been a while."

Asha giggled, and he joined in. "I'll do better next time. Promise."

She pressed a tender kiss to his eyebrow. "I think you did just fine." And then, with her heart in her mouth, she murmured, at long last, "I love you, soldier. Unconditionally."

His whole body softened at her words, and the tenderness in his eyes was palpable.

"I love you too," he replied, then added with a wry smile, "little viper."

She laughed again, and he shifted their position so that he held her against his chest. They lay quietly together, enjoying the afterglow.

"Did you mean what you said?" Asha asked after a while. "About giving me the life I want?"

Cade kissed her forehead. "Of course. Is there something you've got in mind?"

"Maybe," she said, hesitating briefly. "It's just...I've been thinking. About everything I've done. All the people I hurt. And how I want to do things differently. We're freer now. Like we weren't in the gang."

"Sure." He was patient, letting her finish her thought.

"I want to help other women and girls," she finally said. "Or...I want to try. We have room here at Ashburn for more people. Maybe we can give it to people who've been trafficked. Find them and give them a new start, if they want it. Give them freedom. I just feel like...I can't make up for anything I've done. Not with the people I did it to. But maybe now is my chance to do something better. To redeem myself? If there's such a thing."

There was a long silence between them, and eventually, Asha squirmed with nerves.

"You think it's a bad idea," she said, doubtful.

"No," Cade replied gently. "I think it's a wonderful idea, darling."

She propped herself up, and he was looking at her with such hope. Maybe even a glimmer of excitement.

"Really?" she breathed, hardly daring to believe it.

"Really," he answered with a smile, then pulled her down into a kiss. "We can talk logistics in the morning. But I feel good about it."

"Me too. First thing I've felt good about doing in a while."

Satisfied with their conversation, Asha let herself drift in Cade's arms, and when she finally slipped into sleep, it was with the knowledge that the darkness inside of her hadn't won in the end. Her light was still there, a tiny flame that begged to be fed the darkness of this world, to illuminate the path for others like her to follow.

She'd learn to nurture that light that'd been so neglected throughout her life, with the brave captain who'd loved her fiercely and taught her what it meant to fight.

Thank you so much for reading Asha and Cade's story! If you enjoyed it, please consider leaving a rating or review, as this helps me more than anything to reach new readers.

If you're new to my work, *DIB* is a standalone spinoff of my *Wastelander Series*. If you'd like to read about what happened to Asha's friend, Claire, and more about this dark post-apocalyptic world, please check out *The Wastelander*. I'm currently working on the third book in that series, which will release in 2026. That book will also include appearances from Cade, Asha, and the rest of the Blackguard crew.

I also plan to write more books about Leo and Dom in the future, so stay tuned!

Also by E.S. Luck

Acknowledgements

All books are a labour of love, and though authors often work alone, there are plenty of people to thank for making the creative process possible.

First, I would like to thank my intrepid duo of returning beta readers: Bethany and MackenZee. You guys have been amazing to stick with me for multiple releases. I'd also like to thank all the incredible new beta readers who were kind enough to join me for this book: Morgan, Heather, Andie, Hannah, Chelsea, Haleigh, Sadie, Melissa, and Riem. Your feedback is so valuable and makes me a better writer!

Thanks as well to my friends, Kate, Emily and Erin, for always supporting my author career and listening to me rant about banal things like spine width, print costs, and shipping logistics. You're the best.

Finally, as always, I have to thank my husband, Steven, for making it possible for me to pursue my dreams, for loving me at my most unlovable, and for always making sure I have Coke Zero, especially when I'm writing. That's true love right there.

About E.S. Luck

E.S. Luck is a copywriter by day and an author when no one is watching. She grew up in Ontario, Canada, where she still lives with her husband and their adorable dog, Rosie. She holds an honours degree in English Literature, and published an academic paper before moving on to fiction. When she's not reading, gaming, or eating peanut butter, she's probably having an existential crisis while staring at her blinking cursor. She writes post-apocalyptic romance books that blend the dark backdrop of dystopian fiction with the character-driven narrative and irresistible steam of romance.

For more information, you can check out her website at esluckauthor.com, or follow her on Facebook, Instagram, or TikTok.